RAYNA
OF
NIGHTWIND

By R. A. Baker
Published by Apollo House Press

THE TAREN SERIES
Rayna of Nightwind
Beyond Irel's Band*

*Forthcoming

RAYNA OF NIGHTWIND

The First of the Taren Novels

R. A. BAKER

Apollo House Press
Virginia

This is a work of fiction. The characters and events described
in this novel are either fictitious or used fictitiously.

Copyright © 2008 by R. A. Baker

Edited by A. J. Sobczak

An Apollo House Press Book
P.O. Box 3209
Chester, VA 23831

www.apollohousepress.com

Library of Congress Control Number: 2006907046

Publisher's Cataloging-in-Publication Data
Baker, R. A.
Rayna of Nightwind : the first of the Taren novels /
R. A. Baker.
p. cm.
ISBN-10: 0-9787518-7-6
ISBN-13: 978-0-9787518-7-6
1. Taren (Imaginary place)—Fiction. I. Title.
II. Series: Baker, R. A. Taren; bk. 1

PS3603.A468R28 2008
813.6—dc22
2006907046

Manufactured in the United States of America

First Edition

Quality Printing and Binding by:
BookMasters, Inc.
Mansfield, OH

For Avis,
my better half.

CONTENTS

The Twelve Schools of Psi-magic

1. Psi-aquatics—   Water, and that which flows.

2. Psi-botany—   All that is green upon the earth.

3. Psi-clairvoyance—   The divine inspiration of future-sight.

4. Psi-illusion/optics—What the eyes may or may not see.

5. Psi-kinetics—   Control of movement over all solids.

6. Psi-olfactics—   Smells both pleasant and foul.

7. Psi-portation—   Willing oneself to vanish or pass through solids.

8. Psi-pryrics—   The flame and heat of fire.

9. Psi-sensation—   Knowledge and understanding through touch alone.

10. Psi-somatics—   Healing or harm for the flesh.

11. Psi-sonics—   Sounds that can be uttered and heard.

12. Psi-telepathy—   Thoughts unspoken; influence over mind and emotion.

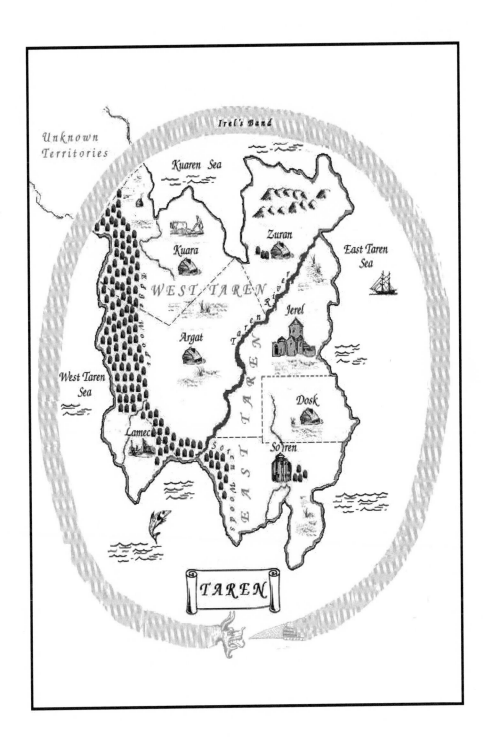

PROLOGUE

The Lake Stone

Under the calm of the star-filled sky, the wrinkled hag shuffled, a crooked cane in her gnarred hand, taking smalls steps so she didn't tire before she reached the guardhouse. Though she lived just inside East Taren, it took her half the night to reach the border of West Taren.

"A dangerous journey for an elder," East Taren townspeople whispered among themselves as she passed, night after night. "The West Taren savages would find a tired old lady traveling alone an easy target."

Her keen ears occasionally caught the idle chatter as she passed, causing her to snicker to herself, knowing the gossips saw only her bent back and feeble walk, and therefore assumed her magic was feeble as well. No brigand who crossed her path and challenged her lived to make that mistake a second time. Just two nights ago, she had cast asunder an entire band of rogues. Lying at her feet, they had begged for mercy. She gave them none.

In need of money, she had reluctantly agreed to train an ignorant guardsman of West Taren—an *Unnatural*. Even though her pupil showed no talent, she had kept her promise, teaching the fool the ways of magic. What she taught, however, were inferior spells that lasted but seconds, ones creating smoke and sparks and little more. An East Taren child might have shown him such cheap, trivial tricks for free, but her pupil knew no better.

Ignorant of magic, as all West Tareners were, he shamelessly overpaid for such worthless lore — ten silver pieces a visit. Tonight, she intended to collect more than silver; tonight, she hoped to collect power beyond imagining.

Her eyes, milky and clouded with age, squinted ahead. There stood the guard, nervously awaiting her arrival. She despised Unnaturals, and this was the second one she had agreed to teach. At least the first one had potential. This one was useful only for the money he paid her and as a pawn, to be exploited as she desired. The guard suspected nothing.

The old woman thought about the success of her deception and cackled. The guard, as he always did, mistook her disdainful amusement with him as enthusiasm for the next lesson. He glanced around anxiously, then hurriedly escorted her into his small guardhouse, containing two wooden stools and lit with only a single lantern. The old woman knew the risks the guard was taking and thought him all the more foolish for doing so.

She loathed the dusty, cramped quarters almost as much as she hated the guard, but she drew comfort in the knowledge that this loathsome project was nearing its end. After so many cycles, the guard was ready. Her magic had slowly crumbled his judgment, like rust ate away at unkempt armor.

Directly outside the guardhouse was the Great Lake of Lamec, and precisely in its center lay the Lake Stone, the talisman from the heavens. The waters glistened and glowed from the mysterious power of the Stone. Soon she would obtain its power.

"For this lesson," she told the guard, "I want no silver." Upon seeing the predictably puzzled look on his face, the old woman went on. "I ask only that you take me by boat to see the Lake Stone for a closer view." She waited awhile to judge the look in the guardsman's eyes. "I wish to touch it."

As she expected, the guard rambled on about how no one was allowed near the Stone and of his responsibilities to guard it. Growing impatient, she cut his pitiful babbling short with a hard tap of her cane upon the stone floor. The guardhouse was suddenly silent.

"Do you not want to continue with your lessons, man? I offer you a chance to save your money, and you insult my generosity with this nonsense." The old woman leaned forward so close, the uneasy guard feared the hag would kiss him. "This is no bandit or vandal who stands before you, guard," she whispered hoarsely. "What possible harm can I, a bent old woman, do by touching the Stone? Even the King himself of this marvelous capital city would grant my simple request if he knew of it. Perhaps I would do better to go to him instead."

The old woman smiled; her teeth were brilliantly white. She backed away, sat on a stool, and waited. The guard looked uncertain, unsure. Not willing to make eye contact, he simply stared at the floor. The old woman was confident in what he would say next. Starting with the guard's first lesson, she had gradually developed a link to touch his mind with hers. Now, he unwittingly exposed his thoughts for her to manipulate and exploit as she pleased. Her grin slowly widened. She had access to his very soul—and thus access to the Lake Stone. She knew the guard feared her as much as he feared getting caught near the Lake Stone—a crime the West Tareners punished with death.

"Very well, witch," the guardsman scoffed. He laughed as if he couldn't care less, but the worry in his voice, and in his mind, betrayed him. "If you wish to forfeit your payment just to lay your wrinkled hands on a rock, then so be it." The old woman waited for him to continue. She knew he was going to add something else. Something foolish.

"However," the guard added hesitantly, "such a special request demands a special lesson."

The old woman was ready with an answer. "Of course, my friend. Did you think I would not reward this favor?" The witch tossed up her gray head and shut her eyes in apparent concentration. A long moment of silence passed.

"I know," she said at last, "I will teach you one of my most treasured enchantments. Would you like to learn the wondrous magic of flight?" Of course she possessed no such power, or she would not have needed a boat to reach the Stone, much less any help from the ridiculous sentry.

The guard did not notice this breach in logic, and though he struggled to conceal his excitement, it shone in his eyes, brighter than the smoky lantern that lit the room. "That would do nicely," he agreed. "I have always wanted to fly like the birds of the air. Let us begin the lesson."

The old woman pointed at the guard, wagging her finger and shaking her head like a mother showing disapproval to a misbehaved child. "In all the time you have spent with me in study, I have always collected my payment first. Tonight will be no different."

The guard frowned. "Very well, but I pray that you do not take long with this folly."

"No longer than it takes you to ready the boat."

In a short while, they boarded a small boat, used only by guards when patrolling the lake. The woman was pleased that her plan, so long in the making, was working so well. She cast hidden glances at the guard as he nervously rowed toward the center of the lake. He had never told her his name. She revealed a cold smile. It was Platus. She loathed the guard's hypocrisy almost as much as his West Taren blood. He spoke of duty and responsibility, and here he was peddling away his loyalty to his King for personal gain, like the well-dressed hustlers of Argat, who would sell their own daughters for profit. He was more of a scoundrel in his shiny, medal-adorned guardsman's uniform, than all the ragged thieves in Taren. That is why most West Tareners possess no magic, she thought. Their corrupt, lazy minds were not suited for the discipline.

Slowly, the boat neared the Lake Stone. The witch could feel the waves of perpetual heat gushing from it, like a mystic fountain. It was such a waste, she thought, that this treasure fell on West Taren land.

Finally, they reached the marveled Stone. The old woman stared in awe at the size of it. From a distance, it resembled a shrunken pearl set in a giant oyster of water, but up close it was immense. Though most of it was submerged, its dry upper half rose higher than three men and more than thrice as wide. It looked smooth in some places and rough in others. Small holes, connected by fine cracks, pocked its surface. In the darkness of the night, she could detect a low glow emanating from within, shining faintly through the cracks. That was the source of its magic, she decided. Somewhere underneath its dull, scarred crust was the core of unimaginable energy—energy that could make her the most powerful being Taren had ever seen. She would become a goddess.

The guard hissed at her side, "Do it now old witch, or we will be seen!"

Annoyed at having her thoughts severed, the woman looked over and spoke harshly to the guard for the first time. "Be quiet, pawn!" Her eyes narrowed with hate. "I will do this in my own time. If I move too slowly for your taste, you may swim back!" Without waiting for his reaction, she turned her back to the now wordless guard and refocused on the Lake Stone. Its strange, silvery glow grew brighter, as if it anticipated this moment as much as she did. So seductive. Entrancing! The Lake Stone was meant for her. The old woman knew it.

She could bear the delay no longer. She leaned forward with outstretched hands to receive its touch. The warmth of the Stone warmed her night-chilled skin and made it tingle. She trembled. The long cycles of pretending to be a lesser mage finally were over!

A blinding flash of light engulfed the boat, spilling outward until it illuminated the entire lake. Night became as day, and a strange humming filled the air. The old woman was alight from the strange fire coming from the Lake Stone. She shattered its outer shell, allowing the power to flow into her without hindrance or restraint. Like daggers, silver-white beams of flashing force bored their way into her trembling body. Fear suddenly gripped her. She could not remove her hands from the burning stone. She could not move at all. The old woman shrieked.

Deciding to take the sorceress's advice, the guard had begun to swim back to shore. He turned to look back and saw the little patrol boat explode in silver flame. His eyes widened in terror when he saw the Lake Stone. It glowed like a fiery coal and was belching out metallic, glittering smoke. "What have I allowed to pass?" he cried out loud.

A jab of pain shot into the guard's head. He struggled to keep swimming despite the agony. In vain, he tried to ignore it and concentrate on staying afloat. Then he heard the sound of laughter — hysterical, screaming laughter. At first, he swore it had to be the witch, but that could not be possible, for he had seen her perish in the strange fire.

The madding laughter persisted. It echoed in his head and made the pain worse. Just before he succumbed to unconsciousness, the guard realized that the insane laughter was his own.

PART I

Exile

CHAPTER
1

Rayna

The headlights of Rayna Powell's car scarcely penetrated the darkness, which enveloped the narrow, rustic road. Rayna had no particular destination in mind; what she needed was some time alone so she could sort through her thoughts concerning the past few days. Tonight was her first night back from college, back with her mother, back in her home on Nightwind Drive. She had convinced herself to sneak out and take the car for a drive, just to get some time alone. That usually seemed to help, and she knew from past experience that she couldn't focus her thoughts while her mother was in the house with her.

To an outsider, Rayna would appear as a frail creature, her slight, five-foot, four-inch frame not up to the task of shouldering the weight of the world's challenges. Her intense eyes belied that first impression, and her high cheekbones, braced by jaws that clenched powerfully when she was concentrating or angry, gave the otherwise delicate beauty of her face a chiseled edge. In many ways, Rayna's appearance mirrored her psyche: fortitude tempered with sensitivity.

As she peered at the bit of dark sky and the road illuminated by the headlights, she began to question the wisdom of going out so late, knowing that a storm was on its way. Through she strained her vision, Rayna could see only a few dozen feet directly ahead; beyond that was only deep shadow that seemed poised to swallow her as the car approached it. She could hear the faint rumbling of thunder in the distance.

Just a few more minutes, she told herself, *and then I'll turn back.* Soft-hued backlighting from the dashboard cast a cool tint of indigo to her reddish brown skin. For a car belonging to a twenty-two-year- old, its interior was uncommonly quiet, outside the subdued hum of the motor; music was distracting, and Rayna found that she focused better in silence. Private reflection had always been her great rejuvenator. She had graduated from Eastlander University less than a week ago with a degree in science, and her philosophy hadn't changed. Her mother had never understood that part of Rayna. If she were awake and discovered that her daughter had gone out driving alone in the middle of the night, just to think, Rayna would never hear the end of it.

With her free hand, Rayna reached for her purse, which lay in the passenger seat, to get her mobile phone. She had been told more than once by worried family members and friends that she was sometimes difficult to reach, and she had promised to make amends by carrying her phone with her at all times—*just in case.* After a brief rummage inside her purse, she realized that she had been in such a rush to get out, she had forgotten to bring her phone. *It's probably still charging on the dresser in my room—right where I left it,* she thought, mildly chiding herself for her absentmindedness. *No matter; I won't be gone long.*

Instinctively, Rayna glanced at her watch, a gift from her mother on her 16th birthday. Over the years, it had served her faithfully, without fail, through exposure to rain and through bumps against various objects. Its face was that of a smiling clown, the two ends of whose bright red mustache served as the minute and hour hands. A clown watch. She sometimes felt ashamed to wear it but could never bring herself to replace it. Now, the mustache showed that it was a quarter to midnight.

Rayna's jaw clenched with the knowledge of her secret. She had already made up her mind, but she hadn't told anyone yet. Rayna sighed as thoughts tumbled through her mind. Her dilemma was not in the decision itself, but in how she would break the news of that decision to her mother. Of course, Rayna reasoned, she was an adult now, and she had every right to make this decision, but that knowledge did nothing to lessen the relentless feelings of guilt.

Her mother would not take this news well. A familiar tremble of anxiety rushed through Rayna's body, and she shuddered. Spindly shadows of the nightscape passed over Rayna as she drove, reflecting in silence.

Ever since her father died of cancer nine years ago, leaving Rayna and her mother to fend for themselves, Rayna's mother had been very protective and watchful of her only child. The entire tragic experience had made her mom stronger; it made them both stronger. Now, her mother ran a small, successful florist shop only a few blocks from the house. Her mother's tenacity, Rayna reminded herself with pride, now flowed in her own veins. Her mother had a tough time letting Rayna go away to Eastlander University, even though Rayna had earned a full scholarship. Her mother was willing to let her go only because she wanted Rayna to be—as she put it—"A woman of power."

A flash of lighting streaked across the night sky, briefly illuminating the car's cabin in a flickering, white glow. During the four years she spent in college, Rayna discovered a part of herself that had lain dormant when she lived with her mother. She was rash, opinionated, and—as she was often told by her few select friends—as stubborn as a pack of mules. She was no longer the passive and painfully shy Rayna Powell that her mother remembered. Rayna sighed again.

Many nights in her dorm room, her dreams were filled with visions of going to bizarre new places and being far from everything familiar. She would awake, amazed and exhilarated at the same time. The dreams, though strange, were fun and promising—all except one. That dream recurred at least two nights a month, featuring an unwanted visitor. She could remember only pieces of it. She knew it involved a mysterious woman urging Rayna to follow her somewhere. It took place somewhere dark, but full of little sparks of light. The woman was dressed in some type of green uniform, unlike anything she'd seen before. The woman's face didn't look threatening initially, but her eyes watched Rayna oddly, in an almost sinister way. In the dream, as Rayna walked toward the woman, she realized she was walking into some kind of trap. Before she could escape, she felt herself falling into a black nothingness. As Rayna fell, she could hear the woman's cold laughter.

Then she would wake up, always troubled and frightened. She had had the dream again tonight, in her mom's house. It so disturbed Rayna that she could not go back to sleep. That was when she decided to go for a drive and perhaps think of some gentle way to tell her mom what she intended to do, some way of breaking the news without breaking her heart.

A lone car, with its high beams on, rushed toward Rayna. She squinted and looked away, toward the side of the road, trying to recover her sight. As the car passed, she noticed that it had its wipers on. Only then did Rayna realize it was raining. She silently scolded herself for letting her musing distract her.

Her windshield was alive with the sound of light drizzling rain dancing on its surface. Thunder crackled nearby. Like jagged, white flames, bolts of lightning blazed from the sky at a startling pace. The pace of the rain increased even as Rayna turned on her wipers. The wet road looked like black glass in the darkness. Rayna decided that the weather made driving unsafe, and she scanned ahead for a good place to turn around. It was time to go home; tomorrow she would tell her mother her decision. If she was truly to become the woman of power her mother wished, it had to be done.

A woman stood in the middle of the road straight ahead; she seemed to have come out of nowhere. Terrified, Rayna slammed on the brakes. The road, slick from the pouring rain, offered no traction, and the car skidded out of control. Rayna fought to regain control of the car, her mind flooded with fear. Time slowed, threatening to suspend the horrible moment forever. Suddenly, the road was gone, replaced by shrubbery and grass. Mud and loose rock bombarded the windshield, threatening to break through. Rayna could barely see where she was going and was still frantically trying to stop the car. A large stone hit the windshield, which cracked, spreading a cobwebbed ripple across Rayna's already severely limited view. She could feel the car swaying and rocking as she struggled to keep it from flipping over.

Graphic images raced through her tortured mind, of her dying amid twisted metal and flames. *Control!* She needed control. She battled with the steering wheel, jerking it wildly like a sea captain of days long gone, fighting the wheel in rough seas. After what seemed an eternity, Rayna felt her wheels grip something solid. The car began to slow, but through the ruined windshield, Rayna knew it would not be soon enough. Directly ahead of her was a large oak, and there was no time to avoid it. Rayna had never felt so helpless in her life. The next instant, she heard a deafening crash. Perfect silence followed.

❋ ❋ ❋

When Rayna came to, she was so lightheaded she was afraid she would lose consciousness again. Her head pounded, crying for an aspirin she didn't have. She managed to undo her seatbelt, then did a quick check of herself. To her relief, she wasn't hurt, besides feeling faint, weak, and queasy. She didn't know if she had passed out from the crash itself and possibly from an impact to her head, or from the fear. She couldn't feel any bumps on her head, and she wasn't bleeding. Her watch told her that she had not been out for long; it was ten minutes to twelve. The rain was coming down so hard, pounding on the roof of the car, Rayna was sure it had awakened her so soon. Or perhaps it was the thunder, she thought, listening as its booming sound filled the air.

Dazed, she carefully brushed shattered bits of wet glass from herself. Bracing herself for the worst, she got out to inspect the damage. The front of the car was pressed firmly against the tree. Steam spouted from the bent hood. The car was the most valuable thing Rayna had ever owned. Though she knew that wasn't saying much, the years of freedom that the old car had provided made it priceless. The modest, blue four-door she had bought used from a friend, with practically no mileage, now appeared smashed beyond repair.

Rayna realized that she had no time to mourn her loss. Hastily, she stumbled away from the wreckage, afraid there might be hidden flames that might cause an explosion. As she fled in the rain, she looked for a way back to the main road. The darkness made retracing her car's tire tracks impossible. Trees and foliage extended in every direction, and the farther Rayna walked, the deeper the woods seemed to get. Rayna forced herself to stay calm, but she knew she was lost. She didn't realize that her car had strayed so far from the road or that the stretch of road she was driving was surrounded by such thick forest. Rayna had to admit, however, that the trees were useful for blocking some of the soaking rain. Mud sucked viciously at Rayna's shoes as she trudged through the woods, looking for a way out. Her eyes spotted something ahead, a standing figure.

Rayna stopped walking, slipped behind a nearby maple, and hid. It was possible, she thought, that the person saw the accident and was there to help, but Rayna wasn't going to take that risk. She was a young woman, alone in the woods at night; she was not about to embrace the first stranger she saw. She would find her way out on her own. As quietly as she could, Rayna turned around, praying the rain would hide her as she crept away in the opposite direction.

After going a short while, she managed a strong, steady jog. Frequent lightning lit her way as she hurried ahead. Looking behind her, Rayna could see nothing but layers and layers of dense forest that closed behind her like dark green curtains. By now, the rain had completely drenched her, aided by strong winds that also gave her a chill. Her dark, wet hair flapped around her head and face in the rushing breeze.

Suddenly Rayna stopped running and stared ahead in disbelief. The mysterious figure stood silently ahead of her, in the distance, as if Rayna had never changed her course. She was being followed. The tense muscles in Rayna's legs were ready to run, but fear paralyzed her. A cold panic descended upon her; she felt herself tremble like a rabbit facing a wolf. The rain and distance made it impossible for her to know if it was the same person. It *seemed* to be, but that was impossible. How did he or she get ahead of Rayna in woods as thick and dark as this? Nobody could move that fast! Gradually, Rayna felt her rational mind return to her.

She had to believe there were at least two people out there, possibly more. Could they be a rescue party? Rayna seriously doubted it. Neither of them had attempted to call out to her or identify themselves, and the accident hadn't occurred that long ago. Whoever they were, Rayna was convinced they were not good Samaritans. The other one was probably on his or her way to join the accomplice. If she tried to run again, she might fall into an ambush.

Rayna knew she had to act quickly. She focused her attention on her present stalker. The heavy showers formed a veil between the two, preventing Rayna from seeing much more than a hazy outline of her pursuer. The chill of the rain on Rayna's taut face suddenly felt unbearable as she saw the stranger begin walking toward her. Whoever it was advanced softly and confidently in the darkness.

Nervously, Rayna called out loudly, only half expecting a response. "Hello? Who are you, and why are you following me?" Hesitantly, she added, "I don't need any help, I'm fine." She swallowed deeply after she spoke, then waited. The stranger said nothing and continued steadily toward her.

Buried anger slowly seeped its way into Rayna's consciousness, washing away her fear. She was letting herself be intimidated by someone she couldn't even see clearly. *Fear of the unknown.* Her intuition told her that whoever was out there was unarmed and was trying to prey on her fear. Rayna decided not to give the person that satisfaction. Caution wasn't working—she would trust her instincts to bring her through this alive. She frantically looked around for something useful.

A nearby storm-beaten tree provided an answer. At the foot of its trunk lay an assortment of branches and twigs of various sizes and lengths. It didn't take Rayna long to find one that suited her, a straight branch about a yard long with enough weight to be an effective weapon. She grabbed one end of it and swung it against the tree as a test.

Braaac! The solid sound of wood striking wood briefly interrupted the steady rattle of the rain. Her headache, however, drew strength from the vibrating impact. Stubbornly, Rayna swung the limb at the tree again, this time more as a warning to her enemy than a test of its strength.

Satisfied, Rayna gripped the branch like a baton. It was strong wood and would not break easily. Strong enough to take a man down, she hoped. She inhaled the damp night air fully and stepped forward into the gloom to meet her unknown adversary. The clouds became alive again with an endless series of lightning flashes. Rayna had never been in a storm as violent as this one. Thunder roared and rolled, testing the full range of its scales. The wind pushed urgently at Rayna, forcing her to push back. It felt like it was trying to turn her away and shield her from what lay ahead. Rayna continued forward, club in hand. As she drew nearer, the shadowy figure slowly took shape, sharpening into a detailed, clear image.

Rayna now recognized the woman as the one she had run off the road to avoid. Though she had seen her face for only a second, it was painted in her memory as vividly as a photograph. Rayna felt certain it was her, with her long, lustrous black hair streaked with gray and her cold, dark eyes. The woman smiled.

"Thank you, Rayna Powell." Her woman's voice was hollow and measured—unnaturally so.

For an instant, Rayna was almost ready to forgive the lady for the fright she had put her through, thinking that the woman had followed her only to offer her gratitude. Then Rayna realized that the woman, a stranger, had called her by name.

As if summoned, a recent memory triggered in Rayna's mind. She stared in disbelief. She *did* know this woman. She was the one in Rayna's dreams, dressed in the strange green uniform, with the same unsettling tone to her voice.

"Am I dreaming?" Rayna heard herself say without thinking.

The lady chortled the same chilling laugh that haunted Rayna's dreams so many nights. "You exist not to dream but to become." She raised her arms high, as if welcoming the icy rain to drown her.

Rayna paused, confused. The air suddenly became alive with heat. A clap of thunder vibrated in Rayna's clenched teeth. Jagged slivers of lightning ripped open the heavens above. Rayna wasn't sure what was happening, but it was getting too dangerous to stand her ground. This was no natural storm, and it was no dream. Rayna knew she had to seek shelter quickly. The woman apparently was in some sort of shock, blind and deaf to what was happening. Rayna considered dragging the woman with her but dismissed the idea. That would make it the second time she would have endangered her life as a result of the uniformed stranger's reckless abandon. The woman would have to save herself this time.

The woman's eyes snapped open as a fresh chain of thunderbolts hurled down like a volley of arrows. Then came more—closer and closer—until Rayna and the mysterious woman were bathed in a continued renewal of celestial light. Rayna could only watch the event in transfixed terror, afraid that if she moved, she would be struck down by one of the bolts in the bizarre lightning orgy.

When her eyes darted upward at the angry sky, she knew her fear was about to come true. Rayna felt herself engulfed in an explosion of pain. Flaming light burned in her eyes, hands, and feet, forcing her to her knees. Only the mercy of unconsciousness rescued her from the onslaught of agony.

CHAPTER
2

Irel's Band

Rayna drifted in the dark oblivion; she felt herself floating freely in its space. Stray noises, with no discernible source, faded in and out of range. Starting as a few, simple beeps and hums, they gradually multiplied and melded into a complex, harmonious symphony of machine sounds. Rayna turned around in slow motion. "A dream?" she wondered out loud. Slowly, a large mirror formed and shimmered in front of her. Rayna frowned. Her reflection was that of the uniformed woman.

"I do not exist to dream, but to become," the reflection whispered. The mirror shattered, sucking Rayna into the void it left in its place. The place of machine sounds and nothingness fell away violently.

✳ ✳ ✳

Rayna's eyes opened to a world far unlike the one she left, with the darkness replaced by the light of day. She lay sprawled on the ground like a discarded rag and struggled to stand, fighting disorientation that lingered from her blackout. After she stood upright and breathed in mind-clearing air, her mouth gaped in disbelief. Gone were the rainy woods and the mysterious woman; barren, flat wasteland surrounded Rayna. The dusty red ground beneath her feet was hard and lifeless, without even a single weed. Trailing networks of small fissures and cracks spread over the earth.

The landscape appeared unnaturally forbidding and Rayna began to doubt her sanity, wondering if such a place could only emerge from madness. The sky was colored a red so complete, it formed a seamless union between it and the equally red ground beneath—obscuring the horizon.

She could not tell one direction from another; there were no trees, hills, or anything she could use as a marker. Various-sized rocks were strewn across the expanse, too haphazardly to offer any navigational aid.

A wave of sickening dizziness came over Rayna, and she almost lost her will to stand. She staggered a few steps before regaining her balance. Her head pounded in a frenzy of pain. No visible sun, no clouds . . . what *was* this place? She forced herself to look down at her feet, and the nausea faded.

Before Rayna could ponder her situation any further, strange sounds made apparent yet another wrong—a terrifying one. Continuous bolts of lightning lanced their way down to the earth. Rayna winced, remembering her recent encounter in the woods, but this was not same lightning. This lightning was unusually narrow, and it came down perfectly straight, like some sort of white laser. No rain or wind accompanied it; the air was as dry and dead as the parched ground on which she stood. In place of a crackle, the lightning made sharp popping sounds, like a bug-zapper. When the bolts struck the earth, they exploded, leaving shallow craters about the size of Rayna's fist.

Rayna noticed that the entire landscape was spotted with such lightning craters. Their pattern, random and wild, made it appear as though the world had been invaded by mad giants with round, spiked shoes. The feeble snapping sound the bolts made did not fool Rayna; she knew she stood in the midst of falling death. She paused. How did she get here? The last thing she remembered was being struck by lightning. If that were true, Rayna proposed, why was she not hurt or dead? She recalled literally being set ablaze from the lightning storm, yet she could find no burns or other physical evidence of having been struck.

Secondly, *why* was she here? She shuddered to think that she had really died and materialized in this hellish afterworld as punishment for some unknown deed. Rayna's forehead wrinkled in worry. It was possible that she was hallucinating. That explanation made the most sense of any. Or, she reasoned, this could be an extension of the strange, dark dream from which she had just awakened from.

Rayna sighed, dismissing that possibility. Unlike the dream, the pain of her headache from the car wreck was present and pounding. Her resolve strengthened, and she deeply inhaled more of the strange red-tainted air. This was no dream, and it was not the time to be second-guessing herself. Rayna's thoughts shifted to the woman she had seen in the woods. What happened to her?

Her concentration was shaken abruptly when a charge of lightning touched down close to her left. The small pit it left behind smoldered with promise of instant death to anyone foolish enough to stay around for another. Rayna scolded herself with fear-laced sarcasm. *Only Rayna Powell,* she thought, *would sit around and debate a situation while unknown energies blasted around her.* She wanted to blame her recent blackout or her headache for the dangerous lapse in urgency, but she wasn't sure. The questions would wait. Survival was first priority.

Rayna started to walk, slowly at first, then faster, until she was at a full run. She didn't know where she was running to; she prayed that she would find a road leading to a neighborhood—any neighborhood. Rayna found solace in the possibility of reaching a phone and calling to have her mother to pick her up. Then this nightmare would be over.

Suddenly, she heard a loud *pop,* and fragments of rock sprayed over her back and neck. As she ran, she turned her head to see a newly formed lightning crater with hot gray smoke ushering out. Rayna panted with relief. If she had been running just a little slower, she would never have seen her mother, or anyone, ever again.

Two lines of the white energy landed almost in the same spot in front of her. Rayna dodged to avoid the flying bits of dust and stone, still running hard. Sweat flowed over the skin of Rayna's tense face. Its salty wetness slid into her eyes, joining with her tears. Her ears heard only the sound of her own heavy, ragged breathing. Rayna's burning lungs coughed in protest; her legs began to buckle. She slowed, then collapsed and folded onto the hard ground, gasping in the stale crimson air.

Rayna groaned. When she was running, every tendon had hurt, and her headache had gotten much worse. Now, the fall intensified the muscle pain so much that her headache seemed trivial. Wearily, she rose back to her feet. Her ankle stung under the pressure of her weight. She wiped her sweaty face to clear her vision and discovered blood. Rayna's body was so filled with pain, she couldn't tell exactly where the blood came from. She felt like a drunkard vainly trying to pinpoint her nose. From the location of the blood, she guessed that she had a nosebleed.

As she limped on, a brief surge of tingling warmth came over her.

Rayna ignored it, not daring to stop walking. She could see and feel the white beams detonating all around her. Eventually, Rayna's sense of terror became as depleted as her body. She no longer flinched with each loud impact. She was no longer in any condition to dodge the bolts; that would take too much valuable energy. Instead, she doggedly hurried down a linear path of cracks at her feet. The fissures in the ground, though jagged, did follow a somewhat straight direction. She refused to let herself die here, in this lonely, bitter place. She found her thoughts drifting back to another, better time. She recalled how she used to help her mother tend her garden many years ago.

Her mother let her do much of the planting, and she was proud to care for that small spot of land. A stray cat delighted in trespassing into that beloved space. The long delicate stalks and stems of lovely flowers were nothing more than green yarn to the cat. Some days, when Rayna came home from school, she would see the cat in her garden joyfully pouncing about and swatting at her beautiful plants—mangling them with its paws. Furious, she would chase the pest away, her ebony ponytails flying in the afternoon air. The cat, no wiser from the ordeal, would return to play in the garden the next day. Rayna stared at her dismal surroundings. This was no beautiful garden.

This place was so desolate and empty that she would gladly have had that miserable cat by her side now. Rayna closed her eyes to the loneliness around her and imagined being back in her garden. She imagined the feel of fresh soil in her hands, the purity of a spring breeze washing over her, blending with the perfume of budding flowers as she worked. A wonderful, cool breeze, so—

She *felt* the breeze! Rayna opened her eyes in shocked surprise. She had grown so used to the windless world in which she was trapped, the change felt almost traumatic. The current of clean air was steady and gentle. She felt its soft touch brush the right side of her cheek. Her fatigue momentarily caused her to forget where she was. She was still walking, her feet on autopilot. Rayna's head tilted upward at the sky, testing the air with her face. Cautiously, she continued onward, letting her sense of touch guide her through the faint, whispering, airy oasis she found. The lightning became less frequent, and she noticed fewer craters as she hobbled on. She scarcely bothered to look up at the sky to predict its descent. The breeze got mercifully stronger. Then, as if an atmospheric veil had lifted, the dim, red world that had become familiar slowly receded, and soon Rayna was standing on green earth.

CHAPTER
3

Kuara

Ragged but determined, Rayna made her way across the grassy plains. The bright morning sun and gentle wind helped brighten her mood and replenish her precious little stamina. It was hot, and the breeze was just enough make the heat tolerable. Rayna removed her sweater and tied it over her head, bonnet style. It gave her much needed shade from the overbearing sun, though by now she was already perspiring profusely. Her blouse, soaked with sweat, made the wind feel blessedly cooler. Rayna couldn't help thinking that not long ago, she had been standing in an icy downpour at night, then awakened in a red, wasteland. Now she was here—a sunny, green, and very warm pasture.

By now, Rayna found that little could surprise her. She wanted only to get back to civilization and go home. Her ankle hurt, forcing her almost to hop forward, putting as little weight as possible on the injured ankle. The countryside was flat enough to see for miles in each direction; it didn't take long before Rayna saw what she was looking for. A small town loomed in the distance, perhaps two miles away—thirty minutes by foot, much longer if one foot was hurt like hers. Several small houses lay scattered at its outskirts, like little children who wandered too far from their mother. Rayna glanced at her watch and saw that it had stopped near midnight, moments after the car wreck.

She unclasped the band and took the watch in one hand, lightly smacking it into the opposite palm to try to get it working again, but to no avail. The grinning clown face stared at her, the halves of its silly mustache saluting upward. Rayna tapped and shook the watch a few more times, then gave up, reattached it to her wrist, and looked for somewhere to rest. The pain in her ankle told her that the injury could not go untreated for much longer and that she needed to limit her walking. As far as Rayna could tell, there was no bleeding, but she feared what she would find underneath her sock. At the very least, the ankle felt extremely swollen. She bent down and explored the ankle with a light touch, grimacing in pain that felt as fresh as the initial injury. She tried to remove her shoe to take some of the pressure away, but even though she handled her foot as gently as possible, the pain forced her to stop. Rayna knew she would never make it to the town like this. She guessed that she might be able to walk for five, minutes at a time, at most ten, before the pain would become too great.

As tempting as the grassy meadow looked, she resisted the urge to lie down. If she rested here, she thought, the swelling would only get worse, the muscles would stiffen, and she might not be able to walk at all. Then she would be stranded—alone and helpless in the middle of a field foreign to her, with nothing to eat but grass.

As if in answer to her worries, Rayna caught sight of a small, green cottage. She hadn't noticed it at first because it was mostly hidden by a gentle slope. Its old-fashioned charm suited the rustic landscape perfectly.

Rayna smiled optimistically. Whoever lives there, she thought, hopefully would drive her to a hospital. However, from her vantage point, she couldn't see any sign of a car or garage. On a sudden impulse, Rayna turned to look back at how far her travels had brought her. Past the waving grasses and sea-blue skies, she could still see the edge of crimson abyss from which she had come. It was like staring back at a nearly forgotten dream—pale and insignificant in the distance. She turned, putting the past behind her, and headed for the cottage.

The door to the cottage was open, as if whoever lived there was expecting her. Beyond the gloom of the doorway loomed a lone figure, sitting at a table. Rayna paused, now uncertain of her prospects here, but her pain made her abandon caution, and she went inside. Upon closer inspection, Rayna saw that the figure was a girl, thin, frail, and sickly. She was dressed in dirty white robes and was barefoot. Rayna guessed that she was about eleven or twelve years old. She looked tired, as if she had not rested in a long time.

The girl held a staff of polished tan wood, both ends wrapped with silvery metal. Something about her concerned Rayna. The girl's skin had an unhealthy tinge to it. Dark hair draped both sides of her long, pale face before coming to rest limply on her shoulders. The overall effect gave her a long, sad, look. Her eyes, like dark, oval pools, reflected sorrow and despair, and Rayna could tell the girl had experienced things far beyond her physical years. Rayna wanted to speak, to ask for help, but the pain muted her.

Thankfully, no words were needed on her part. The youth was aware of Rayna and did not appear to take her unexpected presence as an intrusion. She gestured for Rayna to take a seat in a nearby chair. Without hesitation, Rayna limped over and sat down hard on its wooden seat. She sighed in relief. She closed her eyes and just sat for a moment, her eyes shut tightly in sightless silence; she breathed deeply and savored the simple joy of sitting.

When Rayna opened her eyes, she noticed that her sneakers and socks were missing. The sweater that had been tied around her head was now neatly folded and placed on her lap.

The girl sat facing her, holding one of Rayna's shoes, eyeing it with reserved fascination. Looking even wearier than earlier, she glanced up at Rayna sorrowfully. "So this is what Powers wear on their feet. The paintings that show you wearing sandals are wrong, Irel." Her voice was soft and kind, yet so sad.

The girl's words puzzled Rayna. "I think you have me confused with somebody else. My name is Rayna, not Irel," she blurted awkwardly. "And I need to see a doctor. I think I broke my ankle."

The girl smiled faintly. "I am the only true healer you will find in West Taren. My talent is humble, but I was able to restore your wounded foot to health as you slept."

Even as the girl spoke, Rayna realized the pain was gone. She touched her ankle, lightly at first, then more firmly. She could not find the slightest swelling or redness anywhere. She stared at the girl in disbelief. "How?"

"Your body is strong and healthy. Healing was easy because all I needed to do was focus that strength on your injury." The girl paused and leaned forward in her chair, staring briefly at Rayna's sweater before returning her gaze to the floor. "Forgive me for removing your sacred headdress, but I had to know if my eyes were mistaken. They were not."

Rayna wrinkled her forehead, puzzled. "What are you talking about?"

"Forgive me; I speak in riddles. Let me recall all I know, so you will not think I was not paying attention." She leaned back and slowly closed her eyes.

For the next few minutes, the frail girl sat so quiet and still that Rayna feared she had died. Then, to Rayna's relief, the girl began to speak. "Shortly before you came to me, I was peering through the window for signs of the Red Robes. It was then that I first saw you. Prophecy tells of a day when the Irel will come back and punish those who sent her away. She would cross through the very Band that they used to imprison her."

The girl eyelids opened, revealing dark glistening orbs on the verge of tears. "I lived here in Kuara most of my life and I have seen several people enter into the Band, but no mortal has ever departed from it. And so, Irel—" The girl paused, then began again, speaking cautiously and thoughtfully. "When I saw you pass from the Band, I was afraid my eyes were seeing things not true." Rayna peered out the window. Though it was a strain, she could still see the accursed thing, a crimson stain that would not wash away.

"When you say 'Band,' you're talking about that red no-man's land back there, aren't you?"

The girl nodded meekly, "We know it as the Band but sometimes call it 'the Place of Unbent Lightning.'"

Rayna smirked at the colorful names for something that nearly killed her. She remembered the white lasers coming down all around her and repressed a shudder. Turning away from the window, she faced the girl.

"What is that place, really? Some kind of weird military testing ground? I must have accidentally stumbled onto it after the car crash."

The girl smiled, the kind of sheepish smile people give when they really don't understand what you're saying but are too embarrassed to admit it.

"Do you want me to tell you how I knew for certain that my eyes had not deceived me?" The girl's question was an obvious attempt to change the subject to something more familiar.

"Sure. Why not?"

The girl's eyes widened, looking like sad, ebony saucers reflecting back at Rayna. "Everyone in Taren knows that Powers are round-ears. When I removed your beautiful headdress, and saw your ears, I knew you could be no one other than the Power Irel, free from exile!"

"Wait a minute," Rayna began. "What's a 'round-ear,' and why do you keep calling my sweater a headdress?"

The girl tilted her head slightly, seemingly confused by the double question. In resignation, she apologized and said nothing else.

It suddenly dawned on Rayna what the girl meant. "You mean my ears are round, so you call me a round-ear?"

The girl nodded. Rayna shot the girl a questioning glance from the corners of her eyes. She felt herself becoming annoyed for allowing the childish game to get this far and not catching it from the start. Rayna wasn't good with fast, witty retorts, but she wasn't about to be made a fool by a twelve-year-old. "Well, if *I'm* a 'round-ear,' then what are *you*, a 'square-ear'?" she said sarcastically.

The girl, sensing she was misunderstood, simply pulled back her long, raven-black hair so Rayna could see her ears. They were narrow and long, with a sharp, distinctive point at their top. Astonished, Rayna gawked at the girl.

"How . . . how long have your ears been that way?"

"From the start of my life. All mortal citizens of Taren are as such."

"You're telling me there are more people around here with ears like that?"

"Yes, Irel, many more."

"Please stop calling me that! My name is Rayna, Rayna Powell." Rayna forced herself to look away from the girl's disturbing ears. "I suppose you'll be telling me next that you're a very tall elf."

"I know not what an elf is, Irel."

"That's a relief—and again, for the last time, my name is Rayna."

"Forgive me."

Rayna sighed, realizing how rude she must have sounded. "No, forgive *me*. You let me in your home and somehow healed my foot. I really appreciate all you've done. And I'm sorry about your . . . birth defect."

The girl looked uncomfortable but nodded respectfully, a small smile on her face and a bit of uncertainty in her eyes.

Rayna frowned. "Sorry again. In case you haven't noticed, I have a tendency of putting my foot in my mouth."

"It is not my place to question where a Power puts her foot."

Rayna laughed, and soon the girl's delicate laughter joined Rayna's deeper, throatier chuckle. Rayna relaxed, relieved that the tense encounter had taken a lighter turn. The girl's eyes softened, and for a brief moment she didn't look so ill. To Rayna's surprise, she began to sing, a smooth, enchanting melody. Her ethereal voice perfectly suited the song's haunting lyrics. As Rayna listened, the girl's thought-provoking lyrics became superseded by the spirit in which they were sung. Still, Rayna's sharp mind managed to commit to memory the first few verses:

The club forged of trees
is greater than the sword forged of fire,
for its wood is born of life,
and above life there's nothing higher.

Let not evil dark deeds
bring the sorrow which robs all happiness.
Stand against the hate disguise,
and unite half to make whole our less.

The light is our need
and will take time for us to brandish well.
Winds of wrong blow without toil,
but the labor to make right prevails . . .

When the girl finished, Rayna wanted to ask her to sing again, sad and almost angry that the beautiful song was over. Before she could say anything, the girl spoke.

"That was an old song passed on for many ages. It is customary to offer a Power a gift if one should be fortunate enough to meet one. My father and I are poor. The best gift I could offer was song. My father says my voice is as lovely as the land of Kuara, so I chose to share it with you." She smiled briefly, trying not to reveal her pride.

Rayna appreciated the girl's kindness but knew she was enjoying benefits and courtesies not intended for her. Her analytical mind demanded a rational explanation. Who was this Power called Irel that the girl spoke of? How could Rayna be mistaken for her? And how did all of this connect to her being in this strange place?

Rayna surveyed the small room. The minimal furnishings were spartan, with no upholstery on the wooden chairs and no decorative carving on the small, simple table. She noticed the absence of a television set, radio, and lamps—not a single electric appliance could be seen. The windows had no glass, only antiquated shutters. The table where they sat had one unlit candle in its holder, and a mortar and pestle in one corner, its crushed contents still inside. The girl certainly spoke the truth when she said she and her father were poor. Rayna made a sweeping gesture of the area with her hand, nodding several times.

"Nice place," she lied.

"Thank you."

"I don't suppose you have a phone I can use to call home?"

The girl, predictably, shook her head, a puzzled look on her face.

"You don't know what a phone is, do you?" Rayna asked, softening her voice to avoid sounding condescending.

Again, the girl shook her head.

Rayna leaned back, and the old wooden chair creaked under her weight. She began to massage her temples. "Your song was so wonderful I forgot that I have a splitting headache," she said.

The girl rushed to Rayna's side and offered to heal her. Rayna was tempted to let the girl do for her headache whatever she had done for her ankle, but she reluctantly refused. The girl looked half dead already, and she had looked worse after healing Rayna's ankle than before. Whatever she did seemed to take a lot out of her, and Rayna feared that any more of this mysterious healing could kill her.

Rayna smiled sadly. "I would simply ask for an aspirin, but I don't think you know what that is either."

An awkward silence followed. Rayna was curious about her host and this strange, backward place, but she couldn't think of a polite way of asking for explanations. She was pleased when the girl began to talk about herself. Rayna learned that the girl was born in a providence called Zuran. She had begun to demonstrate healing talents before she could talk.

"No one was sure," the girl said, "why I, a child of West Taren parents, would possess magic. Such people as myself are called "*Unnaturals*" because we are neither truly West Taren nor East. Few of us exist."

"But you do."

"Yes, and I believe my mother would have preferred it if I had come into the world blind or crippled instead. You see, when I turned seven years of age, my mother could tolerate my magic no longer. She begged my father to kill me, and she accused me of being a spawn of evil."

"You're not evil," Rayna assured her.

"Thank you, Irel. That means much to me."

"I'm sorry for interrupting. What happened next?"

"My father, a well-regarded courier by trade, also feared my magic, but he could not bring himself to kill me, his only child." The girl's stare focused down at nothing as she relived the past moment in her mind.

"Soon after my father's decision to spare my life, my mother hanged herself outside our home. The note he found in her pocket said that she forgave him for being too weak-willed a man to perform the deed."

Rayna was stunned into silence.

For the first time, the girl raised her voice in anger. "My father is not a weak man! His body may falter, but his spirit never has. Surely you know this to be true, Irel."

"Yes, of course," Rayna answered, unsure of what else to say.

Reassured, the girl continued. "My father was fearful for my safety, because soon my talents would be too difficult to hide. Even back then, the penalty in West Taren for using magic was death. The only hope a magic user had of avoiding such a fate was self-exile to the land of East Taren, where magicians were not only accepted but welcomed. But my father, as most West Tareners did, regarded East Taren as a foul land not fit for raising West Taren young. Instead, he quit his position and secretly moved us here to Kuara, a West Taren province known for its strong but welcoming people."

Rayna learned from the girl, that though deep in magic-phobic West Taren, Kuarans were rumored to accept magic healers into their community from time to time. According to the girl, her father was a big, strong, hardworking man then and could fit in as a Kuaran native easily. He gambled that the Kuarans would accept them both. They did, and the girl and her father remained in Kuara.

Throughout the conversation, much of which flew against everything Rayna knew to be rational and sensible—places she never heard of before, the casual references to magic. Yet, Rayna found herself intuitively trusting the girl's words, accepting them as truth. If it were not for the bizarre course of events leading up to this point, Rayna would have dismissed the whole story as the product of an over active imagination. Something strange, however, had happened to her in the woods during the storm that night. In that context, the girl's story could make sense.

Rayna recalled the chain of events that had led her here. She had been followed by a woman she had previously known only in her dreams, then been struck by lighting, only to appear in a red wasteland unscathed. Her badly injured ankle had been mysteriously healed by a pointed-eared girl claiming to be a magical healer. Then there was the issue of being mistaken for someone called Irel, apparently a really important person. It all had to mean something.

A feeble cough sounded from behind a closed door. The girl took notice, looking more anxious than ever.

"Please excuse me. I must go now to attend to my father." When she stood, the girl leaned on her staff like a cane, as if young girl's uncharacteristically mature behavior had internally aged her body. As the girl rushed to the closed door, Rayna decided to follow her, partially out of curiosity and partially out of her desperate need to find clues to the growing mystery of what had happened to her.

The girl opened the door quickly, but Rayna slipped in before the girl could object. The pungent smell of decay and sickness rushed violently into Rayna's nostrils. She gently closed the door behind her, sensing that it never remained open. With the door of the windowless room shut, she felt like she had entered a small tomb. A lone candle illuminated the room only dimly. As Rayna's eyes adjusted, she first made out a bed, then the man in it, partially covered by a thin, veil-like sheet. His eyes were shut tight, and his breathing was shallow and irregular. His face, the least ravaged by whatever dark malady that gripped him, indicated he was somewhere in his forties. The rest of his body, Rayna observed, looked much older.

At one time, he may had been the powerful and hardworking man his daughter claimed him to be, but now, all that was left of his frame was a brittle, withered mass of bone and skin. Then there were his ears— pointed, just like his daughter's.

It must be a hereditary deformity, Rayna thought. The dying man spoke no words; Rayna was unsure if that was by choice or due to his sickness.

He appeared blind to Rayna's scrutiny. His pitiful hacking cough eased only momentarily in response to the girl's whispered words of comfort that Rayna could not hear.

She turned to Rayna and said, "It has been a long time since my father has been well enough to work. Ever since he became ill, I have earned our bread by healing the local laborers after they toil in the fields all day. It is a secret arrangement that no one outside Kuara knows of. I earn enough coin to care for my father and keep home, and that is all I need."

"Why can't you heal him like you did me?" Rayna asked.

The girl shook her head tiredly as she brought her father some water and helped him to drink. "I fear that is my failure. My father suffers from a rotting sickness that consumes from the inside out. I can only partially heal such a condition, and at that, only modestly. Healing a sore limb or treating a backache is an easy task for me, and I can do so using only small amounts of magic. You see, the Red Robes, though powerful, cannot sense magic use in such small amounts. I can help the farmers and townspeople with their minor ailments without fear of detection."

"I see," Rayna said thoughtfully. Her thoughts ran briefly to that of her own father, shortly before he died of cancer. She remembered him looking as frail as the girl's father. She cried when the nurse asked her to leave the room. That was the last time she saw her father alive.

"But your father is a different matter," Rayna said, drawing herself back to the present. "His healing would require more than a little magic."

The girl nodded in agreement. "Yes. For years, I have been able to keep him somewhat well through a blend of small healing and herbs that I buy in town. But recently he got worse." She clasped her hands around those of her father. "Last night, I feared that he would die unless I did more."

"So you gave him everything you could muster, the full extent of your power."

"Yes, and it was a great strain on me, but it was not enough, Irel. His illness goes beyond my abilities. Death still grips him, and I know he will die before the sun sets tonight."

Rayna put her hand on the girl's frail shoulder. "I'm sorry."

"As am I, for now I am certain my magic has been detected by the Red Robes. Soon they will come for me, to punish me."

Rayna struggled to swallow all of what the girl was saying. Magic, Red Robes, death. "Maybe we can find you a hiding place," she said.

"There is no hiding from the Red Robes. Once they have caught the scent of my magic, they will track me down and find me. No one has ever escaped the hunt of a Red Robe."

The girl quickly turned apologetic, forgetting that her company was special. "Please forgive me. I am sure a Power as great as yourself could provide me sanctuary. But my father is too ill to come hide with me, and I cannot abandon him in his final hours. I must be by his side through it all."

Rayna remained silent. She wished the girl would stop referring to her as some great Power, but this was not the time to raise the issue. She had to admit, the girl's father appeared to be in no condition to move, and she agreed that any attempt to move him had a high probability of killing him.

Rayna admired the girl's maturity and devotion to her father. Watching her, Rayna couldn't help feeling ashamed of what she planned to tell her own mother before the car accident. The girl spoke, interrupting Rayna's thoughts.

"When I vainly poured out my magic to help my father, I did not know you would be coming, Irel, so I did the only thing I knew at the time would save me."

Rayna didn't like the sound of that. Afraid of what she might hear, she asked anyway. "What did you do?"

The girl walked to a corner of the room, to a small wooden box on the floor. She reached into the box and produced a handful of small dried berries, bluish gray in color.

"I have used these herbs," she said solemnly, "in the past for my father's pain. In small portions, these berries help to ease suffering, but if too much is taken, it sours in the stomach and becomes poison."

Rayna felt her blood run ice cold. It suddenly dawned on her why the girl looked so pale and sickly. "You're telling me you overdosed on that stuff and you're dying?"

The girl poured out her confession, speaking rapidly, in a hushed tone. "I have taken more than what was needed to do the deed. I did not want to risk facing the Red Robes alive when they come." A strange look of resolve passed over the girl's face. "It was my plan to die with my father tonight and cheat the Red Robes of their bounty. Unless . . ." The girl hesitated, looking up at Rayna. "Unless you see fit in your wisdom to change that."

Rayna turned away, unable to look in the dying girl's vacuous eyes. "What do you think I can do? *You* are the healer. Heal yourself—please!" she pleaded. "Whoever these Red Robes are, I'm sure we can talk to them and get them to understand that you used the magic only to help your father. At most, I can see them giving you a few days in prison for breaking the rules. They might even be able to help your dad. Please, heal yourself now. You're scaring me."

"You are the one my daughter spoke of moments ago," a crackling voice uttered behind them. Rayna turned to see the bedridden man, who somehow had managed to prop himself upright, seemingly through sheer will. "Please come closer, let me see your ears."

Rayna took in a deep breath to calm her nerves, then did as he asked. As he peered at her ears, his clouded eyes widened in amazement. "So it is true, the time has finally come," he said. "Irel is here, and my heart is glad. I know you will vanquish the enemy. Please . . ." He broke into a fit of violent coughing, which gradually subsided into low wheezing. His daughter brought him more water to drink. As she slowly moved her hands over both sides of her father's body, Rayna saw a halo of soft light build around the girl's thin fingers and over her hands. The man's body relaxed in relief, and he slid down to a supine position. The girl sat on the bed for a moment, momentarily unable to stand. The strain of healing while poisoned was taking its toll.

Rayna didn't believe in magic, but she had just witnessed what appeared to be magic in action. The conflict between what her mind refused to accept and what her eyes clearly saw formed an unsettling paradox inside her that wouldn't go away. Scientifically, she tried to rationalize the feeling away. The glow she saw on the girl's hands could have been a trick of light in the dimly lit room; perhaps something on her skin reflected the candlelight. But the feeling that she had just witnessed something beyond the explanation of known science remained. Unnerved, Rayna felt an urgent impulse to flee the house and leave the whole depressing nightmare behind her, but she sensed that the girl needed her. Rayna wanted to say something noble and comforting to them both, something worthy of the wise and powerful person they thought her to be. Noble, comforting words would not come to her mind.

"My name's not Irel," she said instead.

In reply to Rayna's feeble and indirect response to her father's plea for help, the girl's voice took on a desperate tone. "Irel, forgive me if I can call you nothing else, but you ask me to deny the only name by which I have learned to know you." As she spoke, the girl added another sheet to her father's coverings. "He has become weaker still. I think the end is near," she wept. "I know they say that sometimes, before revealing his or her true self, a Power will test a follower to see if he or she is worthy," the girl said. "I have done everything you have set before me. I have healed you, even though I know you could have easily healed yourself. I have answered your questions, even though you surely knew the answers already, and I have explained things that you surely understand better than I. And I have accepted the knowledge that you will not cure my father of his illness."

The girl's head drifted downward, then jerked back up again as she resisted the dark sleep as long as she could. "I only ask—no, I beg this one thing of you, for I can feel the cord of death tightening around my neck, like my mother's noose."

Rayna envisioned the poison pulsing through the girl's veins, like hundreds of tainted rivers. She trembled and realized that she too was crying. Though she had known the girl for only a few hours, she felt there was nothing she wouldn't do for her. "What is it you want me do?" Rayna asked.

"My father once told me that I have the soul of a West Tarener but was cursed with the magic of an East Tarener. He often spoke of how wicked the East Tareners are, saying their ways of magic are the cause of the woes in the world. I don't believe all magic is evil; I have done much good with mine. My father would ask that you destroy East Taren and its people. I do not want such a thing to happen. I just want peace, true peace—not this false peace we have been living for so long. I believe my father wants this as well, deep in his heart. Please, do this for us and—"

The girl collapsed, and Rayna quickly knelt by her side. There on the floor, by the dim light of a single candle, Rayna held the dying girl closely.

A faint sound from behind Rayna aroused her attention, and she turned to see a woman standing at the doorway, blocking the only exit from the room.

CHAPTER
4

The Talisman of Light

The first thing Rayna noticed was her black, wide-brimmed hat, made of painted straw. Long, thin, braided locks of her hair drooped down freely from under the hat. Unsurprisingly, the stranger's ears were pointed just like the girl's, and her father's. Several small drawstring sacks, filled with unknown things, hung loosely against her sides, attached by a thin rope tied to her belt. She wore a cloak, a dark gray tunic with matching trousers, and worn black boots. In her hand, she held a long curved knife; her brown face was stern and tense.

Startled, Rayna backed away and hurried to her feet.

"Are you a Red Robe?" Rayna spotted a wooden chair not far from where she stood. She planned to grab it.

"Hardly," the woman scoffed, sheathing her knife. "My name is Keris." Following Rayna's gaze, she added "Chairs make poor weapons—don't make the mistake of using them for anything other than sitting. I mean you no harm. If I did, I would have done so."

"Then what was the knife for?"

"I trust few people—least of all unknown magic users. But I have decided that you are a reasonable sort, so I apologize for appearing before you armed."

Rayna quickly dried her tears. She didn't trust the stranger, and she wasn't going to show weakness. "What do you want?" Rayna asked in a gruff tone.

Keris arched an eyebrow. "I want many things this day: Freedom from oppression, vengeance against my enemies, the sound of my friends near me . . . but for now, your abilities will suffice."

With uncanny speed and grace, Keris reached down and lifted the girl in her arms, gently laying her on the bed. "I wish I had the chance to speak with her," Keris said softly, remorse in her voice. "I did not know her, yet I feel she was far stronger a person than she appeared. If she had joined me, it would have been a blessing to my cause. It is said that healers bring not only healing, but good fortune as well." Keris shook her head. "But it is too late. She is dead, and so is her father," she announced. She held a small mirror near their noses and mouths and failed to see signs of breath. She moved quickly around the room, gathering odds and ends, bits of food, medical supplies, and cloth, shoving them into her knapsack.

Rayna watched her incredulously. "Don't you have any shame? You can't just walk in here and start stealing their stuff just because you can."

"I am no thief," Keris said defiantly. "What I take, I take for our survival in the days that will follow, not profit. The dead have no need for food or medicine, but we do." She handed a blue robe and a shirt to Rayna. "Here, change into these. The garments you wear are too exotic and will draw attention."

Rayna folded her arms indignantly. "I'm not changing clothes, and I definitely am not going with you."

"We do not have time for debate. If what the girl says is true, the Red Robes could be here at any moment. We need to leave now."

"How did you know about—"

"I have followed you ever since I first spotted you limping toward the healer's home. I waited outside by the window as you spoke to the healer, and I heard everything said. When you two moved into the next room, I could no longer hear, so I came inside."

"You were spying on us?"

"As I said earlier, I was planning to recruit this healer for my cause when I saw you. I feared you might be an agent for the Red Robes, so I decided to hide and wait. I could not afford to be detected."

"You make even less sense than the girl did."

"I will explain things in better detail when we are somewhere safer. Now, put these clothes on."

Rayna studied the garments suspiciously. "Whose robes are these?" she asked.

Keris shrugged. "They look too long to belong to the girl, so they must be her father's. They should fit you well enough, though."

"I'm not wearing any dead person's clothes."

"If the Red Robes find us here, we will be dead as well. Now hurry, we don't have much time!"

As Rayna reluctantly donned the shirt and robes, Keris thrust yet another item at her. It was the dead girl's staff.

"You will need protection. You do not appear to have any of your own."

"She was kind enough to heal me, and you want me to repay her by taking her staff?"

"She thought highly of you. Surely she would have given it to you if you had asked while she lived."

Rayna let the staff drop to the floor. "These Red Robes don't know me, and I haven't done anything wrong. I refuse behave like some kind of criminal. Maybe these Red Robes can help me find a way back home."

Keris's voice took on an edge. "By coming to the home of a magic user, you have now made yourself a target. The Red Robes are cunning hunters, and such hunters know not only the trail of their prey, but everything and everyone that prey has recently been with. That includes you. They will associate you with the magic user, and hunt you as well. Any pleas of your innocence will fall on deaf ears. Then they will interrogate you."

Rayna remained skeptical. "What kinds of questions will they ask me?"

Keris looked impatient but answered anyway. "They will want to know of your loyalty to the throne and whether are not you know the whereabouts of other magic users. However, the Red Robes will not trust your tongue. Instead, they will reach into your mind and tear out the information they desire. It is a most painful ordeal."

Rayna, though nervous, tried not to show it. "Why are you so eager to help? What's in this for you?" she asked.

"With the death of the healer, I am still in need of a magic user. I would have preferred a healer—someone who could heal our warriors as they battled. Instead, I will settle for a sorceress, such as yourself."

Rayna laughed out loud. "What? You think I'm a sorceress?"

"Unlike the girl, I do not believe you are Irel, or any other Power for that matter. To do so would lend you more credit than you deserve."

"Thanks," Rayna quipped sarcastically.

"I believe you are a sorceress, though I will not request proof here, at this time. We don't need to add to the scent the Red Robes are following." As if in anticipated response to Rayna's next remark, Keris added, "Do not debate the benefit of my doubt. If I was certain you couldn't help me, I would leave you here for the Red Robes to find. Now gather what you may need and let us go!"

Stubbornly, Rayna refused to move, watching with disgust as Keris hastily rummaged through more of the dead family's provisions, like a grave robber. With reluctance, Rayna concluded it was better to go with Keris, a somewhat known, if unlikable element, than to face the totally unknown Red Robes. The Red Robes certainty didn't sound like good guys, and the girl had been so terrified of them that she had taken her own life to avoid them. Rayna couldn't imagine anyone so evil that would want to harm someone as kind and as harmless as the girl.

Keris stood at the doorway of the room. "Are you coming?"

"Yes." Rayna stepped to join Keris, and at the last minute she grabbed the staff. She might just need it, she reasoned, if not to defend herself against the Red Robes, then against Keris.

✳ ✳ ✳

Rayna felt torn with mixed feelings. She was glad to be out of the cottage and the stale, fetid room, where she just witnessed two people die. On the other hand, she was nervous about being with Keris, who moved with the stealth of an assassin. Rayna couldn't help feeling like a mouse trusting the house cat to help it avoid a mouse trap. It was getting late in the day; they had fled the girl's home and hidden a distance away behind a sloping hill. Though the sun had nearly vanished behind the horizon, it was still very warm. Crouched close to the tall grass, they watched the cottage from their concealment. Keris wanted to be certain the Red Robes had truly sensed the girl's magic and begun pursuit. It didn't take long to find out: The Red Robes arrived within an hour.

Rayna could make out several hooded figures dressed in red, moving in and out of the house. Straining her eyes, she could see them—outstretched hands, touching everything in sight, from the opened front door, to the furniture and walls inside. It was as if they were trying to *feel* what had happened there. Minutes after their arrival, they all gathered outside. One of the figures, who was carrying a torch, set fire to the cottage, and soon the entire home was engulfed in flame. The bodies of the girl and her father were still inside.

"So those are the Red Robes," Rayna whispered, her voice edged with anger.

"Yes," Keris said. "They are the scourge of Taren, and they serve Nephredom and his personal witch."

Rayna didn't hear her. Watching the burning of the small house, she had become fixated on the dancing, popping flames. The fire forked upward at the darkening sky, like a horrid, clawed hand. Silently witnessing the pyre, Rayna mouthed a brief prayer for the girl and father; she found herself again fighting to hold back tears. The whole time she was there, she thought, she didn't even ask for the girl's name. Why didn't she ask for her name?

A warm, tingling sensation on Rayna's left wrist began to bother her. She had felt it almost since they left the cottage and had been absently massaging the feeling away. Now the warmth had intensified to the point that she could no longer ignore it. That was when she noticed the watch on that wrist had a glow.

The growing heat and illumination of her watch's band were nothing compared to the wonder going on within the watch's face. The silly clown illustration looked silly no more—it looked terrified. The idiotic grin it once wore was gone; its expression was of animated fear. Its eyes had widened, and its mouth formed a terror-stricken 'O' that twitched occasionally.

The mustache hands, formerly stuck on midnight, now spun wildly around in opposite directions. No voice came from the clown image, but with a performance like that, Rayna thought, none was needed. Rayna was about to show Keris, but she saw that the woman was already aware of the spectacle.

"So," Keris spoke without expression or emotion, "it seems you are the sorcerer I thought you to be."

"Look, I have no idea why my watch is doing this. This is *not* my fault!"

"Shhhhhhh! We will discuss this later. Now end your talisman's glow before its light and magic reveal our position."

"I can't get it to stop. My watch doesn't even come with a light. It's not supposed to be able to do any of this."

One of the Red Robes looked up in the direction they were hiding.

"I think they are aware of our presence," Keris said. "We must leave now. The town is near—we can hide there for a while."

"Will they chase us?"

"Chasing is not their way. They may follow, but they will never run. Like the spider, they are patient hunters. Now come."

Despite her newly healed ankle, Rayna had a hard time keeping up with Keris as they raced together toward town. Keris glided effortlessly across the land like a feline, her sleek body perfectly attuned for motion. Between gasps for air, Rayna found herself silently cursing Keris's athletic prowess. The heat didn't help. Only the splendid scenery helped to take her mind off the running. Kuara was filled with a natural beauty Rayna had never experienced. Even in the dusk of day, everything was vivid and full with the color of life, with endless, grassy plains and broad, majestic trees. A pleasant warm wind blew from the west; the star-emerging firmament above lay over the land like a sparkling quilt. Rayna noticed two stars that looked out of place. They shined brightly in the sky in close proximity. One was red and the other blue.

Rayna called out to Keris and pointed upward as she ran. "Those two stars. Do you know their names?"

"They are called the Twin Stars of Taren," Keris called back. "Rumor has it that they are mystical eyes placed in the sky by the Powers so they can watch over us. I do not believe in such things."

As the sights of Kuara soothed her soul, Rayna saw that her watch was returning to normal. The glow had died down to a barely noticeable shine, and the clown's ridiculous grin had returned. The hour and minute hands were frozen at twelve o'clock again. As Rayna watched, the shine disappeared, leaving the watch deceptively innocent looking.

They stopped to rest in a blossoming field of wildflowers, with the town in sight. Acres of well-kept farmland surrounded the field in all directions. Keris produced a white scarf from her bag.

"Here," she said, handing it to Rayna. "You must wear this. We will not get much farther with your unusual ears announcing us."

"My ears are not unusual," said Rayna, tying the scarf around her head so that it covered the upper halves of her ears. Her long hair flowed from the top of the scarf, like a plume.

"Why then are there no others with ears such as yours?"

"I don't know."

"Well, time is the greatest solver of riddles. We will see." Keris handed a piece of fruit to Rayna, who bit into it hungrily.

"I haven't eaten in nearly 24 hours."

"You're welcome."

"Oh, thanks."

Keris sat with her knees drawn toward her, watching Rayna as she ate. "Tell me," she asked, "back in the cottage, when the girl was still alive, I overheard part of your name—Rayna. What is your full, proper title and origin, Rayna?"

Keris irritated Rayna. Who did this woman think she was—first bossing her around, and then asking her casual questions as if her previously rude behavior was irrelevant?

"I am Rayna Powell, daughter of Mary Powell and Stephen Powell, the first," she replied, mocking Keris's haughty, proper tone. "I live in the affluent suburbs on Nightwind Drive. Is that full and proper enough?"

"Nearly. Your homeland is unclear to me. Because you are a sorceress, I will wager you are of East Taren. Is that true?"

"No."

"You are a West Taren Unnatural then?"

"No."

"Well, then." Keris's voice took on a cynical tone. "I assume you wish me to believe as the child did, that you are Irel from the Band."

"I did come through the Band, if you want to call it that."

"And this Nightwind Drive you spoke of, is it on the other side of the Band?"

Rayna finished off the last bit of the fruit and crossed her arms defensively. "It has to be. It definitely can't be around here. Everything here is so primitive."

"What a shame we lack the comforts you are accustomed to."

"You don't believe I came from the Band, do you?"

"No, Rayna Powell of Nightwind, I do not."

"Look, there's no way I could make up the kind of hell I went though in that forsaken place. The girl had seen me leave that place, why didn't you?"

Keris pulled out a piece of fruit for herself and began to chew on it slowly. "Perhaps I was momentarily blinded by the brilliant light of your presence," she said. "That is rumored to happen to those who attempt to look directly at a Power without permission."

Rayna fought to keep her composure. "I'm sick of your snide remarks."

"As am I of your lies," Keris replied. "If you prefer not to reveal to me your true origin, then be straight about it and say so."

"But I'm telling you—"

Keris raised her hand in interruption. "Hear and understand this. Primitive I may be, but I am neither child nor fool. No one can walk seven steps into Irel's Band without being struck down dead. No one.

Are we agreed that this joke is done?"

"Fine. It's done."

A moment of angry silence passed before Keris spoke again.

"Aside from your sorcery, what do you do to earn coin?"

"I was a university student, and I didn't *earn coin*. My mother sent me money when I needed it."

"Ah, a student. What is your discipline of focus?"

"I was a science major."

On seeing the amused look on Keris's face, Rayna shot back, "Don't they at least have science here?"

"Science is a most futile craft, practiced by a handful in Dosk. They supposedly study in secret, but their secret is poorly kept."

"Where's Dosk?"

"It is an East Taren province, many days' journey from here."

Rayna was going to ask more about Dosk when she felt a tingle on her wrist. The clown face of her watch grinned on, unchanged, but the watch band took on a steady, faint glow—barley noticeable, even in the fading light. Keris saw it too.

"It appears that your talisman warns you of danger," Keris said, looking at the watch and then back at Rayna with new insight. "I take it the Red Robes are somewhere near?"

"Yes . . . I guess."

"You do not know the magic of your own artifact?"

Rayna frowned. "I'm used to watches telling time, not glowing and making faces." She recalled how earlier, her watch had tingled lightly, then increased in both sensation and light as the Red Robes drew nearer.

"Somehow my watch has turned into some kind of proximity detector," Rayna muttered absent-mindedly.

"In common tongue, I assume you mean that the closer the danger, the greater your talisman's light becomes?"

"I think so."

"Then we need to move on now, while they are still some distance away." Keris rose to her feet. Her black hat looked menacing in the darkness.

CHAPTER
5

The Sharpening Stone

At last, in the middle of the night, they reached town. As if for subtle camouflage, the stores and shops were built with the colors of the soil, grass, and rock.

"We will spend the night there." Keris pointed to a sturdy, rustic-looking establishment a few yards from where they stood, on a main dirt street. Its signpost read *The Sharpening Stone*.

Stepping inside, they discovered that the inn was also a tavern. Rayna and Keris sat at an empty table, near the rear of the room. Rayna noticed that her stool had a square seat and a single leg in the center. She first assumed it was broken, then saw that all the other stools had just one leg. Though it took a bit of balance and skill, Rayna found her stool to be adequate once she got used to it. Somewhere, someone played a fast tune on a flute; at the tables, clusters of men and women sat laughing and drinking together. There wasn't a frowning face in the entire tavern—except Rayna's. She didn't feel comfortable in places like this.

"I thought this was a hotel, not a bar," she grumbled as she surveyed the room.

Near the front of the room, Rayna saw a burly man dressed in shorts.

He sat on some kind of contraption resembling a bicycle. The machine had no tires; its pedals were connected by pulleys and sprockets to a small network of fans attached along the ceiling. The man pedaled the machine steadily to make the fans above turn, producing a pleasant breeze throughout the pub. Judging from the man's occasional grunts, Rayna could tell it was no easy task. He looked happy enough, though, and seemed to enjoy the effort.

Her gaze fell on the man's powerful, pedaling legs. The sweat on his solid calves made them gleam like dark steel in the lantern light. The fellow caught Rayna's stare and gave her a wink. In spite of the breeze, Rayna suddenly felt her face grow uncomfortably warm, and she averted her eyes. Keris watched her with an entertained expression.

"The men of Kuara are interesting, wouldn't you agree?"

Rayna sidestepped the question. "Now that things have slowed down a bit, I need some facts," she declared.

"What do you need to know?"

"First of all, do you have a map?"

"If you hope to find Nightwind on a map, I will save you the trouble by telling you that of all the maps I have seen and places I have been, none bears that name."

"I'll like to see that for myself."

If Keris was offended, Rayna couldn't tell.

From her bag, Keris pulled out a worn, scrolled map, which she gave to Rayna. "You may," she said.

After unrolling and examining the leathery scroll, Rayna was at last convinced that she was a very long way from the place she called home. The towns shown on the map were disturbingly unfamiliar, and the borders were shaped unlike any places she knew. Although geography wasn't Rayna's passion, she knew it well enough to know there was no such thing as the East and West Taren Sea—at least not until she arrived here.

Rayna briefly considered the possibility that she held a fictitious map, but she dismissed the notion like an analyst ruling out a faulty premise. There was no reason for Keris to go through such trouble just to fool her. Rayna's forehead wrinkled with worry and thought. No place on the map gave her a clue on how to get home. It didn't make any sense.

Her pondering was cut short by Keris's even voice. "I take it you couldn't find Nightwind either."

"No, I couldn't. It looks like I'm stuck here, for now."

"Perhaps you fell and struck your head recently," Keris suggested, as she instructed a serving girl to bring them both soup. "That would explain why you remember not from which province you came."

Rayna handed the map back the cloaked woman. "I did fall, but only my ankle was injured. Before that point, I started out in the woods near my home. Then I got lost during a bad storm. After a while, I found myself in the middle of a crazy lightning show." Rayna stopped for a moment to prepare herself for the ludicrous thing she was about to say. "I think one of the lighting bolts hit me, and . . . *magically* brought me to the Band."

"Are we back to the 'Irel of the Band' story again?"

"I'm serious."

"Then tell me, if you were magically brought to Taren, what was the purpose of this event?"

"You're the one from the world with magic! I was hoping you could tell me."

"Transport by magical means requires a rare kind of power, and the use of lightning to accomplish such a thing is unknown to me. The scholars of Dosk would know better than I."

"That's the second time you've mentioned Dosk," Rayna observed.

"Yes, Dosk is the city of scholars and diviners, where one can find out about many things. There are myriad libraries and schools there."

"Where do the scientists stay in Dosk?"

Keris smiled thinly. "The scientists are the outcasts of Dosk, since even the most liberal book learners there scorn their work as worthless. The scientists cling together for safety in their so-called science guilds, like a cult. They are wary of strangers. You would do better seeking the knowledge of the more accepted groups in Dosk."

Rayna was not discouraged. "I don't need the advice of fortune-tellers, soothsayers, and phone-psychics. I don't need somebody telling me 'just click your heels together, and you'll be home in no time, dear!' I want a real explanation of how I got here, and a logical proposal on how to get back. So far, the scientists of Dosk seem to be my best hope."

Keris eyed Rayna curiously. "You said yourself you were magically brought here. Wouldn't a magical solution to a magical problem be—?"

"Absolutely useless to me," Rayna cut in. "I refuse to let go of the hope that somewhere in this backward world, there are people who believe in reality."

The serving girl returned with two bowls of soup. Keris drank from her bowl, her eyes occasionally peering around the crowded room. "You are a strange one indeed, Rayna Powell of Nightwind," she said.

Rayna shifted her weight slightly to maintain balance on the one-legged stool. "I want you to show me how to get to Dosk," she announced. "If you don't show me, I'll find a way to get there myself."

"There are more urgent matters you must attend to than visiting scroll keepers and philosophers."

Rayna scowled. "Like joining you in your crusade?"

"Yes—and lower your voice. Enemy ears are always about."

"I'm not a sorceress, Rayna whispered."

"I believe otherwise."

"I suppose you expect that I will lead the charge flying on a broomstick, while hurling fireballs."

Keris grinned unexpectedly. "Nothing that grandiose, though I must say, it sounds fitting of a magician of your standing." Keris's voice softened and lowered. "I will tell you more of my purpose—but at a time and place more convenient and appropriate than this. You will need time to make up your mind. If you are truly 'stuck here,' as you say, then there is no harm in waiting a while before gallivanting off unaccompanied during times as dangerous as these. I am sure that once you know more of the situation, you will join us."

"How long?"

"At least one day. I do not feel at ease speaking of my cause with the Red Robes so near. We will need to gain a greater distance from them first."

"Speaking of Red Robes," Rayna began angrily, "just who are they, and what gives them the right to burn down someone's house—with the former occupants still in it?"

"Lower your voice when speaking of such things," Keris warned again, as she adjusted the brim on her black hat. "I dare say, I am beginning to truly believe that you are not of this land. You know nothing of common matters."

"I'm willing to learn."

"The Red Robes are the elite magician guard of Nephredom, their ruler and master. They all have been personally trained by Nephredom himself, and they possess very dangerous magic. They wear the color of blood to taunt and strike fear into the hearts of their victims. Their authority is second only to Nephredom and the witch who is his aide. Even the Queen wields no control over them. Since Nephredom declared that magic may not be practiced in East Taren or West Taren, the Red Robes have been punishing anyone they find breaking this law."

"The Red Robes are exempt from the no-magic decree, I assume."

Keris nodded. "The enforcers of rules are seldom bound by them themselves. The Red Robes freely use their magic to torture and inflict pain on whomever they choose."

"This rebellion of yours is against the Red Robes?"

"I suppose it is only fair to disclose that much now. Yes, the Red Robes are one of the evils I and those with me oppose."

Rayna was skeptical "Why should I believe you?" she challenged. You claim to be a recruiter, but you act more like a spy. How can I trust your word?"

"If you searched your heart as much as you did your head, your path would be clearer. The Red Robes violated and burned the home of an innocent, whose only crime was her love for her father." Keris sneered. "The dogs did not even bother to give them a decent burial. They burned them where they lay—their souls un-mourned for, save us two."

Rayna whispered sadly, "I know."

"I remember how you looked then," Keris said. "It was in your eyes, and in your tears. You felt as I did. You wanted revenge."

"I did."

"Then I believe we share a common enemy. That is a good start."

Rayna agreed reluctantly. "But even if I wanted to help you fight those monsters, it would mean postponing my search for home." Rayna paused, uncertain. "You're right, I'll need some time to think about this.

"Agreed." Keris rose and propped her stool against the table. "Now, if you would excuse me for an hour or so, I have some contacts here in Kuara, and I need to meet with them to gather some information. I would welcome you to come with me, but they are not fond of new faces."

Rayna did her best to disguise her anxiety and started to sip on her now cold soup. "Doesn't matter to me," she said dismissively.

Keris added, "Under normal circumstances, I would tell you not to worry about your safety in this place. Kuara is the safest province in Taren, and law is rarely broken here. However, with the Red Robes about, your eyes must be alert for their possible approach. But I believe their trail has gotten cold, and I doubt they will find us, so long as they don't sense any additional magic."

On that note, Rayna checked her watch; it was dormant and cool. That was a good sign.

"And one more thing," Keris cautioned. "Do not remove your head scarf for any reason." Keris briefly spoke to the innkeeper, handed him something, and vanished out into the night.

Rayna wasn't the kind of person to feel self-conscious about sitting alone, but this was different. In a place where almost every table was filled with noisy people, Rayna felt a need to better blend in. To make matters worse, everyone looked as if they worked out regularly in a gym, leaving her to feel like a weak and skinny outcast. At the bar, she noticed a lone, older man nursing a mug of drink—presumably an alcoholic beverage. He appeared harmless enough. She stood up to join him, and her stool hit the floor with a resounding knock. Annoyed and embarrassed, Rayna let the stool lie on the floor. A few heads turned Rayna's way, then lost interest.

Rayna sat on the stool next to the gentleman drinking at the bar and watched him curiously. He was a slightly heavyset man with a short, puffy salt-and-pepper beard. Four mugs of drink were lined up in front of him. He cradled a fifth drink in his large hands. He grinned and laughed a lot, stopping only to swallow more brew. The plain work clothes he wore were worn and frayed from many days of hard labor.

He noticed Rayna and laughed with a yellow grin. "Hi there, lovely woman! What have I done to have such a fetching creature as yourself in my company?"

Rayna wrinkled her nose in disdain. The man reeked of alcohol. "Nothing," she said.

"Hey, Ho! My name is Merlott of Kuara—and yours, lovely lady?"

"Rayna—of Nightwind."

"Come, Rayna, and have an ale with me."

"I don't drink."

"Don't drink?" Merlott threw back his head in laugher. "Nonsense!" he bellowed before gulping down more of the brownish stuff. "After a day of hard work, a mug of ale is all I have strength left to lift! Haw, haw!" He pushed one of the spare mugs of ale over to Rayna. "Here," he chuckled, "drink, and make me happy."

Hesitantly, Rayna sipped from the mug. It had a strong, spicy taste. "I need to gather some information from an unbiased source," she said, wincing from the taste of the ale. "You will do."

Merlott belched. "Huh? Speak plain talk, girl. You sound like one of those lazy Dosk do-nothings, who get tired just turning the pages of those dusty papers they hoard! Haw, haw, haw!"

Rayna defiantly took another sip from her mug and angrily stared the bearded man in the eyes. "Don't call me 'girl'! I told you, my name is Rayna."

Merlott cheered with delight and exclaimed, "Oh ho! A woman with fire! Forgive a silly old man, Rayna. It is only a saying of this town to call beautiful women 'girls.'"

"A bad saying," Rayna mumbled, drinking more of the spicy brew.

"I agree," said Merlott, swallowing more ale himself.

Gradually, Rayna became accustomed to the crowded room, and it bothered her less. She felt more relaxed than she had been in days. On the bar sat a large wooden bowl of something resembling stale, crumbled biscuits. She grabbed a handful of the stuff and ate. To her surprise, it wasn't half bad, though it was a bit salty.

"Tell me about Nephredom," she said.

"Now that's a character for you!" Merlott bellowed, starting on his next mug. "He's the mighty mage over in Jerel." Merlott leaned over and gave a friendly elbow to Rayna. "The East Taren Queen might sit on the throne, but everybody knows Nephredom is the real ruler of East Taren."

"What does the West Taren monarchy think about this?"

"Bah! Surely you jest, Rayna! We all know that ever since we lost the war and Nephredom came into power, West Taren has been forbidden to have a king or queen." Merlott laughed so loud, others in the room took notice and laughed too. "The closest thing we have to a ruler," Merlott shouted, "is that fat weasel of a governor in Zuran—a poor substitute for a king indeed. Haw, haw!"

Rayna looked confused. She looked into her nearly empty mug of ale as if searching its contents for clarity. "You mentioned some kind of war that you lost?"

Merlott managed to belch and laugh at the same time—a strange sound to hear. "'Some kind of war'? You make it sound like a lover's quarrel! No, no! It was the *War of Kings*! When our great King Sunder succumbed to the Lake Stone, East Taren won by default."

"Why?"

"We had no soldiers left to fight with, that's why! They had all gone back to help our King defend the capital city. They never returned. The East Taren King, Bromus, died on the battlefield, leaving his Queen to mourn a bitter victory. She doesn't care anymore, you know. She lets Nephredom and his pets do as they please. I feel a bit sorry for their Queen."

Rayna clapped her hands and grabbed another one of Merlott's ales. "This is a good story," she declared. "Go on."

Merlott's eyes filled with mirth. "There's no understanding that man Nephredom," he said. "He oppresses his own people more than he bothers us. 'No magic,' he says. And who uses magic?"

"East Tareners!" Rayna answered cheerfully.

"Right!"

"We pay our taxes, fill their markets with our crops, and he leaves us alone."

"That's good."

Merlott's eyes narrowed. "But then there's his Red Robes. I don't like them one bit! Sneaky, slippery bullies, they are. Nephredom claims them to be his order keepers, but I say they are pure evil." Merlott began to wobble at his seat. "Now hear me, Rayna. I have no love for East Tareners, but let them die with a blade buried in their gut—not have their minds ripped to pieces by those fiends!"

Rayna miscalculated the proper placement of the mug while drinking, and ale dribbled down her chin. She didn't notice. "Aren't Red Robes East Tareners?" she asked.

The middle-aged man chuckled. "Yes, Rayna, but they are far worse than any normal East Tarener—if you can imagine that. Nephredom has figured out a way to make their magic stronger than anyone else's"

"With great power comes great corruption," Rayna said.

"True, true!" Merlott leaned too far back and found himself on the wooden floor.

The barkeep smiled but sternly pointed to a sign that hung above the stocked kegs of ale behind the bar.

"I know, I know," said Merlott as he cheerfully rubbed his rump, sore from the impact. "'If you can't sit, you must quit!'" Merlott managed to stand and bid Rayna goodnight before swaggering out the door.

Rayna squinted at the words, fighting blurred vision. The sign really did say that. "That explains these stupid one-legged stools," she surmised out loud, saddened over having lost her drinking partner and source of information.

The barkeep began to clear the area of the bar where Merlott had sat. "One can't be expected to work their hardest if they are feeling low from too much drink," he said. "Rules are rules."

Rayna noticed that the tavern was now nearly empty. Apparently, those people could no longer sit either. Rayna was disappointed to see that even the handsome man who pedaled the ceiling fan machine was gone. The flute player had long since changed her fast tune to a much slower one, suggesting to those still remaining that it was time to go to bed. Rayna stubbornly consumed more of Merlott's ale. She refused to go anywhere. Unlike the others, she had been cleverly holding onto the edge of the bar to keep her balance. She rocked back and forth on her stool, like a yo-yo on a short string, but she didn't fall.

This seemed to irritate the barkeep, who watched her suspiciously.

"Perhaps you've had too much to drink, my lady," he said.

"I have not had too much to drink," Rayna declared, her voice as wavy as a flag in a breeze.

"Why then, do you use the bar as a crutch?"

"I don't need crutches! I am an independent person!" To demonstrate her point, Rayna released her hold, then promptly fell to the floor. From out of nowhere, she felt a tap on her shoulder. It was the innkeeper. His voice was full of compassion.

"It is unbecoming of a woman of your beauty to be sprawled on the floor in such an undignified manner," he said quietly as he helped Rayna to stand. "The woman who was with you earlier has paid for your lodging in advance. It is the first room upstairs to the right. Goodnight. Tomorrow promises a new day to work and to be merry afterwards."

After successfully completing the gauntlet of the stairs, Rayna made it to her room. It was a small one, with almost no furniture save a neatly made bed. The night wind from the open window helped to cool the room and make its heat tolerable. Rayna was tired and ready for sleep. She searched along the walls for a switch so she could turn off the lights but found none. It dawned on her that the source of light in the room was not electric. A set of flickering candles mounted on the wall were the culprits. Angrily, she blew out both candles. Standing in absolute darkness, Rayna realized she had made a mistake and tried to relight one of the candles with the other. After a pitiful display of poor dexterity, Rayna was about to give up when she heard a knock at the door.

"Come in, whoever you are!" she called out, her words badly slurred.

It was Keris. She held a small lantern; its light filled the room. "You should not be so open with your invitations," she said. "I caution you, not all inns will be as safe as this one." Keris paused, sniffing the air. "Your breath is foul with drink," she accused.

"Leave me alone. I'm trying to get these two wicks to touch."

Keris cast a questioning glance at Rayna. "Why are you trying to light an unlit candle with another unlit candle?"

Rayna could feel bubbles of laughter fill the back of her throat, until she could no longer hold them in. She giggled loudly and freely. "I knew there had to be a logical reason why it wasn't working!" Rayna tried to look serious in front of Keris, but she couldn't stop laughing. "As we know, fire requires three basic components—fuel, oxygen, and heat. I didn't have the necessary heat!" Another bout of giggles burst from her smiling lips.

Keris was somber. "You don't have the necessary discipline either."

She took the candles from Rayna, lit one with her lantern, and placed both back on the wall. "I heard from the innkeeper that you have become good friends with the town drunk."

"His name is Merlott, and he has pointed ears."

"It was foolish of you to ask commoners questions about the Red Robes—especially with them being so near. You endanger our lives as well as the lives of innocents."

"Go away. I don't like you anymore."

Keris resigned with a disapproving sigh. "I will see you in the morning, when your wits have returned to you." Keris turned to leave when, as if an afterthought, she stopped and handed Rayna her staff. "You left it at the bar," she said, then left.

Rayna lay down on the bed; she was too tired to slide under the sheets. Lying there, Rayna wished Keris hadn't gone.

She wanted to fight her. In such a contest, Keris was sure to lose, she thought. She briefly played with the idea of searching out Keris's room and challenging her to battle, but the softness of the bed made it much easier to just lie where she was and . . .

CHAPTER
6

Judgment

Rayna awoke early the next morning, just in time to vomit into a clay pot that sat at the foot of her bed. Her head pounded so bad she nearly cried. No amount of temple rubbing did any good. *Just when my headache was almost gone, I decide to invite it back with friends,* Rayna thought as she groggily washed her face with water from another pot she found by the bed. There was no mirror to be found, but Rayna decided that was for the best. She really didn't want to see how horrible she probably looked. Then she noticed the tingling warmth on her wrist. *Red Robes!*

She quickly grabbed her staff, left her room, and searched the upper hall for Keris, calling out her name. Keris, her figure shadowy and dark, emerged from one of the rooms with her dagger drawn. Seeing that Rayna was alone, she sheathed her wickedly curved blade. She saw the glow of Rayna's watch and knew. "Judging by the faintness of the glow," she said, "they are not extremely close, but close enough to merit concern."

They made their way downstairs to greet the innkeeper. A crease of worry stretched across his forehead.

"Hail, friend," Keris announced. "How does the start of the day fare so far?"

"Not well." The innkeeper looked bitterly at Rayna. "Must we speak in her presence?" he whispered.

Keris nodded thoughtfully. "I suspect she will need to know this as well."

"Very well. Keris, in all the years I have managed this inn, none of my patrons has ever been condemned, until now."

"I see. Who?"

"Merlott, of course. He was talking about the Red Robes to that outsider." He pointed accusingly to Rayna. "He gets a bit loud-mouthed with drink in him. His words must have been overheard by someone beholden to Nephredom and his Red Robes. They went to his home early this morning." The innkeeper rubbed the crown of his balding head in despair. "Merlott is a kindhearted soul. He wouldn't utter a cross word to a mosquito if it bit him. He does not deserve this! What will I tell his brother?"

Rayna cut in. "Wait a minute, when you say Merlott is condemned, you're talking a few days in jail, right?"

Keris stared coldly at Rayna a few seconds before saying anything. "No, Rayna Powell of Nightwind. He is condemned to death."

Keris turned back to the innkeeper. "When are you going?"

"I was just going to rouse the rest of the lodgers and close the tavern for the day. I will be there very soon."

"We will be there when you arrive. Perhaps you will see us there. Come, Rayna, we need to be on our way."

Rayna leaned against her staff for support, much like she had seen the girl back at the cottage do once. Feelings of guilt consumed her like cold fire. She couldn't bear to look either person in the eyes. "I'm not going. I refuse to go to a public execution."

Keris's voice was forceful. "We have little choice in the matter. All of Kuara will be there. To not be present will provoke suspicion and make it much easier for the Red Robes to single us out. And because your recklessness makes you at least partially responsible for his fate, your sense of honor should obligate you to mourn his passing in person, regardless of your shame. It is how things are done here."

The innkeeper looked at Rayna as if she was an utter fool and silently went up the stairs.

Rayna grimly conceded. "Okay."

❊ ❊ ❊

The condemning was held on the edge of Irel's Band, adjacent to the Edgewoods; that was the customary location. When Rayna and Keris arrived, scores of people had gathered and were talking among themselves. Keris and Rayna pressed forward until they stood near the fringe of the Band. By now, Rayna's watch shone so brightly that only the morning sun prevented it from being seen by others. She hid her hands under her robes, just in case.

Rayna didn't like being so close to the Band. She could see charges of lightning crackling down like a rain of death. Her discomfort was compounded by the fact that Keris hadn't spoken a word to her since they had left the inn. Rayna took the chance that Keris was still willing to answer her questions. "Why are they holding the condemning here, of all places?" she asked.

"The Kuarans are a superstitious lot," Keris explained dispassionately. "They believe that crime is an evil that must be atoned for through human sacrificial means. Irel's Band is such a means. Anyone who commits a crime in Kuara, no matter how small, is sent through the Band as an offering to the Power Irel, so that she may spare innocents from her wrath. That is why Kuara is the safest province in Taren. Even laziness is considered a crime here. Kuarans are the hardest working people you will ever see."

Rayna braced herself against waves of nausea that came crashing onto the shores of her weakened body. The combination of last night's stupidity and the revelation she had just heard was almost too much for her to stomach. These people were using the Band like some twisted electric chair, and they were doing it in the name of Irel, the Power the girl in the cottage mistakenly had thought Rayna to be.

A row of twenty men and women dressed in black sackcloth lined the edge of the Band; their profoundly sad faces were smeared with ash. *The prod bearers*, Keris explained. In their gloved hands, each carried a wooden prod about ten feet long. Rayna remembered what Keris had told her: No one can walk seven feet into the Band without being struck down dead. Gathered on one side of the prod bearers stood a small cluster of tearful mourners—Merlott's family. On the other side stood Merlott, sober and frightened. His beard had been shaved off, and judging by the numerous small, red nicks around his chin, it was done in haste. He was dressed in stiff, formal clothing, unbecoming of his casual nature. He gazed pitifully at the ground as if he sought escape in the dirt.

An elderly man dressed in white, his head held low because of the task set before him, stepped forward and began to speak in a loud voice that belied his old age.

"Oh, people of Kuara, we are gathered here today for a most grave affair. Though it is rare among us, sometimes one from our flock goes astray and must be punished for the good of Kuara." He gestured with an unsteady hand toward Merlott. "Our brother Merlott has strayed. We are . . . thankful to the Red Robes and their followers for bringing Merlott's offense to our attention, for we were unaware that he had committed a crime." The elder and Merlott exchanged a fleeting glance of sorrow and resignation.

"Merlott is charged with conspiracy against the one true throne, and though the standard punishment is full interrogation, we have convinced the merciful Red Robes to allow us to punish our brother in our own way. With that said, I welcome our visitors to come forth as our special witnesses."

The solemn-faced gathering abruptly parted down the middle, allowing five Red Robes through. The ominous party took slow, deliberate steps, allowing time for the hushed crowd to suffer with anticipation with every passing second. Fear was their element. They evoked it. They sought it. They *thrived* on it. The long, red, hooded robes they wore covered them from crown to feet. Rayna couldn't catch even a glimpse of their faces; shadow obscured their dark identities like a sinister shroud.

At last, they made it to the front of the waiting throng. The crimson of their robes absorbed the rays the sun in such a way that they appeared to be surrounded by a faint aura of darkness. The Red Robes stood with the stiff authority of a panel of smug judges. As the tension rose to a nearly unbearable level, one of the Red Robes spoke to the crowd—or, more accurately, *thought* to the crowd. His lips never moved, yet Rayna "heard" him in her mind, more clearly than any mere utterance.

Sharp and rude, the words rang in her head, and in the heads of all those present. ***You may now carry on with the execution.***

Everyone reacted to these dooming words with simultaneous unease. Rayna was filled with dread and wonder. Somehow, the Red Robes had spread out a network of telepathic bridges, on which they sent across their thoughts. Rayna wondered if this was the accomplishment of solely one Red Robe, or a collective effort. Either way, their reputation for being powerful was no exaggeration. The crazy events were happening so fast in Rayna's life—travel by lightning, then healing hands, and now this. She shuddered to think what might come next.

She clasped her tense fingers firmly around her staff for reassurance.

Initially, she abhorred the idea of possessing the staff of the girl who had died. Now she felt differently. The staff was in her safekeeping, and she trusted it, like she had trusted the girl.

The elder popped backed into view and continued his speech. "I know it is our tradition to give family and friends time to speak parting words to the condemned before he joins Irel in her Band, forever. However, the Red Robes have requested, for the sake of . . . brevity that we skip that formality and get on with the condemning. And so, with that said—"

"Wait!" The deep, booming voice of protest came from someone in the group of Merlott's relatives. Like a titan, the brawny man stepped forward. His bulk and powerful seven-foot frame made him stand out in the crowd—an impressive accomplishment, because nearly every man, woman, and child present was strong and well muscled. He was younger and taller than Merlott, and if he had stood before any group other than the Red Robes, he would have looked intimidating. Instead, he looked foolhardy.

The thoughts of one of the Red Robes touched the crowd like icy splinters. This voice sounded different from the first—a woman's voice. *Who delays the execution?*

The man showed no fear. "My name is Arstinax, and it is my brother who will die today. What gives you the right to—?"

Without warning, chaotic thought paralyzed everyone in pain. More feeling than real thought, it was a taste of the contempt the Red Robes held for everything good and pure. A vile essence sprang forth in the form of sound, violating all ears, like embedding shards of hate. Rayna put her hands to her ears in a vain attempt to block the screeching noise from her head. The ghastly sound was like some evil entity, laughing and screaming at once. After a brief burst, it stopped, but it took a while before the echoing remnants of the telepathic assault finally left her mind. Fading moans from the recovering crowd became fainter until the scene was quiet again. Arstinax still stood tall, though his eyes looked troubled.

The Red Robes never moved a muscle; their appearance remained unchanged.

We are the greater servants to Nephredom, keeper of the Gate, they thought in unison. *Our rights are governed by him, and should be addressed only by him. You are a lesser servant to the throne. Your only desire should be that of obedience.*

"My desire is that I be allowed to speak my final peace to my brother!"

Arstinax growled loudly, ignoring murmured pleas from Merlott and others near him to shut up.

Your wishes mean nothing, the Red Robes replied. *Obedience is all.*

One of the Red Robes lifted its head and opened its mouth, from which an orb of cold, green light came forth. The summoned spawn hovered briefly in midair, then suddenly streaked toward Arstinax.

The giant howled in agony, then dropped to his knees, holding a hand to his bleeding face.

This appeared to please the Red Robe. *That is the position appropriate to obedience. You will all do the same.*

Everyone got on their knees. The floating orb of throbbing light returned to the Red Robe and released something red and wet that it slipped into its creator's hand. Rayna gasped when she realized that it was one of Arstinax's eyes.

To Rayna's horror, the Red Robe petted and caressed the orb-thing, like one would reward a dog for fetching a stick. The Red Robe reopened his mouth, and the orb rushed in, disappearing into the maw. As he placed the eye into a bulging satchel, Rayna couldn't help but wonder how many dismembered eyes the Red Robes had claimed for their collection. Dozens? Hundreds?

We adjudged whether to pluck out his eye, or his heart, The Red Robes announced. *Two of us for his heart—three of us for his eye. We are a merciful order, but this such mercy will not endure. The next time this Arstinax brings offense before us, he will die.*

Everyone ignored the quietly suffering man, fearing that a caring hand or a comforting word would rouse the Red Robes' wrath.

No one should have that much power, Rayna thought angrily. *Especially not those things.*

At the Red Robes' command, Merlott was brought to the Band's perilous fringe. The electric charge in the air made his hair dance a troubled dance, like an unseen hand was rummaging through it.

The prod bearers lifted their sharpened poles, and Merlott was directed to enter the Band. He did so without hesitation, looking back only once with concern for his brother, who was still hunched over in pain. The prods lowered behind him and firmly pushed at his back, forcing him to step deeper into the Band.

"And now it begins," Keris whispered to herself. She glanced casually at Rayna. "Now do you understand?"

"Yes," Rayna answered. That was all she could find to say, but it was enough.

The elder called out loudly, "We deliver Merlott of Kuara to Irel. May he know peace in her Band."

In a fatal, brief fury of flashing light, it was over. Merlott was dead.

"The lightning will not stop with death," Keris said. "It will keep striking until there's nothing left."

Rayna remembered when she ran through the Band. She must have been in that thing at least an hour. Lightning descended all around her but never hit her. Merlott was in the Band a fraction of a minute when he was struck down hard. *Why?*

"Cowards!" Arstinax shouted. "You use magic to fight me, when you know I have none of my own to oppose it. You don't have the courage to fight me with honor—with hand and blade. How much blood will you spill before your crimson robes become so drenched, they will no longer hide the stains!" Arstinax now stood as tall and noble as before, his right eye swollen shut.

Silence! The Red Robes commanded.

"I will not be silenced, not now, not ever. You may frighten my neighbors, but you will not frighten me!"

Ungrateful. Disrespectful.

Abruptly, an invisible force effortlessly whisked Arstinax into midair and dangled him there, as if deciding the fate of the massive man. At first, Rayna thought they were going to kill him right there, but suddenly Arstinax was hurled into the Band like discarded trash. As he fell hard against the red earth, Rayna could almost feel his agony in her bones. Without hesitation, she angrily pushed her way past the impotent crowd and into the Band itself. Somewhere in the bustling rush, she lost the scarf that hid her ears. Racing against time, she helped the dazed and bruised Arstinax to his feet and pushed him out of the Band, with strength she never knew she had.

Momentarily amazed at what she had just done, Rayna stood in the Band longer than she should have. A paralyzing panic overtook her. Rods of lightning pelted every surface around her—everywhere except where she stood. Fearing the wrong move could be her last, Rayna gazed wide-eyed at the flashing sky like a stunned deer. Cautiously, she stepped to the side; instantly, the spot where she had stood a moment ago was struck by lightning. She stared at the smoking spot, then back at the watching crowd. Minutes slipped away. By chance, her eyes caught sight of the mostly incinerated corpse of Merlott, adjacent to her. Inhaling deeply, she made a running leap from the Band, colliding with a townswoman. Startled, the woman backed away, as did the rest of the crowd.

"How can it be?" the woman rasped to another.

Nearly everyone was pointing at Rayna's ears, whispering to one another.

"Not even a scratch, not a single one."

"Round ears."

"The bracelet on her wrist glows!"

"Bad omen."

In a short time, the gathering was orderly no more; some ran away, while others looked on timidly from a safe distance. Still others darted though the crowd, manic messengers shouting "Irel has returned!" Only the Red Robes remained unchanged. Dark watchers, they observed the fiasco in grim silence.

A firm hand touched Rayna's shoulder. It was Keris. "You have interfered in the Red Robes' plans, and they will not forget you for it. We must leave now, while they are distracted by the crowd."

Rayna agreed, and they began to slip away, but then she remembered Arstinax.

She stopped. "Wait for me here," she told Keris. "There's something I've got to do."

With shouters and finger-pointers announcing her every approach and whereabouts, Rayna felt like an unwilling celebrity, wishing there was some way she could hide, and shield herself from the overwhelming barrage of attention. When she reached Arstinax, he appeared immune to the din of the mob. He stood humbly at the Band's rim, calmly muttering soft words in the direction of where his brother once lay. He seemed a softer, more approachable man, different from the belligerent protester she witnessed moments ago. Like his brother, he had a quality about him that made him immediately likable.

"What favor, what bounty do I owe the Power Irel for saving my life?" he said, never looking away from the Band.

"You don't owe me anything," Rayna answered. "In fact, I came to say I'm sorry. I'm so sorry."

"What need have I for your sorrow?" Arstinax said. "Be instead sorry for my dead brother, for he will never see the light of morning again. Be sorry for my mother and my father, who will weep for many days after this one. Be sorry for my neighbors who would rather live in fear than fight the evil that oppresses them. Your sorrow is wasted on me."

"All right, then I'll go."

"Wait."

Rayna paused.

"Forgive me," Arstinax said. "My brother Merlott was sacrificed in your name, but it was not your ruling that forced him into your Band. I have heard many tales about your exile in the Band and your prophesied return to Taren. I remember as a child lying awake at night with my brother in fear, after my mother had scolded our mischief, warning us that Irel of the Band would one day come for us if we did not behave better. Now, what was once a story to frighten little children into obedience has come true, and I am not afraid. After a day as cursed as this, another curse would make little difference."

"I'm not here to curse anyone, and my name's not Irel, it's Rayna."

Arstinax shook his head. "You are Irel, the Power of change and of chaos. The selfish Power that never helps without a price. That is what I know. That is what I *know*."

He sighed. "I once failed to understand why anyone would crave change. I was content to work and grow old here, in this village, just as my father did, and my father's father, and all of those before him. Tradition is what makes a Kuaran strong. But that was before the blight of the Red Robes. They care nothing of our traditions, and they mock our ways. Now I welcome the change you will bring, Irel. Whether it be for the better or worse, I no longer care. I only hope that whatever change you bring, it will mean the many deaths of East Tareners like the ones that tore out my eye, killed my brother, and disheartened my people."

"There's something else you should know," Rayna said slowly. She bore a mixed expression of guilt and fear. "I don't know exactly how to say this."

Arstinax turned to face Rayna for the first time. "It involves my brother?"

Rayna nodded sadly. "Arstinax, I am responsible for the—"

"It would be better," Arstinax interrupted, "if you didn't tell me. My mind is burdened with more pain than it was meant to bear. To know of a bane great enough to trouble a Power would surely drive me mad. Maybe another time," Arstinax suggested, turning his attention back to the Band.

"Another time," Rayna echoed absently. Miserable and dissatisfied, she departed.

Keris waited watchfully after Rayna disappeared into the crowd. Rayna intrigued Keris; nevertheless, the lingering mystery of this woman bothered her. Keris wondered if she would be better off without the strange mage, who had stood in the Band long enough to condemn ten men, yet walked from it unharmed. Could she trust this one, who claimed to live beyond the Band? Finally, and most important—would Rayna still be willing to go with her to Soren to see Ciredor once she discovered the whole truth?

Her thoughts turned to Ciredor. In the light of the day's misfortune, it felt forbidden to think about such a sweet thing. It had been so long since she felt the warm embrace of his arms around her. Regrettably, her anticipated visit to see him in Soren would be more business than the pleasure she hoped for. If the mage Rayna accompanied her to Soren, Ciredor would surely back the plan. Keris was certain Rayna possessed great power and that Ciredor would see this, too. With Ciredor's support, and his following of loyal men, it would be possible for her to take back what was hers. She was never one to covet the favor of another, yet she secretly worried how Ciredor would receive her proposal—and perhaps, even her.

Keris shifted her position. She had been careful to remain inconspicuous; she was well skilled in stealth and guile. The constantly moving crowd made such a task difficult, and her worse fear became manifest: One of the Red Robes saw her. All five slowly made their way toward Keris, mentally shoving aside anyone unfortunate enough to be in their path. Keris drew her dagger.

She turned to see Rayna taking up a defensive position beside her. "I was beginning to wonder if you would ever return," complained Keris, her voice tenser than usual.

Rayna ignored the remark, her nervous eyes fixed on the nearing Red Robes. "Why have they singled you out?" she asked. "I just spoiled their circus act, so I wouldn't be surprised if they went after me, but why you?"

Keris remained expressionless. "I'd rather not say, and it makes little difference at this point. We need to fight our way past them and make our way into the Edgewoods. It's the only chance we have of losing them permanently."

"How do you propose we do that?" Rayna asked in dismay. "They have the power to snatch out eyeballs, hold people in midair, and who knows what else."

"I suggest you weave a spell to distract them. I will hold them off as long as I can."

"I keep telling you, I'm not a—"

Return with us to Jerel, Princess. We have been instructed not to harm you—so long as you do not resist. The Red Robes were addressing Keris only, but somehow Rayna could "hear" as well.

Keris stepped forward boldly with her weapon ready. "I've often wondered if there is flesh and blood beneath those robes," she called out. "Today, I would like to find out." She shot an urgent glance at Rayna. "Whatever you plan to do," she hissed, "do it soon!"

This is crazy, Rayna thought to herself. *What could she do against those things?* She watched Keris circle and dodge around the robed tormentors, careful not to get too close. Lashing at the air dividing the two parties, Keris formed a precarious barrier. Every thrust and slash was carried out with the skill of a master, though Rayna suspected it would do Keris little good against her current adversaries. Eventually, one of the Red Robes ran out of patience and lifted his half-clenched hands in the air, as if he sought to pull the sky itself down upon Rayna and Keris. Rayna swallowed with fear. The Red Robe was about to cast another accursed spell. She had had her fill of Red Robe magic to last a lifetime. She yelled at the Red Robe to get his attention and possibly disrupt whatever dark conjuring he had started. Her words had no effect. The spell was unleashed, and air suddenly began to ripple and become hot, then hotter.

When Rayna realized she was on fire, a panicked, frenzied sense of self-preservation came over her in her desperation to find a way out of dying a horrible, burning death. Every inch of skin on her body felt the searing touch of the fire. Keris was also ablaze and had wrapped her cloak around herself tightly, rolling along the dewed grass to snuff out the flames. The fire, being magical in nature, would not extinguish. Keris shrieked in pain as the deadly flames spread over her like a death blanket. It was the first time Rayna ever heard fear in Keris's voice.

Teary-eyed from flame and emotion, Rayna made up her mind to fight. The Red Robes weren't going to kill her, or her dreams of getting home. Charging out with her staff—a passionate but badly aimed effort—she managed to graze one of the Red Robes' outstretched hands.

A sharp rupture of cold pressure and bright light formed at the point where Rayna's staff made contact. The powerful force pushed her back so fast she stumbled and landed embarrassingly on her posterior. For a few seconds Rayna assumed the force came from the Red Robes, then realized with astonishment that it was her staff. In her grasp, she could feel currents of throbbing energies pacing up and down within its wooden shell.

The Red Robes writhed and howled in agony, like a pack of wounded wolves. They huddled together, fighting the unseen hurt, oblivious to everything else. The fire had vanished; the spell that sustained it had been broken.

Rayna's wrist tingled with a familiar sensation. The face of her watch had been very much in tune with her situation. The clown face looked petrified with fear, its alarmed expression easing only a fraction now that she was no longer on fire. She was still in grave danger.

"Are you injured?" Rayna heard Keris's voice ask.

Rayna looked up to see Keris standing before her. "I'm fine," Rayna breathed in reply, "just scared to death. How about you?"

Keris wearily helped Rayna to her feet. "My clothing and hair are singed and unsightly, but I will live."

The two made their way quickly to the Edgewoods, leaving behind the Band and the stunned Red Robes. The rows of tall trees—the gateway to the woods—seemed to convey the promise, or threat, that the journey on which they were about to embark would not end anytime soon.

CHAPTER 7

Nephredom

Jerel. It was a majestic city, worthy of its majestic role as capitol of East Taren—the seat of its royal government. The city's glistening marble domes and sky-reaching towers left no doubt in the minds of the casual observer as to its claim as the most beautiful city in Taren. A rainbow of stained glass adorned every window; in the sunlight, they shone like a parade of precious jewels. Even the chilled East Taren air was perfumed with smells of sweet spices and incense. And yet, beyond the spender of polished stone monuments, delicately arched walkways and sculptured evergreen hedges frosted with frozen dew, lay something ugly.

The ugliness hid beneath the city's golden skin—a cancerous, rotting thing, consuming and replacing healthy muscle and bone. Only in the hollow stares of the citizens, their eyes like dark channels, could one peer past the illusion and glimpse at the source, naked and undeniable, staring back: Nephredom.

Often whispered, but seldom spoken publicly of as the "subjugator of joy", Nephredom brooded in his study alone, in the Palace of Jerel. His position as Council to the Queen and Keeper of the Gate earned him the fear and awe of many. He was a tall man, who's straight, formal posture made him appear even taller. A well trimmed and groomed beard and mustache framed his chiseled face. Like many Tareners, his hair and eyes were like ebony and his skin a dark reddish tan, though the Eastern Taren cold, coupled with his tendency to stay within palace walls, made him paler than most.

Today was the twenty-first day of the fourth cycle—the Queen's birthday. Outside his doors, he could hear myriad aides and servants scampering about in preparation of the upcoming festivities. His mood was a festering wound, too foul to be festive, too bloated with venom to issue anything but hatred. The anniversary of the Queen's birth was the same day as his father's death. But there were no mourners here. No one to speak of his greatness. No moments of silence in respect of his memory. Just an array of grinning underlings, nosily exalting their sickly Queen. Another voice for the chorus.

"Curse them!" he shouted aloud. "Curse them all!"

Suddenly, he dug his fingers deep against the sides of his throbbing head and then hastily clamped his hands around nearest corners of his writing desk, clenching his jaws shut. The venom flared anew. It blurred his vision, and splashed over his brain like lava-fire. His eyes rolled back far in his skull, red-veined whites superseded his irises. The episode lasted for a few minutes, and then eased.

Every year he tolerated this charade, and every day, the pain in his head, like the waves of a growing tide, became harder to ignore. The torments of the past and present had huddled together and joined the chorus of enemies against him. Nephredom broke out in a bout of unexpected sobbing. He was not a man prone to the whim of tears, but today they came, and for all his power and title, he could not hold them back. What would his father think, he wondered, to see his son now, weeping like an old woman.

Nephredom paced the room slowly, occasionally stopping to listen to the muffled bustle outside. He was High Mage Lord Nephredom, Regent to the East Taren Queen, and Keeper of the Gate. With their King dead, he was the most powerful man in Taren. Not simply was he a great man politically. The sheer magical force he wielded was mightier than that of ten mages and more. He was a man slow to speak, but when he did, his strong words alone could bend men to his will. Indeed, in all aspects he was the perfect East Tarener. But he was of West Taren, and the secret rebelled in his heart now more than at any other time before. His father would have agreed that there was no greater test of a man than to live in the stronghold of his enemy, with patience, not striking until the moment was right. How he wished that moment were now! However, the last line of Bromus had yet to be brought forth.

The faint sound of knocking interrupted his thoughts.

"Am I intruding, my liege? I have news you might find interesting."

Nephredom glared at his aide, Aric, standing in the doorway before him. Colorfully dressed and adorned with many necklaces and rings, she stood in stark contrast to him in his simple robes. Truly, he had to admit, she was the most beautiful woman he had ever seen, but by whose mandate was such beauty awarded to an East Tarener?

He replied sharply. "You may tell me on the way to the throne. Guards, post yourselves here until my return."

Two Red Robes, previously hidden, materialized before them and stood watch where they were told. A moment later, their stealth magic resumed, and they were invisible again.

"Requesting my ear during my time of solace shows disrespect," Nephredom said, walking with Aric at his side through the palace halls. "I assume you have good reason."

A gleam crossed Aric's eyes, and she bowed. "I dare not offend your Greatness without just cause." She leaned closer to him than necessary and whispered, "I bring curious news, my liege. The Red Robe searchers have at last spotted the Princess."

"Where?"

"In, of all places, the backward province of Kuara. The Robes were on a routine assignment when they saw her hiding in a crowd."

"You will not speak unkindly of Kuara, or any West Taren Province."

Aric gave an exaggerated bow, so low that her locks of tightly braided hair swept the marble floor. "My apologies, my liege. I'm sometimes forgetful of your generous affection for West Taren. It's a most unusual trait for an East Taren High Mage, wouldn't you agree?"

Nephredom paused. "The day is too young for your games." His intense eyes focused on her. "Are you questioning my loyalty?"

Aric smiled slyly. "I assume that is a rhetorical question, my Regent, for only a fool or suicidal would answer anything but 'no.'"

Nephredom chuckled softly in spite of himself. "And I suppose you are neither?"

Aric tilted, then lowered, her head. "A man as great as yourself can be no employer of fools."

"And suicidals?"

"Only when it suits your needs, my liege."

Nephredom laughed. "Now that you have told me what you are *not*, finish your report before my fading patience proves you wrong."

"I fear there is not much more to report. Pardon my awkward approach, but the Red Robes are famous for their efficiency, so speaking of them and failure proves difficult to my tongue."

"They have failed?"

"Miserably, Regent. The Princess escaped into the Edgewoods."

Nephredom's face hardened. "How did she do this?"

"Reports say it was a magical assault of an unknown nature. It paralyzed all five Robes—they barely made it back to Jerel. They suffer from profound shock and confusion, and our healer is tending to them now."

"Would you insult my hearing by having me believe that the Princess, a novice mage at best, brought forth enough power to overcome five Red Robes?"

"Perish the thought, but it was not the Princess's doing. She was accompanied by a young, unknown she-mage."

"A rogue mage dares defy my decree?"

Aric nodded. "It would seem so."

"I see. The Princess always had a talent for finding powerful allies, and this bold she-mage apparently is a powerful one."

"Master-mage powerful, I'd wager, my liege."

Nephredom didn't like what he was hearing. A mere rogue mage was a threat to his reputation, but a rogue master mage was a threat to his life. With a pass of his hand, he motioned for Aric's silence, and they entered the throne room. Nephredom took his place in the seat of power, one he had occupied for nearly three years, since the Queen's illness had kept her mostly in bed. Aric laid a silk spread over a nearby couch and then reclined there on her side, her head propped and resting in her hand. Along the walls of the vast room stood sixty leather-armored bodyguards, motionless save for the eyes of a few of the males, which occasionally met the flirtatious smile of Aric.

Aric pouted and muttered to herself, "For West Taren mercenaries, they are well behaved. Far too boring for my taste, I'd say." She looked at Nephredom, who nodded, giving her unspoken permission for an unspoken act. Her eyes glazed over, and the muscles in her face slackened, giving her a blank, withdrawn expression. The connection was made.

Nephredom stared intently at the doors before him, and he appeared to be deep in thought. His mind called out to Aric: **Have you finished the probe? What of their loyalty?**

Aric replied in thought as well: **None of these newly hired guards** harbors any thoughts of betrayal or ill-intent about you. Nevertheless, I must voice my concern over the increasing number of West Taren mercenaries in the capital. I understand you are sending the message that West Taren is now a friend of the throne, but a dozen would have been symbolic enough. This many threatens the integrity of the empire.

Nephredom's thoughts bellowed loudly in Aric's mind: *Question not my reasons, Aide! Perhaps I should have someone give you a loyalty probe.*

As your chief administrator, my liege, I would be remiss in my duties if I did not voice my concern over possible threats to your rule.

Enough. I let you come into my head to discuss the matter of the Princess and her accomplice, not my military policies.

Of course. Forgive my forwardness.

This upstart magician has undermined my authority by using magic and publicly embarrassing my men.

Then, may I humbly suggest her public execution to atone for a public disgrace? A slow and painful execution, of course.

So it should be.

Good. I was afraid our good Princess would feel lonely dying on display alone.

You speak of two captures when you have yet to produce even one. The Edgewoods is dense and difficult, and the Princess is a well-learned pathfinder. It will be no easy task to find her.

I have a remedy for that ailment, my liege. Before they were defeated, our Red Robes were able to perform a fast scan of the Princess's recent memories. It will take some time before the Robes' findings are brought forth, due to their injuries. Nevertheless, we will certainly learn of the Princess's contacts and her most frequented hiding places. With this knowledge, there should be no need to track her down. Our Red Robes can simply lie in wait for her when she tires of cowering in the woods. We will then have our elusive Princess—and the she-mage too, if she is foolish enough to still be in the company of the Princess. If not, the mage's shameless disregard for your law will no doubt compel her to use her power again, and our Robes will be ready to catch the scent of her magic. The she-mage surprised them before with her unexpected attack. This time, they will be amply prepared. Her capture will be swift.

Good. When the Princess's contacts are discovered, I want them killed immediately. The Princess and the she-mage will wish their deaths were as quick.

Would you expect any less from me, my Regent?

Pray I never do. Leave me now, and inform me when the information from the wounded Red Robes is ready.

Forever and always in your service, my liege.

Aric pulled her mind back inside herself, then walked over to where Nephredom sat, close enough so that only he could hear what she said. "Fear not, my Regent. What I say is of little security significance, scarcely worth your time. In fact, I nearly decided to dismiss it as worthless West Taren superstition. However, I am anything but incomplete; my thorough nature behooves me to report all. The locals in Kuara claimed that the she-mage was the Power Irel of the Band, come back to reclaim the land— or something like that. The Red Robes who were there confirmed that the young woman did have rounded ears, as all Powers supposedly have. A distracting trick, I say it is."

Nephredom did not reply; instead, he stood and walked out. Aric did not follow. Back in the solitude of his office, he contemplated what he had been told. Could it truly be possible that Irel of the Band had joined with the *Princess* against him? His eyes widened in revelation. *Yes, of course!*, he exclaimed to himself. Irel had become envious, envious enough to break free of her Band prison to seek him out. Irel must have sensed that his powers had risen to a caliber that threatened to dwarf her own, and she had come to challenge him. It was destined to happen, he thought; greatness such as his would attract great attention.

A troubling notion came to mind. Because Irel was a West Taren Power, she would use West Taren loyalists to do her bidding. If so, he could not count on the loyalty of his fellow West Tareners. Nephredom's dark eyes shifted nervously toward the door. Irel's spies could be in this very palace, he thought, plotting to kill him. He would double the amount of Red Robes, he thought—then hesitated and reconsidered. No, Irel was the Power of change. She would not do the expected: She would use the East Tareners against him. He sat down and rubbed his chin thoughtfully. He would triple the number of West Taren mercenaries in the court.

Nephredom clenched his fist so tightly that the nails of his fingers drew blood from his palms. It was clear to him now. As a Power, he postulated, Irel knew far more than most. Surely, she knew he was not of East Taren. *She knew who he was.*

Irel must have known that 16 years ago, a father could no longer conceal the fact that his son was an *Unnatural*. To avoid a scandal, King Sunder, then ruler of West Taren, had his son, Prince Sunder sent away to the East Taren Province of Dosk. To ensure the safety of his only son and sole heir to the throne, he had the boy's name secretly changed to Nephredom. *Nephredom.*

He had lived in Dosk under the guise of a common student. Although the caretakers his father had sent with him as his protectors protested his decision to improve and refine his developing magic, they dared not argue with the King's son—even if he was an exile. An old she-hermit who lived in the Soren Woods journeyed to Dosk to teach him at the estate where he lived. He knew little of this woman, for she was the secretive sort. She did tell him that the local schools did not appreciate her skills and banned her from teaching there because they were envious of her strong magic. The woman, known only to him as "Teacher," taught him how to fully harness the power that smoldered inside his being. Most mages considered themselves fortunate if they mastered one school of Psi-magic in their lifetimes. Under his teacher's tutelage, Nephredom had mastered two: Psi-kinesis, the magic of movement, and Psi-pyric, the magic of fire. His teacher was a master of those two schools, and incredibly, a third—Psi-telepathy—the magic of mind-speak, mind-read—and on weaker minds—*mind control.* Though he practiced diligently, he never rose beyond the level of adept in that school. He did become skilled enough to mind-speak to his teacher, which made their lessons mostly wordless affairs.

Talking would better help spies learn the secrets of my teachings, she had explained to him mentally. He did not understand her then, and believed her to be a worrying, senile old woman. But now he understood. Spies were everywhere.

What, Nephredom wondered, did Irel know of his past? No doubt, she knew that he had studied under the old woman for nearly ten years before he banished her in a fit of rage. He had learned a complex magic lesson that day. Proud of his progress, the old woman had said, "You have done well, Sunder. Very well." It was not the praise that incensed him, for he had grown to respect the woman and value her opinion; it was the use of his real name, the name that was his birthright. He had been careful never to reveal any clues to his true origin, and his caretakers had sworn death-oaths to keep his secret. The only way she could have known his name was by stealing it from his mind.

The teacher realized her slip and quickly began to babble lies and excuses. Nephredom did not listen. She knew his name and thus, she knew he was the Prince of West Taren. Countless cutthroats and bounty hunters in East Taren would rub their palms with greed at the idea of having a prince to offer for ransom. If news of his identity got out, he would be an exile in both lands. Nowhere would be safe, and he would be forced to wander as a pariah, a wretched nomad.

His first, furious thought was to kill his teacher, and with her the knowledge of his secret. In his studies, he had surpassed his teacher in many fire spells; he could hurl a fireball so large and intense even she could not block it. Then a sense of pity and mercy—unusual emotions for the Prince—overcame him. He told the old woman to flee to her home in the woods and never return to Dosk. He assured her that death awaited her if she were so brazen as to venture onto the city streets again. His caretakers, armed with swift, deadly arrows, would see to that. He never saw the old woman again.

Nephredom lowered his head with the burden of old grief. The next year had been one of pain and despair. Late one night, he was awakened and told the news about the Lake Stone in Lamec. The great Stone, a symbol of West Taren's solidarity, had been defiled. At first, no one knew what caused the Stone to weep silver tears and vomit silver smoke. What dark omen was this? Why did it tremble so?

The guard who had watched over the Stone had gone missing but was later found, laughing to himself like a madman. In brief bouts of lucidity, he revealed that he had allowed an unknown East Tarener to touch the Stone: It was East Taren magic that changed it.

The great Lake Stone, it was said, had fallen from the heavens long ago, at the beginning of recorded time. Because it landed in the lake of the West Taren capital, it was accepted as a celestial gift to the King. The un-submerged half of the stone shone like a metallic mirror by day, reflecting with pleasing clarity the blue skies whence it came. The Stone held value beyond its immense beauty. It made the fish in its lake multiply twice as quickly and grow to twice the size of fish elsewhere. Lamec prospered in trade because of its ever-full fishnets. Lamec's other trades also had prospered, simply from the tourist traffic of curious outsiders willing to pay to see the Stone and hear scholars tell them of its past.

The Lake Stone had sat undisturbed for hundreds of years. When it was corrupted, all the lake's fish died, and the city had become blanketed with a chilling, silvery mist that flowed from the Stone. The Stone's guard, after revealing his story, was put to death for his crime, but a larger crime had yet to be dealt with.

Exactly one night after the Lake Stone incident, Nephredom received a letter from his father requesting him to return home. King Sunder had declared war on East Taren, vowing that the magic users would pay for their insult with blood. Thinking back on that moment, and giving in to a sentimental calling, Nephredom sat in a wide, ornately decorated chair and reached into his desk drawer. He opened a secret compartment behind a false backing and pulled out a slightly wrinkled sheet of parchment. He read:

My son,
The dawn of a great war has come upon us. The East Tareners have betrayed our kindness. They have broken our most solemn law and have used magic on our lands. One of their kind has enchanted the Lake Stone and made it unclean. If King Bromus cannot control his own people, then it is time his people were under our control. I suspect the war will favor us in the end. I have been preparing for such a war for some time. My army is vast and ready. We will sweep over the East Taren Empire like a great hand, and crush every province in our grasp. Son, I need you here by my side—public opinion be damned. If by chance I should fall in battle, you must be here to take the crown. Your exile is over. My eyes will weep with joy to see you again at last.

The first time Nephredom had read the letter, four years ago, he had been elated. He was finally allowed to go home. He had hastily made preparations and set out toward Lamec the next day. Then weather had become poor; a great snowstorm swept over East Taren and ruled the skies, forcing Nephredom to travel slowly. Passing some skirmishes along the way, he could clearly see that the war was going as his father had foreseen. The declaration of war caught the East Taren government by surprise, forcing it to recruit unskilled civilians to supplement the minimum core army. This makeshift military posed no threat to the seasoned warriors of West Taren. As a bonus to this advantage, the East Tareners were too arrogant and proud to wear armor. The fools marched onto battlefields dressed only in flimsy robes, confident their magic would protect them.

Armed with plentiful bows and spears, Sunder's men had killed many of the mages before they could cast a single spell. By the time Nephredom approached the Taren River, the natural border between the two halves of Taren, he had heard that Sunder had lost only a tenth of his forces and had taken all the East Taren provinces except Jerel. The East Taren forces had been cut nearly in half by death and injury, and their King Bromus had been killed in battle. The vanguard of their forces had retreated to Jerel, the last sanctuary of East Taren, to protect their widowed Queen. Nephredom remembered his pride at what his father had accomplished. Never before had a war been won so decisively and so quickly. Soon East Taren would surrender, and all of Taren would be ruled by King Sunder's iron fist.

Then something went wrong. He noticed that his father's troops were marching in the same direction as he, toward Lamec—not toward Jerel, the East Taren stronghold. This angered Nephredom. Why would they retreat when victory was in their hands?

When Nephredom had entered the outskirts of Lamec, he first saw the beasts—hideous, monstrous beasts. Dozens of them roamed wildly, attacking anything in sight. They were dumb and mute, making hissing sounds rather than speech. One of the beasts had spotted Nephredom and his caretakers and charged at them. Nephredom, brash and fearless, had bathed the beast in white fire, hot enough to melt steel. The creature shrugged off the attack as if Nephredom had thrown dirt at it. Sharp swords in hand, his bodyguards charged forward, but their blades barely scratched the beast. A viscous, oily coating on its scaly skin made most sword blows glance off harmlessly. If by luck the creature's skin was pierced, the wound sealed and healed itself right before their eyes. Nephredom had never seen anything like these beasts, and not even a healer who was a master of the Psi-somatic school could heal that quickly.

The West Tareners soon learned that the best way to harm the beast with their weapons was by thrusting, not slashing. They fought the beast, stabbing it so frequently that it could not heal itself quickly enough to stop the blood loss. After a fight lasting nearly half an hour, it expired. Seven of Nephredom's ten caretakers were dead as well. Too disillusioned to venture onward to the city, and needing to care for their injuries, the remaining four West Tareners camped out on the fringes of Lamec, camouflaged their encampment to prevent being seen by more wandering beasts. Days passed as Nephredom and his three men lay hidden, listening to the sounds of battle echoing in the distance. Now Nephredom understood why the army had come back, but what of the beasts in the West Taren capital? What kind of East Taren magic created them and brought them here?

On the fourth day after the battle with the beast, Nephredom saw a lone man fleeing from the city. The young prince stepped out from the brush that concealed him and demanded that the man tell him what was happening in the capital.

Forcing himself back to the present, Nephredom stood and looked out his office window, tears forming in his eyes. Through the glass, he could see the many banners, of various sizes and shapes, flying in honor of the Queen's birthday. "Surely you know what happened next, Irel!" he cried out, in spite of there being no one else in the room. "You are a Power, after all—master of master mages—common history should be a simple matter for you!"

Confronting the pain of the past once more, Nephredom recalled the words of the man whom he had accosted. "It is the Lake Stone, sir! The Stone is turning the citizens into monsters! The army is fighting them as we speak, but the mist from the Stone is turning the army into beasts as well! Soon all of Lamec will become a den for the beasts!"

Nephredom was about to release the man when he noticed scales forming on his face. His nails already were pointed like claws, his teeth like fangs—the man was becoming a beast before his eyes! Quickly he drew his dagger and put an end to the man's life, before he could utter a single protest.

Nephredom's mind was on only one thing now: his father. He had to find him, before this new and terrible danger became too great.

He called for his caretakers to go with him into the city, but they refused, citing the danger and their various wounds. Disgusted by their cowardice, Nephredom flamed them dead where they sat, then headed to the city alone. At the gate of Lamec, Nephredom could sense a powerful magic about—airborne magic. Summoning the forces of Psi-kinesis, he created a personal force shield and walked through the gate.

The memory of what Nephredom had found inside the beloved city of his childhood was too painful to revive in detail; his mind skipped ahead. After a brief tour of the once-mighty Lamec, Nephredom had returned to the gate. There was nothing for him here: The capital was no more, the people of Lamec were no more. His father was—no more.

He later learned that the entire army had been recalled to fight the beasts but had been slaughtered or become beasts themselves. These mindless creatures—once proud Lamecans—threatened to escape the gate of Lamec, spill out in large numbers, and slaughter the rest of West Taren.

From outside Lamec's walls, Nephredom studied the gate to the fallen city. It was sturdy but scalable. The walls surrounding the city, however, were much higher than the gate and were smooth, making it impossible to climb without a ladder or hook. The gate was the weak point.

To protect the remaining West Taren provinces, Nephredom prepared to cast the most difficult spell he had ever attempted. He closed his eyes and focused on his magic. Once again calling upon his Psi-kinesis, he ripped the existing gates from their hinges with a force equal to that of a hundred strong men, then mentally dragged the gates out of the way. Next, he gathered the surrounding sands, making them rise up and fill the gap where the gate had once been. Sand, mixed with natural salts, was plentiful around Lamec, and tons of it now towered before him, in piles dozens of feet high. He commanded the sand to form a wall six feet thick. He knew he had to act quickly, for though his eyes were shut, he could hear the hissing of many beasts nearing the entrance.

Next, he evoked the power of Psi-pyric and ignited the wall of sand with a sheet of searing flame. The effort of the magic and the nearness of the fire drenched his body in sweat. The fire melted and fused the sand. Nephredom extinguished the flame, and the air cooled and tempered his creation, a wall of smooth glass. Then the beasts arrived.

Nephredom stood and watched silently as hordes of the creatures clawed and spit at the glass barrier, unable to reach him. They tried in vain to climb its polished surface; they clumped together in vicious packs searching for an opening—any opening. They were tenacious, Nephredom observed. If he stood in the same spot for twenty days, he imagined that they would still be there, determined to get at him. Eventually, if enough beasts clambered and piled upon each other, some could reach the top of the glass gate and escape. For the future of his people, he thought, that must not happen.

Sighing deeply with exhaustion, Nephredom thrust both arms forward in a shoving gesture. The glass wall shattered in a deafening roar that drove most of the beasts back. A few bold ones stayed, waiting to see what would happen next. The wall had broken into thousands, perhaps millions, of pieces, some of them immense. By the force of Nephredom's will, the largest of these shards, dozens of feet long and pointed like spears, stayed suspended in space, their sharp, deadly ends aimed at the beasts. Nephredom imprinted a simple animation onto the shards. Whenever any of the beasts came too close to the gate, the glass shards would thrust several feet forward in unison, impaling any of the beasts in their way. Then the shards would momentarily tilt themselves downward to drop the skewered beasts to the ground. The wall would then return to its original location to wait for the next victim. In the event that some of the beasts learned and adapted, he imprinted a few surprise animations in the glass.

After witnessing the deaths of dozens of their comrades, the horde of beasts turned away, hissing, and disappeared into their mist-filled city. Nephredom set up the blockade as a one-way door. If any of the free beasts were to return to the city, this Gate would let them in, but once inside, they could never leave.

Satisfied with his work, Nephredom collapsed, unable to stand and barely able to stay conscious. Suddenly he felt a sharp pain in his shoulder—the impact of a rock the size of his fist. He turned to see a handful of dirty, ragged children, who apparently had fled the city when their parents started to change. They were the smart ones, Nephredom thought, or at least lucky. He had seen the half-eaten remains of children who had stayed in the city. The magic that came from the Lake Stone was not absolute; it did not affect children. The ones that stood before him were mostly older children—eleven, perhaps twelve years of age— though a few younger ones were present as well.

Another rock hit him, then other. It would be a ludicrous fate, Nephredom thought, to survive the beasts only to be stoned to death by the young of his own people. He tried to re-summon his personal force shield to no avail. Creating the Gate had left him too drained to cast even the humblest of spells. Bloodied and broken, he called out to the children, trying to make them understand that he had just shielded them from the beasts forever. But even as he spoke, the stoning continued. The children apparently saw only a magic user—no different from the one who had cursed the Lake Stone and turned their mothers and fathers into monsters. Too weak to protect himself or to flee, Nephredom covered his head the best he could and had resigned himself to die when the stones stopped. The children had run away. He saw a figure dressed in robes, displaying the crest of Jerel—an East Taren soldier on West Taren ground!

Too weak to resist the young soldier, Nephredom allowed the man to help him to his feet. Captain Ciredor of the East Taren army. Nephredom thought carefully about his next move. If this captain knew of the letter in his pocket, proving him to be the crown prince of the enemy, he would no doubt finish what the children had begun. To draw attention away from himself, he asked the captain what brought him to Lamec. Ciredor gave Nephredom a suspicious look, but explained.

The captain and his men had taken advantage of the retreat of Sunder's forces, regrouping and taking the offensive for the first time since the inception of the war. They also encountered and fought some of the beasts, finding their flame attacks as useless against their resistant hides as Nephredom's had been. The seldom-used daggers they carried for emergency protection saved their lives. They too learned that quick thrusts were the only known way to defeat the creatures. They were about to return to Jerel to plan what to do about the new, unexpected menace when they sensed Nephredom's great magic and chose to investigate. Nephredom could tell that they were amazed at what he had done and grateful that the remaining beasts were safely caged. Because Nephredom was a mage and was dressed as a Dosk student, the captain assumed he was of East Taren. He asked Nephredom why was he in West Taren during this time of war.

With false humility, Nephredom answered: "When I heard rumors that strange beasts walked about in Lamec, my zeal for learning overtook my wisdom, and I came to study them. When I realized how dangerous they were, I erected this Gate to prevent their possible attack on East Taren hamlets and villages. This feat I dedicate to the glory of the East Taren Empire."

To Nephredom's relief, Ciredor believed his lie and relaxed his guard. The captain wanted Nephredom to go with him and his men to have an audience with the Queen and tell her what he had done. Nephredom agreed. His father was lost to him because of her people's callousness. By pretending to be one of them, he thought, perhaps he could get close enough to the Queen to cut her neck and avenge his father's death with her blood.

Nephredom was offered a horse, and the party reached Jerel the same day. Before going in the palace, Nephredom remembered being told to be of good humor, for it was the Queen's birthday. Nephredom had smiled and said, "Then may she have many more."

The Queen, impressed by the potency of his power and the service he had done for East Taren, appointed him court mage and titled him "Keeper of the Gate." That was one of her last official acts before she secluded herself to mourn for her lost husband, King Bromus. Nephredom realized at that moment the opportunity unfolding before him, with the potential to deliver much more than the simple murder of the Queen.

Nephredom's thoughts returned to the present. For a long time, he glared hatefully at the cheerful banners celebrating the Queen's birthday. He abruptly turned away from the window, as if offended by a bright light. His memories would not give him peace. The chorus in his head would not stop its constant singing.

What he saw when he entered Lamec that day the beasts had spawned nearly drove him insane. To see an entire population of his kindred deteriorate into something . . . no longer human . . . into those terrible beasts . .

Only one thing, he thought, saved him from the embrace of madness:

Vengeance. As a high-ranking member of the court, he could enact vengeance on not just the Queen—she was half-dead already with grief—but the entire line of Bromus! Every relative, every friend, every sympathizer—they all would be held accountable for their war crimes!

He would not rest until they were all dead, but patience and time would serve him far better than a hasty blade. Nephredom smiled. The expression was alien to his grim countenance. He had risen to become Regent of the East Taren throne—with authority to rule the Queen's people as he pleased.

It was nearly time to release the Gate and direct the beasts into East Taren. Being creatures of magic, they would be attuned to the cause of their long-term imprisonment and angrily seek him out here in Jerel. To be sure of this, he allowed the essence of his magic to fill and saturate the Gate—it's burning scent forever familiar to the beasts caged by it. Like tracking animals, Nephredom was certain the beasts were capable to following that scent to its source, if given the chance. He was not merely "Keeper of the Gate," he was also secretly keeper of the beacon in which the beasts would soon follow—here.

They would destroy every East Taren province along the way, like locusts consuming the land. As he so often did, Nephredom wished he could release the beasts right then. The strain of maintaining the Gate for so long was excruciating; his psionic seizures were getting more frequent, and the one this morning had been the worst yet. If he did not release the Gate soon, it would kill him.

With fortitude and resolve, Nephredom forced his rising, internal dissension to be still. The Princess still lived, and he could not trust her death to the beasts. Before he released the Gate, he had to be certain that she paid for her crimes. Nephredom crumpled the letter from his father in his hand. Slowly, flames began to lift up and devour the ball of paper, until only ashes remained in his unscathed palm.

The misguided Power that guarded her, he thought, would do the Princess no good, for he was a very powerful mage, and Irel was a very weak Power. Her long stay in the Band had no doubt enfeebled her. Irel had returned, apparently to stop him from achieving his goal and to steal his magic for herself.

Nephredom was determined to outmaneuver this Power. When the additional mercenaries were in place, he speculated, Irel would be unable to use her agents to reach him. She would be forced to face him directly, one to one. Then he would kill her, thus becoming a Power in his own right.

CHAPTER
8

Keris's Tale

R ayna stopped running and leaned heavily against a nearby tree. "That's it," she panted. "I'm not going any farther. It feels like my heart's about to explode any second." Keris heard her from a short distance ahead and stopped. She turned and walked back to the tree where Rayna rested. Breathing heavily, she urged Rayna, "We must keep going."

"I'm staying right here."

"Have you no concern for your life?"

Rayna panted back, "I don't see how running myself into unconsciousness is going to do any good." She raised her wrist so that they both could see it. "Look, my watch is back to normal, so there's no danger."

Keris, unconvinced, spoke in a hushed tone. "Your charm is mistaken. I am certain we are being followed."

Rayna glimpsed backward, a crease of newfound worry forming under her knitted brows. She whispered back, "I thought you told me Red Robes don't chase. I was under the assumption we were running just to get out of their range of detection."

Keris nodded in agreement. "It is true that they do not chase, but I suspect the Red Robes sent someone after us who does. A mercenary, perhaps.

Rayna pushed herself from the tree with a weary groan. "Why didn't you tell me this two miles ago?"

Keris drew her dagger and darted behind a large oak a few feet away. "There's no more time for questions. Your delay has allowed our pursuer to gain ground, and we stand little chance of losing him at this point. He is a large man, but alone. I can hear his approaching steps even now—prepare yourself."

Rayna cocked her head to listen. She could hear the rustling leaves of surrounding trees, and occasionally the sound of a bird singing from its perch. She listened more closely and detected a barely audible, distant crackle of twigs being snapped underfoot. The sound was faint, and she never would have noticed it if Keris hadn't brought it to her attention. Rayna had to admire Keris for her keen perception, but how, she wondered, did she know—

Keris interrupted with a hiss. "If we are to succeed in this ambush, we would have a much better chance if you hid yourself rather than standing in the open, waiting to be seen!"

Annoyed and embarrassed, Rayna took cover behind a tree a few feet from where Keris hid, cursing herself silently for letting herself become distracted yet again. Rayna had always taken pride in the capable image she projected to others; it was particularly distressing that whenever she tried this with Keris, she ending up looking like a bumbling buffoon. Rayna crouched and listened for the stranger's arrival. Every minute felt like ten. The situation eerily reminded her of how she felt after her car crashed in the woods—the same adrenaline-fueled, panicky feeling. Fortunately, she thought, this time she did not have to go through the ordeal alone.

Rayna was relieved when she finally heard the sound of someone entering the clearing where they waited. At least the suspense was over. She squeezed her staff reassuringly and cut a quick glance to where Keris hid, to see if she was going to give a signal to strike. She was gone.

"Where *are* you?" Rayna cried out, before realizing she was speaking out loud. "Where is she?"

The sound of the man's footsteps paused, then resumed in Rayna's direction. Certain that the element of surprise had been lost, Rayna readied herself for the worst. At that very moment, she heard Keris gave a yell from an overhead limb. Keris pounced upon the distracted stranger, her blade bared like a talon. Rayna realized that Keris had not abandoned her but had sought higher elevation to better spot and surprise the enemy. She scolded herself for not thinking to do the same.

Keris had landed neatly on the tall stranger's back, her long dagger held dangerously close to his neck. Rayna rushed to Keris's aid, searching for the best place to target her staff. She was just about to deliver a spirited whack at the man's knees when Keris shouted to her, "Hold! We know this man."

Rayna blinked at the captive in disbelief. It was Arstinax. A square patch of brown leather, attached to a cord bond around his head, covered his missing eye. Keris now stood before him, her dagger still in hand. "Explain yourself," she demanded evenly.

Arstinax apologized. "Forgive me for startling you two, but you both move like the wind. I have been trying to catch up for some time. I wish to join you, wherever your travels may take you."

"Why?" Rayna and Keris asked in unison.

"Because you two are unpopular with the Red Robes. That makes you very popular with me." Arstinax sighed heavily. "And because there is nothing left for me in Kuara. I have angered the Red Robes, and my parents' lives would be in peril if I stayed. They have suffered enough without me making things worse."

He addressed Rayna. "I have also come to atone for my earlier disrespect, by serving you however you see fit. Having my life saved by a Power has created a great debt I must find a way to repay."

Keris relaxed her posture and looked up at the solemn giant. "Then welcome, friend, Arstinax of Kuara. The people of Kuara are known throughout the land as dutiful, loyal, and strong. I have personally witnessed your willingness to stand bravely against that which is wrong. You have earned my respect, and that is something I do not easily give."

Arstinax managed a humble smile and looked back at Rayna, who was lost in a daze of resurfacing guilt. "And am I welcome to you as well, Irel of the Band?"

"Yes, of course," Rayna blurted, wishing at that moment she could crawl into a nice, deep, secluded cave. "Welcome, and please don't call me that. My name is Rayna. Rayna Powell."

✳ ✳ ✳

The three of them made camp, set up temporary lodging, and prepared a small cooking fire. Searching her pack, Keris found a standing metal rack, unfolded it, and placed it over the flames. She set an iron bowl on top, emptying into it some of the dried contents she carried in the small sacks around her waist, then added water. Soon the mixture spread into a thick broth. The rich smells of onions and herbs filled Rayna's nostrils, reminding her how hungry she was.

As they sat eating quietly, a tugging at Rayna's conscience compelled her to speak, but her words refused to communicate what her heart had to say: "Arstinax, how's your eye? I mean, how's your missing eye—never mind."

"I believe," Keris interceded, "that my friend wishes to know how you are coping with your injury, as would I."

Arstinax pointed to his patch casually. "I can work just as hard with one eye as I could with two. My wound does not slow me, and my good eye will not fail me."

Changing the subject, Keris presented Arstinax with an empty sack and asked if he would be willing to gather fruit for their long journey. Arstinax, bored and restless, gladly accepted the chance to work and eagerly set off, promising to be back before nightfall with enough fruit for a feast. Keris watched Rayna staring off at nothing, her thoughts far away from the surrounding woods.

"Now that we have invited Arstinax to join us," Keris began, "your indulgence in self-guilt is a luxury you can no longer afford. Shall you tell him or shall I?"

Rayna glared resentfully at Keris. "I don't need your advice, and I certainly don't need you speaking on my behalf. The only reason I agreed to come this far is because you can get me to Dosk."

"My question remains unanswered."

"I'll tell Arstinax, but in my own time."

"And in the meantime, I suppose you expect him not to notice your awkwardness around him and your tendency to avoid looking him in the face? In time, he may get the impression you think he has very handsome feet."

"Fine! I'll just walk up to him and say, 'Oh, by the way, I'm responsible for your brother's death.'"

"You were reckless and unthinking, but it is the Red Robes' hands that bear Merlott's life blood, not yours."

Rayna said nothing; an uneasy moment of silence passed.

Keris removed her hat and dusted the soot from her Red Robe encounter. "Your stubbornness is denser than these woods, Rayna Powell of Nightwind. I did not send Arstinax away so that I could argue this matter with you. At the Sharpening Stone, I gave you my word that I would answer your questions when the time was right. That time has come."

Rayna straightened, her confidence returning in floods. Expressing herself about emotional issues never came easy for her, and the chance to escape the ordeal for the far more comfortable process of digging for facts was a welcome change. "Back at the condemning," she asked, "I overheard the Red Robes communicating to you. I got the impression it was for your ears only. They called you a Princess. Why?"

Keris nodded. "I see you waste no time on small questions. Can I trust you to be silent about what will I tell you?"

"I won't tell anyone."

"What the Red Robes called me is indeed my true title. I am Princess of East Taren."

Rayna stared at Keris, not saying a word. The thirtyish-looking woman was in better physical shape than many athletes, definitely not the type to sit around waiting to be catered to all day. Rayna seriously doubted that a princess would know any of the survival skills Keris had expertly demonstrated, much less be caught roaming the countryside like a vagabond, possessing only the few items she took from a dead person's house. It was hardly a princessly thing to do. And that wicked looking dagger she carried, Rayna thought, was not exactly a golden fan.

Rayna's face bore the familiar wry expression of blatant disbelief Keris had come to expect. Keris cautioned Rayna, "This is no jest. Before you judge me with prejudiced eyes, you should give your ears a chance to listen first."

"I'm listening."

"I am the daughter of Queen Aknata and King Bromus."

"I remember hearing about Bromus back at the bar. Something about a war?"

"Yes, my father died in the War of Kings, four years ago."

"How did it start?"

"It is said that an East Tarener started the war by touching the sacred Lake Stone of Lamec."

"A war was started over a rock?"

"Yes, yes. You know nothing of this?"

"Sorry, but they didn't teach me much Taren history in class."

"Are you willing to learn?"

"I'm always willing to learn."

"Then know this. The Stone incident is but one curse of many. For as long as time has been recorded on paper, East and West Tareners have been killing each other in war, long after either side could remember its cause. There are many on both sides of Taren who believe that their people should have dominion over the other. Those of the West believe magic to be vulgar, and those that practiced it evil. Those of the East believe the non-magical West Tareners to be inferior and envious of what they do not have.

"Sometimes in secret, and sometimes openly, both sides have plotted to undermine the peace that the wiser ones worked hard to maintain. Even before the ink had dried on treaties, armies were secretly multiplied and weapons for mass death forged. It had come to be expected that any peace between East and West Taren was only a lull between storms to give the other side time to prepare for the next war. History tells of many bloody disputes between our two lands. The War of Kings was simply the most recent."

Crickets began to chirp their nightly song, and the heat of the sun started to wane.

"The War of Kings did not go well for our people," Keris continued, "for we were not fully ready for war."

"But you won by default," Rayna added, recalling her ill-fated conversation with Merlott.

Keris smiled thinly. "That is one way of putting it. West Taren was defeated by the same darkness that prompted it to declare war. Our remaining forces, though few and wounded, were left without an enemy to fight. It was as if Destiny had changed its mind just before Fate could stamp its final seal."

Rayna was about to ask what specifically killed off the West Taren troops when another question popped into the forefront of her thoughts. She asked critically, "What did you do during the war?"

More from reluctance than from surprise, Keris flinched at the question as if pricked by a thorn. That was not something she cared to talk about. Her honor and her pride did not always agree, but Keris knew the disbelieving mage would never join her without a gesture of trust. Too much was at stake to let walls of vanity stand in the way. Pushing her reservations aside, she told Rayna her tale.

"I was not the same person then that I am now," Keris began. "I paid little attention to the war or the affairs of the government, and instead entertained myself in athletics and training sports. As hundreds of East Taren soldiers died, I enjoyed a privileged lifestyle, free of care or worry. When my own father died, I learned a valuable lesson about the misery of war."

"I lost my father too," Rayna confided. "It was cancer. I was just a kid at the time. The day it happened, in was in the room with him, when the nurse told me to go outside. That was the last time I saw him alive."

"Then perhaps you can understand how I wished at that moment I had spent more time with him while he lived."

"Yes," Rayna said, now regretting asking Keris to talk about her past pain, just to bolster her own wounded pride.

"With the news of the King's death," Keris explained, "my older brother became King. Days later, a strange mage was brought to the court. He had somehow sealed the evil that was loosed from the Lake Stone, and saved many lives by doing so. In gratitude, my mother bade him to stay and gave him power over many. His name was Nephredom."

The sound of the familiar name sent a chill through Rayna. *He was the one in charge of the Red Robes*, she remembered.

"At the start," Keris went on, "Nephredom was kind and benevolent in his ways, so I did not concern myself with the East Taren mage of Dosk. Then relatives began to die. First, distant cousins would be found murdered in their beds while they slept. Others would keel over dead after a poisoned meal. Later, my uncles and aunts all met similar fates. My mother's thoughts were forever on the grave of my father, so she left the charge of finding the killers to my brother, the King. Alas, my poor brother, in his arrogance, believed no harm could befall us behind the safety of the palace gates. He did nothing but delegate the matter of finding the assassins to Nephredom."

Rayna shuddered. "Somehow, I think that was a mistake."

Keris laughed bitterly. "Would one ask the thief who robbed him to guard his vault?"

Rayna absently tossed a twig into the dying cooking-fire. "So you believe Nephredom had a hand in the assassinations?"

"Yes," Keris said. "I am certain of it." Her eyes narrowed in bitter reflection. "You see, my brother was vain and believed that a beard covered up his better features. He demanded that he be shaved with a fresh blade each morning by a servant. I was on my way to see my brother that morning to discuss our mother's worsening state when I saw that the servant who usually shaved my brother had been replaced with another I did not recognize. Her name was Aric. She said was a new servant appointed by Nephredom himself. I remember becoming angry that Nephredom would put the hiring of handmaidens above investigating the murders.

"I let the servant go on her way and decided to see Nephredom to demand an explanation. I had nearly reached the study where the villain made his den when I realized that my brother's life was in danger. It made little sense for Nephredom to hire a new servant when we had many. It made even less sense that a skilled and trusted servant be replaced by an outsider—one who would be allowed past the guards to put a blade at the King's neck.

"When I reached the King's quarters, the deed had already been done. My brother was in a strange trance, and his freshly shaven face had been deeply nicked many times by the servant's razor. Blood rolled freely down the sides of his face, and I cried out. Aric saw me and was not surprised. So confident was she that I could do nothing, she told me her murderous scheme. She confessed that she was no mere servant, but a master mage. The spell Aric placed on my brother would dissipate once she left the room—its only function was to block from the King's memory that which she was telling me. The blade with which she shaved the King was coated with a slow-acting poison. She gloated at what she had done, and told me that the King would go about his daily business, then suddenly drop dead.

"The mage said in her own words: 'Surely you can appreciate the beauty of my plan. All who see him fall will agree that his heart failed him, and nothing more will come of it.' She asked me to join her and Nephredom, promising that I would be made Queen in a year so long as I acted in their interests."

"In other words," Rayna surmised, "they wanted a puppet. They felt your brother was too proud to fit the bill, so they picked you."

"Perhaps. Or perhaps they wished to bribe me into silence long enough to murder me later, with fewer consequences. One thing was certain: With my brother soon dead, my mother and I were all that stood between Nephredom and the throne. The fullness of Nephredom's treachery was then clear to me. Piece by piece, Nephredom had been dismantling our power, by buying the loyalty of those willing to support him and intimidating or killing those who would not.

"I suspected the guards would refuse to obey any order I gave against Nephredom and his hireling. There was only one choice left to me, however desperate it may have been. I drew my knife on Aric, hoping to stop her, and then to stop Nephredom before his usurpation became manifest. The knife I held then was unlike the dagger I hold now. It was a decorative blade, issued only to royalty and encrusted with the crest of Jerel. It was richly embroidered and meant more for show than for combat, though it could be used well enough against the unwary.

"Aric, however, was not unwary. I was poorly prepared and was of little challenge to the master mage. With just a thought, she tore the knife from my grasp and pinned me against a wall with such magical force, I could not move. She took my weapon and stabbed my brother in his heart with it, saying, 'I applaud you for providing me with such a splendid opportunity. To your credit, I must admit this plan is far superior to the first. With your knife, I will kill two monarchs with but a single blow.' With that said, I knew she planned to accuse me of killing my own brother, claiming that my thirst for power had driven me to fratricide. I feared she would succeed, for I was well known to many for my preference to the knife over magic, and my quiet nature made me a mystery to most in the court. My mother was too withdrawn to help me, and no one else bore witness to the crime.

"Grief welled up in my heart like a dark spring, and I knew then that one of the assassins who had been slaughtering my family stood before me. She magically peeled the King's blood from her reddened hands and sent it to fall on me. Soon Aric was clean of all blood, and I was splattered with it, like a mad butcher. She put a shallow wound in her side with my knife, then let it fall to the floor, stained with her blood. She called out to guards screaming, 'murderer!'

"The pain of her self-inflicted wound had disrupted her magic, and I could stand. I could have freely attacked the injured witch right then, but if I took the time to do so, I would surely have been captured and executed for a crime that was not my own. Part of me wanted to stay, even if it meant my death. I did not want to leave my mother to that vulture. Aric knew this too, and she waited. Her eyes were as cold as winter ice, and nothing good could be seen in them.

"I ran quickly from the palace and fled the city, hoping that one day I would come back to reclaim what they had stolen from me. Nephredom proclaimed himself Regent and declared me an escaped murderer. He offered to any citizen of Taren a thousand gold pieces for my return. With such a price on my head, I have been forced to live a life of disguise and secrecy."

"But the Red Robes said they wouldn't harm you," Rayna tried to assure her.

"A convenient lie. To kill me here, on West Taren soil, would leave some suspicion and doubt in the minds on many. Instead, they would give me a mock trial, at which I would be found guilty. This would give them the legitimacy they require to publicly drain the life from me in my capital, in front of thousands.

"For the last two years, I have survived on my wits and the generosity of those who would grant me shelter. I have been working on building an army great enough to overthrow Nephredom, but it has not been easy. The Red Robes are his eyes and ears, and anyone they suspect of supporting me is soon killed."

"How large is Nephredom's army?"

"About five thousand."

"And how many people are in your army?"

"Ninety-eight. One hundred even, if myself and you are included."

Rayna was incredulous. "That's all you've managed to recruit in two years?"

Keris's normally calm voice took on an agitated tone. "This is no contest, no game. There is a bounty worth a small fortune open to anyone able to find me. Lest I fall to betrayal, I have to choose my allies carefully, and slowly. These are dangerous times, and Nephredom's power is daunting at best. Most of my contacts were willing to provide me with information and services, but not willing to risk their lives and their families in open defiance."

"Sorry. I see your point. Still, you can't expect me to help you retake a kingdom with ninety-eight men. The only way we'll get as far as the front door is if the guards are too busy laughing to stop us."

Keris agreed. "You are quite right. That is why I want you to accompany me to Soren."

"Soren?"

"It is a large town in East Taren. I know the governor there. With his help, we will have an army of more than three thousand men."

"That sounds a lot better. What's his name?"

"Ciredor. He is a good friend of mine. He was once Captain of the East Taren army. There is no better leader to be found in Taren."

Rayna was far from enthusiastic. "Why do you need me to go with you? Can't you just drop me off at Dosk on your way?"

"I need you there to convince him to commit his men to my cause. You are a master mage. Your presence will prove to him that our chances of winning are favorable."

Rayna held up her hand in protest. "First of all, I'm not any magic mage master. Second, if he's such a good friend of yours, why does he need convincing to help you?"

"Ciredor has many things to consider. Rising up against his own people is no trifling affair. I would be asking him and his men to slay other East Tareners. A civil war on such a scale has never been fought. He may be going against popular opinion as well, for Nephredom had ruled acceptably, albeit ruthlessly. As with magic, he has outlawed song and dance, but the hungry are fed, and the homeless are given shelter. Even if we are successful, there is a small chance the people will rebel if Nephredom continues to keep them content. Also, any action against the throne may be perceived as an attack on the Queen, even though everyone knows Nephredom does the ruling."

"What about you? Wouldn't the people want a legitimate heir to rule them?"

"You forget, Nephredom has poisoned the people's minds against me. I am despised in most circles. They call me 'brother killer.'"

"I take it Ciredor is a lot more popular than you are."

Keris nodded. "He is regarded as one of East Taren's greatest heroes. He had gained the respect of both commoner and noble. If he supports me with his army and his good name, I am certain we will have victory."

Rayna let out a tired groan. "I don't want 'victory.' I just want a way back home."

"Without you, Ciredor will not commit."

"What's so special about me? You said yourself, you originally wanted a healer. Why not find another one?"

"That is not as simple as you say. Healers were rare and precious even before Nephredom took over. Once in power, the dictator declared that all healers who were not members of his Red Robes be killed. The healer who died in Kuara was one of the last free healers left in the land. It would take too long to find another, if any more still live. That is why I chose you. Master mages are second only to healers in rarity, and nearly all of them serve Nephredom."

Rayna's response was broken off by the sound of Arstinax returning from his chore. The sack he carried was pregnant with fruit, indeed enough for a feast.

"As a boy," he exclaimed, "I used to go exploring in these woods, and never got lost—" He paused. "Am I interrupting something?"

"Not at all," Keris said. "It has been decided that we shall go to Soren. Agreed?"

Arstinax scratched his puffy beard thoughtfully. "An East Taren town, eh? Well, of all the places in East Taren, Soren strikes me as the least offensive. I will gladly go."

"Good." Keris turned to Rayna. "Are we agreed?"

Rayna folded her arms, walked away from them both, and stood at the edge of the clearing to sulk in private.

"I will take that as a 'yes,'" Keris said. She began working with Arstinax to prepare sleeping pallets for the three of them.

Rayna was furious. She resented Keris, with her bossy demeanor. Princess or no princess, she had no right to arbitrarily decide where they were going! She had no right to interfere with her search for home! Keris's fight was not her fight, and she had no intention of being a part of it!

Looking up at the ebony sky with its starry sparkle, Rayna felt calmer; momentarily distracted from her anger, she began to study the stars. Thanks to a passing interest in astronomy, she was able to recognize a few constellations. For the second time, she noticed what Keris referred to as the "Twin Stars of Taren." One red, the other blue, they shone down from the sky like jewels of the night. "Were they planets?" she wondered. There was something about the unusual intensity of their colors and their dominating presence in the sky that made Rayna doubt it. But then what where they?

The surrounding bramble of the woods looked foreboding and dangerous in the lonely darkness; the inviting light of Keris's campfire beckoned.

✳ ✳ ✳

Late in the night, Arstinax gently woke Rayna for watch duty.

"It's my turn already?" she mumbled, rubbing the blur from her eyes.

"Yes, you have the last watch, but I would gladly stand guard in your place," Arstinax offered earnestly.

Rayna shook her head, yawning. "I expect to do my share. Anyway, it's only for a few hours."

Arstinax handed her a small hourglass, stretched his mighty arms, and settled down to sleep.

As her traveling companions slept, Rayna busied herself scrutinizing her staff, hoping to discover its secrets. She lifted her staff high before her. Constructed of dark, smooth wood, tipped at both ends with studded iron bands, it gave no impression of a hidden power source. It had clearly shown its effectiveness against the Red Robes, by somehow paralyzing them and neutralizing their attacks. The staff was normal enough now; the vibrating pulse she felt in its core during the confrontation had long since ceased. If she were to face the Red Robes again, would she be able to summon its power again, or was its earlier demonstration a random fluke?

Rayna swung the staff back and forth in mock combat swings. Nothing happened. Her imagination briefly toyed with the mischievous idea of testing how the staff would react if it "accidentally" hit Keris on the head. However, Rayna had seen how well the Princess handled a dagger, and to do anything but fantasize about such an attack would be tantamount to suicide. Besides, as much as she disliked the woman, she didn't want to cause her serious harm if the staff activated again. She sighed and turned her attention back to her staff.

She wanted to rely on the staff with the same certainty as one would a flashlight or a telephone or a toaster, but for that to happen, she had to understand it. She examined the metal bands closely. Was the power in the staff strictly contact oriented, somehow channeled into the bands for direct attacks? If she encountered the Red Robes again, she doubted they would let her get close enough to tag them with her staff, now that they knew what it could do. She believed her chances of getting back home alive would be greatly improved if she could find a way to control the power in the staff and figure out how to evoke its magic from a safe distan—

Rayna caught herself in mid-thought.

It's bad enough I trust a broken watch to alert me of danger, she brooded. *Now here I am observing a rod of wood for so-called magical properties. I suppose next I'll be looking for a crystal ball to complete my collection.*

The first signs of morning's pale arrival shed no light on the puzzle of the staff's powers, and even less on her darkening mood. Looking up sleepily, Rayna greeted the early sun with a frown. The scientists of Dosk might have the answers she needed, answers that could lead her home.

As the last sands funneled into the lower chamber of the hourglass for the second time, Rayna heard the stirring movements of her traveling companions getting up. Their bodies apparently were accustomed to starting the day at the crack of dawn, without the need of a wake-up call. Keris sprang to her feet, nimble and alert, like a coiled spring, while Arstinax rose up groggily, scratching his beard and yawning fiercely, like a great bear roused from hibernation.

"The day is new," Keris said to her companions. "If we don't idle ourselves by taking too many breaks," she glanced warningly at Rayna, "we should reach Soren by moonrise, one cycle from today."

Rayna cut in, "Wait, what's a cycle?"

"I see they did not teach you the calendar in class either," Keris added dryly. "A cycle is about thirty days. There are twelve cycles in a grand-cycle or year, in case that was your next question."

"A month? There's no way I'm roaming these woods for a whole month! Can't you rent a couple of horses somewhere?"

"Horses are rare, and the few that exist are hoarded by the resourceful and the rich. In any event, your feet are too young to pass on their burden so quickly. We will make do without the aid of a horse."

"What about Dosk?"

"If you can recall from the map I showed you, Dosk is even farther from here than is Soren—about one and one half cycles." Rayna was about to say something else, but Keris waved her hand in a definitive gesture. "We must not waste any more time standing about. Gather your things. We will go now."

Rayna pressed her lips together tightly to prevent them from putting to words the unpleasant feelings she had toward Keris. The idea of being stuck with the intolerable Princess for so long was enough to give her a flaring headache. It frustrated Rayna that such a simple goal as going to Dosk would have to be postponed. Instead, she was to embark on a month-long hike to help Keris beg a captain to join in a conflict—one in which Rayna wanted no involvement. But as it stood, her options seemed close to none. Taking up the rear, Rayna followed grudgingly behind Arstinax, with Keris leading the way.

※ ※ ※

They had journeyed for fourteen days, stopping to rest sparingly, and only after much protesting from Rayna. The toil of the journey was taking its toll on her. Nothing she had done before had prepared her for this. She had been sleeping on grass for so long, she had nearly forgotten what a mattress felt like. The heat left her in a constant sweat, and she got little relief from drinking the infernally warm water Keris stored in skins. Her stomach was always queasy— probably from a combination of sleep deprivation and the heat. The woods seemed exhaustingly endless, and she knew they were only halfway to their destination.

Arstinax helped eased the tedium. Each night as they camped, he would entertain his companions with wild stories of his great-grandfather and his magical, talking poleax. As she listened to his jovial tales, Rayna was sadly reminded of his brother and of the secret debt she could never possibly repay.

The following day, the party came across a wide stone road, partially covered by grass and earth. Despite its neglected appearance, Rayna could see that it was a major thoroughfare, likely leading somewhere important. She quickened her pace to catch up with Keris. "Shouldn't we be following this road?" she asked.

Keris did not share Rayna's enthusiasm. "No, we will continue south."

"Why?"

"That road is forbidden, for it belongs to the lost city of Lamec."

"The city that has the rock that somebody touched and caused the War of Kings to happen?"

"Yes, and do not expect to rest until we have put that place far behind us."

Arstinax nodded in agreement. The normally confident giant looked vaguely unsettled. He whispered to Rayna, "Lamec carries a curse. The less said of it, the better. Let us leave this place."

Rayna persisted. "If this place is so bad, why are we here to begin with?"

"The Edgewoods is the safest haven we have from the Red Robes," Keris explained hastily. "As fate would have it, the fallen city of Lamec lies in its center, and there is no way completely around it, save leaving the woods. My best hope was to avoid all visible signs of the city, lest your curious mind fill my ears with countless questions"

Rayna knew she was supposed to feel insulted, but she couldn't help feeling pleased with herself. "I'm sorry you failed," she lied with a smirk.

"Then I pray you let your sorrow liven your steps, Rayna Powell of Nightwind. I have heard many bad things about this place, and I do not intend to wait for one of them to introduce itself."

"Ghost and goblins?" Rayna quipped sarcastically.

"No, darkness and death! I will share with you the horrors I know of Lamec when we reach the safety of Soren. Until then, I choose to forgive your ignorance." Keris brushed past Rayna and Arstinax rapidly, forcing them to break into a jog to keep up.

As they hurried along, Arstinax touched Rayna softly, on her shoulder. "Why is it that you and Keris argue so? Have you had past quarrels with her?"

Rayna smiled, in spite of herself. "Maybe in a former life," she replied.

"I don't think she believes you to be a Power as I do."

"You shouldn't. I'm not a Power. I'm just a person who is tired of taking baths in muddy ponds, and eating bulbs and roots—and seeds!" She raised her voice loud enough that Keris could hear. "And I'm tired of being walked to death, like a camel!"

"But are those things what truly make you so unhappy? If mere comfort

was your only concern, you would never have bothered to save my life."
Arstinax hesitated, then added, "It is said that fear will make even the
meekest creature bite."

Rayna looked away defensively. "How did you know?"

"I have seen it enough to know. I have felt it enough to know."

"You? I saw how you stood up to the Red Robes. You were fearless."

"And was it not you who faced them with your staff of charms and
defeated them with a single blow? Was there no fear in your heart?"

"Yes, plenty—but I overcame it."

"And I as well."

"But how can I overcome a fear of never seeing home again?"

"By building a new home."

"I wish it was that easy." Rayna was eager to change the subject.
"Enough about me. What do *you* think of Keris?"

"It is true the knife wielder is firm and demanding, but I trust her
instincts. She has proven to be an able leader."

Rayna grumbled, "But a little common courtesy like 'please' and 'thank
you' would be nice from time to time."

"A hand that is too gentle sometimes loses its grasp," Arstinax pointed
out calmly. "Keris has not chosen to tell me all she plans to do in Soren,
but I suspect that kind words alone will not get her what she wants."

Rayna slowly relaxed her guard. Arstinax had a way of doing that to
her, despite her fear and guilt. "Then I suppose you think it's unreasonable
and irrational of me to want decent food and a horse?" she asked flippantly.

"Tell me this," he challenged. "If Keris had horses and better food,
would she not share them with us?"

Rayna grew silent. The gentle-hearted Kuaran had told her in so many
words that she was acting like a spoiled brat, and deep in her heart she
knew it was true. Suddenly, she felt unworthy of Arstinax's kindness, or
even Keris's, for that matter.

Arstinax could see by her silence that Rayna wished to be alone
and marched ahead to leave her to her private thoughts. Rayna began
to slow down, trailing farther and farther behind. Keris and Arstinax
didn't notice. She had wanted to tell Arstinax what she planned to
do, but she knew he would only try to stop her. She had to agree;
Arstinax was right—Keris was an able leader. Rayna wasn't a leader,
but she wasn't a follower either—she was a loner. She wasn't going to
get home by following somebody else's lead or somebody else's agenda.
An opportunity had presented itself, and the decision to investigate was
hers, not Keris's, to make. If the people in this mysterious Lamec could

show her the way home, or at least help her get to Dosk, she owed it to herself to find out.

Slowly, carefully, Rayna came to a dead stop and let her companions drift out of sight. When she thought her footsteps would be out of their earshot, she turned and ran back quickly the other direction, toward the road. Branches seemed to pop out of nowhere to hit her spitefully in embarrassing places; hidden rocks stumbled her movements, and slippery mud holes seemed to find her every step. She had taken for granted Keris's expert path-finding skills—and she no longer did so. For the first time since she entered the woods, Rayna began to worry about wild animals lurking about.

"I hate hindsight," Rayna thought nervously.

Like a creeping blanket, green moss coated the forest bed and all the loose bark and bits that rested upon it. The trunks of the trees were literally sheathed by its draping, dragging, clumping layers. Rayna noticed that the overall effect was to make the forest appear as if it was *bleeding green*. The towering trees abounded with leafy boughs that stretched wide, like yawning arms, forming a living canopy above. "I really hate hindsight," she repeated, and she began looking up at the overlying branches for snakes.

At last, to Rayna's relief, she reached the worn stone road. There, she found yet another reason for worry: Which way? East or west? Rayna wished at that moment she had a map, but since she didn't, she settled for her less-than-scientific intuition. She went east. It didn't take long before Rayna could see she had gone the right way.

The city stood like an ancient colossus in the forest. Stone parapets— moss-coated and unoccupied—wreathed Lamec's lonely borders. Rayna struggled to remember the details she had learned about Lamec from Keris. The city had fallen, a victim of the war, but what happened then? Is it occupied by the East Taren military? Or were the people of the city allowed to rebuild and keep their independence? Or maybe the city was so heavily damaged it was abandoned and forgotten. If that is the case, Rayna thought, she wasted her time trying to get there. Then she saw the Gate.

At first, Rayna thought she was seeing things; she walked closer to get a better look. She stared in amazement. It was beautiful. Hundreds, possibly thousands, of pieces of green glass decorated the entrance to the city, like a sparking curtain. Fascinated, Rayna walked up and touched it. Immediately, the curtain of glass parted slightly, allowing enough room for her to enter.

Rayna looked for evidence of hidden strings or wires that could support such a magnificent mobile and found none. This glass was floating! Each shard in the odd mobile was at least two feet long, and some were much longer. She shook her head, both bewildered and awed. The glass appeared to have been formed containing large traces of iron impurities, she noted, studying a piece up close. That would account for its greenish tint. Rayna felt reassured. The city was not abandoned. Nothing as delicate and as graceful as the glass mobile would last long without a keeper.

It would be great, Rayna told herself, if she could find the architect responsible for the mobile and learn the secret of its suspension. With renewed hope in her heart, Rayna entered though the jade gates. And it draped shut behind her.

CHAPTER 9

Aric's Dance

Aric posed before her mirror, pleased at what she saw. She understood that before one could expect to be appealed to, one had first be appealing. She wore a long silk dress that bore a pattern of many colored rings of different sizes, looping one into the other. It clung to her shapely form in such a way that most male eyes would follow without hesitation. She applied a matching scarf scented with perfume, then smiled with satisfaction. She had looked into her mirror thousands of times in the past and never grew bored with the image it reflected.

Beauty. It was a tameless, cunning craft she had nourished and seen blossom in herself, much to her gain. Of course, she also had the advantage of youth. *The beauty of youth is so often wasted on the young,* she thought as she began to braid her glossed, black hair methodically, pondering the irony with amusement. *Only when gray hairs began to sprout on their heads like weeds, and their faces start to gather wrinkles from Time's fated harvest, do women ever realize what they've lost.* A knock sounded at her door.

"Enter, guards," Aric called out, not moving from where she stood.

Two West Taren mercenary guards stepped inside her quarters and were amazed. Four polished marble pillars braced each corner of her bed, and ruffled strips of velvet, embedded with precious stones, crossed loosely from one pillar to the next. A great wardrobe sat in one corner, its ornate surface painted with gold leaf. The walls also were painted in gold, which brightened the room with a warm, luxurious glow. Looking down, the first guard could scarcely believe his own eyes. Even the floor beneath his feet featured an elaborate tile mosaic of gold, silver, and marble.

The second guard blinked repeatedly. *The opulence of this woman's quarters is second only to that of the throne room,* he thought.

"Only second?" asked Aric in an amused tone. "I dare say, I had this room designed with the specific intent that its splendor surpass that of the throne room. No matter. When I become Queen, the throne room shall be mine as well."

The two guards turned quickly to see Aric standing in a niched corner of the room, facing a mirror. Aric turned and smiled seductively. "Well, my handsome friends, are you content to gawk at me all morning, or did you have another reason for disturbing me in my quarters?"

The first guard inhaled abruptly and sputtered, "Forgive us, my lady, we are newly assigned here and not used to such beauty. We have been sent to inform you that the accused have been captured. Would you have them put to death?"

"No, no, no. It is very important that their deaths be properly administered, not to mention the delicate matter of interrogation—which has not been attempted yet, I hope."

"No, my lady they have not been—"

"Good." She cut him short. "That is a task best left to myself, lest it be bungled."

Aric lifted both arms dramatically, and on impulse, she began a lively dance. "Come now, my newly assigned friends," she urged, taking the first guard by the hand. "The good news you have brought me has lightened my spirits, and I desperately need a dance partner. She winked at the blushing second guard. "Preferably two."

The reluctant guards looked at each other nervously. Aric stopped dancing and eyed them with disapproval.

"There is no music to dance by," the first guard offered lamely.

Aric laughed coldly. "Don't insult my intelligence, West Tarener. If my memory still serves me adequately, I believe Nephredom, in a dour fit, prohibited all music and dance within city limits, and declared all who disobeyed the edict as fit to die. That is why you jilt me so, is it not? Being new recruits to the empire, I cannot expect you to understand, nor do I have time to explain the many intricacies of the political game. Let it be enough for you to know that punishment for all criminal offenses that are set by the court must be approved by my pen before being carried out." She reached out and softly ran her fingers down the second guard's cheek. "And pens, my shy attractive friend, have a tendency to run out of ink."

Aric paused, suddenly aware of the presence of another mind. A woman with stern eyes, wearing full leather armor, had walked confidently into the room; at the sight of her, the guards suddenly straightened to attention. Her voice was clear and sharp: "My men had ample time to perform their duty. Why are they still here? Have you found fault with their report?"

Aric bowed formally "Ah, Captain of the Kuaran Shields, I presume? I've heard so many delightfully good things about you. But you travel about so much, I've never had the honor of meeting you—until now. Let me first say that of all hirelings we have dealt with, you command the best behaved group of West Taren mercenaries we've ever had the pleasure of contracting. You should be very, very proud."

"We do what we are paid to do," the captain replied. She looked critically at her men and with a stiff motion, of her head, silently dismissed them. "Nothing more."

Aric's smile faded as she evaluated the woman in a new light. "And your purpose for being here?"

"To inform you that the last of my company will arrive tonight."

"And?"

"And I was informed that you are the one in charge of minor arrangements that Nephredom is too occupied to bother with. So I trust you will see to it that additional barracks are made ready for my men before they arrive. They will be tired from their long journey, and I will not have them sleeping in the cold."

Aric's eyes narrowed with disdain. "You don't like me, do you, Captain?"

"No."

"Good. I appreciate honesty in those under me."

"I am not under you, for I do not take orders from minor officials or petty functionaries. My employer is Nephredom."

Aric forced a dry laugh, "You are a direct one, to be sure. As a military type, I'm certain you're familiar with a quaint little concept called the chain of command. You answer to me, Captain, not to Nephredom—to *me*. I am your superior, and if you ever go over my head," she permitted herself a wide grin, " I'll have yours,"

"I do not take well to threats," the captain sneered.

Aric looked offended. "Threats? No, no, no. Think of it as a little healthful advice from one woman to another. You see, I could not help but notice that every time we mention Nephredom's name, your thoughts instantly turn from testy to tender." Aric snapped her fingers as if something had suddenly sprung to mind. "Could it be that we have—how shall I put it—*feelings* toward Nephredom?"

The captain clenched her teeth in rage. "You dare reach inside my head? Magic is forbidden by all except the Red Robes!" She placed her hand on the pommel of her sword.

Aric took pleasure in the other woman's rage. "Don't be naïve. And I wouldn't be too rash if I were you, dear. I assure you that you would be quite dead long before your blade left its sheath." With that, the captain released her grip on her sword.

"Honestly, I can't blame you," Aric continued cheerfully. "Nephredom is a powerful and handsome man—a rare combination, if I may say so. That would certainly explain your jealousy, for it is plain to see that a man of such refined taste would naturally gravitate toward someone like myself, and that you are hopelessly beneath his class."

Aric glowered and held out her hand. "Take, for example, my hand here." Aric casually spread her fingers. "My nails are well trimmed and as colorful as a rainbow, while yours are broken and unsightly. My hair is soft, long, and adorned with beads of pearl, while you hair is matted and unkempt, and smells of . . . Well, I believe you understand my point. Though your face may be somewhat pretty, don't ever become so deluded as to think—"

A scream echoed from down the hall, cutting off Aric's monologue. The scream itself was not important to Aric, but there was something else. *Nephredom.* Aric hurriedly ushered the captain into the hallway. "I deeply regret that pressing matters of the court demand my immediate presence elsewhere; otherwise, I would indulge myself with more of this delightful chat. Nevertheless, you look smart enough to grasp its gist, and as long as you remember your place, I foresee us getting along famously—good-bye."

Aric made her way down the hall to behold the drama in mid-action. Two young East Taren servant girls pitifully cringed before Nephredom, their brooms and dusters scattered at their feet. Nephredom wore his civilized guise straight and convincing, like a well-made mask. But a mask could cover only one's face, and Aric could tell plainly that his heart blistered with rage. She began to feel giddy from the reverberating currents of malice emerging from the Regent's unguarded thoughts. He was nearly ready to kill the servants.

Nephredom slowly shifted from the sobbing girls to Aric. "Be gone, aide!" he yelled. "I will deal with these slanderers myself!"

Aric bowed deeply. "Far be it for me to impose, my liege. However, may I humbly ask what has transpired that has vexed you so?"

"A strange dream woke me early, and I could not return to sleep. I was on my way to find peace in my courtyard when I overheard these rebel spies speaking ill of my good name—plotting my downfall!"

Aric could feel it. His volatile temper was taut and unyielding, like the tightening string of a crossbow. She arched her brows, peering down at the girls. "Rebel spies, my liege?"

"You doubt my words, Aric?"

"I would sooner die a thousand deaths. I merely meant that spymasters are uneager to enlist juveniles with the task of spying on a man of your caliber. The wills of these young girls have not yet fully formed and would be easy to break if they were captured. If that were to happen, they would utter all they know, including the names of the ones who sent them, and from where. Truly, in the unlikely event that our enemies have manage to circumvent the safeguards we have erected in this mighty fortress, it would require the skills of hardened veterans rather than the likes of these two."

"And so you believe these maids to be innocent?"

"Innocent? No, my liege. Unfortunately, the nature of my job has taught me to expect treachery and question loyalty."

"Yes, you do well to know that."

"But I am nevertheless hesitant to see these youths die until I am certain they have committed a crime worthy of death. I must know if they truly intended you harm."

"I have seen children kill. I myself was nearly killed by youth barely weaned from their mothers' milk. It matters not how old the serpent is that bites you, for its venom changes not."

"Your wisdom stretches far and wide, my liege."

"But my patience does not. I heard their slander with my own ears, Aric, and I will deal with them with my own hands!"

Nephredom unclenched his gloved fists so that all could see the deadly magic that flickered upon his fingertips.

"As you wish, my Regent, but before you burn them to ashes, may I first have a word with you, *in private?* It is most urgent."

With a thought, Aric bound the girls were they stood, and she and Nephredom walked to a nearby alcove. Nephredom nodded, giving Aric permission to enter his mind.

You test me one time too many, Aric.

My liege, I must strongly advise against taking their lives. Your reputation as a . . . fierce ruler has frightened off many of our best help, and I have heard that some laborers would rather starve than serve here. I know it is my responsibility to attend to staff matters, but surely, you can appreciate the difficulty of my task when the only domestics willing to work here are crazed zealots and naïve children. I fear that if you kill these girls and word of it gets out, which is all but certain, the palace will fall into disrepair due to labor shortages. Appearance is everything. If we no longer look the role as head power, our enemies will lose their fear of us. I beseech you to show the girl servants a merciful hand.

You would ask me to spare the lives of spies?

Please, permit me to question them. If I see them to be enemies of the throne, I will gladly step aside and let you punish them as you will.

A waste of time, but you may proceed, so they may suffer longer still before they die.

Thank you, my gracious Regent.

Aric went back to the girls. "What is it you said about our great ruler—*exactly?* Cease your slobbering and speak loudly. I warn you, if you lie to me in the slightest, I will know, and your lives will be forfeit."

The taller girl trembled and spoke with a quavering but easily heard voice. "I only said, 'No one likes Nephredom because he does not allow us to use magic, and his rages are so very bad.' I swear that is all. We are not spies!"

Aric suppressed a smile. "I believe you." She ran a finger across the edge of wood molding that bordered the lower wall, producing a small clump of dust. "You cannot even spy dust in plain sight!" She scolded harshly. "I doubt you can spy anything else with any better success! Your bones have become idle and your skin soft up here. One of our stable hands recently died after being kicked in the head by a horse. You will take his place. There, you will be too busy feeding the horses and cleaning up their dung to find time for gossip."

Aric addressed the other girl. "Well, have you nothing to say in your defense?"

The child opened her mouth, but only intelligible grunts and hoarse squeals sounded forth.

"Ahhhh," Aric surmised, "a mute. This does not free you of guilt, however. It is as bad a crime to listen to wrong as to it is to speak it, for only when one listens can one be influenced. You are to switch places with the one who keeps the dungeon. From this moment on, your sole purpose in life will be to clean rat droppings and feed the wretched lot imprisoned below, as a reminder to you the price of committing wrongs against the throne. I will inform the guards there of your arrival. Go now, the both of you, while the Regent is still in a benevolent mood!"

With the girls gone, Aric walked back to where Nephredom had been watching her.

"Are you Regent, that you would contradict my wishes?" he demanded. "Is this now your court, aide? *Is this now your court?* Answer me!"

"Of course, not my Regent; I am only your aide." She lowered her head shamefully. "Forgive me. I have—overstepped myself."

"There can be no forgiveness for this disloyal act!"

"I would never be disloyal, my Regent. In fact, it was my devotion to you that guided my actions."

"Your double-talk will not spare you my wrath this day!"

Aric smiled. "If you mean the echoing words of respect and gratitude that naturally issue from my lips to you—this I cannot help. But such respect does not end with words. If you must pass judgment on me, I hope you do so knowing that a lesser aide would have brought you shame."

Nephredom's exasperated voice hinted intrigue. "You are never bereft of riddles, woman. Tell me, why would a lesser aide bring me shame by honoring my intentions?"

"I prefer to see it as you testing my integrity, my liege. I need not remind you that it was by your wisdom that I was granted the position as administrator and chief aide. It would be an insult to you to perform my duties anything short of my best. My decision reflects that perfectly."

"The maids were to die!"

"I was granted your approval to question the girls, in order to find evidence worthy of their deaths."

"Nothing she said proved their innocence!"

"I recall the girl saying you have banned magic, and that your rages were getting worse: the first, a statement of fact, the second a misguided grievance. The latter certainly deserves punishment, such as I had given— but death? What's more, the dust I found proves my earlier point that they are no spies. True spies would never indulge in such a gross inattention to detail," she laughed, "lest they be fired before their mission is done."

Aric moved in dangerously close to Nephredom and eased her arms over his stiff shoulders. "I know better than most," she whispered, "for I was once a spy. *Your spy.*"

Nephredom managed a low, throaty chuckle. "You plead for the lives of the homely cleaning wenches as if they were you own children!"

"I only want what is best for the empire, my liege. Killing them would produce no good fruit."

Nephredom pressed her close. He kissed her deeply, the final flames of his ire quenched with her soft lips. Then he pushed her away, perhaps perturbed by her ancient eyes, which seemed to look through him as if his flesh were but a transparent shadow.

He thought of when he first met Aric. Three years ago, she presented herself before him as a former student of a nameless old woman she referred to only as "Teacher." Her descriptions left no doubt that she was speaking of the same old woman who had taught him. Aric begged him to accept her as his apprentice, saying the old woman had recently dismissed her and would teach her no more.

Nephredom agreed, not because he was in need of an apprentice, or even because of her stunning beauty. He took her in because he feared the old woman had divulged his true identity to Aric, and if that were so, he would kill her. Careful not to reveal his past, he questioned the young mage. Aric claimed that her teacher never so much as mentioned any of her previous pupils and told him that she knew nothing of the old woman's whereabouts.

But Nephredom was slow to comfort, and he watched his new aide closely for many cycles, keeping her forever near his side. It became obvious that she possessed exceptional wit and a gift for social finesse—talents that could prove useful to him. In time, he increasingly entrusted her with more authority, freeing him from the ever-demanding bureaucratic quagmire that encumbered his actions at the start of his ascension to Regent.

He was not blind, however, to the fact that though she had served him well as secretary and assistant, she had never once requested a lesson of magic from him. Odder still, she was a master mage in her own right, hardly in need of a new mentor; her Psi-kinetic skill was strong and her Psi-telepathy perhaps rivaled his own. It was not a desire to learn spells that brought her to him, Nephredom reflected. Any fool could see that. It was him. She wanted his heart and all the spoils that came with it.

This in itself was nothing new. Fortune hunters and fame seekers abounded, but none as beautiful or as clever as Aric. How many countless times had she coaxed him into her embrace, only for him to turn from her just before his desires overtook him? It was a most dangerous game, but he had to admit, it was an addictively enjoyable one as well. He relished a good challenge, but a game was all it was. He could never love someone of East Taren blood.

"Very well," Nephredom conceded, and he began walking to the throne room. "I will permit your decision to stand."

Aric bowed and followed close behind him, her gait as regal as his own. "I am forever and always in your service. By the way, the dream that woke you so excitedly—was I in it?"

Nephredom smirked. "It was a dream like none I've had before. Something about my Gate—I cannot remember. It does not matter. A foolish dream was all it was."

The walls of the throne room were lined with even more West Taren guards than Aric had anticipated. *Nephredom has been busy*, she thought cynically, smiling all the while. The West Taren captain stood stern beside the throne.

With a single clap of Nephredom's hand, two previously unseen Red Robes shimmered into view.

"Well?" Nephredom demanded. "What news have you of the injured Robes who saw into the Princess's mind? Can they now tell us what they know?"

The Red Robes seemed to recoil and shrink at the question as if attacked, then rebounded back to normal. *No, Master Nephredom, they are still comatose.*

"Are the healers close to restoring them?"

No.

"Then you have chosen to waste my time, by appearing here with nothing."

No, Master Nephredom. There is another way. We do not need them aware to get what we need.

"You have a suggestion, then?"

We will link our minds as one. We will see all they have seen and know all that they know.

"How long will this take?"

Their minds are deeply buried . . . their physical shells . . . weakened. Preparation is needed. One cycle.

"Then leave me now, and do not enter this room again until you have the information."

It will be done.

A serving girl, summoned by Nephredom's beckoning hand, stepped forward with a silver dish of fruit and drink and offered its contents to him. The Regent sat on the throne brooding, gnawing a bit of fruit. He eyed Aric. "Have you nothing to add to their report, aide? Or have you been too busy redeeming worthless servants to care about such things?"

"Actually," Aric replied, "I have some news you may find interesting, and far more pleasing than what the Robes had to say." She glanced at the sneering captain. "Both are confidential, of course."

Nephredom nodded, and the magically formed walls of his mind opened a crack, allowing her consciousness to slither through and mingle with his own.

My Regent, the Queen is dying.

There is no news in that. She has been dying ever since her husband failed to return from the field of battle years ago.

True, and I must confess, the Queen's endless lingering on has been a dragging dirge of many verses. A shame it couldn't have been shortened to a more respectable length—say a ditty. However, it appears the process is finally at its own end.

So she will soon die?

Yes, my liege.

Her attendants have verified this?

Yes. They say she will no longer have food or even lift her head up from her pillows. She cares nothing more for life.

How long?

A few weeks at most.

Good.

May I ask why you wanted the old mourner alive? I could have easily made her death look natural enough many cycles ago.

It was necessary that the old facade did not topple until the new regime was ready.

That, my Regent, is a most profound wisdom. I must endeavor to keep that one close to my lips.

There is very little you don't keep close to your lips.

You flatter me.

Perceive it as flattery if you will. Is that all?

Just one other thing. Ever since we've suggested to all that our runaway Princess would most likely seek sanctuary among her kin, we've been able to eliminate members of the royal family in a way that made the risky business of assassination no longer necessary. Indeed, our newest policy of openly convicting and executing royal relatives as secret supporters of the Princess is beginning to sway public opinion in our favor. The Queen's silence is perceived as her given consent—and endorsement. As a result, the people see you as a strict but strong champion of justice. They feel safe behind your back.

Aric, you have an annoying talent for stating the obvious. Cease this meandering and speak your point!

Sorry, I'll be brief. My point is simple: I have found another royal sacrifice to present before the people, and another opportunity to boost your popularity.

You have found more kinsmen of the Queen and her dead husband?

One. I was informed earlier this morning that the political prisoner is ready for your inspection. He sits below us now, chained in the dungeon.

What is this man's name?

Finus—a distant cousin to our beloved Princess. He is perhaps the last of the royal bloodline, save the Queen herself and her fugitive daughter.

Why was he not found sooner?

Finus was no dunce. He must have known that all royal relatives brought to the palace eventually found themselves charged with something that merited execution. He took on a name common to the family of his wife, and he abandoned his old estate nearly two years ago. He was living in a modest home near the river's border in anonymity when we discovered him. They call him Nebitt now.

Hiding. I swear the whole royal breed is rife with cowards! What was this one's undoing?

Taxes, my liege—or, to be more specific, the lack of funds to pay them in a timely manner. Even before the war, Nebitt was a noble in title only. At least then, he could use his prestige to solicit financial favors among the elite. Now he had nothing and had to work for meager wages as a cobbler to the neighboring hamlets where he lived. His wife worked as a seamstress, earning even less than he. At tax time Nebitt always found himself short, and it would have been brought to my attention on many occasions had not the tax collector allowed him to pay late. Needless to say, that tax collector is no longer among the living.

What of Nebitt?

After I discovered the frequent delinquency, I had another go to collect our dues, and he recognized Nebitt for who he truly was. The collector did not utter this to Nebitt, but instead returned and told me.

And you charged Nebitt, and sent him here for execution.

Yes, but circumstances required that I be somewhat delicate. Within right of the laws, I penalized Nebitt for paying his taxes late, by ordering him to pay not only this season's taxes but also next season's taxes in advance as well. When he failed to do so, he was charged with tax evasion and the illegal influencing of a court official—two very serious charges.

Worthy of execution. Well done. What of his family?

He had only his wife, and because she lived under his house, she was subject to the law as well. She too was seized and awaits her fate in prison beside her husband.

Does her lineage reveal any royal blood?

None. Apparently, she was trying to marry up.

Any children?

Surprisingly, she failed in that area as well. She is barren.

Now Aric, you have outdone yourself. I shall grant you ownership of Nebitt's estate with all the land it holds.

Truly, my Regent, your generosity is unparalleled.

Bring the accused here so that I may see the fear in his eyes.

Shall I bring his wife as well? Husband and wife executions are never soon forgotten.

No. Only the man's veins have the blood of my enemies. The woman is not worthy of my time or presence. Her death will come differently.

As you wish, my Regent.

✳ ✳ ✳

Nebitt was a thin, nervous little man, preoccupied with biting his nails. He was shoved roughly into the throne room by two West Taren guards, where they then painfully restrained him by both arms.

With nails no longer accessible, Nebitt anxiously bit down on his lips until they bled, then sniveled. "Oh, please, please, I have done nothing wrong!"

"Oh please, please shut up!" Aric mocked, and she placed her hands across his forehead.

Nephredom made a cursory motion to Aric with his hand, commanding, "Interrogate him. Fully."

Aric nodded. "My pleasure."

She dug her fingers into Nebitt's temples, like claws, and closed her eyes.

Nebitt writhed and struggled, but the guards held him tight. Suddenly, his chest heaved forward, the muscles in arms and legs convulsing wildly.

His mind. No way to keep it out. *Something unclean.* No way to keep it out! It's inside now . . . *something foul–digging–ripping–tearing* . . . mind!

Nebitt parted his lips in a silent scream. The presence inside him slowly withdrew, leaving tangles and ravaged strips of his former mind behind.

Aric calmly opened her eyes to greet Nephredom. She whispered into his ear: "I was hoping he knew something about the Princess we could use to hasten her capture, but all I could find was gibberish about his wife and making enough shoes to live by. I don't believe he has even met the Princess."

"Dispose of him."

"A public affair, as usual?"

"Yes."

✳ ✳ ✳

The palace was opened to the public as scheduled. However, fewer than a hundred visitors were allowed into the throne room itself. These hand-chosen few—who were permitted an audience with the Regent—were inspected carefully, passing through several guarded checkpoints before finally being allowed to grace the polished floors of the throne room. Most who were granted an audience were rich opportunists and merchants, vying for political or social gain, with bribes in hand, to be presented as gifts for Nephredom. To promote the illusion of an open-door policy, a few commoners were allowed in as well. They were usually the only ones who bore gifts for the ailing Queen.

This day, however, rather than being filed into a single, rigid line to the throne, the guests were encouraged to gather into small, informal groups, as if at a fashionable party. Refreshments were served, and soon the room was alive with the idle chat of polite society.

With Nephredom looking on, Aric assumed the role of hostess as comfortably as old leather. Clapping her hands to call attention, she addressed the curious crowd. "Greetings, everyone. We thought you could all use a welcome change of pace, and what better way to do than with an execution?" She walked over to Nebitt. Though he was still restrained by the guards, it was obvious to all in the room that he was being held up for support and showed no signs of resistance.

"If I may, I would like to introduce you to Nebitt the cobbler, or Nebitt the tax evader, as we have come to know him." Aric paced lightly around her captive. "Some of the more keen-eyed of you might even recognize him as Finus, cousin to the brother-killing Princess."

A few gasps and whispers escaped the mouths of those watching.

Aric nodded. "You are quite right. It *is* Finus, and we have proof that he has been secretly helping the Princess and thwarting our efforts to bring her to justice! The evidence against him is so overwhelming, it was decided that we forgo a trial, since anyone can plainly see this man is guilty. We have even found correspondence in his home—in his own handwriting—detailing a long history of harboring, feeding, and transporting the Princess—"

A moan sounded, interrupting her. It came from Nebitt, who was very much a changed man. Slack-faced, with wild eyes that no longer blinked, and twisting lips that had forgotten how to form the words he struggled to speak. Though he tried hard to express himself, he looked and sounded like a madman, or a fool, or both.

"I . . . nothing wrong." He could say no more.

Irritated at having her speech so severed, Aric spoke sharply to the guards. "Silence him!"

One of the guards delivered a rib-cracking blow to the side of Nebitt's chest with his fist. Nebitt coughed wretchedly and was quiet.

Aric cleared her throat warningly to the guards. "Be careful. I don't want you to bruise him too badly; otherwise, we might sully our pretty, clean floors with blood." She turned to face her guests. "And we wouldn't want you, our distinguished company, to think we are uncivilized. Save the blood-filled executions for the uncouth peasants of the streets, I say."

"How will he die, if not with blood? Poison, then?" someone from the crowd called out.

Aric shook her head vehemently. "For this execution I've chosen a refined method of punishment, befitting a royal person like our friend Nebitt here. In all fairness, I must say it is rather experimental, inspired in part by the powerful teachings of science!"

Laugher filled the room. As it subsided, Aric continued. "Yes, it's true. Having consulted the fools—I mean the *scientists* of Dosk—I have learned that the heart is not the sole representative of our mortality, as some may think. They say there are many lesser hearts—if you will—of various shapes and sizes inside us all, just as important to life as the heart."

Aric chuckled dryly. "Now I don't know about you, but aside from my entrails and brains—which are both very much intact—I know nothing of what they speak. However, since disproving their theory would require my rummaging through the innards of countless cadavers, I will take their word for it."

Roaring laughter ensued, and Aric bowed.

"With that said, I will attempt to prove a theory of my own, which is simply this: Although these lesser hearts exist, as the scientists claim, I believe they are frivolous redundancies our bodies can make do without. To demonstrate my point, I will use—with our Regent's permission, of course—an ancient Psi-pyric technique that allows one to burn an encased object while keeping its covering intact, much as hot water boils an egg with no damage to its shell. For the less visually minded among you, I simply mean I will target his lesser hearts—and burn them from the inside out. You see, I told you there would be no blood."

"What if you are wrong?" a bold spectator yelled out.

Aric shrugged indifferently. "No great loss, I suppose. This is an execution, after all. But if my theory is to be disputed so soon by skeptics . . ." She paused with a feigned wounded expression. "Perhaps it's best this trick be saved for another day."

Her teasing seemed to bring out the crowd's more fiendish nature; they stood around like hungry hyenas, eager to see the miserable man die at Aric's hand.

"Show us!"

"Yes, show us please!"

The wicked mantra of the crowd's calls grew strong and persistent, prompting Aric to "relent"—exactly as she had intended.

"Very well," she said with a dark smile. "Let us have our science lesson."

An orange aura encircled her hands.

"Remove his shirt," she commanded one of the guards, and it was torn from Nebitt.

"My, my!" Aric exclaimed. "I'll wager that this one would have fancied a last meal, for I can see his ribs all too well. It's a pity it's too late for that now." Thrusting her palms like firebrands, she pressed them onto one of his arms.

Nebitt screamed as an orange-red glow spread over the tense surface of his arm, then shrank and faded away. The startled guard released the arm, which dropped limply, then sagged unnaturally against Nebitt's side—useless.

Coolly inspecting her handiwork, Aric remarked, "Save your cries for what is yet to come, Nebitt. That was merely a test." Her dangerous hands next went to Nebitt's side.

It buckled in on itself, like stone turned to jelly. Whatever had filled that spot beneath the layers of flesh had been consumed. His abdomen was next. Pleading in vain, Nebitt could do nothing to avoid Aric's hellish touch. A numbing calm suddenly overcame him, and he no longer felt the need to resist. His eyelids fluttered and closed.

Aric frowned and slapped him soundly across the cheek. "Not yet, Nebitt," she objected. "I've only just begun. Don't disappoint me by dying too soon."

Disregarding her wishes, Nebitt had died.

Realizing this, Aric said, "You may release him now." The guards let Nebitt's body slump to the floor. "It appears the scientists were right, for a change," Aric said. "We now know with certainty that the heart is but a captain in an army of many." Her eyes briefly met those of the lady captain. Aric walked her fiery fingers across her victim's chest, stopping where his heart would be, and pressed down hard. "However, one can never be too certain, wouldn't you agree, Captain?"

The mercenary captain wore a mixed expression of fear and hate.

Aric grinned mischievously to her guests. "Now you can see why our Regent, Nephredom, wisely prohibited all but a trusted few from practicing magic. She nudged the fallen Nebitt with her foot. "Someone could get hurt!"

The captain muttered something under her breath and left the room in disgust.

Aric clasped her hands and laughed. "Now, that was true entertainment. I'm afraid you all must now return to your dreary, mundane lives—until the next execution."

To the music of cheers and applause, Aric bowed in bliss. Clusters of satisfied onlookers began talking among themselves; she chatted with a few and politely dodged the rest. Stepping up to the restricted throne area, Aric approached Nephredom with a suggestive swagger. If Nephredom was tempted, it did not show.

"Shall I leave you to your legion of admirers, my liege?" she asked with a wink.

Nephredom forced a tight smile for the benefit of the public and murmured in a hushed tone. "A legion of leeches would be more accurate, but you may go."

On her way out, Aric gestured for a guard. "See to it that news of this execution is posted on every street," she commanded. She paused at the exit and pointed back at Nebitt's remains. "Oh, and get someone to clean up that rubbish."

✳ ✳ ✳

Back in her room, Aric heard a knock at the door. "Yes?" she called out.

A guard opened the door halfway, far enough for Aric to see that he held a wrist of each of the two servants Aric had rescued earlier. "These two cleaning girls claim they have business with you," the guard said. "A scraggly pair, they are, m'lady, hardly needing to speak to someone like you. If you like, I'll give them a boxing on the ears for disturbing you and send them on their way."

"No, I was expecting my little friends, and they've come right on time. Let them in please, and then you may go."

As you say, m'lady." The girls were allowed inside, and the guard withdrew back into the hall, closing the door behind him.

Aric gave the girls a serious look, and without a word spoken, she linked with their minds. *Now girls, you've done well. I now have you where you can do me some reasonable good, and it would not have been possible without Nephredom's unwitting help. The dungeon and the stables are two places where my eyes and ears are a bit dim. You two will remedy that nicely. I suspect there are some goings-on in the dungeon that our seizure-ridden ruler has kept from me. You will find out what it is. The stables are a more practical concern. I like to know who's going where and when. You will see to it that I do. Well, my precious little spies, we will stay in touch as we always have. Good-bye for now.*

Aric dismissed them, then rolled and stretched on her back across her oversized bed, like a pampered cat. "The old facade must not topple until the new regime is ready," she purred softly to herself. "How prophetic."

"Guard!" she called out.

Soon, her door opened, and the guard marched in. "You called for me, m'lady?"

Aric gazed lazily at the tall sentry. "What is your name?" she inquired.

"Platus, m'lady."

Aric sat up with interest. "Platus, you say? I knew a Platus once; he was a West Taren guard as well. A hairy brute, and a poor learner at that. Denser than dirt he was—a shame to your kind. Oh, well, forgive my digression. That was a long time ago, and you are far more handsome than he." She beckoned him with a curve of her finger. "Come keep me company, and don't fret about your post or your captain. I think the good captain and I have come to an understanding.

She won't object to my borrowing you for a while."

"What would you ask of me?"

"Oh, nothing difficult, Platus," she promised, moistening her lips. "I have grown bored in this bed alone, and perhaps you can help me. But before we get to that, I would like to dance. Forbidden as it may be, I simply *love* to dance. It is my passion, and I think you are agile enough to serve my needs . . . as a dance partner."

Platus swallowed nervously, then slowly walked to her bedside and offered his hand to help her up.

Aric playfully but firmly nudged her foot into Platus's crotch. Platus suddenly felt his trousers become uncomfortably tight where the aide had touched him. Aric looked at him, an amused expression on her face, and said, "My, you are a *fit* one, Platus. I had no idea you were so happy to see me."

Before the embarrassed guard could speak, Aric took his hand. "We will need to take care of that . . . condition of yours before you leave," she said with a throaty laugh, "as it would not be very becoming of my guard to be standing to attention in quite *that* manner while at his assigned post. But first, we dance!"

Aric bounced to her feet, and the two of them danced with reckless abandon. A full-length mirror reflected their waltzing images: a well-built, robust guard, holding a young beauty in his arms. Aric saw herself in the mirror and smiled, revealing brilliantly white teeth that were slightly pointed.

CHAPTER 10

Inside Nephredom's Gate

S omething's not right about this Lamec place," Rayna finally admitted to herself. Her previous denial made her overlook the cracked-fenced gardens, overrun with weeds, and the chipped fountains spouting vines rather than water. She had rationalized the armless, headless statues in the city square as classical monuments, and the absence of people as some unknown holiday observance. All of that changed when she saw the Lake Stone. Nothing in Keris's brief description of the Stone had prepared her for this.

The Stone shone like a small sun, partially submerged in the water. The top of the enormous object featured three triangular sections that separated slightly and closed repetitively, venting a mysterious vapor each time. Rayna knew she was looking at something far more sophisticated than a rock in a lake. The so-called Lake Stone was no stone; clearly, it had been manufactured. That bothered her. Why was something so advanced located in a crumbling city like Lamec? Aside from the delightful glass mobile at the entrance, the city looked only slightly less low-tech than Kuara. Did the Stone really fall from the sky, as Keris said?

Rayna failed to find a logical connection, and on a less logical level, she had an unsavory feeling about the Lake Stone. She couldn't shake the feeling, and it made what she was about to do all the more difficult. She took in a deep breath, then released it slowly, drawing strength from the calm it gave her. She paused briefly, and then began to walk toward the Stone.

There was a chance the Stone could offer some insight on how to get home, Rayna thought. She owed it to herself to get a better look. Her watch began to glow and tingle warmly around her wrist. She ventured closer. Her watch became hot; its clown face was contorted with fear. Testing a hunch, Rayna took a step back, and the watch's reaction lessened. When she stepped forward again, its reaction increased in intensity again. *Danger*, the clown's ruby lips seemed to mouth. *Turn back!*

Rayna stubbornly ignored the warning. As she approached the Stone, she could make out more detail: An abandoned guardhouse rested at the southern bank of the lake. Nearby was a boat landing made for two boats, but only one was there. Rayna peered cautiously into the small boat. Made of blackened planks that had seen better days, the floor of the boat was mostly covered with dank, moldy water that had seeped in slowly over time. Rayna found it amazing that the vessel still floated. For all its flaws, the boat appeared to be the only means of reaching the Lake Stone, other than swimming. Rayna peered into the ramshackle vessel a second time and shook her head. There was no way she was getting in that thing. The oppressive midday heat made swimming an appealing option—if she only knew how. She puzzled over her dilemma. There had to be another way to reach the Stone.

The glow of Rayna's watch began to pulsate, and then it suddenly shot out a charge of energy that revolved around her like mystical armor—a spectacular cylinder of light. Rayna stopped abruptly in her tracks, startled. She looked at her watch with newfound respect. "You did that?" she exclaimed aloud in a broken voice. She could sense it was trying to protect her from the Lake Stone, but why?

Flee! She felt her flashing watch urging her silently. *Run! Run now! Flee!*

Unnerved, Rayna ran. Though the energy shield disappeared after she had put a few more yards between herself and the Stone, fear and momentum pushed her blindly on. When she finally stopped to catch her breath, she realized she was in the heart of the city. A crowded labyrinth of multistory brick buildings blocked her line of sight, and she discovered she was lost, off the main road and unable to find it. Her watch, dormant since she fled the Lake Stone, began to tingle and glow once more.

Frightened and angry, Rayna barked at her watch, "Now what?" The watch gave its reply by flaring brighter. And brighter. Rayna experienced the feeling of warning again. *Danger!* This time, however, she wasn't walking toward danger—the danger was coming to her. Taking heed of her watch's warning, Rayna quickly hid herself behind the corner of an old brick building and shoved her glowing hand in her pocket. Then she saw . . . something

It stood more than eight feet tall, and it oozed dripping, green ichor from every pore of its scaly body. Its face resembled a nightmarish hybrid of boar, dog, and lizard, creased and knotted like heavy clay molded into monstrosity. Its bulging eyes had lids that closed horizontally, and as the creature squinted in the daylight sun, only its elongated, red pupils showed through. It was an undeniable rendition of evil personified. Its pointed-toothed mouth opened and closed repeatedly, as if rehearsing for its next meal.

Rayna dared not breathe, and she feared that even the sound of her own pounding heart would give her away. The monstrous thing rounded the corner and disappeared behind a set of stout buildings, leaving a putrid trail of muck behind. Rayna let out a gasp of relief, amazed that the thing hadn't seen her. Still looking in the beast's direction, Rayna carefully followed the wall against her back until her hand found a doorknob. Eager to get somewhere inside in case the gruesome creature decided to make a return visit, Rayna turned the knob and went in.

Inside was a small square foyer; another door faced her ahead. To the left was solid wall, dirty and cracked. To the right loomed a narrow stairwell leading upward. The foyer was too empty and confined to make a good hiding place, Rayna thought. If someone, or some*thing*, opened the outside door, she would be seen. Rayna fiddled with her staff nervously. The hulking, red door that lay ahead looked interesting, but Rayna decided to try the stairs.

The stairway opened up to an isolated balcony, overlooking an enormous room—the size of an amphitheater—below. Her eyes quickly adjusted to the gloom. To Rayna's frustration, her watch refused to stop shining. Looking over the edge of the balcony, she found out why. Hundreds of creatures, similar to the gray-skinned horror she had seen moments ago, huddled around a single beast—a mother, Rayna assumed. The creature held a squirming newborn monster tightly in her arms and began meticulously removing the bloody remnants of birth-sac from the baby's tiny body with her teeth. Rayna stared in amazement.

Unlike its mother, the child-beast had wings—long, leathery, bat-like wings. Apparently, it was too young to fly, and it contented itself by hissing to its mother for food. The mother produced a live rat that she had kept firmly secure in her clawed hand, and dangled it by the tail over her child's gaping mouth.

Rayna strained her eyes to see what would happen next.

Without warning, a stream of something green and slimy gushed from the infant creature's mouth. In moments, it melted both flesh and fur off the rodent's body, and they slid down into the infant's waiting throat. All that remained of the mouse was its furry tail—still being held by the mother—tenaciously attached to the skeleton. Baby was fed.

In addition to the main horde, Rayna noticed several smaller, younger beasts in the crowded room. While the adult beasts gathered around each other to watch the winged baby with its mother, the younger winged creatures entertained themselves in a game. One of them grabbed a wingless young beast and tried to fly with it as high as possible. It nearly managed to take its live toy as far as the lofty ceiling, but it slowed its ascent, even with its wings flapping in huge strokes. The weight was too much for its wings to bear, and it released its passenger. The fallen beast hit the floor and arose, seemingly feeling no pain, screeching urgently for its playmate to start again.

Two other winged creatures, both fully-grown and just as hideous as their wingless counterparts, flew around the room, their wings making faint but menacing flapping sounds in the air. Rayna ducked to avoid being seen by their airborne eyes. Suddenly, a leathery hand clamped firmly across Rayna's mouth, stifling her attempt to scream.

The attacker slowly turned Rayna around to face it. Gripping her staff tightly, Rayna braced herself for the fight of her life. Instead, she found herself face-to-face with a very angry-looking Keris. At that moment, Rayna half-wished it had been a beast. Keris put a finger to her lips and removed her gloved hand from Rayna's mouth.

Rayna fumbled for an apology to atone for the predicament she had gotten herself in. Keris cut her short with a scornful tone, whispering, "I will hear no more. What is done, is done. But do not think I will soon forget how you decided to abandon your companions in pursuit of this suicidal wandering." She handed Rayna a long strip of dark cloth. "Wrap this around your talisman quickly. Your charm is leaking rays of light through your pockets. In this dimly lit place, it is a miracle you were not seen! Tell me, what were you expecting to find in this city other than death?"

"A telephone," Rayna replied candidly, careful not to reveal her pleasure in seeing the resulting puzzled expression on Keris's face. As Rayna better concealed her watch's glow, Keris peered over the balcony, with much the same reactions of dread and disbelief Rayna had had.

"Some of the beasts have wings," she whispered. "This should not be, for I was told the beasts had no wings. What does your science say of this?"

Rayna shrugged. "I don't know. Maybe it's some kind bizarre mutation as a result of too much inbreeding. Based on what you told me back in the woods, they haven't been around nearly long enough for those wings to be an evolutionary trait—so hereditary mutation is the most logical hypothesis."

"You sound like a true scientist—full of words that make little sense. What is clear to me is that the beasts are adapting and changing so that they may eventually overcome the Gate."

Rayna tried to follow Keris's reasoning. "That's why they're making such a big to-do out of the birth of the winged infant?"

"Yes. There appear to be only a few winged beasts—a score of them, perhaps. If they were to fly out of the city now, they would eventually be singled out, hunted down, and killed. They are no doubt waiting until the winged among them are of a sufficient number. Then each winged beast could carry an unwinged beast over the city walls in a relatively short period of time. I'd wager it would take only about fifty winged beasts a few days to fly a thousand land-beasts over the Gate—a hundred of them could do it in even less time."

"I see," Rayna said, realizing that the "game" she saw of the younger beasts was actually a kind of adolescent prison-break training—to strengthen their wings to support the payload of a fellow beast. "Then the entire beast population would be outside the city."

"Yes, and all of Taren would rue that bloody day. The winged creatures would attack from above, while their wingless counterparts acted as foot soldiers. With thousands of them attacking at once, no province could survive. This lot may be unsightly, but they are organized, and more intelligent that I had once thought. If they are successful in this plan, they will take everyone by surprise—even Nephredom himself."

Rayna had to admire Keris's sharp deductive skills, but something didn't quite make sense. "There's just one thing I don't understand," she said. "Why hasn't it occurred to the beasts to just take the front entrance, like we did?"

"Haw!" Keris exclaimed under her breath. "You never cease to amaze me, Rayna Powell of Nightwind. If it were that simple—" Keris fell silent.

The beasts had started chanting. The haunting sound filled Rayna's heart with feelings of despair and impending doom. The mother beast walked through the crowd, proudly displaying her prized offspring.

"I know not the language of the beasts," Keris muttered, "but I have no doubt they are singing in celebration of the winged child, for it brings them closer to the day they will leave their prison. You have stumbled upon a discovery that may save both halves of Taren. I am grateful."

Uncomfortable accepting praise she felt she didn't deserve, Rayna simply nodded.

Keris glanced down warily at the wailing creatures below. "Now we must leave here and tell of this news to Ciredor. He will need little convincing to ready his army when he hears of this."

As they darted down the stairs, Rayna was suddenly aware of Arstinax's absence, and old guilt sprang fresh in her voice. "Is Arstinax okay? Don't tell me one of those things—"

"I left him by the entrance to this building," Keris said, "for I did not want us surprised from behind." On seeing the look of relief in Rayna's face, she added, "He has been worried about you since you disappeared. He will be pleased to see that you are well."

They crept back down the stairs.

"I have seen more beasts creeping about in the streets," Arstinax announced gravely as the three met in the foyer. "It will be difficult to make it to the Gate unseen."

Rayna tried not to show how happy she was to see the young, bearded Kuaran, but her broadening smile betrayed her. Arstinax returned a grin of his own and gave Rayna an unexpected hug. "I had feared the worse, brave Power," he said with a hearty laugh. "My heart is glad you proved me wrong."

Rayna didn't know what to say, but no words were needed. The embrace of the moment was enough.

"Let us be on our way," Keris said. "With every moment we wait, the greater our peril becomes."

Following Keris's example, they kept close to the shadowy sides of buildings and trees, avoiding the open streets. It made their trek safer but much slower. Rayna filled Arstinax in on what she and Keris had seen on the balcony.

"The ceremony involving this rare birth of the winged beast-child must be the reason the streets have only but a few," Arstinax said.

"That was most fortunate for us," Keris whispered. "Had we entered this city at any other time, we would be long dead by now."

Rayna shivered. "How many of those ugly things do you think are in this place?" she asked.

"When the Stone was violated," Keris explained," many of the citizens were said to have died from its magic. The thousands that lived became beasts."

Rayna thought about that for a moment. "And because they've been breeding all this time, it's fair to assume their numbers have significantly grown since then, right?"

"Yes."

"Not good," Rayna muttered.

The flying beast would have landed its swiping, clawed paw on Rayna if Arstinax hadn't pushed her out of harm's way before the blow could connect. Keris lunged forward, just missing the creature with her blade as it glided skyward for another pass.

Rayna was shaken. "That thing came out from nowhere!"

Arstinax strained to lift a wide slab of granite fragment that once served as a base for a forgotten statue. "Full of guile, these beasts are," he agreed, grunting from his exertion.

"Prepare yourselves!" Keris yelled.

The creature swooped low again. This time, its target was Keris. She dodged the attack and thrust up her dagger as soon as she found an opening. To her amazement, her blade slid across the beast's mucus-coated chest without making a mark. A lightning-fast backhand from the beast sent Keris sprawling to the ground, barely moving.

As the creature went in for the kill, Arstinax gave a mighty cry. When the beast turned to see from where the bellow sounded, Arstinax swung his slab of stone like a great discus, releasing it with startling force onto the monster's snarling maw.

The slab, which was half as heavy as Arstinax himself, would have killed any human instantly. It only served to enrage the beast. Its bleeding gums now revealed broken front teeth that allowed dark green saliva to dribble though. Wiping gravel fragments from its furious face, the creature flew high into the air, and then dove down to rake Arstinax's shoulder. Arstinax groaned in pain. "In my haste to leave home," he lamented, "I left my poleax behind. If only I had it now!"

The winged beast descended once more, leaving a bloody claw trail across Arstinax's back. In agony, the mighty giant sagged to his knees, and for a brief moment, it appeared as though he would rise to his feet again. Then, like a toppling monolith, he collapsed.

Rayna looked distressfully to Keris; she was still only semiconscious.

Keris was down, Arstinax had fallen. Rayna was alone.

Beneath the cloth, she had used to hide her watch's glow, Rayna felt burning against her skin. Rayna yelled at her wrapped watch, "You think I can't see I'm in danger? Tell me something I don't know!" The beast turned its attention to Rayna.

To her own surprise, Rayna stood her ground. It wouldn't do any good to try to outrun the creature, she figured. Staff in hand, Rayna prayed it would save her life like it did before, against the Red Robes, but the vibrating flow of magic she once felt in its core was absent. What was she doing wrong?

The beast charged at Rayna. She half-ducked, half-fell to the ground, but still managed to scrape her staff against the beast's side as it rushed past. Nothing happened. The beast effortlessly shrugged off Rayna's pitiful attack and made a series of high-pitched squeals. Rayna recognized the sound for what it was: Laughter.

Rayna clenched her jaw in anger. The beast found her more of an amusement than a threat. She was nothing more than a joke to the snickering, slobbering thing.

Suddenly, in the throes of tension and humiliation, the floodgates of Rayna's mind burst open and she felt a calling deep within her, suppressed for so long. *Too long!*

A fetid breeze splashed over Rayna as the beast flapped its great wings and maneuvered in preparation for its descent of death. Rayna had expected to see her life flash before her eyes. What she got instead was clarity. The dynamics of magic were no longer absurd to her. If fact, magic *almost* made perfect sense. Above, the beast spread its wings wide and began to dive; its dark shadow fell over Rayna like a cloak of impending doom.

Rayna held her staff before her, pointed it at the beast, and concentrated. Sparked by the mental energy of her thoughts, her staff released a kind of energy of its own, showering it outward in a fierce deluge of power. It cascaded over the beast, boring tiny holes in its wings that wreaked havoc on its ability to control its flight.

Before the beast crashed to the rocky ground, flailing its damaged wings, it gave an earsplitting shriek and issued from its jagged mouth a spray of green droplets. Rayna managed to avoid getting the foul-smelling stuff on her face, but some splashed on her arm, seeped deep into her robes, and absorbed into her vulnerable skin. It burned going in, like acid. Focusing her thoughts, she briefly managed to summon the same watch-shield, that had activated when she was near the Lake Stone, but the damage had already been done.

Her arm was splotched with the green substance, and it began to itch and swell painfully. She turned to see Arstinax and Keris rising groggily to their feet.

Keris picked up her dagger and crept, limping slightly, to where the broken beast lay. "It is dead," she declared with relief in her voice.

"I shall shed no tears over its demise," Arstinax grumbled, rubbing as much of his sore, bleeding back as his hands would reach. Keris looked at Rayna's wound and quickly searched her through her bag.

"I'm all right," Rayna said. "Save your medical supplies for Arstinax."

Keris shook her head. "Indeed, Arstinax was badly scratched by the creature, but you were poisoned by it. During the war, all who tasted the beasts' venom died."

"'All' is not very good odds in my favor," Rayna said, suddenly woozy.

With deft precision, Keris used her dagger and cut away the poison-soaked sleeve of Rayna's robes. She produced a small, metal jar with a stopper, allowed several drops of venom from the saturated fabric to drip inside, and sealed it. "This foul flow may one day be useful," she said, returning the jar to her bag.

Keris then quickly cleaned Rayna's blistering wound and treated it with a brown salve. "You are fortunate," Keris continued. "Your robes absorbed a good deal of the poison. Otherwise, you probably would be dead by now."

"Your bedside manner leaves much to be desired," Rayna quipped, trying to appear stronger than she felt.

"I know an herbalist in the city of Argat, not far from here," Keris said, giving Rayna a drink of water. "Though she uses no magic, your best chance of survival lies in her hands."

A ghastly chorus of howls sounded in the distance.

"They know we are here," Arstinax said.

"Yes." Keris agreed. "They have heard the cry of their comrade dying at the master mage's hands, and so they fill the streets in search of vengeance."

Rayna leaned heavily against her staff, fighting bleary vision and shortness of breath. "Is it very far to the Gate from here?"

"No," Keris said, "but we must hurry."

In spite of their wounds and Rayna's worsening condition, the three trudged onward and soon found themselves standing before Nephredom's Gate. The hounding call of the beasts was not far behind.

Rayna felt herself wobble and used her staff to regain balance.

"Why are we stopping so close to the exit?" she huffed. "Those things will be here any minute. Let's get out of here!"

Keris picked up a rough piece of brick and tossed it at the Gate. A sudden transformation overcame the Gate, and its many glass teeth pointed in the party's direction, jutted out menacingly. The brick met its end at the tip of a glass shard, shattering into bits. Then the Gate withdrew; its green blades turned downward, as if it had never moved.

Startled, Rayna gasped. That was no benign mobile. She felt like such a fool.

"Did you not know that Nephredom's Gate permits all, but releases none?" Keris asked with an edge to her voice.

"No!" Rayna shot back defensively.

"Can you defeat the Gate's magic so they we may pass safely through?"

"No!"

"No?" Keris responded, then added, "The food supply of the beasts is no doubt made up wholly of rats, a few wayward woodland animals, the occasional lost child—and foolhardy adventurers like us."

"I guessed that much," Rayna grumbled. They didn't strike me as the agricultural-vegetarian type."

"Joke if you like, but the thought of the beasts' unsated hunger alone should bring to your memory the necessary spell."

"Irel should not be rushed," Arstinax warned softly, in his deep voice. "I trust she will do what needs to be done when the time is right. That is the way with all Powers. In the meantime, I will defend her with my life."

Keris was not impressed. "We entered this city assuming you possessed a secret magic that could overcome the Gate," she emphasized. "Instead, you say you can do nothing."

Rayna steadily met Keris's angry eyes with her own. "First of all," she began, "I'm not a magician. Second, I made a bad decision, but it was *my* bad decision. I didn't ask for a rescue operation."

"That blame lies with me, Irel," Arstinax said. "After Keris and I determined you that you had gone to Lamec, I volunteered to go after you. I told Keris I did not believe you would enter such a forbidden city unless you could leave whenever you so desired. Not wishing me to risk going alone, Keris joined me, and she helped me find you once we got here."

The thud of heavy footprints sounded behind them. The party turned to find yet another beast before them. This beast was younger and smaller, but still large enough to threaten the wounded crew. Rayna was getting sicker by the minute and could hardly stand on her own; Keris and Arstinax still suffered from the pains of their previous encounter. With the unforgiving Gate at their backs, however, there was only one option: *Fight!*

Keris limped forward, brandishing her curved dagger, while Arstinax took up her left side. Instead of accepting the challenge, the junior beast turned and ran.

"That was easy enough," Arstinax said. "We are victorious."

"No," Keris disagreed. "It was only a scout. Its job was not to fight, but to find. Now it will go and tell the hordes of our location. Against such numbers, we cannot prevail. It would have been far better had we fought and killed the creature before it had such a chance."

Keris looked at Rayna. "I ask you again, have you not the means to open this gate? Your coming to this city has revealed to us the inevitable escape of the beasts. But what good is this knowledge if we die before others hear of it? We must depart from this place now!"

Rayna nearly collapsed, but she found support in Arstinax's arms. "I'm still coming to terms . . . with my own mag–abilities," Rayna said, her speech throaty and slurred. "I need . . . I need some time to think . . . do some troubleshooting . . ."

"There is only time for action," Keris countered.

"I . . . can't."

Keris turned her attention to the Gate. "Then we must find another way to leave this place—and quickly."

"The city walls are too smooth to scale," Arstinax said, "and we have neither rope nor hook."

"We need only our wits," Keris replied. "There is a short moment's rest between when the Gate attacks and when it slides back. If we time it right, we can use that pause to climb the glass pieces to the top and back down on the other side."

A concerned expression crossed Arstinax's face as he tugged his beard. "The Gate is very high. If one of us falls—"

"It will be a kinder death than at the hands of those fiends," Keris cut in, handing the last remaining scraps of cloth in her pack to Arstinax and Rayna. "Wrap these around your hands to protect them from cutting." She picked up another piece of brick. "I will go first to show you both that it can be done."

Although she had been fading in and out of consciousness, Rayna had heard most of what Keris said. She had a bad feeling about Keris's idea, but before she could protest, Keris walked closer, in measured steps, to the Gate and tossed the brick at it.

In uncanny synchrony, the glass shards drew their dreaded tips and pressed forward, stopping only inches from the brim of her hat. Keris's lithe body jumped smoothly onto one of the shards and held on tight. As before, the Gate lowered its sharp points and slowly retracted, taking Keris with it. Rayna breathed a sigh of relief. Keris had really done it. She watched in awe as Keris gradually made her way up the treacherous Gate. Keris had climbed nearly halfway up when everything went terribly wrong.

The shards erected and began shaking violently. The Gate rippled as if caught in a tremendous wind. The glass sawed through Keris's gloves and bit deeply into her flesh. She nearly fell, but clung relentlessly to a shard that had stained red with her own blood.

"By my beard!" Arstinax shouted. "Nephredom's accursed Gate is as devious as it is deadly! It is trying to brush her off. If she falls from such a height, she will most certainly die!"

Rayna nodded weakly. "At this rate, the glass will get her before the ground does."

"Then I should climb up after her. The glass will have to work hard and long to hinder me. I'll have her down safely in the blink of an eye."

Rayna shook her head, whispering hoarsely, "Unless you can leap approximately twenty feet in less than a second, while carrying Keris, it won't do any good. I'm certain the Gate's programmed to pop out the second you let go of the glass."

"I do not understand, Irel. Are we to turn our backs on her and do nothing?"

"No," Rayna said calmly, "but it's my fault you two are here." She removed the wrapping around her watch to reveal its near-blinding light. "It's time I did something about this."

Arstinax look worried. "You are ill. If you use your magic now, it could kill you."

Rayna managed a thin smile. "I appreciate your concern, Arstinax, but if we don't get out of this awful place soon, we're all dead. Now please stand back. I'm about to try something experimental, and I'm not sure how it's going to turn out."

Arstinax reluctantly did as he was asked. Rayna carefully removed her watch, fastened it to the tip of her staff, and pointed it at the Gate.

Keris fell.

"Keris!" Rayna cried out. Was it too late?

In that same instant, the watch exploded, hurling the brunt of its fury at the Gate. The recoil shoved Rayna backward, her staff ablaze and smoking. The unloosed magic of the watch hit the Gate, which buckled and shifted unevenly, its shards losing their cohesiveness and pointing wildly in opposing directions. Arstinax caught Keris as she fell. The Gate was too preoccupied with its own troubles to retaliate.

As Rayna put out her flaming staff, she noticed that all that remained of her watch was some blue-white dust, which the hot wind was quickly scattering into oblivion.

"There are now openings in the gate!" Arstinax alerted. "Let us pass through quickly, while we still can!"

The three slipped through the Gate. They had gone only a short way when the Gate crashed in a thunderous roar. The party was sprayed with glass bits, but only their covered backs felt the sting. A mountainous heap of green glass was all that was left of Nephredom's Gate. Just as the din of settling glass ceased, the sound of hissing filled the air. The beasts had come.

Rayna's eyes widened in fear. *How much longer?* she wondered. The venom overtook her once more, and she passed out.

The beasts, numbering in the thousands, were initially hesitant at nearing the newly smashed Gate. They were aware of the pain and death the Gate was capable of inflicting. Many soon lost their fear, however, and hungrily lurched and shambled forward.

"The Gate is down and will do little to keep them in," Keris said somberly. "In our state, we cannot hope to outrun such an army."

Arstinax broke off a heavy limb of a nearby tree and began to snap off its leafy branches until he had fashioned a formidable studded club. "Then we will fight, and take as many of those creatures as we can with us to death."

Keris nodded silently and drew her blade.

Before the beasts could cross the Gate's threshold, the glass magically arose in a shimmering ocean of green. Smaller in size, but more numerous, the shards resumed their former order. Like well-trained soldiers, the glass spikes aimed at the first wave of advancing beasts and ran them through mercilessly. Another wave of beasts charged the Gate, and again it attacked. Another wave followed, with the same result. Hundreds of beasts threw themselves at the Gate, unable to accept that it had been restored just as they had come so close to freedom.

In time, as the number of impaled beasts mounted, the remaining horde turned from the Gate, dragging their dead with them, screaming bitter howls of discontent.

Rayna regained consciousness in time to feel the hatred exuding from the retreating beasts. It was almost as if she could read their minds. They would remember this insult, Rayna thought, and when the time was right, they would make everyone on the other side of the Gate pay.

Keris crossed her arms, quietly taking in the events that led to the Lamec fiasco. She looked at the Gate, then at Rayna, and spoke only one word: "Explain."

Rayna strained to keep her eyes in focus, but although the conflict against the beasts had been won, she was losing her battle with the venom. "A theory of mine," Rayna said. "I speculated that if one were to combine a purely defensive magic with a purely offensive one, the two elements would explode and . . . cancel each other out. I further speculated that such an explosion would create a . . . neutral field of 'anti-magic,' in which all magic-based objects would be rendered temporarily inert . . . and—"

"You can tell us more when you are better," Arstinax interrupted. "You need to conserve your strength to better fight the poison."

"No, wait," Rayna persisted. "I need to tell Keris something. I need a favor. I don't think I'll be able to do it myself."

"Thrice I owe you my life," Keris replied. "I am eager for the chance to clear my debt."

Rayna breathed laboriously. "Good. I want you to tell my mother I'm sorry—do you know what I was going to do?"

Keris and Arstinax briefly looked at each other and returned their gaze to Rayna. "No," Keris said. "What were you going to do?"

"I was driving in my car the other day, deciding how I was going to tell her that I was moving out. I was going to get my own place—leave her all alone."

"There is no shame in departing one's nest of birth to start a new one," Keris said, wrapping a blanket around the shivering mage. "It is the way of things."

"Then why . . . why do I feel so guilty? Please tell her I'm . . . I'm sorry."

"That is one favor I fear I cannot honor. That task can be done only by you."

"But . . ."

"Enough. Arstinax is right. Save your energy. You are not thinking clearly, for the venom clouds the mind. You are strong, Rayna Powell of Nightwind. You will survive."

Rayna's head began to reel; her friends began spinning beyond her control. Giving in to her heavy, fluttering lids, she closed her eyes. The approaching darkness of night became one with the darkness within.

CHAPTER 11

Emawin

Even with closed eyes, and lying flat on her back, Rayna could tell she was once again in the large room from her college-day dreams. She could hear the soft hum of machines nearby. And wind. No, it wasn't wind—it was the sound of ventilation fans blowing. Rayna tried to turn her head and discovered she couldn't move. Then she noticed the weight, an oppressive force that bore down on her chest, becoming heavier with each strained breath she took. Her lungs began to wheeze and burn under the burden. *Heavier.* Rayna struggled to sit up, but something held her fast. She could no longer breathe—suffocating. Her eyes felt glued shut, and they rolled about in panic inside her skull. *Heavier.*

With her remaining strength, Rayna forced her eyes open, and she saw, standing on her chest, the green-uniformed woman from the accident—smiling at her in an odd, mechanical way. One of her eyes was red and other blue, and they shined and twinkled in their dark sockets.

The voice sounded in the darkness. "Why do you fear death, little ghost? You are already dead."

It struck a chord in Rayna that felt like cold fingers on her soul.

Rayna screamed.

"Easy now. It's all right," a gentle voice coaxed.

Gasping for breath, Rayna could see only the uniformed woman's haunting face. Slowly, the image of her nightmare faded, and she realized that looking over her was an elderly woman she'd never seen before. The memory of what had happened to her in Lamec was triggered, as the full misery of the venom's effects reminded her in its unsubtle way that she had been poisoned. She thought she had died, but she was alive, and lying on a strange bed.

She felt sick to her stomach, and every muscle in her body was tight and sore, as if she had tumbled down a flight of stony stairs. Her vision was blurred, and as she rubbed her eyes to better see, she found her face to be hot and clammy with sweat. Strangely enough, her scarf was still in place.

"A bad dream that was. No doubt it was brought on by the venom," the old lady said. She was a short woman, with sunken shoulders and a slightly stooped back. She had a warm smile that spread to her eyes, cheeks, and chin—all wreathed in a network of creases and wrinkles, formed by years of laughing and smiling. Her most distinguishing feature was her ears. They poked through her puffy, gray-white hair like two brown pyramids, leaning in opposite directions. That produced a comically disarming effect, putting Rayna's fears at ease. She smiled back in spite of her fever and body-aches.

"Who are you?" Rayna asked, her hoarse voice barely audible, even though she had intended to speak loudly.

"Me?" the old woman answered. "My name is Emawin. I'm an herbalist in this city, and grandmother to whom you call Keris."

"Grandmother?" Rayna repeated, surprised.

"I have many children here at the shelter, though Keris is one of my favorites."

"Shelter? I thought you said you were an herbalist."

"I am, I am, child. But I can't simply turn my back to the homeless children of this unforgiving city, now can I? This house has many rooms, you see—a gift from my dear husband, since passed. Part of my home is a shop of herbs, and part is a shelter for the wayward girl-child. That is how I met your Keris, you know. Now I usually don't take in someone as fully grown as she, but she had need of a home, and something about her refused to let me turn her away. I don't just take in anyone, mind you. The streets of this city are filled with girls who can't stay here. Too late for them, you know. The evil of the streets has taken root in their hearts, it has, and I am too old to deal with it. You understand—stealing and swearing and the like. No place for that here! Even the fourteen or so good ones in my care require a firm, guiding hand."

"I can't imagine. It must be difficult to run a business and care for them too."

"Oh, it is a labor, full of joy and sometimes pain. But don't think they lounge around all day, taking in the city view! No indeed! The ones who are old enough help me go to the woods to gather the herbs I need for my mixes. The brighter ones, I have sit in and teach the younger ones their lessons, when I'm in shop. And the truly gifted ones, ah! *Them* I accept as apprentices. I tried to apprentice Keris in the trade, but she's too restless to stay here longer than a cycle or two at a time. Then she's off again. She's fairly adept in the basics, I suppose, but she needs to work on her salve mixing. The stuff she was giving you could have used a pinch more purple loosestrife."

"Are there any boys in this shelter?" Rayna asked.

Emawin sighed. "This place is a haven for girls and young women—some of whom haven't had very good experience with those of the opposite sex, if you know what I mean. Besides, I am only one person, and it's hard enough to keep up with a crowd of rambunctious girls, without adding boys to the mix! There is one exception, though, a young boy-child named Quan.

It all started about ten years ago, you see, when I heard a knock at my door in the middle of the night. Well now, the shop was closed, and no customers would be knocking at that hour. I ran and got my sword. I might not look the part, but I can handle myself well enough with a blade against any bandit trying to enter my home with less than honorable intentions! It was my late husband's sword, you know, and as sharp as the day it was forged. For good measure, I always kept the blade coated with a cream made from lizard root—burns a wound like fire, it does! Well, I waited by the door for what seemed like an hour—just waiting for the scoundrel to break in, so I could whack at him good. No one tried to come in. When I felt I could wait no longer, I decided to open the door and see if anyone was about.

That is how I first met Quan—as a baby, wrapped in a quilt, sound asleep, and no mother to be found. I didn't have the heart to take the boy to the orphanage, for they treat their children so cruelly there. And so I kept him. A good boy he is, and talented too. He plays a flute, you see. Where he learned to play it, I don't know. He earns his keep by playing to the crowds as they go about their daily business. They sometimes drop coins into his hat. Now, I don't allow my children to beg like unloved paupers, but I suppose playing music for a few coins is respectable enough. Humph, it's that noisy stray dog of his that needs to go. Eats enough for two children, it does. Well, I suppose it earns its keep as a good watchdog and the younger children seem to love—my goodness! I've been rambling again. I suppose you feel bad enough, child, without me bending your ear so."

"No, not at all, ma'am," Rayna respectfully replied. "In fact, you kind of made me forget about the pain for a while."

Emawin nodded, pleased with the compliment. "You make an old woman feel good, you do, Rayna Powell of Nightwind."

"Keris told you my name?"

"Well, it wouldn't be very polite to drop a sick person on your bed without at least telling what that person's name is, now would it?"

"No, I guess not."

"Rayna. That's a pretty name, it is."

"Thank you."

"Your husband, is he somewhere worried about your roaming the countryside with my granddaughter, getting in all kinds of trouble like this?"

"I'm not married."

"I see. Hmmmmm. You are an uncommon one, Rayna."

"Why do you say that?"

"There is something different about you, but methinks it is a good kind of different."

"I don't understand."

"Well, for one, you are not from the streets—your speech is too polite and proper for that. Remind one a little of Keris, you do."

"Oh, really?" Rayna said, trying hard not to look offended. In vain, she shifted and turned to find a more comfortable position to lie. "How long have I been in your care?" she asked, changing the subject.

"Oh, I'd say about five days now."

Rayna suddenly sat up. "Five days! It's been that long?"

"Oh, yes. The poison that got you was very strong. Never seen the likes of it before. Took all my wits and my best herbs just to keep you from dying before your time, it did. Your body would wake up every now and then to eat or drink a bit, but your mind was still asleep, you see. Bad fever it was. Thought it would never break. Today is the first time you've been well enough to talk in whole sentences. That is good!"

Rayna sighed in disbelief. "I don't remember any of it."

"That is probably for the best. The poison was not kind to you. A very strong poison, it was. How did you get poisoned so, child? Keris wouldn't tell me. She can be the secretive sort sometimes."

Rayna saw no need to lie to the old woman. "I was poisoned by a creature in the city of Lamec," she said.

Emawin put her hands to her mouth in surprise, grabbed a cold wet cloth from a basin, and applied it under Rayna's scarf, firmly against her forehead. "Stubborn poison! Stubborn, stubborn! I thought the fever had broken, but I see you are still going in and out of nightmares. No wonder you shouted in your sleep so. The poison has you dreaming of such cursed places!"

"But—"

"No 'buts.' Here now, drink this brew, while I have you sitting up so nicely."

Rayna took a few sips of the bitter-tasting concoction and suddenly coughed up some recently consumed soup, its taste soured with bile.

"What was that stuff you gave me? Rayna demanded."

"Oh, it wasn't the brew's fault," Emawin explained, wiping a stained, sopping, wet rag around Rayna's squirming face. "It was the poison. It doesn't want you to hold down your food, you see. It wants to kill you, and it can't very well do it if you're fat and well fed. Hush, now, and try to be still. Finish your brew, and I'll give you some more good soup to replace what you've brought up."

Rayna held her breath and downed the rest of the frothy brew. It had a soothing effect, and she reclined to give her stomach a chance to calm its turbulent churning.

"No, no child," Emawin scolded softly to a small girl who had entered the room. "This is bayberry root. I have that already. I need you to fetch me some black snakeroot on the bottom shelf—and some silverweed while you're at it. And hurry, child. A poison will not wait long for you to find the herb best to beat it!"

The girl returned promptly with the herbs, and Emawin began to boil the ingredients in a small pot over a stout, wood stove, adding water and various other herbs. For at least fifteen minutes, she stirred her brew with a long-necked spoon; it made curious scraping sounds against the bottom of the pot as she cheerfully hummed some unknown tune.

"Here, it's ready now," Emawin offered, pouring the pot's steaming contents into a bowl. "Something to warm your aching bones."

Rayna eyed the bowl with reluctance.

"Go on, now, drink. It's soup. Tasty soup, it is."

Rayna held the bowl to her chin and drank. It wasn't too bad, though it had a strong onion taste.

"Arstinax has a surprise for you, he does," Emawin whispered, with a hint of mischief in her frail voice.

That got Rayna's attention. "Surprise?" she echoed, turning away from the remaining few swallows of soup.

Emawin scratched her head, trying to recall something. "It's a lady's trinket. A piece of fancy jewelry methinks. Yes, that's it. Very lovely it is."

Rayna smiled. She could feel the soup's warm touch spreading in her belly. It was an exciting, invigorating feeling. At least she *thought* it was the soup.

"Poor thing was too shy to give it to you himself," Emawin went on. "He asked me if I would give it to you as soon as you were feeling a bit better."

"I think I'm feeling a lot better now," Rayna said.

Emawin laughed, "Ooooh, I bet you are!" She went over to a nearby table and returned with a small, bark-covered box, sealed with a single red ribbon.

Rayna carefully untied the ribbon, set it aside, and lifted the lid from the box. Inside was a silver bracelet inset with a smooth stone of pale blue in its center. Rayna had to agree with Emawin; it was lovely—more than she deserved from a man to whom she had caused so much pain.

"Your Arstinax sold his warrior belt to purchase that pretty bauble, you should know," declared Emawin abruptly, saving her best news for last.

Rayna stopped admiring the bracelet and stared back at Emawin with a look of utter sorrow.

"True it is!" Emawin assured her. "A nobler deed you won't find anywhere!"

Rayna stammered, "I didn't know he had to—"

"When I first heard of this," Emawin continued excitedly, "I wove him a broad belt of sturdy cloth. It is as strong as his leather one was, perhaps stronger." Emawin giggled with almost girlish delight. "Otherwise your smitten friend would be little good in battle, you know, with his pants always falling down and all!"

"Oh, I don't think he's smitten with me, ma'am," Rayna corrected. "A little protective maybe, but not smitten."

"Are you sure, child? I have seen the eyes of many a love-struck to know what I'm talking about."

"It's just that I know that someone like Arstinax wouldn't find me attractive in that way."

"And why not? You are young, and prettier than many. You are bound to catch the eye of many a suitor—some good suitors, and some scoundrels. But methinks this Arstinax fellow is a good catch, he is."

"You think so?"

"Absolutely!"

"Oh. Well, he is very nice."

"More than nice he is—never mind nice! He's well mannered, hardworking, smarter than most his size, and very handsome. Even with the patch. Methinks it gives him character, it does." Emawin placed a wrinkled hand on Rayna's shoulder in a comforting gesture. "Now I'm not the kind to meddle in young people's affairs, but when a man is willing to sell the very belt off his waist to make a particular young woman happy, that particular young woman should take notice, for he is a rare find."

"You are a very perceptive woman, Mrs. Emawin."

"At my time of life, I had better be! There is no place in Argat for old fools. Young fools perhaps, but not old ones."

Rayna looked at the bracelet, her lips turned down in a regretful pout. "I couldn't wear this with a clean conscience, now that I know what he did to get it. I'll have him take it back."

"Heavens no, child!" Emawin admonished. "That would do more harm than good in the lover's game. You have a pretty bracelet. That makes him pleased. He has a strong, new belt. That should make you pleased. Balanced it is. No need to mess it up."

"But I think—"

"Ah, you think too much! Let your mind rest. Enjoy what your heart is telling you."

Suddenly Rayna felt the undeniable urge to throw up. "Right now," she cried, "I think my stomach is trying to tell me something!"

"Goodness, goodness!" Emawin ran and fetched a clean basin. "I just can't seem to keep any soup in you, can I? Oh well, at least some more of the poison will come out with it. Here, right into this pan."

A knock sounded at the door.

"That sounds like the knock of a strong man," Emawin said. "Your Arstinax, I'd bet. I'll let him in."

"Not now!" Rayna called out miserably from a bout of retching.

"Don't worry, he doesn't seem the type to think less of you just because your hair isn't fixed up and all. I promised to let him speak to you as soon as you were able, and Emawin always keeps her word."

"But I smell like vomit!" Rayna hissed back.

"What better way to test a love's mettle, don't you see? Any man can love a woman at her best, but only a man truly in love can see a woman at her worst and love her just the same. When you reach my age, you'll understand."

"But—"

Emawin opened the door, and Arstinax walked inside.

"Now, my patient needs her rest," Emawin advised softly, passing Arstinax on the way out, "so don't stay too long." She added, laughing, "I'll be in the shop, making sure my children aren't giving away my herbs cheaper than rain!"

As Arstinax came forth, Rayna put out a hand in protest. "Wait. Please don't come any closer."

Arstinax paused, puzzled. "Why?"

"I don't want you to . . . catch what I have. And I can see you perfectly fine from here."

"If that is your wish."

A moment of awkward silence passed before Rayna spoke. "I received your gift."

"Let me explain. You see, because your former bracelet was destroyed in Lamec, I thought you might like a new one. It has no magic, of course, and I could not afford a more lavish one, but I felt—"

"Arstinax, it's so beautiful! How did you know my favorite colors are blue and silver?"

The tips of Arstinax's pointed ears turned red, and the blush spread down to his cheeks. "I did not."

Rayna put the bracelet on. "Perfect fit."

She wondered if she was worthy of Arstinax's friendship or respect; she worried if accepting the bracelet would prolong the ruse and somehow validate her role as a deceiver—pretending to be innocent of any guilt. She wanted to tell Arstinax about that fateful night she spoke to his brother in the Sharpening Stone. She urged her mouth to form the right words, to say all the right things, and say them in a way that they could still be friends. Or perhaps more.

Yes, that would be so nice. But the reality of the matter was that Rayna was no elegant speaker, and she wasn't brave enough just yet to even attempt the task of trying to undo the damage that had already been done.

Nevertheless, she had to say something—perhaps in stubbornness, or perhaps because she found herself helplessly tumbling down a spiraling slope of emotional and physical attraction she could not free herself from, nor did she wish to.

Rayna nervously pointed to Arstinax's belt. "Looks new," she said, smiling, realizing too late it was inappropriate.

Arstinax sighed. "She told you."

"Arstinax, it was a very sweet gesture, but I think you should take—"

"Very sweet indeed," Keris replied from behind Arstinax. Rayna and Arstinax turned their attention to Keris. Aside from her bandaged hands, the clandestine Princess gave no physical clue that she and Rayna had shared the same misadventure a few days earlier.

"How did you do that?" Rayna demanded. "I'm facing the door, and I didn't even see you come in."

Keris smiled faintly. "Perhaps you were distracted."

Rayna fumed. "I was having a private conversation!"

"It is all right," Arstinax said to Rayna. "This is Keris' home, not mine. I will come back at another time. May you enjoy your gift for many seasons to come."

Rayna watched Arstinax depart the room and shot an angry look at Keris. "I hope you're satisfied. You scared him away."

"Back to your old self, I see," Keris quipped. "Since you are so adamant about private conversations, you should not object to my having one with you now. I will be brief. You nearly died; we brought you to this place not a day too soon. In this sick room, my grandmother was able to pull you beyond death's reach. With rest you should be fully restored in a day or two."

Rayna couldn't shake her newly sour mood. "I don't think she's really your grandmother," she grumbled, drawing her bed sheet nearer her chin. "I don't see the family resemblance."

Keris laughed briefly. It was so unexpected, Rayna nervously wondered where Emawin put her staff.

"It is good to see that your powers of observation have not dulled with illness," Keris said. "You are correct. Emawin is not my grandmother by blood, and we are very different in both feature and temperament. But I love her dearly, and she has become more family to me than most of my blood relatives had been when they lived. She took me in when I needed sanctuary most. She taught me many things and cared for me as her own."

"Your real grandmother, is she . . . ?"

Keris nodded. "Both mothers to my parents died mysteriously in their sleep. Assassination by poisoning."

Rayna suddenly felt like a heel. "Does Emawin know about your past, and the death warrant that's out on you?" she asked quietly.

"She knows only that I am of East Taren, and that something happened that forced me to hide in this land. I would tell her no more, and she has asked no more."

"I see," Rayna mumbled softly to herself. She knew Keris was playing a risky game, seeking refuge from someone who could turn them both in for a handsome profit if she ever found out the whole truth. Rayna was still weak and could do little if that were to happen. Besides, Rayna reasoned, why would a West Taren citizen care about the fates of an East Taren Princess and her companions?

"Emawin's compassion does not end with the Taren River border," said Keris, guessing what was on Rayna's mind. "Otherwise, she would have let you die on the very bed you privately accuse her from, when I told her you were of East Taren. You need not doubt her intentions, for she will not betray us."

Rayna turned silent.

Keris removed her hat and shook her black woven hair, damp with sweat. "Argat's heat is no less fiery now than my last visit," she commented casually, her voice scarcely above a whisper. Looking back at Rayna, she added, "Forgive me, I did not wish to be short with you. I understand your concerns. Outside of yourself, the only ones who know my full tale are a few trusted informants—and a boy that lives in this home named Quan."

Rayna ventured a cutting remark: "You won't tell Emawin, but you trust your secret to a boy."

"He is attuned to the happenings in the streets and keeps me abreast of possible dangers upon my returns. I have known him for years; he has been a valuable resource—and a second brother to me. Do not judge him lightly, for he is far more than he appears."

"Is it really true he's the only male living here?"

"Yes, this place is devoted mostly to girls, so that they may not defile themselves with the filth on the streets. Argat is a dangerous place—especially for girls. If it were not for this place, many of the children you see here would be in forced servitude to the highest bidder."

Rayna winced at the thought. "I hate this city already, and I haven't even seen it yet."

"It is time I told you why I came to see you. I sense a tide of evil is brewing as we speak, and it threatens to blot out the light of all that is good."

"You're going to try to talk me into going to Soren again, aren't you?"

"I've come with this promise: If you accompany me to Soren to see Ciredor, and if are not still convinced to fight with us to reclaim Jerel by the end of the talks, I will personally escort you to Dosk. In these troubled times, it would be folly to attempt the journey alone."

"You really think I would make a difference in this personal war of yours?"

"Yes."

"And if I get there, hear the sales pitch, and still want no part of it?"

"As I said, you would be free to go to Dosk, and I would accompany you. However, I am certain, once you meet Ciredor and see his great army with your own eyes, you will agree to lend your talents to our cause."

Rayna was secretly impressed. This was the first time she felt Keris had approached her as an equal, and not some royal subject to boss around. "Even if you convince me," she said, "what makes you think Ciredor will go along with your plan?"

"You must leave that to me. I know Ciredor best. He will listen to me."

"Okay, you have a deal. I'll go with you to Soren to see Ciredor and his army you've been talking so much about."

"And I have your word you will make no further attempts to leave our company until then?" Keris questioned, her tone critical and serious.

"I promise."

"Then it is agreed."

As Keris turned to leave, an afterthought came to Rayna's mind. "Keris?"

"Yes?"

"I think I owe you an apology. I know how important this Soren thing is to you, and I'm sorry my um—earlier diversion cost you so much time. Emawin told me I've been out for five days."

Keris shook her head. "An apology is not needed. Coming here to Argat has been good for me. I have not seen my grandmother, the girls, or Quan for over two cycles. Moreover, I now have the opportunity to conclude some dealings I have with one of my contacts here."

"Well, at least let me say thanks for bringing me here."

"That gratitude should be given to Arstinax. It was he, and not I, who carried you in his arms all the way here. I was not up to the task, for I could scarcely carry myself at that time."

Rayna stared up at the ceiling, mentally kicking herself for unspoken deeds. "Why is it," she began, her voice brimming with emotion, "when I think it's the right time to tell Arstinax what happened with his brother, he does something so ridiculously kind, I can't bring myself to do it?"

"There will be no right time."

Rayna did not reply; she was lost in quiet contemplation.

"I see you have much to think about," Keris said. "Rest well. I will see you with the next sunrise."

CHAPTER 12

The Blade in the Table

R ayna arose the next day feeling much better; her fever was gone, and so was her nausea. She noticed there was a fresh, clean tunic and pair of tan leggings laid out for her beside her bed. With a little searching, she found her robes and staff tucked away in the closet.

For the first time since her arrival, Rayna took the opportunity to scrutinize her accommodations. It was a small but efficient room with everything an herbalist needed to care for a sick customer: racks of drying herbs, colorfully hung on a black iron rack behind her bed; a sturdy cauldron; and cooking implements lining every wall on shelves and hooks. Rayna smiled. Of course, there was the rustic soup stove.

In the corner lay a tub-sized bucket filled with clean water, with a washcloth draped over its rim. A lump of semi-clear soap floated shamelessly inside, as if in playful parody of the smooth, sleek bars she was accustomed to.

Not exactly a jacuzzi, Rayna mused to herself, *but it'll do.*

After bathing, Rayna hurriedly got dressed, ready to see what awaited her beyond the door. A long hallway led Rayna to a large room displaying myriad-labeled jars and bottles of tonics, potions, and elixirs. The shop had a sweet, earthy smell, like an indoor garden. The feel of the place gave Rayna a certain sentimental peace she hadn't experienced in a long time. It reminded her of the times she helped her mother run her florist shop. She pictured herself abandoning her troubles and working alongside Emawin as an apprentice. No more running from Red Robes, no more talk of joining lost causes, no more reminders of stupid mistakes . . . and no hope of seeing home again. Rayna pushed the temptation from her mind. This home, she thought, as inviting as it seemed, was no substitute for her own.

Emawin had just finished selling some kind of flowering plant to a customer and grinned at the sight of Rayna. "There you are, child. Poison's all gone, I see."

Before Rayna could reply, Keris entered the room, holding the hand of a small boy.

"Rayna Powell of Nightwind, meet Quan of Argat," she introduced formally. "It is good to see you have recovered. Let us go outside in the fresh air."

"Very good!" Emawin agreed enthusiastically. "I've done all I can do here, in this stuffy place. Our Rayna needs to move about a bit and see the sights! Do her good, it will." Emawin smiled, remembering the days of her youth. "It is good for the young to walk around and see things." She raised a bony finger of warning. "Just keep her away from the bad spots!"

The three stepped outside, and Rayna was nearly blinded by the suddenness of sunlight. It had been a long time since her eyes had seen the sun, she thought, grateful to feel the wind on her face again.

Keris gave Quan a firm nudge in Rayna's direction. "Quan has something he wishes to say to you," she said.

Quan stared intensely at Rayna for a moment, as if assessing her. He abruptly broke into a relaxed posture, beaming her a smile so warm it was contagious. Rayna found herself smiling back at the brown-eyed boy.

"Well?" she asked.

With a single, fluid motion, Quan reached into his pocket and pulled out Rayna's bracelet. "It came off while you slept," he explained, his charming smile growing brighter still. "I kept it safe for you."

Rayna noted that the boy's mild words came out smoothly formed and molded like those of a polished speaker or theatrical performer, carefully timed and articulated. She found this unusual for a child his age.

"Tell her *how* it came off—and why," said Keris sharply. "Speak the whole truth!"

Quan took on a defensive slouch and his confident grin began to falter. "I . . . I took your bracelet . . . and I asked Keris to help me sell it." Scowling angrily at Keris, he declared with emphasis in his voice, "I've been betrayed!"

Until that moment, Rayna had not noticed her bracelet was missing. She snatched the bracelet from the boy. "You little thief!" she accused.

Quan was not the kind to be defeated easily. On command, bright tears began to form in his eyes. "I'm sorry," he sobbed. "I was curious—nothing more."

"And that's why you tried to sell it?" Rayna barked back, restoring her bracelet to her wrist. "Curiosity?"

"I was only thinking of Grandmother, and my sisters. We are hungry, and—"

"Enough," Keris said, putting an end to the burgeoning story. "Your deed has been brought to light, Quan. Only cowards hide behind lies and false tears."

Quan made a face at Keris and cheerfully reached back into his pocket, pulling out a gleaming silver flute in pristine condition. "Wish to hear me play?" he asked Rayna, all signs of remorse gone from his seemingly innocent face.

"No," she growled.

He played anyway. It was a perky little tune, treacherously difficult to follow, full of frivolity and whimsy, yet skillfully done. Misgivings aside, Rayna had to admit Quan was quite good with the flute.

Drawn to the music as if it were but a variation of its master's voice, a brown and tan dog—something of a collie and retriever mix—raced from somewhere behind house and playfully jumped against Quan, nearly knocking him over.

"Bard!" Quan cheered, rubbing the dog's thick coat vigorously. "You mustn't wander off like that again. I've been looking for you all day!"

Tail wagging, Bard sprang over to Keris but did not jump on her. He briefly sniffed Rayna, apparently decided that her scent wasn't interesting enough, and went back to jumping around Quan.

"Now that you've met Quan and his dear friend," Keris began stoically, with a touch of sarcasm, "I would like you to accompany me to see someone."

"One of your contacts?" Rayna presumed.

"She shouldn't know that!" exclaimed Quan in protest.

"Calm yourself," Keris said to him. "She knows my past and is here to help us."

"If you say so," Quan warned, and then began playing with Bard.

Rayna yawned, looking with longing at the front door to the shop. "I'll stay here, until you've ready to travel to Soren. Maybe I can help Emawin with something."

"I must insist," Keris replied. "The last time I left you to visit a contact, I found myself at a condemning the next day. It is best you come with me."

Rayna grimaced. "Thanks a lot. Look, I feel bad enough about that without your reminders."

"My intention was not to wound, but merely to point out a fact—something I know you to respect."

Rayna's gaze drifted to her feet. "You're afraid I'll endanger Emawin?" Keris did not answer, but she didn't need to.

"All right, lead the way," she breathed, sad but resolutely grateful of the decision to go. The last thing she wanted was another person getting hurt because of her. To Rayna's disliking, Quan tagged along, skipping, with Bard trotting at his side.

❄ ❄ ❄

Emawin's home lay on the outermost tip of a well-trod road that gradually thickened and grew straighter with time. From the perspective of a bird flying above, the three travelers could be likened to wandering ants on a vast world-tree of many branches, moving from the leaf-tipped fringes toward its great trunk.

In a short time, the quiet sound of their own feet against the road became drowningly displaced by the growing din of wagon wheels rolling along cobblestone streets, and multitudes of people yelling, talking, and laughing. The sound of music was everywhere, and the city seemed bathed in perpetual festivity. As they entered into the market square, they saw dozens of umbrella-covered stands, tents, and various other canopied structures lining both sides of every thoroughfare, selling aged cheese, smoked meats, dried fish, and roasted nuts. Covered tables were laid out, displaying incense and fragrant oils that clashed with the sharp smell of animal carcasses that hung on bloody hooks.

Boisterous clothiers stood outside their shops whipping garments about, declaring their prices to be lowest. In fact, everyone seemed to be shouting about sales and bargains just waiting to be claimed by the lucky prospective buyer. Rayna was suddenly accosted by a hooded merchant, selling lock-picks. "Go anywhere at any time!" the salesman hissed annoyingly, with a wink. "No door shall be a boundary with this fine set of tools in your hands! And nowhere will you find them cheaper than here!"

"You should ask him," Rayna retorted as she passed, pointing to Quan. "He's the thief."

Brightly dressed merchants roamed about offering water for sale. These water merchants were quite possibly the quietest of the bunch; the sweltering heat of the sun did their selling for them.

"This city is too distracting," Rayna complained, feeling vaguely claustrophobic. "How can anyone hear themselves think in all this commotion?"

"This is not actually Argat," Keris pointed out, "but rather an outlying hamlet bearing the same name. The true Argat—commonly known as "Argat City"—is further down the way, marked by a great city gate. It is far more crowded than this."

Rayna cast a questioning eye around her, noticing beggars dressed in rags with outstretched hands, crying, "Mercy for the poor! Mercy!" Prancing prostitutes casually offered their services in broad daylight. Kitten-sized rats, fat and bloated from feasting on the sewage and filth frequently tossed from overhead windows, brazenly stood their ground as people passed by—moving only when in immediate danger of being stepped on.

"A suburb? This place?" Rayna asked, wrinkling her nose. "You've got to be kidding."

They happened upon a jester juggling fruit. Catching sight of the party, he walked their way. His painted face twisting in silly expressions, he joked, "Have you ever see an East Tarener work? I have, and I say it was the strangest half hour I have ever seen! Haw haw!"

Rayna groaned. "He should stick to his fruit juggling act," she muttered to Keris.

The jester's keen ears overheard the comment, and he made an exaggerated face of offense, then feigned as if he had been struck by an arrow in his heart. He hunched over in mock pain and buried his face in the crook of his arm, then suddenly popped back up, his crimson smile returned. "Didn't like that one, did you?" he said, carefully noting Rayna's robes and staff. "Well, East Tarener, I'll bet this riddle brings laughter to your lips! Do you know why Kuarans shun the use of oxen to help them in their labors?" The jester began juggling fruit again, waiting awhile before delivering the punch line: "It's because they hate the idea of working with anything smarter than themselves! Ho, ho haw!"

Rayna pointed her staff at the jester, shouting, "I happen to have a friend from Kuara, and he's more intelligent than anything I've heard you say!"

The smile on the jester's face vanished; the fruit he tossed was allowed to drop in a basket at his feet. "No harm intended, lady," he said, scarcely moving his lips; one of his hands had slipped under his bright tunic and rested there.

Rayna felt a tingling on her wrist but ignored it.

Quan began running in circles, weaving between Rayna and the jester, playing his flute and singing between tunes; Bard raced happily at his heels. Quan sang:

> *A fight! A fight!*
> *There will be a fight!*
> *Who will win? Can no one tell?*
> *The jester shall tell another bad joke.*
> *The she-mage shall cast a forbidden spell!"*

Keris quickly pulled Rayna away and ushered her back to the road. The jester watched Rayna for a while, then resumed his act.

Keris scolded, "You are not skilled in staff fighting, yet you wag your staff about as if you were. Never raise your weapon unless you are prepared to use it!"

"But I didn't like—"

"Know this: The people here are street-wise and deceptive. The jester may appear to be a harmless fool, but I assure you he is not. He could have slit your throat with a single pass of his blade, and no one would have tried to help you, or even attempt to punish him—especially since you wear the garb of an East Tarener."

Rayna sulked. She wished Arstinax were by her side. If he were here, she thought, that jerk would have found another joke to tell.

"He tried to pickpocket you five times," Quan said to Rayna matter-of-factly, "but I moved in his way every time so he could not."

Rayna could scarcely believe her ears. "But how can he pickpocket when he's juggling fruit?"

"A good pickpocket can pinch your purse and make it a part of his juggling act without the victim being the wiser," Keris explained patiently. "You should watch these so-called entertainers with better care, Rayna Powell of Nightwind. Only three of the items the jester juggled were fruit. The other two were coin-bags he had filched from the unwary as they listened to his jokes. Now come. My contact is to meet us in a tavern not far from here."

✳ ✳ ✳

They came to a junction where the road split in two, to encircle a large statue, and rejoined.

"I just want to say, for the record," Rayna stated, as they came to a stop, "it wasn't my fault. I didn't like his jokes, and I had the right to express it."

Secretly amused that Rayna was still brooding over the earlier incident, Keris responded more sensitively than she would have otherwise. "You are a woman of learning. Never let your emotions undermine that—even if it is for someone you care much for."

"Now wait a minute. I admit I lost my temper, but it wasn't over Arstinax, if that's what you're thinking. It was over the fact that that clown was insulting all Kuarans."

"If that is what you say."

"That is what I say."

"Then the matter is closed."

Keris lowered the brim on her hat, to hide all but a fraction of her face.

"Wait here with Quan a moment," she told Rayna. "Caution must not be forgotten. I must check the area first—unaccompanied."

Keris vanished into the crowd, and Rayna found herself uncomfortably alone, save a young thief she hardly knew. And a dog.

"Who's that?" Rayna asked Quan, pointing to the central statue they had passed earlier. As depicted, the figure had a certain arrogance in its face Rayna didn't like.

"Oh, that's Nephredom," Quan replied, pulling out his flute again. "He has statues of himself everywhere."

"You're going to play that now?" asked Rayna caustically with a frown. After the jester incident, she wasn't in the mood to hear flute music, especially not the jumpy little tunes Quan was fond of playing.

"This is my favorite spot to play," Quan explained. "People with money come through here."

"You're going to pickpocket them, aren't you?"

"I'm not a thief!" Quan replied indignantly. "I'm a musician, and musicians play music. Bard is my minstrel, and he sings to my music."

Rayna laughed. "A singing dog?"

Quan made a face at Rayna. "Laugh if you like. My flute is magic. It can play music that only Bard hears, and when he hears it—he sings.

You'll see. Come, Bard! Let us earn some coin!"

Quan took his place by the statue in the circle and began to play. Surprisingly, it was an unhurried, delicate tune, comforting and inviting, like the memory of a childhood friend. Then Rayna remembered—It was the song sung to her by the young healer before she died. Even without the words, Quan had captured the song's beauty perfectly. Reliving that moment once again in her mind, Rayna mouthed the words she once heard the healer sing:

> The club forged of trees,
> is greater than the sword forged of fire.
> For its wood is born of life,
> and above life there's nothing higher.
>
> Let not evil dark deeds,
> bring the sorrow which robs all happiness.
> Stand against the hate disguise,
> and unite half to make whole our less.
>
> The light is our need,
> and will take time for us to brandish well.
> Winds of wrong blow without toil,
> But the labor to make right prevails.

Rayna's reverie was broken suddenly by the crude sound of howling. Bard! A sizable crowd had gathered around Quan, clapping for the wailing mongrel and tossing money at Quan's feet. Rayna realized that although Quan was still blowing in his flute, no sound came forth. Bard apparently felt the need to fill in for the vacancy of sound with his own voice.

Her ire at having the song take such an offensive turn was dissipated by a surprising conclusion: Quan's flute was playing a note too high-pitched for her ears to detect. It was capable of acting as some kind of silent dog-whistle. The public seemed captivated by the sight of a dog "singing" to the melody of a flute only he could hear.

So that's Quan's game, Rayna thought, crossing her arms in fascination. Playing music to draw a crowd, then putting on an animal act as the main attraction. Smart.

The show was soon over, and the satisfied crowd went on their way. With Bard standing guard, Quan gathered and counted, with the nimble fingers of an expert, the money he had earned. He quickly stuffed the assorted coins into his pockets.

Better trained than Rayna initially suspected, Bard was watchful and rigid during this process, growling at anyone who might try to rob Quan as he pocketed his sizable earnings. When the last of the coins were safely tucked away, Bard reverted to his tail wagging and pouncing, waiting eagerly for Quan's next move.

"Alas," sighed Quan lamentably. "I am but one coin short."

"Short?" Rayna scoffed. "You made a small fortune back there."

"But I desire to buy my grandmother new pots, and they cost more than what I have," he explained. "Grandmother's pots are chipped and cracked—surely they will not hold up much longer. Then she will not be able to support us, for what good are herbs if one cannot prepare them properly?"

Rayna had her doubts, but the boy's soft eyes looked sincere and showed no hint of trickery. She was coming to realize that Quan had a way of bypassing her usual analytical scrutiny in a way that was almost frightening. *I guess it would be nice*, she thought, to *surprise Emawin with a gift.*

Rayna searched her pockets and presented Quan with a small cylinder object, telling him, "I don't have any money to give you, and even if I did, I don't think my kind of currency would do you any good. Maybe you can get something for this."

Quan marveled at the strange item. "What is it?"

"A pen," Rayna replied curtly. "I know it's not much, but that's the best I can do."

"How does it work?"

"You twist the pen here, and it's ready to write—see?" Rayna scribbled a few stray lines on the palm of her hand to demonstrate.

"Magic!" Quan shouted.

"It's not magic. It's just a pen."

"But where is the inkwell to dip it in?"

"It's built into the pen, and it's not called an 'inkwell'; it's called a reservoir."

"Are you certain it's not magic?"

"Trust me, it's not magic. Now here, take it."

Rayna gave the pen to Quan with mixed feelings. It was the only reminder of home she had left, now that her watch had been destroyed.

"Why do you want to go to Dosk?" Quan asked all of a sudden, as he tucked Rayna's pen away with the care with which one would handle a priceless artifact.

"How did you know about me wanting to go to Dosk? Did Keris tell you?"

Quan wiggled his pointed ears, grinning. "I hear things."

Rayna chuckled in spite of herself. "Between you and Keris, I'll never have any privacy. I want to visit Dosk because I believe there are people there who can help me find my way back home."

"Your home is far away?"

"Yes, so far away you won't find it on any Taren map."

"Who are the people in Dosk that will help you?"

"I don't know any of them personally, but they're called scientists." She added with touch of pride, "I guess you can say I'm a scientist."

Quan brightened, eager once again to put his flute to his mouth. "I was taught a song about a scientist! Care to hear it? Please say yes!"

Rayna's interest was piqued. "A song about a scientist, huh? Sure, I'll be happy to hear it."

Quan ran back to the statue and began singing, playing his flute hurriedly after each refrain:

> Oh the folly of science!
> The folly of science!
> Heaven save us all,
> from the folly of science!
>
> This tale's of a scientist,
> armed with his sword.
> Alone in the woods!
> Alone in the woods!
>
> He traveled a bit,
> and soon he was bored.
> Alone in the woods!
> Alone in the woods!
>
> He noticed his blade had a spot of rust.
> It baffled him so, and he made such a fuss.
>
> In a hot fire,
> did he melt the blade down.
> Alone in the woods!
> Alone in the woods!
>
> Along came a bear,
> who beside him sat down.

Alone in the woods!
Alone in the woods!

Said the great bear, "How has one such as you,
come so far without a weapon or two?"

The scientist said "Hush!
I've no time to chat."
Alone in the woods!
Alone in the woods!

"I'm studying this rust,
and that is that!"
Alone in the woods!
Alone in the woods!

With the news of this did the bear delight,
it gobbled the scientist in ten bites.

"Fool!" the bear said,
when his dining had passed.
Alone in the woods!
Alone in the woods!

"I knew that but only
ten bites you would last."
Alone in the woods!
Alone in the woods!

"For as you studied your rust for a clue,
all the whole while I was studying you!"

A couple of passersby, amused by the song, dropped a few more coins at Quan's feet.

Rayna, however, was not amused. "When you told me you knew a song about a scientist," she said to Quan, "that was not what I had in mind. Who taught you that song, anyway? It's gross."

Quan grinned. "Emawin did."

"So much for an appreciation for my major," Rayna mumbled to herself.

"What's that?"

"Never mind. You can give me back my pen now. You've earned your one extra coin."

Quan pouted; his face sagged, as if every muscle in his face had lost its tension, drooping pathetically, pulling down his button-round eyes, as if a pair of invisible hands was tugging at his cheeks. He looked so completely sad, it teetered between the tragic and the hilarious.

Who needs magic, when all one has to do was be young and cute? Rayna thought to herself, resisting the impulse to hug the boy. "All right," she told him. "Keep the pen."

Quan cheered up quickly, taking off with a start. "I will sell the magic quill and buy my grandmother *two* sets of pots! A wealthy scribe lives not far from here, named Sirek. He will find this quill worth the price of a few pots, or more."

"Wait a minute! Aren't you going with us when Keris gets back?"

"Emawin has forbade me to go in any of the taverns," he called back; then he and Bard darted into the city throng and faded into obscurity. Moments later, Keris returned.

"Where is Quan?" she asked. "He should not have left you alone here."

Choosing to ignore the implication that she needed a ten-year-old to watch after *her*, rather than the other way around, Rayna simply said, "He went to buy Emawin some pots."

"What?"

"Pots."

"That I heard. What I wish to know is why. I recently purchased Emawin a goodly set of pots but three cycles ago. She has no need for more."

"But I just gave Quan my magic quil—pen to sell so that he could get a bunch of pots."

"It makes little sense. To whom did he say he would sell this pen?"

Rayna took a minute to remember. "A scribe that lives—Sirek, that was his name."

Puzzled, Keris shook her head, "Sirek? I know many names in Argat, and I cannot recall . . ." She paused and revealed a knowing smile. "You've been duped. Sirek is merely my name in reverse. There is no such person."

"Quan did the right thing, leaving when he did," replied Rayna calmly. "Otherwise I would be strangling him right now. I can't believe I actually fell for that—the little sneak."

Keris motioned to Rayna to walk with her. "I regret to say," she voiced, after they had gone some way, "that you are not the first person whom

Quan has beguiled so. Because of my constant travels, I cannot keep as close an eye on him as I would like. Emawin tries her best, but she is old, and she knows not of Quan's less than honorable ways."

"Then maybe you should tell her."

"No. Emawin is generous, but if news of this reaches her ears, she would not take it well. She may turn him away."

"I heard Quan play today. He's pretty good, and he earned a nice little pile of coins—*twice*. If Emawin stopped providing everything for him and required that he be more independent, it might force him to make an honest living as a musician—unless there are child labors laws preventing such a thing. Based on what I've seen since I've been in Taren, I doubt it."

"What he earns now is but a pittance of what he would need to survive on his own. The large copper coins they toss at his feet may look impressive to you, but they are of low value—far less than the smaller gold and silver ones, carried by merchants. And troubadour bands rarely accept new musicians these days. Without Emawin, he would have to steal much more to earn his living. The local thieves' guild would soon discover that Quan is more than a minstrel and would not take kindly to his freelancing, to say the least."

"Join or die," Rayna summarized.

"Yes. And when they see how clever he is, they will drain the decency from his soul and make him work as a street jester, like the one you encountered earlier, or worst still, a prospector."

"What's that?"

"Vultures that prey on the weak. This city is infested with them, and I do not wish that fate to befall Quan."

They rounded a corner and turned down a narrow, muddy road.

"It sounds like you've put a lot of thought into this," Rayna said, fascinated by the "big sister" side to Keris previously unknown to her.

"I have. I believe Quan's intellect can be used for good with the proper training."

"You know, it's only a matter of time before Quan runs out of luck, gets caught conning somebody, or stealing something, and Emawin finds out."

"Yes, I know. That is why he is coming with us to Soren."

"What? You're not serious, are you?"

"Quite. It is my hope that some exposure to men of a more venerable nature will do him lasting good; he has taken well to Arstinax, and that is a good sign. Perhaps Ciredor could find a respectable job for him in Soren."

"Fine, but I'm not a baby-sitter," Rayna shot back, only half determined. She found it hard to stay mad at the boy for long.

"We are here," Keris said. They had stopped outside of a tavern with the words "The Sword and the Lizard," faded and barely legible, on a grubby sign nailed to the door. "Keep your wits about you, and say nothing when my contact arrives."

As they entered the seedy place, the sharp stench of unwashed feet and body musk wafted past Rayna's nose. She was annoyed at Keris for having brought her there. "What kind of contact would want to meet here?" she whispered, sneering, afraid to touch anything as they made their way to a vacant table.

"A contact who wishes to remain anonymous," Keris whispered back. "In this place, the owner has a policy of looking the other way on acts most foul."

Rayna took a firmer hold on her staff. "Just who exactly is this contact you're meeting?"

"An illegal arms dealer by the name of Jharet."

"Sorry I asked."

"He knows we are here, and will approach us in his own time."

Rayna couldn't help noticing the lustful leer from one of the patrons sitting one table across. Dressed in scarecrow-like rags, the ugly man wore an unkempt beard and a mustache with white bits of something encrusted in it—possibly the remnants of a long-forgotten meal. There were too many unattractive things about the man for Rayna to list, but the most apparent was a long, swollen scar that traveled down one side of his face to his lower chin, like a serpent trying to crawl from his ear into his mouth. He watched Rayna and Keris with wild, bloodshot eyes.

Pretending not to see the man, Rayna spoke to Keris in a low, hushed tone. "Why is that guy staring at us like that? Don't tell me that's your contact."

Keris shook her head slowly. "He is a prospector."

Rayna carefully allowed Keris to see a glimpse of her bracelet; she had been keeping it under the cover of her hand since they sat down.

Keris's brows knitted together in astonishment. "How can this be? It glows as though it were your old talisman."

"I don't know how, but I do know why. It's that prospector—he's trouble."

"Hummph. All prospectors are trouble."

Rayna heard a chair pull away and saw movement from the corner of her eye. "What do we do?" she asked, tense and worried. "I think he's coming our way."

Keris smiled and mouthed softly, "I recognize this one. Show him no fear. I will deal with him."

The prospector approached their table, revealing a rotten-toothed smile, pocketed with blackened gaps. "Me was enjoying the view of you two pretty females, when me decided to do you both a favor."

"Like doing something about your breath?" Rayna muttered.

The stranger eyed Rayna suspiciously. "Uh? What's that you say?"

"What my friend said," Keris interceded, "is that we need no favors, and that you should go on your way." She added smugly, "A vendor down the road sells peppermint leaves for chewing. Perhaps you should invest in a bushel, or two."

The man savagely yanked his filthy beard and crossed his arms. "Pah!" he spat. "You know not who you be playing games with, female! But there be too many pieces of gold I can be making to kill you, so listen up. You two be mine now. The streets be not safe for pretty young females, so I will protect you both—make sure no *harm* comes to you."

Keris arched an eyebrow in feigned curiosity. "In exchange for?"

The prospector grinned nastily; long droplets of drool slipped through the spaces in his lower teeth, running down his chin, beard, and shirt. "We'll be discussing that later, after I take you to my boss."

As he reached over with both hands to grab Keris and Rayna by the wrists, Keris delivered a quick, snapping blow to his already-broken nose. The scruffy man staggered back, startled and stunned. No one in the tavern seemed to notice.

"Let that be a warning to you, scoundrel," Keris said "Now leave us be. We have no interest in your brand of protection."

Wiping the blood from his nose, the stranger glared hatefully at Keris with his red eyes. Unsheathing his dagger, he held it up menacingly before Keris and then stabbed it into the wooden table where they sat. "There, you see! I mean business!"

The blade was an impressive weapon, broad, long, and sharp.

Unflinching, Keris looked bored, staring back at the prospector with her usual stoic expression. Then, with a mirthless smile, Keris produced her own dagger and laid it gently on the table. The exotic blade had a series of downward, curved spikes, like the flickering tips of a flame. It was the kind of weapon that would hurt even more coming out than it would going in. The gleaming edge of her dagger was so sharp it threatened to cut from the sight of it alone.

Rayna winced. Keris's dagger made the prospector's weapon look like a pocketknife.

The prospector made a move to take Keris's dagger, but with eye-blinking fast reflexes, she had already recovered her blade, and she held it dangerously close to the brigand's exposed wrist.

"Be very still," Keris warned, "or you may find yourself with but a single hand."

"That be a beautiful blade you have," he laughed nervously.

Keris's eyes grew cold. "And it would be a shame to mar its beauty with your foul blood, wouldn't you agree?"

"Yes. Yes, me lady, it would."

"Then leave. Now!"

The would-be "protector" bolted from the table and out the door, not bothering to retrieve his weapon. It remained where he left it, solidly buried in the wood of the table.

Rayna leaned over. "He looked as if he recognized your weapon."

Keris replied, "That is because he did. One year ago, I met him in Zuran, where he tried to offer me his so-called protection."

"What happened?"

"His broken nose, I know not how he got that, but the scar you saw trailing down his face is mine."

"And he was stupid enough to provoke you a second time?"

"Though he recognized my blade, he did not recognize its owner. I often travel in disguise for obvious reasons. My hair, my garments, and even my speech were different then. That trash was not smart enough to see through it all."

Another stranger approached the table. He was a tall, distinguished looking man and neatly clad—a far cry from their previous visitor. "Quite a show," he commended, clapping as he pulled up a chair beside Keris. "I am Jharet. May I offer you two ladies a drink—ale, perhaps?"

"I don't drink," Rayna barked rudely, bitter memories of her drunken mishap in Kuara resurfacing.

"No, thank you," Keris replied. "Now, let us dispense with the niceties. Will you be able to deliver the shipment?"

Jharet smiled. "To the point as always, Keris. The answer is yes. If Ciredor will pay, we will provide."

"They are all ready?"

"Of course. Enough to furnish an army—an army of pike-men to be exact. It took quite a bit of convincing to get my associates to commit to the manufacture of ten thousand customized weapons, but ultimately we decided you were a good risk. I mean, if by some strange reason you fail to pay us, we could always recoup much of our loss by cashing in on the generous bounty that hovers over your head, Princess."

"Spare me your threats. Ciredor will buy your weapons. What proof have you that they will pass inspection?"

The mysterious contact got up and walked over to another person, who was standing in the shadows on the far side of the room. The shaded man handed a long object to Jharet, who returned to the table. "Pardon the wait," he said with a nod, "but I never bother to show my merchandise unless my customers are smart enough to ask."

"It's just a staff," Rayna blurted out, having forgotten she was not to speak.

"An astute observation, my lovely woman," Jharet said with an unsavory grin. "A wood staff just like yours, minus the elaborate metal tips. Or perhaps," Jharet continued, "the metal is somewhere else." With his thumb, he pressed a hidden button at the top of the staff, and a wickedly serrated blade, more than a foot long, sprang out from the staff's bottom with a coiled springing sound, strong and loud—*Clicktkk!*

"Impressive," Keris responded.

Jharet laughed coldly. "Indeed. If this staff can fool a clever looking lady like your companion here, it will undoubtedly fool any bumbling guard who may decide to stick his nose into our bag of goods on its way to Soren. We are well aware of the bladed weapons embargo imposed there, and have no intention of landing in one of Nephredom's prisons, as popular as they may be." Jharet raised the spear-tipped staff high with both hands. "And if the question of quality is your next concern," he said, "then please allow me to demonstrate, though forgive me if I lack the prospector's flair."

The staff-spear came down hard on the table, which nearly split in half under the shuddering impact.

Rayna gasped.

"Trust me," the dark gentlemen went on, "this arm will hold up in any battle. Finer workmanship I challenge you to find anywhere. If you do, please let me know. We are always looking for fine craftsmen." Jharet wrenched the weapon free and pushed the button as he firmly nudged the business end of the staff against the floor. The blade slid neatly back into the wooden casing, completely undetectable to the eye.

Satisfied, Keris nodded. "It will do."

"Excellent. We will wait one cycle for Ciredor to contact us to begin payment for shipment. If we do not hear from anyone within that allotted time, we will assume you have reneged on our agreement and are subject to all the unfortunate consequences that involves."

"Understood."

"Good. Now, if you will excuse me. I have an engagement elsewhere with another client." Jharet stood and paused for a moment, then added, "Perhaps if you are successful in killing your opponent and win the favor of the people once more, you will remember us, your friends who helped you. We could use friends in lofty places."

"I think not," Keris responded indifferently. "Do you take me for a dunce, Jharet? I am full aware that it is your people who supply swords to the very mercenary army I oppose. Our relationship ends with the weapons in my hands and the gold in yours."

"As you wish, Princess."

Rayna waited until she was sure Jharet and all his cronies had left the tavern. "You are insane!" she accused. "You're striking a deal with the Mob?"

Keris nodded. "If you mean that I have dealings with the underworld, yes."

"Why?"

"It was unavoidable. As an accused murderer, my options are limited."

"He knew who you were."

"That too was unavoidable."

"You trust him?"

"Of course not. He is a necessary evil I must endure for now."

"Just when I think I know you, you throw me a curveball—like dancing with the devil."

"What?"

"Never mind. Can we leave this place? It's starting to get to me. Besides, old scar-face might decide to come back with friends for a rematch."

✳ ✳ ✳

Rayna and Keris had made their way back to the main road when they heard the shouting. "Hear all! Hear all! The Queen of East Taren is dead! The Queen of East Taren is dead! Regent Nephredom proclaimed King! Hear all! Hear all . . ."

"Just what we need," one man said, whispering to a friend as the shouting herald passed. "Another pompous magic user telling us what to do! We need a revolution—that's what I say!"

Rayna could feel something dangerous brewing—a kind of unease so profound it was almost tangible. Like the prospector's blade in the table, the unmentionable dread had embedded itself in her heart. *King Nephredom.*

Rayna shuddered, looking over to Keris. "Are you okay?" she asked.

"No," Keris replied, "but that matters not. By my mother's dying breath, I swear Nephredom will not rest easy on his stolen throne. I swear it. Come, we must bid farewell to Emawin quickly, for we depart for Soren—tonight!"

CHAPTER 13

The Dawn of the Dark

*O*bedience. Servitude. Respect. We are the Red Robes. We are one. Our goal was clear, our purpose defined. Then the unknown mage came, and we failed because of her. It was she who brought down the magic of stillness upon us, and five who represent us in body were cut off from ourselves. But now we have undone the injury dealt us and have reunited with all our minds, and we know all.

"Quite honestly," Aric complained as she conversed with one Red Robe, in a massive room of many, "it's becoming more and more difficult to tell when you're talking to me, or simply babbling among yourselves in some sort of dreadful self-acknowledgment."

Shared consciousness.

"Annoying, by whatever name you choose to give it. Now, you say you finally have the information?"

Yes.

"Excellent! Nephredom will be pleased—or as pleased as one can be in his mood as of late." Aric paused, twitched her sniffing nose, and pointed to the multitude of red-clad figures kneeling and bowed with their backs to her. "When was the last time your Givers bathed?"

Worldly matters are of little concern.

Aric smiled and suddenly stepped up on the back of a Giver. She leaped from one Giver's back to the next, without any of them arising from their huddled state.

The eccentric aide gestured dramatically, saying, "Behold, the mighty elite mages of Taren! Four hundred strong, two hundred of which are forever meditating on the floor, going days without knowing food, drink . . . soap."

Aric's smile left her face like a fleeting vapor. She rolled her eyes upward with distaste, then sat down on a Giver's back, regarded as no more than furniture to her. "Nephredom's vision of an elite force of mages to serve the throne has indeed come to fruition—albeit with certain disadvantages."

There is no disadvantage. We are as we are meant to be. Yes, two hundred of us are Givers. It is us who see and lend sight to us who walk. It is as Nephredom intended.

"How can I ever forget? Quite clever of our leader, wouldn't you agree? For every Red Robe he appointed a Red Giver, whose sole purpose in life is to sit on this filthy floor, sense the illegal use of magic, and dispatch its mobile counterpart to investigate."

No. Our purpose goes beyond seeing. We increase the magic also. It is us who lend magic to us who walk. We offer the power of two represented in one.

"I stand corrected," Aric said, fanning herself with her hand. "You Givers have two purposes in life, and neither of them lessens the stench." She jumped to her feet and gave a bow. "Well, don't all applaud at once," she said, laughing mockingly at the Red Givers.

No reply came. The Red Robes too were silent, their hooded heads bowed as they stood motionless in fixed rows, like machines stored in a warehouse when not in use.

"Depressing," Aric went on, her eyes closed in concentration. "So many men and women gathered together in this great chamber and not a single arousing thought to be found—other than my own, of course. Obedience. Servitude. Boredom. Nephredom has you trained like dogs. Does not your famed East Taren blood rebel against such blind conformity?"

It is not wise to speak ill of us, for to speak ill of us is to speak ill of our master, Nephredom.

Aric sneered. "And I am to listen to you about what is wise? You who let yourselves become as puppets attached to one string? How many times must I tell you? Nephredom may be Keeper of the Gate, but it is I who is keeper of the Red Robes."

Nephredom does not know of this.

"Of course not. He is ignorant of many things I do. Now do you see the disadvantages? You are only as strong as your weakest mind—for to control one of you is to control you all."

Shared consciousness.

Aric gave a series of gleeful nods. "*Precisely*. You understand at last. I'm proud of you. I can speak ill of anyone I choose, and you will do nothing. Even if you desperately wanted to tell your precious Nephredom how naughty I've been, you could not, for I have long since bound my will to yours, and my will wins every time."

Yes.

"I'm glad you agree. Anyway, you mustn't deny me the one place where I can safely vent my frustrations out loud. When one spends as much time as I do mind-speaking, the good old-fashioned moving of the lips is rather liberating. Well, you didn't honestly believe I come here every day just to enjoy your smelly company, did you? I must confess, I adore the sound of my own voice."

Aric beckoned to the Red Robe she had spoken to earlier. "Well, come on, we must inform Nephredom of your news. I dare not speak on your behalf this time in light of Nephredom's rampant paranoia. If what you say is not to his satisfaction, it shall be you and not I who will be thrown in the dungeon to rot."

With the sound of distant thunder, the two hundred Red Robes lifted their heads and stepped forward simultaneously.

Aric waved them back with fluttering hands, "No, no, no, not all of you! Just one. And don't forget to conceal your presence, or you'll frighten everyone off."

Aric and a Red Robe ascended by stair from the cold belly of the palace's east wing, where the Red Robes and Red Givers made their home, to the Royal Corridor, which served as the building's main artery of traffic. The stale basement air was gone, and the smell of rose petals poured in from all direction. Servants dressed in black went about their business, stopping only to bow before Aric before moving on.

Aric wore a flowing yellow gown that complemented the polished pink marble floors nicely, prompting many heads to turn as she and her invisible companion made their way to the throne. The guards saw her approach and flung open the double doors to the throne room, announcing her entrance to Nephredom as he sat upon his seat of power. "King Nephredom to receive Lady Aric!"

Stepping forward, Aric smiled and curtsied deeply. "Your Majesty, our wait is at last over. The Red Robes have restored their injured five and have retrieved the information they've gleaned from the Princess's mind."

Nephredom had been listening to the hurried whisperings of the mercenary captain, and his thoughts were not on what Aric had said. With the dark eyes of a predatory cat, Aric took careful note of the woman captain who had exercised dominion over the mercenaries and sought to do the same with the King. To Aric's frustration, her warning to the captain had fallen on deaf ears.

Indeed, the she-warrior made no pretense about her intentions. She had abandoned her stiff, leather armor in favor of soft silk. Her dull hair was covered by a lustrous hairpiece, handpicked by the King himself. Her painted face and polished manner gave little reference to the coarse, cantankerous captain of months past. Though taller and more muscular, the captain looked remarkably similar to Aric, so much that they could be mistaken as sisters.

The irony was lost to all but Aric. The woman captain had become a genuine thorn in her side, and for the first time in ages, the master she-mage felt threatened. Aric's ambition had always been to rule. She had the intellect and the charm but not the authority. That is why she needed Nephredom. But now, with his eyes forever on the bosom of the opportunistic captain, Aric found herself in the awkward position of no longer being needed by him.

The King gave a parting squeeze to the captain's hand before letting it go, turning his attention to Aric.

"The Princess," Aric repeated. "The Red Robes now know where to find her."

With widened eyes, Nephredom jerked his head wildly about. "Lower your voice, woman! Have you no sense of discretion? Those loyal to my enemies are everywhere!"

"Of course, my King," Aric whispered. "Shall we continue our conversation the usual way?"

"No, not this time. What you have to say may interest the captain, and because she possesses no Psi-telepathic ability, she would have no voice. We must talk aloud. But be sure to speak with a soft tongue."

Aric cleared her throat. "I thought we agreed that the mercenaries . . . and their captain be regulated to guard duty, my King," she said flatly. "Surely this goes beyond that."

"It does indeed," Nephredom agreed. "But the Kuaran Shields are mercenaries no longer. I have disbanded our untrustworthy army and replaced them with the Kuaran Shields. The captain has assured me that she will increase her force's number to ten thousand strong before this cycle is done." Nephredom paused to vigorously rub his temples.

The captain broke the silence, eagerly saying, "I have been appointed military advisor to the King. I will stay by his side to give him sound advice in this matter. My lieutenants will have the duty of maintaining the troops from now on."

Aric bit down on her lower lip and quietly asked, "And what of the Red Robes?"

"They will stay for now," the captain replied.

"I wasn't talking to you," Aric said with a false smile to the captain before returning to face Nephredom. "My King, I beg of you to reconsider using hired hands to represent our crest, especially hired hands from whose land we've recently ended war with."

Nephredom slowly removed trembling fingers from his head and clawed at the armrests of his throne chair before finally speaking with a weakened voice. "Question not my judgment . . . I am not to be...questioned . . ."

"Are you to waste more time," the captain snapped, "or will you not report what you have learned?"

"Very well," said Aric, "but I thought it would be best if the King heard it from its source." She clapped her hands, and the Red Robe appeared.

Startled, the captain stepped back, instinctively reaching for a sword that was not there. Nephredom stared at the Red Robe with nervous eyes that had lost their ability to see the unseen. "How safe is this creature?" the King muttered.

"The Red Robes are your own personal elect, my King," Aric replied. "Surely you remember. You've groomed each one of them yourself."

Nephredom dismissed her reassurance with a pass of his palsied hand. "Yes, that's all very well and good, but this could be a spy disguised as one of my own!"

"Well," Aric began, preparing herself for an extended explanation, "the spy would have to be a master Psi-illusionist, since the invisibility spell can be achieved only by such. All of the known Psi-illusionists are Red Robes— twenty-nine altogether, if my memory serves me well. This Red Robe is not one of the twenty-nine, however; he is merely borrowing the Psi-illusionic talent from those who are."

Shared consciousness.

"Do not speak unless asked by His Majesty!" Aric hissed to the Red Robe.

Nephredom shook his head. "I do not trust that one. Bring me a Red Robe whose hiding magic is its own!"

"As you wish, Your Majesty. At once." Aric turned to the Red Robe. "You heard our King—replace yourself! And be quick about it!"

The exchange was made, and the new Red Robe met with Nephredom's approval. He said to Aric, "Now the four of us can talk freely."

Aric revealed a devilish smirk. "Mmmmmmm. Four-person discourse. How . . . sensual."

"Speak!" Nephredom commanded, and the Red Robe promptly obeyed, his droning thoughts sounding in the minds of the four, but no others: **Nephredom, we have seen where the Princess hides, and we know with whom she hides.**

Nephredom looked pleased. "Go on," he whispered.

She dwells in the West Taren province of Argat.

"Where in Argat?" the captain demanded. "Tell us now!"

The Red Robe paused for a moment to access some shared thought, bringing to surface the secret their master had sought for so long. **An apothecary's shop that is also a shelter for unwanted girls, in the hamlet east of Argat's main city.**

Aric applauded. "Delightful! Now would you care to impart a name to match the place?"

Emawin. It is she who has hidden the Princess. Emawin is her name.

"What business would the Princess have with a keeper of an orphanage?" Nephredom asked.

"Well, she is clearly an orphan now," Aric quipped. "And she couldn't very well dwell in mansions and rest on fine linen with no money. Princess or not, she has few options. It is satisfying to see she has been reduced to taking refuge in a throwaway home."

"Your job is clear. Why do you tarry?" the captain asked, bristling with envy. "You must go to Argat and bring to us the Princess!"

"I know what my job is," Aric said curtly. "It is unlikely that the slippery Princess will still be there when we arrive."

Nephredom looked troubled. "Then how shall we find her?"

"I'm glad you asked. Red Robe, does the Princess care much for this Emawin?"

Yes.

"There, you see? Just as I suspected. The Princess always had a tendency to get overly sentimental with any riffraff that may happen to cross her path, and *that* will be the key to our success."

The captain frowned. "I don't understand. You speak over my head!"

Aric would have loved to tell the flustered warrior maiden just what she thought of that comment, but with Nephredom watching, she politely explained. "The Princess has an impressive network of informants, who can warn her the moment we arrive for her capture. But this Emawin is the perfect bait for luring the Princess to us. She will ensure that our prey wanders not far from the snare. Needless to say, I plan to stage a little surprise at the orphanage. Something that will get her attention."

"You propose an ambush," the captain concluded.

"I prefer to think of it as a little 'welcome home' party, complete with myself, and, say, ten Red Robes. The invitation will be delivered by her own unwitting informants. The occasion will involve a certain misfortune to befall a certain herbalist in Argat—tragic enough to bring our shy Princess there upon first hearing. My method? Well let's just say it's my specialty."

Nephredom nodded. "Very well, this scheme of yours, but you will take all of the Red Robes."

"*All* of the Red Robes, my King?" repeated Aric, her words drenched with disbelief. "All two hundred of them?"

"Yes," Nephredom responded placidly. "I do not want a repeat of the last failure." I suspect . . . I suspect there is more to the she-mage. Her power must not be underestimated. The Red Robes must prevail against her—they must!"

Aric looked down and away from Nephredom's piercing stare as she questioned, "Surely you don't believe, as the commoners do, that the Princess walks with a Power?"

"That is not your concern! You will take them all!"

The captain gloated. "It would seem your aide does not have confidence in your right to rule, or in my company's ability to defend this city without the Red Robes."

Aric bowed low before the King and the captain with an air of shame and humility. "I have transgressed greatly, but even in the thick of my folly, I now see the wisdom of your plan, great Nephredom. I think I know why you wish it that I go with all the Red Robes." Aric began to pace and gesture around the room, enthralled with revelation. "Yes! How silly of me to have not seen it sooner! By taking the Red Robes to Argat, it will be they who will receive the credit and the praise for bringing the Princess to justice. Don't you see?" Aric said excitedly smiling into the angry face of the captain. "And I must agree, taking all of our Red Robes makes for a far more dramatic victory."

Before the captain could say a word, Aric continued on with great enthusiasm. "By leading this soon-to-be legendary victory, I will win the hearts of the people everywhere! And most important, Nephredom, as King you will receive the highest honor of all. The stuff of songs! This is a privilege I know not that I deserve."

Aric propped herself again a wall to calm herself. "Now I understand my wise King. This assignment has too much at stake to leave to mercenaries, not to mention far too complex and dangerous. As you say, the renegade master mage is not to be underestimated. It is best left in the hands of our own."

Nephredom's scowl slowly dissolved into a look of amused suspicion "What kind of games are you playing at, Aide?"

"Games, my King?" Aric replied innocently.

The captain kneeled clumsily before Nephredom's throne. "King, I beg of you to let me and five hundred of my men lead this campaign. We have horses and will get there faster. Your aide can follow our rear flanks with the Red Robes and join us when they can."

"You seek the glory Aric speaks of?" Nephredom asked.

"We must prove to all that we are warriors worthy of the crest, and I will get favorable recognition for bringing the Princess back here."

"And what of the she-mage? She is a powerful one."

"I have yet to meet a magic-user who wasn't vulnerable to an archer's arrow. We will shoot her down."

Nephredom's gaze fell upon the captain's ample bosom, and he took her hand in his. "I do not want you leaving me now." His voice struck a rare chord of compassion. "Can you not send your men out without you? You are an advisor now, and a solider no more."

The captain shook her head. "My warriors' blood cries out for one final test. I want to personally bring to you the object of your unease, for your enemies are mine as well. Allow me to win this victory for you, and I will forever be at your side afterward."

The usurper King let her hand fall from his clawed grasp. He looked away from her, saying, "Then go. Do well with this, and I will reward you. Fail me, and I will denounce you."

The captain clenched her jaws resolutely. "I would sooner die than fail. You will not be disappointed."

The King looked to Aric. "Aide, have you nothing to say to this?"

"No, my King," Aric said mildly, fiddling with her hair. "I respectfully relent, for it is all too plain that the captain is more deserving of this . . . *reward* than I."

"Then leave me, the both of you. The leaden burden of the gate demands my attention."

"You should give that chore to the Red Robes, so that you may be free of its terrible weight." The suggestion came from the West Taren captain.

A livid expression passed over Nephredom's face; a sharp rebuke poured from his mouth like bitter wine. "Foolish woman, none but I is worthy to keep the Gate. It is my charge—my charge alone!" The moody King settled back into his throne like a weary lion too tired to maintain its roar. "Now leave me be while you still carry my favor."

This time, it was Aric's turn to gloat.

In the halls, the captain, seeking to soothe her wounded ego from its scolding, accosted Aric, demanding, "Aide, where are you off to? Looking to find another of my guards to dance with? Yes, I know about your dance partners, but none of them will tell the King about it. Is it because you do more than dance with them?"

Aric shrugged. "Dancing on the floors, dancing between the sheets—it makes little difference to me."

"Haw! Spoken like a true harlot."

"Oh?" Aric responded, unperturbed. "I rather thought that honor belonged to you—which reminds me, 'military advisor' sounds a tad drab as a title for one such as you, especially in light of your new look. How about royal mistress? Head Concubine? Strumpet-at-arms?"

"If I were wearing my sword, I would cut out your offending tongue!"

"I believe we've already trodden that path before. If you were foolish enough to give me a legitimate reason to kill you, say self-defense, I would gladly fetch your blade for you. I hope you take comfort in knowing that your . . . familiarity with the King is the sole reason you are alive to enjoy this pleasant chat."

"Your words are hollow and feeble, like the bite of a toothless dog. We both know you have lost favor with Nephredom, and when you speak of my relationship with the King, you know not the half of it."

Aric laughed in the captain's face. "As perversely interesting as it may be, I prefer to be spared any details of your bedroom romps."

"Cast your eyes on this. It will quiet your jesting tongue!" The captain showed Aric a sparkling necklace of many precious stones. "Do you know what this means?" she asked, looking for signs of jealousy in the other's eyes.

Aric grimaced at the sight of it and spoke, more as a personal observation to herself than a response. "Before the West Taren royalty was dismantled, it was customary for a king to give a necklace of great value as a gift to his prospective bride."

The captain snatched the necklace from view. "It means that I am to be Queen soon. Nephredom has asked me not to wear it until the time is right."

"Probably because he knows that announcing his betrothal to a West Taren mercenary so soon after the Queen's death would not be taken well by the people."

"They will accept it in time."

"Perhaps you should bear him a few bastards in the interim," Aric suggested in mock consideration. "It may persuade him to marry you sooner, public opinion be damned."

"You think yourself clever, don't you, Aide?"

Aric shook her head. "No, not really. If I was truly clever, it would be I who would stand to become Queen, would I not? No, I see that I have been bested, and it has caused me to accept my station in life. I am but a humble aide and would do well to serve you, Oh Queen, as best I can."

"You speak mockingly, but those words will ring true soon enough, and then we shall see how clever you look then."

Aric simply gave a nod and turned to leave.

"Hold. You never did tell me where you were going."

"If you must know all my business, I am going to see the stable hands and make sure the horses are ready for your long trip to Argat."

"Hmmph. Then I will keep you from your servant duties no longer."

Aric went about her way, leaving in time to let the tears of her fury fall undetected. As quickly as they came, they passed, and an odd smile came over her. Soon her walk sprang into full prance, and she felt alive again, drawing comfort from the fact that someone was going to die soon.

PART II

The Mettle of Queens and Mages

CHAPTER
14

The Path to Soren

"Y ou didn't tell me Ciredor was a priest over a bunch of monks!"
Rayna shouted irritably.

"Does that matter?" Keris asked in her usual nonchalant fashion.

"It matters if I don't like wasting my time—and I don't!
I mean, how can a priest and a bunch of monks help us? What is he
going to do when we meet Nephredom's army? Preach them a sermon?
Or maybe he can convince them to peacefully lay down their weapons,
hold hands, and sing hymns."

"You do not understand."

"Then make me understand! It's bad enough that you've convinced
me to reenter these horrible woods, and halfway to Soren you just *happen*
to mention that this great and powerful Ciredor you've been talking so
much about is a priest. A *priest!* How in the world are we . . ."

"Do they always fuss like that?" Quan asked Arstinax as he polished
his flute with the tail of his shirt.

For three days, Keris and Rayna had been leading the party south,
walking through the Edgewoods with Quan and Arstinax following a
short distance behind.

Arstinax nodded philosophically. "As long as I have known them, their quarrels have been ceaseless. Perhaps they are as the sun and the moon—forever in battle for dominance of the sky, yet bound by a circular cord of mutual need that can never be broken."

"Or maybe they are too much alike," Quan said.

Arstinax knitted his ebony brows skeptically. "Irel and the cloaked woman alike?"

"Mother says that when two people are too much alike, they fuss again and again, but deep inside they are the best of friends."

Arstinax laughed. "I like your mother Emawin's explanation better than my own. She is a wise woman, and you do well to quote her words."

Rayna took time from her rant to glare back at Quan. "Look at him," she said accusingly. "Casually carrying on a merry old conversation without the least bit of remorse." Rayna called out to the boy sardonically. "So tell me, Quan, how's old Sirek doing? He must have been doing pretty well to have given you a new outfit, leather boots, and a fine feathered hat! The only problem is that he forgot to give you the pots!"

Quan wisely kept quiet.

Rayna turned back to Keris as they carefully negotiated a dense patch of stinging nettles. "I still can't believe he got so much from the sale of an ink-pen!"

Keris said, "Though most West Tareners shun magic users, they do have a great lust for magic items. It is said that a master mage can make a small fortune imprinting bits of magic onto trinkets and selling them on the West Taren black market."

"Yeah, but an ink-pen?"

"What you may consider insignificant is prized by others. Quan adores his enchanted flute, and your Arstinax speaks fondly of his grandfather's talking poleax."

"A flute capable of making a dog howl is hardly enchanted," Rayna scoffed. "Ultrasonic sound-making devices are not that uncommon where I come—" Rayna paused, replaying the last part of Keris's words in her mind. "'Your Arstinax'? I think that's the second time I've heard him referred to as 'your Arstinax.'"

Keris shrugged. "He did self-appoint himself to your protection. In that sense, he is more your Arstinax than any other." She paused, curious. "Am I missing something?"

"He's not my Arstinax. He's not my anything. He's just Arstinax."

Keris arched an eyebrow. "Just Arstinax? Is that all?

"All right. A very nice Arstinax."

"Nice?"

"Attractive."

"I see."

With a flustered-faced frown, Rayna whispered back harshly, "Okay—he's sexy. Satisfied?"

Behind them, Arstinax commented on the apparent change in the two women's conversation. "Now look at them," he said, puzzled. "They're laughing and giggling like schoolgirls."

"It is good to hear Keris laughing again," Quan replied. "She has been so sad since she heard the news about the Queen's death."

"I had no strong affection for the East Taren Queen, but I like Nephredom far less. Now that he is King, I can only hope Irel will guide us well during these uncertain days."

"Rayna—the one you call Irel—she's confused most of the time. I wouldn't expect much guidance out of her. My sister, Keris, on the other hand, is a natural leader, you see. And she always has a plan. She'll know what to do."

Arstinax patted the boy on the back. "Well, then, my young friend," he declared with smiling eyes, "between the Power Irel and your wise sister, we need not fear the intentions of any evil man."

The path to Soren had taken them south, along a great stretch of dense forest known as the Edgewoods. Rayna knew from experience how hot West Taren could get, but the scorching heat of the Edgewoods exceeded tropical proportions. Steamy moisture from the neighboring West Taren Sea drifted over the woods, soaking the area in a dense soup of hot, humid air. Rayna wasn't sure which was more difficult—trudging through the heavy vegetation or merely trying to breathe. The group had left the West Taren province of Argat only three days ago, but Rayna had found them to be some of the longest days of her life.

In spite of herself, Rayna regretted leaving. It was not the town itself she missed; the crowded streets with their loud, intrusive citizens were hardly congruent with Rayna's reclusive, moody temperament. Rayna sighed in reflection. She would miss Emawin. The old woman was kind to Rayna during her stay in Argat, and her mastery of herbs had saved her life. Perhaps, she thought to herself as she stepped over an overturned tree, she would visit Emawin one more time after finding the scientists in Dosk.

Rayna mused about her time in Taren so far. She noted the distinct lack of technology: no cars, airplanes, telephones, radios, electricity—not even indoor plumbing. It was as if she had crashed through a window into the distant past. If it wasn't for the fact that everyone she had met had pointed ears, Rayna would have sworn she had traveled back in time. She decided that if anyone could make sense of how she had arrived in this strange world—and more important, how she could safely return to her own—it would be the scientists of Dosk.

At least that was her theory. According to Keris, the "scientists" of Dosk were little more than lunatic members of an obscure guild. Either way, Dosk would have to wait. She promised Keris she would first see this Ciredor of Soren. *What a waste of time,* she thought. What good would it do to appeal to a monk-priest to help fight a war—even if he was a former captain in the army? It annoyed Rayna that Keris couldn't recognize that it was a waste of time.

Rayna forced down her rising impatience. She knew it was her most terrible bane. It caused her to carelessly get an innocent man condemned to death within the Band, and it nearly got her killed when she left her companions to investigate the beast-infested city of Lamec. Perhaps that was the true reason Rayna wanted no part of any noble quest. Death seemed to follow her, and she did not want to endanger her friends any more than she already had.

Rayna looked back at Arstinax. He had been so good to her these past few days, sharing his water with her until they could find more and faithfully responding to her rather childish cries of fear at every stray spider or bee she saw. Rayna didn't like to show weakness, but when it did show, Arstinax was always there—never judging, just *there.* Rayna wondered how responsive he would be to her needs once he learned the truth—that she was partially responsible for the death of his brother. Rayna shook her head at the mess she had made. She had to get home, and the sooner she fulfilled her promise to go with Keris to see Ciredor, the sooner she could head to Dosk and begin her research.

The four travelers journeyed south until they could hear the raging torrents of the Taren River. For as long as anyone could remember, the great river had served as a natural border between East and West Taren, dividing the two lands more or less in half as it snaked past.

As they drew closer, a rushing wind assailed them, accompanied by a mist so thick that Rayna found herself choking on the blowing bits of suspended water. Through her squinted eyes, she found her companions reduced to muddy forms shifting slightly in the distorting mist.

Keris had referred to this narrow region by the river as neutral territory between the two lands—unsuitable for either side to claim. Even most brigands and highwaymen had long ago given up the idea of profiting from the situation, as the blinding mist and howling wind made it impossible for them to spot their victims with any consistency. As best as Rayna could tell in the swirling mist, no one was bold enough to have built a home here. It was truly unclaimed territory.

Shielding their faces from the wind, they pushed their way through the mist zone. With the damp and wind behind them, the party stood upon frozen ground.

"Welcome to East Taren," Keris said calmly, drawing the collars of her dark gray tunic more snugly to her face. "I hope you all have brought ample winter gear with you, for the torrid days you have been accustomed to have come to an end."

Rayna felt her bones turn numb from the sudden drop in temperature. It was if she had stepped out of a roasting oven into an icebox; she could feel the sweat on her face beginning to freeze. She frantically searched the meager contents of her traveling bag for a strap of cloth she could use to reinforce the limited warmth her scarf provided to her head. She found a flimsy piece of fabric and hurriedly put it on. "Isn't this a bit abrupt?" she complained, stunned and in awe of the new ice-covered landscape.

"I once told you that East Taren is as cold as West Taren is hot. Did you not heed my words?"

"What I heeded," Rayna growled, "was what I thought to be a description of a gradual decrease in seasonal temperature as we got deeper into East Taren territory. What reasonable person would expect to go from sweating like crazy to freezing to death just by crossing a half-mile border? Doesn't this extreme climate change strike you as just a bit strange?"

Keris ignored her questions and motioned for the party to follow her. "There is a bridge a few meters from here," she said. "It will provide easy passage for us over the river. From there we shall be well on our way to the city of Soren. All the better, since some of us have come poorly prepared for the journey and chosen to blame the weather."

The lengthy bridge arched over the river like the crook of a giant's arm. Amazed, Arstinax stood gazing at its weathered, gray stonework. It was truly a testament to the masons' skill to have built a structure to cover such a broad distance and yet remain solid, he thought with admiration.

Keris had other concerns on her mind. The clandestine Princess motioned for everyone to stop and remain still. Wordlessly she sniffed, testing the air, tuning her pointed ears with the alertness of a hare.

"Someone is waiting for us on the other end of the bridge," she said, breaking the silence.

Rayna squinted and followed Keris's gaze. Shaking her head, she replied, "I don't see anything."

"Neither do I," Arstinax agreed, focusing his one good eye ahead.

"Wait, I think I see something," Quan whispered eagerly. "A guard?"

"Yes," Keris responded calmly. "Unarmed and sitting."

"I can't see a thing," Rayna resounded glumly.

Keris unsheathed her dagger, with the same unblinking calm with which one would pull out a handkerchief. "I heard that East Taren bridge-guards were monitoring access to the city," she said, "but I thought they wouldn't bother with this old bridge, since its western end leads only to woods. We may have to dispatch this one."

"Hey, wait a minute!" Rayna interjected. "Before we do any dispatching, I want to know what's going on. Why can't we just walk up to the guard, show him our passport—or whatever it is he wants to see—and move on?"

"Nephredom has seen to it that access to the city is closely monitored. The guard will ask questions we won't be able to answer."

"I thought you said that East and West Tareners can enter each other's provinces without much trouble."

"For the most part, that is true; however, Soren is an exception. The Regent sees Ciredor as a threat to his rule. His spies fill the city to report back any hint of betrayal. His guards watch all who enter to ensure that no weapons or women get in."

"Women?"

"Yes. Soren is a city of celibate holy men and priests. No women are allowed inside."

Rayna spread her arms widely in dramatic frustration. "Now that's a nice little tidbit of information I wish you had shared with me before dragging me all the way here—especially since we've both *women*."

"I had not foreseen this obstacle." I have used this bridge to enter this region of East Taren many times before. This is the first time I've encountered a guard here. We very well cannot turn back now. We will have to kill this one. I find no pleasure in this, but it must be done."

"I can't go along with that. It's one thing to help you remove a dictator, like Nephredom, but it's another to kill someone just because he's in the wrong place at the wrong time. There's got to be another way."

"I am in agreement with Irel," Arstinax said, arms crossed. "What harm has this guard done to us to deserve such a fate? I doubt he is a soldier, being posted out this far. It is common practice to give such remote posts to civilians. He is no doubt but a poorly paid sentry guarding his assigned post, and I will not cut a man down for earning an honest coin."

"Besides," Rayna added, "as soon as Nephredom's men see that something has happened to the guard, they'll flood the city, looking for blood. We're being pursued enough as it is. We don't need to drop bread crumbs."

Keris resheathed her weapon. "You two cannot even see him, yet you defend him. Very well. We will find another way."

Quan's small body squeezed into the circle of adults, causing all heads to turn his way. "I have an idea," he suggested with a cunning smile. "We will need the spare wrappings from my pack. Just one other thing—can you all cough convincingly?"

The guard was a graying, portly man with a protruding belly that pressed tightly against the buttons of his tunic. The tunic bore the emblem of a simple sentry, confirming Arstinax's suspicions. His garments, though clean and well cared for, were showing signs of wear, and his sandals could have used restrapping in a few spots, though they showed his efforts to keep them looking new. The "post" was not deemed important enough to merit a guardhouse, so the guard sat upon the cold, stone flat of the bridge's approach. A small fire burned there, and he rubbed his hands above it, warming them against the chilled air.

The uneventful remoteness of the post had dulled the guard's sensitivities, and the sudden approach of footsteps on the bridge startled him, as it was too early for his reliever to arrive. He jumped up quickly to face the party. As stout and tough looking as the guard was, he looked like a fat dwarf before the approaching Arstinax.

"Halt!" the guard commanded, appraising the big man with apprehension. "You there, tall one. You are a West Tarener—a Kuaran, right?"

Arstinax nodded. "Yes sir, I am."

The guard's confidence was restored by the gentle voice coming from such a fearsome looking man.

"Then tell me, Kuaran," he demanded, "why have you left the hot lands of your birthplace for the cold winds of the East?"

"I could be a wandering tourist," Arstinax said with a smile.

The guard snorted and laughed. "Haw! You are a funny one, Kuaran. I think my cold and aching bones would be far happier if I was a tourist in your land! But jokes be done. I need to know your purpose here before I can allow you to pass." The sentry pointed to Quan. "For one, he's a little young to be coming out of woods to visit monks." He then pointed to Keris and Rayna, whose faces were veiled and wrapped with cloth, revealing only their eyes. "And this pair makes me more suspicious still. Why are they wrapped up so, and in such a strange fashion? Are they hiding their faces from the cold—or from something else?"

Arstinax let out a sorrowful sigh under his breath, perhaps in penitence for the string of lies he was about to tell. "I am missionary," he replied. "The boy is my son. The other two are in my charge. We wish to go to Soren for spiritual reasons. We mean no harm."

"Perhaps, but understand that I have my duties to abide." He gave Arstinax a dirty look. "You can't fool an old dog like me, son. These two are curvier than most men. I think you came from those woods intending to sneak women into the city." He winked and gave Arstinax a friendly elbow to his side. "Perhaps to help give the monks a little nighttime company, eh? Well, you know I can't let you do that. Nephredom and his lot would have my head if they found out. You look like a reasonable sort. Turn around and go back from where you came, and I'll forget the whole matter."

Keris started coughing; Rayna picked up the cue and began coughing too.

"You must let me pass," Arstinax persisted. "We don't have much time."

"I was trying to spare you a fine," the guard grumbled, grabbing his staff and a thin stack of parchment bound with string. "Have these two remove their coverings so that I may have a better look at them."

Arstinax looked hesitant, with an expressional of regret. "If that is what you want, I will do it, but I must warn you first. These two both have a terrible disease. No medicines can cure them. I have brought them to this holy province so that the prayers of the monks can bless their departing souls when they die."

"Disease?" the guard echoed.

"Yes. It starts as a tingling in the throat, then it becomes a bad cough, like the ones you hear coming from these doomed wretches. Soon it fills the chest with so much diseased fluid, one chokes dead from lack of breath."

"That sounds like a bad way to die."

"Yes. Surely you must have heard of it. It is called the Rasping Death."

Rayna and Keris let out another round of coarse hacking. The guard's apprehension found him again. "This disease—is it catching?" he asked nervously.

"Yes, very catching. That is the reason we took the Edgewoods to get to Soren. It lessened the chance of accidental exposure."

The guard anxiously fiddled with his pockets. "Is that so?"

"Indeed." Arstinax pointed to Rayna. "That one gave it to the other simply by removing the scarf about his mouth to speak."

Arstinax paused to let out a short cough and massage his throat. "Forgive my delay," he said. "I understand you must do your duty. I will loosen their coverings."

"No!" The guard shouted. "There is no need—you may pass. Just hurry along. Off you go!"

"Thank you," Arstinax said gratefully, escorting his friends safely past the guard, leaving the wide-eyed sentry behind to wonder in solitude about the tingling he now felt in his throat.

❋ ❋ ❋

The steel sky poured forth a powdering of brilliant snow, which bonded to the clothing of the travelers like crystalline paint. It made for a curious spectacle, the four adventurers resembling creatures of frost making their way through the ivory forest. The Edgewoods as they had known it was no more, for the woods had transformed on the east side of the river. It was known there, Keris explained as they marched ahead, as Soren Woods now. This southernmost tip of the Edgewoods was claimed by the monks of Soren and had been converted into the largest and most famous winter garden in Taren.

Tiny meadows abounded like cheerful oases. Amid pine needle droppings, their green blades of grass sprouted through the snow. Giant evergreen spruces stretched toward the waning sun, providing shelter for winter birds and other small woodland animals. What the party noticed most of all, however, were the flowers. A multitude of plants baring countless hardy blossoms of gold, lavender, and white, with foliage equally as colorful, sprayed the woods like strewn jewels of many colors. Colored pebbles formed a narrow path, which the party followed.

Breathtaken, Rayna had temporarily forgotten how cold she was. Instead, she wished she had time to identify each variety and pick a fragrant bouquet from the incredible bounty of blooms. How so many beautiful flowers could survive such frigid weather was a mystery to her.

The scenic path gradually widened to form a road, which proudly led to the secluded city of Soren. Keris said that Soren was nicknamed 'The City of Walls', and for good reason. The city itself was bordered on all sides by a lofty stone wall, made of stones ranging from the size of boulders, to pebbles that could fit in the palm of one's hand. From the outside, the city appeared more like a fortress than a holy city. Additionally, as they passed through the gates, they noticed that many of the buildings were built of similarly heavy stonework, and were each surrounded by a lower wall—perhaps three or four feet tall. Arstinax suspected that the same skilled masons responsible for creating the bridge leading to the city also architected these fine dwellings. *What a masterwork of achievement,* he thought.

In contrast to the splendor of their lavish gardens, the people of Soren humbly went about their business in an unremarkable way, stopping only to give a modest greeting before moving on: "Peace to you, brothers." True to Keris's word, each citizen was dressed in clerical garb, and all were men. Rayna and Keris were still well-covered with wrappings, their gender unapparent. The group made their way to the largest building that lay directly ahead.

"Ciredor will be found here," Keris said, with rare jubilance in her voice.

"It's huge," Rayna commented, tilting her head back to better see the structure's peak.

"As it should be," Keris replied. "It is here that acolytes and young clerics from all corners of Taren train their bodies and develop their minds in regard to spiritual matters. When clerical students leave this place, they are ready to teach others."

The monastery's imposing stone walls were generously dressed with a blend of ivy and climbing roses. Everything but the polished oak front door smelled heavily of perfumed buds.

"*I suppose,*" Rayna mused, deeply inhaling the brisk, aromatic air once more before following her companions inside, *if you're going to reflect on spiritual matters, this is the place to do it.*

CHAPTER
15

Nightfall

The dimming of the Great Torch had begun, for the sun was setting and the skies above grew darker and colder. If one could peer down with the watchful eyes of an eagle, one would spy, amid vast stretches of brush and frozen soil, a large campsite with scores of small fires burning fervently against the approaching night. There, a great legion of mercenary soldiers waited. Some rested their bruised bodies while others stood guard or tended to their wounded.

Even in the waning light, the frustration in the fighters' faces was plain to see. Though their bleeding cuts and shattered bones cried out for vengeance, what profit does it a man to draw his sword upon a curse? Nearly all in the camp believed the Power Irel was punishing them for deeds unspoken. They had heard how the exiled Power had escaped from her prison in the Band to punish her captors and all allied with them. Yes, they were men of hire, but it was a dangerous business to be a hire for a doomed man—even if he was a king.

Nephredom. They had all heard the stories, supported by whisperings in the hallways and hushed utterances coming from his bedroom chambers, where he slept alone. They heard a rumor that the new King saw himself as greater than Irel—so great that he would believe himself able to kill her. The mercenaries all agreed that only a madman would want to challenge a Power. And they worked for him.

What if, they wondered fretfully, Irel's vengeful wrath did not stop with Nephredom but included his retainers as well? Perhaps they had just witnessed but a taste of what was to come. They had been on their way, at full gallop, to carry out a job in Argat, when—without warning—their horses began to give out from underneath them, falling dead to the ground. The riders fell with them; a few landed on their heads and died instantly. Most of the mercenaries survived. With limping gaits and bloodied hands, they decided to set up camp to recover before resuming their journey by foot at daybreak.

It was the harm to her men's morale, rather than their flesh, that concerned the mercenary captain most. Though she herself had struck her knee when she fell from her mount, the pain of her injury did not leave her unmindful to the fears rising around her. She knew that the loss of the horses and the strange manner of it had eroded much of their courage. Tomorrow, she would strengthen their confidence with a speech to stir their souls again. For the sake of her plans, she would promise them fame, more gold, whatever it required to renew their willingness a while longer.

The captain rested solemnly inside a large tent, in the center of the camp. A weathered helm hid her ebony locks, and hardened leather armor covered her pleasing form, yet there was no mistaking her beauty. It was that beauty which spared her life at birth, when her father told her mother he would allow only his male children to live. Her beauty caused her father never to suspect that she would eventually kill him to claim the family business, or turn a pitiful training camp into one of the largest mercenary companies in Taren. Her beauty additionally made it easy to draw out and remove envious female members, who would betray her out of spite, and to reveal weakness in her male members, who could be compromised with a kiss.

Now, this beauty stood on the eve of her greatest conquest. When the eccentric East Taren King, Nephredom, hired her men to be his personal guards, she could see that he was taken by her beauty. Carefully, she reached under the shell of her armor and lifted from her bosom a sparking necklace bearing more stones than could be counted at a glance. It was a necklace of betrothal, and the King had given it to her.

The captain's thoughts fell on Nephredom's aide and sorceress, Aric. The witch tried to frighten her away but could not. With her recent failures to find the Princess as well her immodest ways, Aric had lost much favor with the King. The mercenary leader fondly cradled her jeweled prize in the cradle of her hand. It was for the King to decide whom he would marry. Nothing Aric could do would change that. She would be Queen.

She sat up in her makeshift cot of straw, then forced herself to stand. Her swollen knee jerked slightly but held. A *queen must stand tall and proud*, she thought, ignoring the pain; she laughed out loud in spite of her discomfort. No one would have foreseen that she, a woman of humble birth and only a modest education, would one day become a Queen. Even Aric, with all her grace and cultured words, could not prevent her from stealing the key to the King's heart.

Only one task remained before the deal was done—the detail of snaring for the King the renegade Princess and the mage who accompanied her. A trap would be set to lure the disposed Princess to Argat. Royalty though she may be, she was unpopular with her people and carried a tall bounty on her head. The reward from that alone would more than squelch her men's jitters, for it would make for a handsome bonus to them all. The last rays of daylight passed away and the captain lit a small lantern, setting it on the ground. Nightfall had come.

It would not be hard, she thought, to catch a slippery princess and eliminate one troublesome mage. Aric and the Red Robes had botched the job because they relied on magic instead of steel. A blade to the gullet cannot be dispelled; an arrow to the heart cannot be warded off. The she-mage who protected the Princess was dangerous only if allowed to be, she mused. Her archers will shoot the magic user down at first sight, the captain resolved, her eyes fixed on the lantern's flame. With the Princess delivered and the mage dead, the King would be so pleased as to end the betrothal and marry her at once.

Doing her best to keep her injured leg steady, she clumsily strode around the lantern in tight circles, with the most regal gait she could manage. She imagined, with dark pride, how lovely she would look with her head decorated with the dead Queen's crown.

"Are you drunk, or just naturally awkward?" The disembodied voice sounded behind her.

The mercenary turned to face the voice quickly and nearly fell.

"My, my, my!" the amused voice chirped. "Captain, you must learn to take better care of yourself. Your leg doesn't look well." A moment of mischievous silence passed. "How was it harmed, I wonder?"

"I demand you reveal yourself!" the captain shouted.

From the voice's source, the air shimmered faintly and a thin outline of gray light in the shape of a woman formed. In seconds, the outline became less sharp and defined, gradually transferring its detail inward to reveal the master mage, Aric. She dressed in loose golden robes of satin, bearing the royal crest of Jerel. A wide brush graced the helm she wore, like a golden fan.

"You!" the captain cried accusingly. "You were told to follow our rear flank!"

Aric shrugged with a false air of innocence. "And follow you we did, until you gave us no more ground in which to follow. So we decided to pay you and your brave little battle-merchants a concerned visit."

Aric swaggered to the opposite side of the tent and sat down on the ground, crossing her legs and arms as she faced the befuddled captain. "May I ask why you are not riding with the wind at this very moment, in haste to reach Argat and claim credit for finding the Princess?"

The mercenary captain eyed Aric suspiciously. She didn't trust the master mage, and her unannounced presence at this time bothered her. Her first thought was to seize her sword, which lay under her cot, but discipline kept her still. "Our horses gave out from under us in full gallop. They dropped dead for no reason," she responded curtly.

Aric clapped her hands cheerfully as if the captain had told a clever joke. "On the contrary," she chuckled. "They dropped dead for a *very good* reason." Her face suddenly grew cold and serious. "You see, I had them all poisoned." Aric's petite, lithe frame effortlessly unfolded and stood erect as she sprang to her feet. She began skipping around the captain, clicking her tongue rhythmically to imitate the sound of horse hoofs on cobblestones. "It was a slow-acting kind. Surely you know the sort—one moment you're a happy and gay little steed, trotting and frolicking along under saddle without a care—and the next moment you're dead. Food for the maggots." Aric stopped in front of the captain, frowning. "Sad, isn't it? Especially because horses are such a rarity these days."

The captain stared incredulously at Aric, her words strained through clenched teeth. "You dare stand there and gloat about your crime? When word of your treachery reaches Nephredom's ears, your career and your life will be forfeit!"

"Scolding words from someone who can barely stand, but I'm touched by your concern for my life and career. But never you mind about Nephredom and his ears. You and I have business here and now to attend to."

"I have no business with you," the captain sneered contemptuously.

"I'm inclined to disagree. You see, your—how shall I put it—personal involvement with the King has weakened the faith of those you command. More important, it has made you quite a few enemies in the court."

"Like you?"

Aric grinned, baring pointed teeth. "Especially me."

"I do not fear you, witch, or any other petty member of the court. The King sanctions my actions, and it is he who holds the power of the Tarens in his hand."

"Is that so?" Aric questioned, sounding genuinely surprised. "And all this time I thought it was I who held such power."

The captain scoffed. "You? And what powers do you possess, other than that of angering kings and whoring with my hirelings?"

Aric snapped her fingers excitedly. "I was hoping you would ask that." With another snap of her fingers, three Red Robes shimmered into view. They waited wordlessly near Aric, blocking all chance of escape from the tent.

Taken aback, the captain struggled not to look at or even think of her sword—the Psi-telepathic witch and the Red Robes could read minds. Instead she kept her eye on the mage while slowly, with cautious small steps, backing her way to the straw cot, where her weapon was hidden.

Startled cries of alarmed mercenaries sounded outside the tent.

"The mercenaries can see the Red Robes now," Aric continued. "There are nearly two hundred Red Robes scattered throughout the camp. Your men are seeing them *everywhere*." Aric leaned over in the captain's direction with a glint of sly malice in her eyes. "Now ready yourself for this. Here comes the truly fun part!" She closed her eyes and clasped her hands before her, smiling as if in some meditative trance.

The cries from outside turned from yells to screams as the killing began. The captain's eyes shifted to the exit of the tent, and she peered past her captors into the night. She could see dark figures darting past, followed by even darker ones that seemed to float rather than run. Sounds of chaos echoed from all directions—tables of crockery being overturned, weapons being drawn, clothing being ripped apart. More screams.

"Stay here," a voice sounded nearby, "and fend off as many of those things as you can! I must go and see to our captain's safe—" The voice was suddenly replaced by a soul-wrenching scream, joining countless others in the camp.

The captain edged her way nearly at the cot, apparently without the Red Robes noticing. It was impossible to know for sure because their crimson hoods shadowed their faces so well.

Aric suddenly opened her eyes and let out a sadistic howl of laughter. "What's this? Our great captain of more than five hundred strong, brave men is able to compel only a single one to attempt her rescue?"

The captain clinched her jaw in a resolute grimace and calmly recited her company's oath:

> We are the Kuaran Shields.
> We are the soldiers of hire who go where others fear to tread.
> We march into battle for those who care little of our sacrifices.
> We die for those who will never morn our deaths.
> And so we lend our sword not for the cause's sake, but for our own.
> With our presence we swear might, but never allegiance.
> With our blood we swear battle, but never peace.
> With our hearts we swear respect, but never love.

Aric put on an exaggerated knit-browed expression, mocking with a throaty voice, "and with our mouths we swear foul breath but never witty conversation!" Spreading her arms wide, Aric gave herself a low bow. "Your guild's pledge sounded a bit lonely, Captain," she said. "Now I wonder if it was that very loneliness that drove you into the arms of a wealthy king—or was it avarice? I know! It was profound loneliness caused by avarice! The more riches you saw, the more you longed for their company. I'm not so blind that I cannot see your ambition to marry a king. For a start, it would make you the wealthiest woman in Taren. I must admit, it appears that you indeed hold the key to Nephredom's heart."

Aric took in a deep breath and let it out slowly, drawing deep satisfaction as the air escaped through her pursed lips, like the sound of fall wind. "With that key, you would open wide the vaults of the royal coffers, so that the hoarded gold might spill forth and cover you whole!"

The captain simply stared at Aric. "Your rebukes mean nothing to me, and my reasons for wanting to marry the King are no business of yours. My betrothal to the King would not be if the King did not wish it."

Aric forced a short, dry laugh. "And you made sure that he would wish it, didn't you, my dear? When I first met you, looked like a true warrior, and I could respect that, for that is what you claimed yourself to be. However, recently you have shown yourself to be no better than any other woman hoping to become well off through matrimony. Look at you. Even in armor, it is plain to see you've gotten yourself all tarted up in hopes of catching the biggest fish in the sea."

"It is no fault of mine if the King no longer cares for your affections!"

"What's the matter, dear Captain? I sense none of the boastful arrogance I noted the last time we spoke. Now you seem oddly defensive—one might even go as far as to say *fearful*. I wonder what could have possibly brought that on?"

The wails of death from outside continued, and Aric sighed thoughtfully. "I must confess," she said in a soft voice, "I underestimated you when you first came to work for the King. I thought you to be a thick-witted barbarian with no mind for politics. I soon realized that in place of polished intellect, fate had endowed you with a sort of raw cunning."

Aric approached the captain and lifted a hand to the level of her forehead. "May I?" she asked. Without waiting for an answer, Aric gently removed the captain's helm to get a better look at her distressed face. "I suppose the gossip is true. We do look very much alike—in face, if not in body. Perhaps we think alike as well."

The captain gazed back bitterly. "My mind is nothing like yours."

"Well, that's certainly true enough, but I think you will inevitably come to the conclusion that we do share some common ground. Did you not slay your own father so that you would have his business? Granted, he did treat you and your mother like dogs and deserved to die like one, but—"

"Stay out of my head, witch!"

"Stay out? Why, I never left it in the first place! The duty Nephredom charged you with—do you know why he wants the Princess?"

"Everyone knows she murdered her brother and fled to avoid punishment."

"Hmmmmm. Truth be told, *I* murdered her brother. I killed him because Nephredom told me to. The unfortunate Princess is merely fodder to the people seeking what they think to be justice. With the Prince's blood, I paved the way for Nephredom and eventually myself to claim the throne." Aric wrinkled her nose disdainfully, as if she had caught wind of a nasty smell. "You can image my displeasure when my investment became . . . threatened."

"We can share the power," the captain offered.

"Pardon?"

"The throne. We can share it. You are a powerful mage, and I have the trust of the King. When I am made Queen, we can overtake Nephredom and rule the Tarens jointly."

Aric clapped gleefully. "We have scarcely gone half a day's journey from the throne of the king you hope to marry, and already you are prepared to change employers! I applaud you, for you are a mercenary heart and soul! Now you must forgive my suspicion, but I must question if your offer is born of true ruthlessness or mere desperation."

Aric shook her head decidedly, then grinned cruelly. "No, I'm afraid that arrangement just wouldn't do, especially since we both know you would betray me at the first chance, as I would you. More important, Cattana—I simply don't like you."

"You know my name!"

"Of course I do. I have never understood why so many West Tareners obsess about keeping their name a secret."

"Only to those they don't trust."

"In your case, I suppose that would be everybody."

"One's name is the key to their inner being."

"Let me guess. That poetic little morsel of Kuaran wisdom was passed down through the ages by some primitive tribe of yours, was it not?"

The captain could feel the heel of her foot reach the cot, but she dared not make a grab for her sword now. If she stalled until just the right time, she could grab her sword and smite all four of them—giving each one a fast swipe of her blade. She forced herself to remain calm, focusing her thoughts away from the weapon and instead on the idle conversation.

"You know nothing of my tribe's ways," she said.

They heard the brief thud of someone falling outside the tent, begging for mercy. "Please, I have family! I only did this for them. I didn't mean to anger—No!" The scream echoed in the night.

Aric stared at the flickering lantern at her feet with newfound fascination. Her eyes returned to Cattana, and she asked, "Do you play chess, Captain?"

The mercenary leader scoffed, "No, I do not. It is a game for the idle. I am a warrior of action. I do not waste time on games—especially not ones played while sitting."

"Spoken like a true Kuaran. Pity, though. I think you would appreciate the game if you understood its rules. You see, if one becomes careless—as I regrettably have—and let the game go on too long, a pawn of one's opponent can advance up the board and eventually become Queen."

"You never change, Aric," Cattana hissed back with contempt. "You babble in riddles and expect those who hear your nonsense to understand."

Aric smiled. "Quite right. Quite right, indeed." She began to whisper. The horrid sounds of dying that poured into the tent had diminished, so it was easy to hear her faint voice. "I will speak in a way you can understand: You are a petty player in a game far too big for you. Your small, limited mind can't begin to comprehend the events that are unfolding before you. No matter. I think it's time we retired your piece, little pawn. I fear you shan't be Queen after all, for this night . . . you die."

Cattana already had her sword in her hand, and was drawing it near the master mage's throat, when the muscles of her arm no longer heeded her commands. Though she strained to get her blade to complete its mission, she instead found her weapon against her throat, by her own hand. The blade pressed harder against her taut skin until she could feel the wetness of blood creeping down her neck. Apart from her eyes, Cattana found she could not move at all; it was if her body was not her own.

"No need to worry," Aric said reassuringly. "I won't allow you to die that way. That would be far too neat a demise for the likes of you." Aric frowned disapprovingly at the frozen captain. "Do you have any idea the kind of death you've earned yourself, my dear Captain?" Aric's icy eyes narrowed to slits, growing colder still. "*Do you?*"

Cattana could feel the hilt of her blade, clutched in her hand, becoming warm and supple to the touch. She watched aghast as the sword began to writhe and stretch into a silvery serpent of steel. Slithering out of her hand, it fell to the ground with a dull metallic clang. The squirming thing stretched and lengthened further still, until the coiled mass resembled a vine. It crept up the captain's leg in a slow, fluid, spiraling fashion, squeezing tightly as it went.

Cattana stood in horror and anguish, witnessing herself being laced and bound through magic. The metal held her firm while it sliced into her leather armor, biting deeply against her flesh. Like a statue, she toppled, crushing the small lantern and extinguishing its flame with her chest. The tent became nearly pitch black, save a faint shine of magic that surrounded the captain like glowing death.

Her stricken body would not permit her even a cry of pain for her suffering. She could only stare miserably as her own blade made its way to her throat.

"Oh my, I almost forgot!" Aric exclaimed. She bent over and carefully unclasped the necklace of betrothal from the mercenary captain's neck, just as the gleaming finger of twisting blade began to encircle her throat.

"I can be so forgetful sometimes," the mage explained apologetically. "You shan't be needing this anymore, and it would be an absolute shame to let such a beautiful trinket go to waste, don't you agree? Forgetful, forgetful." Aric paused in thought and added, looking straight into Cattana's dying eyes, "Well, I suppose I shouldn't be so hard on myself— I should count myself fortunate, really. Mind you, I do occasionally lose my head in a spell of forgetfulness, but *you*, my dear, are about to lose your head altogether!"

Aric turned her attention to the Red Robe nearest her. "Yes? You have something to say?"

The Red Robe quivered slightly and spoke with words not of breath and sound, but of thought: **Nephredom will not be pleased.**

Aric yawned dispassionately as she slipped on her newly acquired necklace. "Nephredom has more serious things to worry about than lost brides-to-be. He is in no condition to challenge me, or my actions. In his precious role as Keeper of the Gate, he has allowed himself to become weak. The strain of it has taken its toll on his power and his mind. As it stands, he needs me more than I need him."

Are we to continue to Argat?

Aric paused in consideration, then answered. "Oh, why not? It will be fun. I couldn't care less about the Princess at this point, but this master mage protector of hers has piqued my interest. Have you discovered her name? I mean her *true* name, not 'Irel of the Band.'"

Yes. As you ordered, we interrogated several villagers where we last encountered the mage. One patron at the local tavern recalled overhearing her true name. We plucked it from his mind before he died.

"Well? Don't keep me in suspense! What is it?"

She is called Rayna of Nightwind.

"Impressive name, the name of a worthy enemy. If our good captain was right, I now hold the key to Rayna of Nightwind's inner being, whatever that means. I'm desperately curious to see what lies behind the door this key opens. Yes, we will go to Argat as planned. Nephredom will have his damnable Princess, and I will get an opportunity to test the mettle of a mage powerful enough to have nearly destroyed five Red Robes—powerful enough to have been mistaken for a Power." Aric paced excitedly around the tent. "Besides, I went through the trouble of planning the ambush, so we might as well carry it out. I think we will prepare a warm reception for the Princess and her mage. A *very* warm reception."

She headed for the exit, motioning for the Red Robes to follow. "Come along, poke-alongs. All the horses in the camp are dead, so you must walk, while I take turns riding on your backs. I told you this would be fun!" As they left the tent, Aric looked back at the body of the fallen mercenary, then uttered a single word: "Checkmate."

CHAPTER
16

Crossroads

Rayna and the rest of the party stood at the entrance of a large room, whose walls curved gently around them, like the interior of a great clay pot. The room was nearly devoid of furnishings, with only a few rectangular cushions arranged in the center. A series of three frescos, with life-like detail, covered the wall immediately opposite them. The first depicted a great battle scene, with robed monks hurling balls of blue light at leather-armored barbarians bearing long swords. The barbarians were hairy, hunched men with scowling expressions and gaping mouths; they appeared to be shouting silent war cries at their enemies. The monks were sorely outnumbered, and many of them suffered from arrow wounds. The artist nevertheless portrayed them as confident, noble-faced defenders against the apparently wild marauders.

The next painting depicted a middle-aged woman sitting on an oversized throne. In one hand she held a sealed scroll; her other hand stretched out in a gesture of goodwill. Streaks of pale gray rolled down each side of her long dark hair in perfect symmetry, stopping at her narrow shoulders. Her set jaws and a piercing stare, an expression of determination, looked almost angry, as if she were bracing herself for something thoroughly unpleasant but equally necessary. Of the three frescos, this was the only one with a title. Under the portrait were the words, "Our Beloved Queen."

The last fresco pictured only a simple garden, with an assortment of wildflowers and leaf-heavy trees near a small stream. It was the kind of art, though plainly modest, that could be studied for years and never grow stale in its tranquil beauty. Rayna found the fresco arrangement interesting: A queen flanked by war and peace.

A lone monk, on his hands and knees, scoured the stone facing of a large curved fireplace that graced the wall to their left. Though he dipped his cloth in a bucket filled with steaming water, not a drop did he spill, nor a sound did his washing make. He had been so quiet, Rayna hadn't noticed him at first. He slowly lifted his head, took note of the party, and then left the room without a word.

Moments later, another monk entered the foyer, dressed in burlap-like robes and carrying a simple wooden staff. Like the other monk before him, his head and chin were shaved smooth, making it difficult for Rayna to discern his age, but his easy smile made him appear relatively young. He was a tall man, nearly as tall as Arstinax, but with a thinner build. The bones in his face were angular and pronounced, stopping just short of making him appear gaunt. His probing eyes, as keen as his dark olive face, were a shade of deep brown; they wore their laugh lines proudly as proof that humor was no stranger to them. His smile was bright and sincere; it complimented his already handsome appearance. As he approached the party, he carried himself with the authority of a man used to leadership. Rayna correctly surmised that this must be Ciredor.

Ciredor greeted them warmly, his eyes focused mostly on Keris. "Now this is a grand occasion! It's not often one is reunited with an old friend—and I presume with friends of her own?"

Keris stepped forward to meet Ciredor, and they briefly exchanged understanding gazes. "These," Keris introduced, "are my companions, whom I trust without fail. This is Quan, my orphan brother; Arstinax, an able warrior and wise friend . . ."

Keris hesitated, searching for the right words. "And this is Rayna Powell. She hails from a mysterious region called Nightwind, and it is to her that I owe my life."

Ciredor raised an eyebrow of surprise, looking at Rayna in a new light. He said, "Saving the life of someone so dear to me has earned you my eternal gratitude. Keris is a most capable soul, and if she owes her life to another . . . the threat must have been a considerable one." Ciredor's and Keris's eyes met with an unspoken agreement to discuss the matter in greater detail later, in private.

Ciredor clasped his hands, exclaiming, "Well, enough of that glum business! Tell me, Rayna Powell of Nightwind, how do you fare this day?"

Rayna suppressed a shiver, muttering cheerlessly, "Cold."

"Shocking!" Ciredor replied jokingly. "I've lived in this ice hut so long I forget that there are some, upon coming in from the cold, who actually expect to get warm!" Ciredor motioned to a passing monk. "Quickly! Stoke the fire and make it twice as hot—no, *thrice* as hot. One of our guests is uncomfortable, and I will not have uncomfortable guests in this place!"

The monk bowed before Ciredor and set to work.

Rayna realized how rude she must have sounded and added, "It's not your fault. I was poorly prepared for this weather."

Ciredor chuckled. "I doubt that anyone can truly be prepared for East Taren weather—including East Tareners!" He cast his smiling eyes on Arstinax. "Now here's a fine fellow from the West, though I can see from the looks of you, my friend, that the chill would hardly bother your sturdy Kuaran frame!"

Arstinax permitted himself a modest smile and lowered his head with a single, polite nod. "You are an astute man," he replied, "for it was not announced from which province I hail."

"Ah, but your broad shoulders and chest did the announcing for you, my friend! Now, if I am truly as astute as you flatter me to be, then I would also guess that you are eager to work and earn your keep while here, yes?"

Arstinax was impressed. "Indeed I am. It is the Kuaran way to keep oneself busy with meaningful work. In fact, in my land, idleness is a crime."

"Then say no more. Although legally, idleness is not a crime in Soren, most of the holy brothers here view it as an outright sin, so you are in good company." Ciredor returned his attention to the monk he had beckoned before, calling out to him as he stoked the fire, "When you are done, and once our guests have eaten and settled in, you will show him all of the chores that have yet to be done. This is not something we normally share with guests, but one man's toil is another man's joy. We can learn much from a man such as this. Give him all the work he desires, for you will be his Hand."

The monk nodded and bowed silently, first to Ciredor, then to Arstinax.

Ciredor patted Arstinax on the back with a heavy-handed thump. "Worry not, we will do our best to keep you busy every day you are here. Enjoy your labors."

"Hand?" Rayna wondered out loud. She was still mulling over the peculiar designation Ciredor assigned the monk.

Ciredor turned his attention to Rayna, with a look of amused hesitation on his face, like someone waiting to hear the funny answer to a riddle. His expression quickly became apologetic after seeing that Rayna wasn't joking. "I'm sorry," he said. "I thought everyone knew. It is customary for temples to assign a monk to any honored guest who visits after a long journey. The monk acts as humble servant, guide, and perhaps teacher for the length of the visitor's stay. No task would be too menial, no question too small. Originally, many years past, this sacred title was 'The Hand of Friendship,' which in time was shortened to simply "Hand." Don't worry, we will assign one to you as well, of course."

Rayna couldn't think of anything more unappealing than the thought of having someone following her around, hovering near her shoulder like an ingratiating chaperon. All she really wanted after her tiresome trek halfway across the continent was a decent meal, a bath, and a nice quiet room, preferably with some reading material to help her wait out her stay while Keris begged Ciredor for military support. This time Rayna was careful to watch her tone. As politely as she could, she stated "No, thank you, I don't need a Hand."

The monk stopped stoking the fire and turned to stare at Rayna. Even Ciredor found the humor in his voice faltering, as he asked, puzzled, "Forgive me, are you saying that you are refusing a Hand?"

The room was awash in silence, awaiting Rayna's reply. Before Rayna could confirm her answer, Keris cut in, "No."

Rayna shouted back, in disbelief at Keris's audacity. "I can answer for myself, thank you! What I was going to say was that I don't want—"

Keris cut in again, growling with a smile pasted on her face. "Your Reverence to think that she has committed the grave offense of rejecting a Hand. Rayna fully knows what a great insult that would be."

Rayna's thoughts halted in mid-track, reflecting on what Keris had just said. *Grave offense? Insult?*

"In fact," Keris continued, "she was telling me before we arrived how she was looking forward to receiving her Hand, for it would help her learn more about Soren ways and traditions."

"I did?" Rayna whimpered sheepishly.

"Rayna is a seeker of knowledge—so much so, I have sworn to her on my word that I would accompany her to Dosk once my affairs here have ended."

"Dosk is said to be the seat of learning and the mecca of scholars," Ciredor said, rubbing his smooth chin.

"Indeed," Keris agreed. "Rayna is a scholar of countless interests. She seeks answers to many questions."

Ciredor smiled, pleased. "Then perhaps fate has brought you here to find some of the answers you seek. Perhaps it is here that you will receive clarity. The people of Soren have always considered those seeking clarity to be divinely inspired. We have a series of scrolls in our temple written entirely by my Second, Orin." Ciredor motioned briefly to a man sitting diagonally to Rayna, on her right. "He has a gift for words, and his poetry is quite good. Though it's not quite scripture, I feel compelled to recite a few verses from one his poems." With the vocal control of a seasoned speaker, the priest's voice took on just the right pitch and tone.

> There is a robber that comes to steal one's peace.
> Enlightenment dies amidst angst and fear.
> Troubles will come to despair the heart
> And the path of confusion draws ever near.
> If anyone seeks deliverance from this path,
> May they be forever blessed.
> And if anyone helps them find such clarity,
> May they also be forever blessed.

Ciredor mulled over the words he had just spoken, as if hearing them for the first time. When he spoke again, it was with an air of inspired excitement. "Please allow me to assign you two Hands. The road to clarity is best traveled when the mind and body are in harmony. With that said, one of your Hands will be your *Hand of Mind*. He will introduce you to our library and the knowledge it contains. He will also teach you the history of Soren, the ways of the temple, and anything else within in our power to explain."

"I get to have *two* Hands?" Rayna repeated, stunned.

"Please don't thank me. It is my pleasure. A hunger for understanding should always be rewarded." Ciredor gestured to Rayna's weapon. "I see you possess a staff." The other Hand will be your *Hand of Body*. He will teach you in the art of staff fighting as practiced in Soren—that is, assuming you are not already a master of the staff."

"She is far from such," Keris quipped with her back turned as she studied the fresco of the garden. "I am a personal witness to that."

Ciredor coughed an amused laugh, and then said with a good-natured grin, "Then I suggest you get plenty of rest tonight, Rayna Powell of Nightwind. Our staff master believes in long sparring sessions and . . . well, he hasn't worked recently with novices, so he may seem somewhat demanding to an outsider. But to quote the Kuaran people: 'Work brings forth strength, and strength brings forth work', eh?"

Rayna didn't like the sound of that but decided not to inquire further, lest she commit another faux pas.

✷ ✷ ✷

That evening, they had dinner in the great hall. As the first course was served, all the party had been seated except one.

"Where's Quan?" Keris asked, noting his absence with casual calm.

"It was decided that the young boy needed another bath—this time with supervision," Ciredor replied.

"His Hand?" Rayna asked, curious.

"No. Those as young as the boy are rarely assigned a Hand. Instead, he has a keeper to see to it that he is watched after and instructed on proper behavior for a monastery, and that his basic needs are met."

Rayna added, "In this case, hygiene."

Ciredor found himself unable to hold back a chuckle and laughed. "Apparently, his keeper, Levit, detected—in his words—'an odor of unpleasant character.'"

The others at the table began laughing as well. The warm, bright sound of gaiety filled the great hall.

"Isn't Levit a Psi-olfactic?" Keris inquired, breaking the flow of laughter so that it diminished to a restrained chuckle.

"Yes," Ciredor answered, stifling another laugh, "and sometimes he's a bit oversensitive to unfamiliar smells."

The table spread was modest in variety but generous in portions. Rayna could tell by the lingering stares of the attending monks that it was not often they served such feasts. She found the food to be filling and tasty; it was a far cry from the root bulbs and raw nuts that provided the majority of her diet while crossing the Edgewoods. There was only one kind of meat, roast quail, but there was plenty of it to go around. The dark, grainy breads possessed a satisfyingly earthy taste. There was also an abundance of leafy vegetables, which Ciredor used to roll beans and bits of meat.

Several bowls contained fruits Rayna could not readily identify. Feeling bold, she decided to sample each one. The first looked like a lopsided apple and tasted like a ripe banana. Another resembled kiwi fruit, but with her eyes closed, Rayna would have sworn she was eating watermelon. Rayna next took a small bite from a small, cone-shaped, freckled fruit; it tasted like no fruit she had before.

Seeing the pleased look on her face, Ciredor commented, "I see you find the moodberry to your liking."

Rayna nodded. "This is so sweet. It's delicious."

Those seated at the table began smiling to themselves; Rayna stared suspiciously at the fruit and put it back on her plate, inquiring, "What?"

"No, no, there's nothing wrong," Ciredor assured her. "Finish your fruit. It is only a superstition, and a woman such as yourself would hardly have need to hear such a thing."

Ciredor let Rayna fume in red-faced exasperation for a short while before shrugging playfully. "Well . . . if you insist, legend has it that moodberries have magical properties, and one's inner feelings are reflected in how the fruit tastes on the tongue. To most, the fruit is juicy but rather bland. If you have harmed an innocent, it is said that the fruit will taste salty; if spurned by a lover, bitter; if untrue to oneself, sour . . ." Ciredor paused, smiling broadly. "And if the fruit tastes sweet, it is said that one is in love but does not yet admit it."

The room softened with silence, in anticipation of some sort of confession. Rayna forced herself not to look at anyone in the room— especially Arstinax. She helped herself to more food and began chewing, her eyes focused on her plate.

After a brief moment of awkward suspense, the room once again filled with the hum of small talk.

One of the monks who sat near Ciredor eyed Rayna with fascination. "Tell me, Rayna Powell," he said, his voice like soft brass, "I have traveled many places in both East and West Taren, and yet I have never heard of the land you call Nightwind."

"It's a very small land," Rayna answered, then continued with her eating.

"Come now, Orin," Ciredor cautioned. "It is plain to see that Rayna prefers a private life. Let us not bother her with unwanted questions about herself."

At that moment, Quan, accompanied by a short, frowning monk, entered the dining hall. "Forgive the intrusion, Your Reverence," the monk apologized. "The boy insisted on seeing his sister now."

"It's no intrusion, Levit." Ciredor added, with a straight face, "I understand the child was, um, less than satisfactory as far as cleanliness goes?"

Levit wrinkled his nose vigorously, as if he had caught whiff of a rather nasty odor. "Indeed!" he declared passionately. "I had no choice but to reacquaint the lad with soap and water! He was in dire need of a thorough cleaning—behind the ears especially!"

Ciredor sniffed. "And from the smell of things, it looks like you have succeeded."

Quan wiggled free of Levit's grasp and ran to his sister.

Keris sniffed him. "You smell like—" she paused to sniff him again. "*Roses.*"

"Heavy rose oil," Levit explained proudly. "I save it for my foulest cleaning jobs. I added some to his bathwater."

"I hate this place," Quan whispered to Keris.

"I think you smell very nice, Quan," Rayna offered.

Quan glared at her. "Rose scent is for girls!"

"Nonsense," Levit said, wrinkling his nose. "The fragrant aroma of the rose is to be enjoyed by all. Consider yourself fortunate. Heavy rose oil is very expensive. The temple can afford only a few small vials at a time."

"Has the boy eaten?" Keris asked, changing the subject.

"Yes. I fed him in the kitchen. He eats enough for two, I've noticed."

"You have been most kind, caring after Quan."

The compliment softened Levit's rumbled face. "That is kind of you to say. It has been my experience that the young require a very a firm hand."

Keris glanced momentarily at Quan before returning her gaze to her food. "You will go with Brother Levit now and complain no more. I am sure he has duties for you to complete."

Quan dropped to his knees, pleading, "I want to stay here! He does nothing but talk about smells and cleaning things—it's maddening!"

Keris ignored his dramatics, taking another mouthful of food. "Quan, please do as you were told."

Quan turned a desperate plea to Ciredor, pouting sorrowfully, "Am I not a guest in this house?"

"Enough of this foolishness, Quan," Keris told him sternly. "I will not take you with me anywhere else if you continue to act this way."

"I shall never want to go anywhere else if I keep smelling like this," Quan grumbled. Levit whisked him away, lecturing, "A clean body reflects clean thoughts. Clean thoughts reflect a clean heart. A clean heat reflects a clean soul. A clean soul . . ." His voice faded as the two left the great hall.

The remainder of the meal was uneventful, save for the occasional scrutiny of the monk called Orin. His stony stares made Rayna feel uncomfortable. Equally annoying was how cleverly he managed to stare at her when Arstinax and the others weren't looking. As other monks began clearing the table, she could still feel the bony finger of his narrow gaze poking her from the side. Angrily, she turned and stared back at him furiously, teeth clenched. Though no words were exchanged, Orin shuddered and sank back in his seat, sharply turning his head from Rayna's direction as if her glare had burned him.

Rayna sighed silently in relief. He had finally taken the hint. Normally Rayna may have been somewhat flattered by such attention, because men never seemed to notice her before she arrived in Taren, but being the focus of his steel-gray eyes was unsettling, as if he was looking through her rather than at her. Creepy.

❋ ❋ ❋

Orin paused for moment outside the Meditation Room. Ciredor had asked to meet him there for a private meeting. Keris and her companions had arrived two weeks earlier, and he could feel a sense of urgency in the air regarding what to do about them. Orin, having collected his thoughts, took a deep breath and opened the door.

Ciredor was sitting on the bare, wooden cross-legged and facing the door. He looked at Orin and smiled. "I suppose you know why I called you here," he suggested in his characteristically amused tone of voice.

"Yes," Orin replied simply. He waited.

"Well, before we begin that, I'd rather we start off with a lighter concern. Please, join me." Ciredor motioned to a spot on the floor across from him

Orin sat down on the floor, avoiding eye contact, instead staring over Ciredor's shoulder.

"Am I so unsightly that you cannot even look at me? I must remember to come better groomed next time." He smiled slightly.

Orin waited, saying nothing.

Ciredor observed him closely, noting the lines of worry between his thin eyebrows, the sharp definition of his jaw line, and the absolute seriousness of expression. Ciredor sighed. Despite the odds, he had hoped for a laugh or a chuckle, but the man was hopelessly devoid of humor.

Ciredor did not hold that against him. Orin had always been that way, even when they were men of the battlefield rather than of the cloth. Ciredor clapped his hands sharply in fast procession, a signal that a lower-ranking monk was free to be at ease. Orin bowed his head once and turned to face the high priest with an unwavering gaze.

"Tell me," Ciredor requested, "did you hear from any of the others on how they thought my sermon went?"

"Brother Ferrel thought that your comparison of the curved shape of the chalice to the female form, a bit racy for an early morning sermon."

Ciredor shrugged. "I have noticed lately that the eyes of many of my fellow monks often appear a bit glazed. I hoped that innocent analogy would capture their attention."

"It did."

"For my next sermon, to clear up any misunderstandings, perhaps I should be more specific as to which areas of the female form I was referring to," Ciredor said.

"I'd rather you didn't," Orin responded, failing to see the humor in the remark. "Unorthodoxy may suit you, but it is I who must listen to the complaints."

"Are there many complaints?" Ciredor asked.

"Overall, no. The Order is quite pleased with your handling of things, considering the circumstances. But I suspect that you did not call me here to discuss your popularity."

Considering the circumstances. Ciredor took careful note of that qualifier. He was, after all, not elected by his fellow monks to lead them, but rather thrust upon them by Nephredom's mandate.

"Very well," Ciredor replied. "Enough of easy conversation. I've brought you here to tell me what you have seen in the future that involves the woman."

"You are referring to the exiled Princess who has taken refuge with us and is the rightful Queen now that the old Queen is dead."

Ciredor nodded. "That was hardly a test for you, was it? It is as if you had pinched the knowledge from my mind."

"Pinched it from your mind? No. The ability of Psi-telepathy has always been denied me. The visions I see, however, offer clues that give me far more insight than a mere mind reader. A mind reader learns only what someone else knows. I can see what no one may have seen, or what may not yet have occurred."

If Ciredor thought Orin capable of vain pride, he would have interpreted that comment as a boast. Instead, he took his words at face value and uttered faintly, "I see."

Ciredor's thoughts drifted to Keris, as they often did. This meeting was, after all, about her. He had known her for years, long before her name became cursed by rumors and lies. Before he had become captain of the East Taren army, he used to teach magic and short-blade combat at the prestigious Twin Star Academy of Learning. He was a talented mage and bladesman, and the King himself saw it fit to enroll his own daughter at the academy.

Though Keris was never adept in magic, more of a dabbler, she excelled in the dagger. They spent hours training together . . . and eventually fell in love. It was a forbidden kind of love affair—a mere instructor could never hope to win the King's approval to marry his daughter—so they kept their feelings secret. The secret was not as closely held as they thought, and as a result, the King decided to conscript Ciredor.

Although East Taren was not at war with West Taren at the time, many barbarian and rogue military bands roved the borders, threatening the peace. In spite of his youth and inexperience, he was appointed captain of a small army and sent out to disperse the threat the bands posed. That is when he first met Orin, his lieutenant. He was even younger than Ciredor and had joined the army specifically to displease his father, who had insisted that Orin become a priest like himself, rather than a traveling poet, Orin's own calling. The King had given Ciredor a small army of poets, laborers, fishermen, and farmers. Most were poor at magic and even poorer with a blade.

Thinking back to that time, Ciredor managed to find amusement in the bittersweet memories. By purposely supplying him with substandard troops, the King had sent him out into battle with the intent that he killed. *Sent out into battle to die.* That was the price to be paid for being in love with the King's daughter. Even if he had been given a veteran crew, his was a dangerous mission—suicidal, perhaps, considering the relatively small number of men under Ciredor's command. But Ciredor was not a man to be dismissed easily; he possessed an uncommon talent for strategy and tactics. He rallied behind his forces and led them to victory after victory. As his popularity grew, the King was forced to grant Ciredor more men, with better skills, and with that came more victories. Eventually, the barbarian threat was eliminated, and King Bromus was forced to concede that there was far more to the young warrior-mage than a desire for women above his station.

Soon after the barbarian campaign, the War of Kings broke out. Ciredor's new duties prevented him from spending more than a few moments with his beloved. When that war ended in its own bizarre fashion, Regent Nephredom removed Ciredor from Jerel altogether by sending him to Soren. It was then that Ciredor heard that the Princess had fled the palace as a wanted criminal, accused of murdering her own brother. The stink of Nephredom's lies—that Keris killed her brother so that she could rule—spread throughout the land.

Ciredor was one of the few people who knew Keris well enough to know just how absurd the accusation was. Keris had loved her brother and would have died in his stead if she could. She had neither any interest in holding power nor a taste for glory. Because she opened her soul to few people, however, many mistakenly thought her to be cold and uncaring, the type of person who could be mercilessly power-hungry. People's ignorance became perfect fuel for Nephredom's lies. When Ciredor first heard the accusations, he wanted to send out his men to find her and bring her to his side. He realized, however, that Nephredom's many spies probably hoped he would do this so they could tell their master her whereabouts. He knew that Keris would be safer on her own than with him. When the time was right, she would contact him.

At last, she had. Ciredor braced himself for the next question on his mind: Could he help her get what she wanted? More to the point, *would* he? Lately, his heart had been plagued with indecision. Since he first heard of Keris's escape, he had known this day would come, and he had mentally prepared for it, in part. He imagined himself many times talking to her . . . listening to her voice again, after so much time had passed. He knew the conversation would eventually come around to her asking for his help. But it was there that he faltered. What thing next? He had too much to consider to blindly embrace the obliging answer his heart so wanted to give. Of course, he thought, the choice would be far easier if he didn't love her. *But I do love her!* The words rattled inside him, caged in a prison of his own design. Captive or not, those words refused to be silent. *But I love her!* They echoed in his soul as they had ever since his arrival in Soren.

"Before we discuss the Princess," Orin suggested, I believe I should start with the one who wears the scarf around her head, Rayna Powell of Nightwind."

With Ciredor's mind focused inward, Orin's voice seemed to come from nowhere. The sound jolted Ciredor back to the small room. Mere seconds had passed, yet a seeming eternity of soul-searching had transpired inside him, leaving him suddenly feeling weak and too ill at ease for conversation. His face must not have belied those feelings, for Orin did not seem to notice.

"Yes, I remember," Ciredor replied. "The young lady to whom I assigned two Hands."

"You asked me the night of the dinner why I seemed distracted by her presence."

Ciredor laughed. "Yes, I recall it clearly now. You could not seem to tear your eyes away from her. I know it's been a while since we've seen a pretty woman, but you seemed particularly entranced by that one."

Orin smiled briefly, more as a courtesy to his leader than an expression of true emotion. His silvery eyes stared at Ciredor, waiting.

"You told me you needed time to reflect on what you experienced," Ciredor continued. "I am about to meet with Keris, and if what you found in her companion holds any significance, I need to know now."

"She is a master mage, Ciredor."

"Are you certain?"

"Yes. I could sense at least three separate magics flowing through her, all of them very strong. When she noticed that I was probing her, she stung me with one of them. It took all of my discipline to keep from crying out."

"What types of magic does she possess?"

"That is what puzzles me. I haven't been able to identify any of them. They are none of the twelve Psi-magics known to exist. They felt wild, chaotic. Ciredor, I believe she is the sign I had warned you about."

"Ah, the infamous sign! Now, how did your poem go?" Ciredor began to recite from memory a poem Orin had once shared with him:

> The Mistress Wild Magic bears the sign
> Of yesterday and tomorrow in her hand.
> Truth and Confusion flank her sides.
> And behind her lies the accursed Band.

"Sounds more like an ode to Irel than a real person," Ciredor noted. Don't tell me you've gone West Taren on me."

If Orin was annoyed, he tried not to show it. "Sir, do you know why the Princess is here?"

"Of course I do. She is here to ask my help in restoring her to the throne. I don't need a Psi-clairvoyant to tell me that."

"More specifically," Orin said, "she is here to make an attempt at overthrowing Nephredom by force and clearing her name, so that she may be accepted as the new Queen. I've seen this image before, many times, coming about in many different ways. But only in a few such visions did I see the master mage with her, and of those few, fewer still had the Kuaran and the boy-child in them."

"The rest were false visions, then?"

"No. No vision is ever false. What appeared in any of them could happen, depending on crucial decisions made at crucial times—far too many to count or track. As time passes, some possible futures become impossible, and clairvoyants no longer see their images; the many possible visions become fewer and fewer. Eventually, as time goes on, there is only one vision—and there is little anyone can do to change the outcome at that point."

"Then I was right to call you here. I have a feeling there will be some 'crucial decisions' made tonight, and I need your advice."

"You desire to know whether to support the Princess or to turn her away."

Ciredor sighed as he nodded, meeting Orin's gaze with his own. He was not accustomed to seeking counsel in others; he had once prided himself in having better judgment than most. But lately he wasn't so certain. *But I love her!* "Perhaps it was one of my own crucial decisions—one I made in the past—that has caused us to lose our way. I don't want the problem to get worse."

"You are referring to when you first introduced Nephredom to the Queen?"

"Yes, and I had no way of knowing the Queen would eventually grant regency to that devil."

"The Subjugator of Joy. Respected, but hardly loved."

"He harasses and taxes our people mercilessly. He denounced the use of magic among common citizens—the one thing that defined us as a people. Magic gave us our strength, made us whole. Now, to practice magic openly, one must undergo the secret training of the Red Robes—and no honorable man would desire to become one of those things!"

"They are an abomination."

Ciredor smiled a dark smile. "If I had known the kind of man Nephredom was, I would have let those young urchins stone him to death back in Lamec."

"I believe you would have."

"And yet, now that the Queen is dead, he claims she declared him King with her dying breath. If this is true, to oppose him would be high treason—punishable by death."

"Indeed."

Ciredor turned an irritated eye to Orin. "Seer, if I desired a yes-man, I would have gotten one years ago. This is not the time for cautious conversation. I seek your sight, not slavish agreement!"

Orin stared at Ciredor with his piercing gray eyes. "You mistake confession of truth with false harmony. You know me better than that, *Your Reverence.*"

Ciredor tensed his lower lip, pressing it firmly against his teeth. The only time Orin called him that was when he was offended. *Your Reverence.* Coming from his calm lips, it sounded like a curse.

Orin smiled, then uttered softly, "doubting in the darkness, sifting through the ashes, I cry out, but death has plugged all ears."

Ciredor sighed. "A verse to a new poem?"

"Yes." A short silence passed before Orin spoke again. "I have been your lieutenant in war, your Second in peace, and your friend in both. If you want my opinion, then I will give it freely: You are being foolish."

It was difficult at times to tell if Orin was speaking of the present or of the future. Did Orin mean that Ciredor was being foolish now, or was he referring to a future time? Ciredor laughed in spite of his displeasure. "You are a man of extremes, I'll grant you that. I think I liked you better as a yes-man." Ciredor's tone grew serious. "Is that what you truly believe?"

"No, but you are missing my point. Being foolish implies that one commits foolish acts. *Foolish mistakes.* It is what you fear most—the consequences of a foolish mistake."

"Is that what you see in my future? That I will make a foolish mistake?" Ciredor paused, then added the next logical assumption. "One that could cost us all dearly?"

"That is one possible future, yes. Furthermore, as time has passed, the other possibilities have begun to fade, and the few that remain still show the path you most fear."

"Which involves me making the mistake you mentioned."

"Yes."

"I don't suppose you will tell me what it is, let alone how to avoid it."

"You know I have sworn never to influence the future in that way. Besides, my visions are muddled and unclear, and I never see the whole picture at once. What may start as a bad path may eventually right itself, and what may appear to be the good path may ultimately lead to ruin."

Ciredor chucked humorlessly. "It never ends for you, does it?"

"No. The futures I see are endless arrays of branching roads that shed some avenues and grow new ones based on the choices people make."

"One damned decision after another."

Orin sighed. "Nevertheless, it is sometimes better to make a decision that could damn than to do nothing and be damned."

"Another line for a poem?"

"No, a warning for a friend."

"Is that all you have to say?"

"That is all I can say, without saying too much."

Ciredor clasped his hands behind his back and slowly paced the length of the small room, back and forth, deep in thought. Each time he turned around, Orin thought that his face seemed to age. Abruptly, Ciredor stopped moving; he envisioned himself standing at a critical crossroad, with nothing in his experience having prepared him to choose which road to take.

Orin was the most gifted Psi-clairvoyant Ciredor knew. If this man was worried—and he *was* worried, Ciredor could tell—then something great or terrible was about to happen. Or both. *A great and terrible event.*

The priest privately scolded Orin for not being more forthright. Too much was at stake for guesswork—he had to know! He could use his position as high priest to force the answers from him; he could drive him to break his vow and tell Ciredor all he knew of the future. He turned to face his friend and found the young seer-poet kneeling in prayer, his gray eyes shut to the world. His lips moved swiftly as he mouthed words too faint to hear.

Ciredor's heart grew heavy, and he knew would not pursue the matter further. *Now here is a true man of faith,* he thought. He wished he could say the same for himself, but he was filled with more questions than faith, more doubt than conviction. He was once a man absolutely sure of his way. How things had changed. *But I love her!*

It had been three years since the Queen made Nephredom her Regent, and two since Ciredor had been "promoted" to be High Priest of Soren. Ciredor sat down in a cushioned chair in a darkened corner of the room. He scoffed at the absurdity of the word. *Promoted.* That is what Nephredom called it. In reality, it was little more than imprisonment in slightly better trappings than the average dungeon could offer. He could not leave the city, because doing so would give Nephredom a means to construct a plausible reason to kill him and the few former soldiers still under his protection. Spies roamed freely in the main city posing as citizens. He had to be cautious of whom he allowed to join the temple as an initiate, lest a spy slip into the Order itself.

Ciredor's eyes followed the curved stone walls of the room, noting their subtly imposing presence, and resisted the ever-growing impulse to scream abruptly at his surroundings in response to the lonely, cold feeling those walls placed in his soul. Orin would think he had finally gone mad, and the action certainly was inappropriate for the highest ranking cleric in Soren. Still, it amused him to think about it. He was banished to this holy city to serve as high priest, awkwardly usurping the rights of ranking monks who had served there since before Ciredor was born. Never mind the fact that he possessed no previous temple training. Being true clerics of faith, the monks would hold no malice, and they called him "Your Reverence" with the same respect his own men used to call him "Captain."

All the same, Ciredor knew he was living a lie. Unlike Orin, whose father and grandfather had been in the clergy, the transition had been more difficult for Ciredor. When he was a battle mage on the field, he could be who he truly was. He could be at ease with his men and casually tell raunchy jokes while they all warmed their hands by campfire. He could hold a drink in his hand without guilt, could curse without consequence, and could laugh merely for the sake of laughing. Not so now.

The monks here are as solemn as these stone walls, he thought. They expected their new leader to be the same. They expected him to run the Order as if he had been groomed for the position all his life.

To his own surprise, he did. He gave Orin credit for this. It had impressed and inspired him to see the youth go from promising battle mage to pious monk so quickly.

Orin is a good lad, Ciredor thought—a bit depressing, sometimes, but a good lad.

Ciredor felt that he owed Orin and the rest of his men a chance to make the most of this new kind of life. Ciredor felt the tug of time around him; he knew what must be done. It was time for crucial decisions. Gently, he placed his hand on Orin's shoulder. The kneeling monk opened his eyes slowly.

"Are you ready?" Orin asked.

"Yes, I suppose I am. Please bring Keris to me. Wish me the luck I will need to decide wisely."

Orin smiled. "I will do far better than that. I will pray that the Heavens smile upon you and bless this meeting with holy favor."

Ciredor smiled back, sadly noting that those words should have come from his lips instead.

✳ ✳ ✳

Rayna leaned heavily against the door of Keris's room, wondering if she should knock. As she hesitated, her exhausted body slumped to the floor, where she lay, staring vacantly up at the ceiling.

Keris opened her door and looked down to see Rayna sprawled on the floor. "I take it you've just finished training," she said. She opened the door completely and went back inside.

"Torture is more like it," Rayna breathed, painfully rising to her feet.

"Close the door behind you. I will bring you some tea. It will help take some of the ache from your bones." Keris paused for a moment, noting how much her words sounded like those of Emawin.

Rayna sat down and looked around. Like all the rooms in the temple, this one was sparsely decorated with few furnishings. The red clay walls gave the room a warm glow as bright sunlight poured in from a nearby window. After Keris brought the tea, Rayna sipped it and tried to relax, but her impatience wouldn't let her. "Aren't you going to ask me why I'm here?" she demanded.

"No, but I'm certain you are going to tell me."

"We've been here for two weeks. Haven't you and Ciredor come to some kind of decision yet?"

"No."

"Is that all you have to say?"

"We arrived during the Second Calm."

"What's that?"

"It's a period during the year in which the High Priest and a few of his chosen clerics undergo a special kind of spiritual and physical purging. The First Calm involves fasting; the Second, reflection; and the Third, penitence. The higher ranking monks are somewhat inaccessible during this time. We were fortunate that Ciredor was able to see us when he did."

"You mean—all this time Ciredor has been meditating somewhere—not talking to you?"

"That is true."

Rayna bit the tip of her tongue quietly, then sipped her tea. "Do you know what I've been going through for the past two weeks?" she asked, straining to keep her tone even.

"Please, tell me."

"Every morning before the sun is even out, I get a wake-up call from Brother Aknon."

"Wake-up call?"

"He stands outside my door, banging on it door like a madman, until I answer. Then it's off to the practice room, where we spar for four hours straight. At that point, I'm allowed to eat a few slices of fruit. Then it's back for four more hours of practice before I can eat lunch. And then I have to practice for four more hours before I'm allowed to go back to my room and wait for my *second* Hand, who finds a different scroll to lecture about every evening. It wouldn't be so bad if he were lecturing on a sensible topic like math or science, but no! I'm subject to four excruciating hours of him droning on about the Powers, prophecies, and ancient myths. By the time he's done, I have just enough energy to my crawl into bed and do the whole thing over again the next day."

Keris raised her eyebrows in the smug way Rayna found particularly annoying. "You have an exceptional talent for explaining how much you *don't* like something," she noted as she topped off their cups of tea. "Have you nothing good to say of your experiences?"

"Well . . ." Rayna started grudgingly, "I have gotten better with the staff. I think I can really defend myself with it now."

"Then your sacrifice has not been in vain. Hard work has its rewards."

"You sound like Arstinax."

Keris smiled briefly. "Speaking of whom, how is Arstinax? I trust he is not as eager as you about my concluding business here?"

Rayna sighed. "I don't think he even knows how much time has gone by. He's too wrapped up in all the chores the monks give him to notice anything else. It's like he's in a workaholic's paradise."

"Perhaps you are envious that he is spending more time with his duties than with you. Are you falling in love with him?"

To Rayna, the question came like cold water splashed on her face, unexpected, direct, and shocking. She didn't have a retort ready. *Was she falling in love with Arstinax?* she asked herself. Rayna chose not to reply, instead asking a question of her own. "Where's Quan? I thought he was staying with you."

Keris took another sip from her tea. "Quan will no longer be with us. He is gone."

Rayna's mouth opened wide with alarm. "You don't mean he's . . ."

Keris frowned. "Don't be daft! He is perfectly healthy. I simply meant he is being sent back home."

"When was this decided?"

"Early this morning. He is riding with one of the monks, using the horse they keep for emergencies."

"And the emergency is . . . ?"

"Brother Levit was adamant that he could not stay in the city a day longer, something about thieves not sullying the holy walls of Soren and all that."

Rayna leaned forward, mouth gaping. "He didn't . . ."

A pained expression passed over Keris's face, telling Rayna her hunch was right, but knowing Quan's fate gave her no satisfaction. It had become clear to Rayna that Keris loved Quan like a brother. "Brother Levit says he saw Quan pilfering a small item from the storeroom," Keris said. "Quan admitted to the deed but swears he was only curious and intended to put it back."

"He told me something very similar when he stole my bracelet," Rayna said, not bothering to hide her disbelief in Quan's story. She added, "Keris, I'm sorry. I know how much you were hoping this trip would help Quan." She shuddered to think how Emawin would take the news once she found out.

Keris seemed distant. "It matters not, now. What will be, will be."

The melancholy words lingered in Rayna's mind. Her thoughts drifted back to what Keris had said earlier. She stood up. "I have to go. I want see Arstinax before my second Hand finds me."

As Rayna turned to leave, she nearly bumped into Orin. The quiet monk apparently was unflustered by the awkward encounter, though he did take extra care to avoid eye contact with the young she-mage. Orin waited until Rayna left the room, then looked up at Keris. "It is time," he said dispassionately. "Ciredor will see you now."

CHAPTER 17

From Lions to Lambs

Keris looked at Ciredor with sudden sorrow in her heart, noting his awkward posture, his distracted eyes, and the way he fiddled with his robes as he stood in front of a stout, heavily carved table covered with religious scrolls and papers. Two ornate chairs were in the room with carvings that matched those of the table, and a fresco of a monk kneeling prayerfully in a garden, decorated the facing wall.

Why was he so nervous? She thought. She knew Ciredor had been given a tremendous responsibility and was handling it as best he could, albeit with much trepidation. He was a warrior in a city where there could be no warriors. She wanted more than anything to ease his burden, but she knew her own burdens could not wait. She thought of the risks he was taking simply having her in his presence. She thought of the sacrifices he must have endured as punishment when Nephredom exiled him to this gray-stoned place called Soren. She then thought of better times, when they used to sneak off to make forbidden love, far from the watchful eyes of her father's men. She thought of how deeply she still loved Ciredor.

"It has been too long," she said softly. She let the words fade away quietly, then added, almost at a whisper, "I've come for your help."

"I know," Ciredor said as he walked over to remove her hat. He set it on the table and gently stroked her hair.

Keris closed her eyes for a moment, enjoying the tenderness of his touch. "Is this appropriate for a leader of monks and priests?" she asked, smiling, returning his touch with her own.

"No more appropriate than this," Ciredor said, before kissing her softly on the lips.

"When he lived, my father was very determined to keep us apart, and yet we always found a way to be together."

Ciredor laughed. "And then Nephredom decided to take up your father's cause by sending me here!"

Keris smiled, but he could see the pain on her face at the mention of the name. *Nephredom, subjugator of joy.*

"Your mother's death was not in vain," he said.

Keris stared back calmly. "That remains to be seen. We have much to discuss."

Ciredor nodded, and they both sat down. "The other woman you came with—the scarfed woman with the staff."

"You mean Rayna."

"A bit odd, isn't she?"

"Odd or not, she is my friend, and she has proven herself more times than I can remember."

"Perhaps odd is too strong a word—*different*, then."

"Different. Yes, with that I can agree. Many of the words she uses are uncommon and in a dialect unknown to me. Even the way she phrases her speech is awkward to the ear at times."

Ciredor ventured another chuckle. "That sounds like half the scruffy beggars in Taren, who babble to themselves on the way to the tavern. They also tend to hear voices in their heads—all without the aid of a Psi-telepath."

"Rayna is no drooling dunce. She has an impressive mind."

Ciredor grew serious. "Fair enough. I know you would never waste your time in the company of drooling dunces, and I can see you think highly of this person. Does she know about . . ."

"Yes. I had to tell her. It was necessary, to persuade her to come this far." Keris studied Ciredor, noting the line of doubt that creased his smooth face, just above the ridge of his nose. "Is there is a reason you ask so much about Rayna?" she questioned.

"Master mage?"

Keris arched her brows, vaguely surprised. "How did you know?"

Ciredor smiled. "You are not the only one with informative friends. Orin, my Second, told me. He's a Psi-clairvoyant. He expressed a bit of concern over this Rayna."

"Don't tell me that he, too, believes she is the Power Irel? She's getting quite a following. Arstinax has appointed himself as her personal guard." Ciredor feigned apathy, and said in a tone Orin would use, "I suppose even Powers need protection from time to time." Then he paused, recalling Orin's poem quietly to himself:

> The Mistress Wild Magic bears the sign
> Of yesterday and tomorrow in her hand.
> Truth and Confusion flank her sides.
> And behind her lies the accursed Band.

"Tell me more about her," he requested. "Why would one associate her with a West Taren Power?"

"For a start, she claims to have come from the Band, which of course is impossible. I would have sooner believed her if she said hailed from the bottom of the sea."

Ciredor suppressed a sudden chill. "I see," he said.

"On the other hand," Keris went on, "she certainly acts as if she were from some otherworldly place. She seems to know nothing of the ways of this land. And her ears . . ."

"Yes? What of them?"

"A most peculiar deformity. Her ears are as round and smooth as river stones. The West Taren natives and some East Tareners believe it to be the sign of Irel."

"And so explains the scarf."

Keris nodded. "The fact that she repelled five Red Robes in public sight only adds to the myth."

"Why did you bring her here?"

"Is that not obvious? She is the one of the greatest mages I know of—greater perhaps than Nephredom, for it was she who helped us escape his Gate."

This news disturbed Ciredor. "You were in *Lamec*, behind the Gate? How did this happen?"

"That is a lengthy tale. Needless to say, we made it out alive, thanks to Rayna." Keris reached into one of her pouches and removed a narrow metal vial containing a greenish liquid. "I have proof," she said, handing the vial to Ciredor. "While escaping from Lamec, the master mage was sprayed with this venom. I removed as much of it from her wound as I could, and I placed some of it in this vial. Perhaps you will recognize it."

Ciredor studied the vial in his hand. "It looks like perfume."

"You may call it that if you like," Keris replied, "but I do not recommend putting any on."

The warrior priest laughed, removing the stopper from the vial. He sniffed. His laughter was cut off with the sudden absoluteness of an axe-fall. He nearly swore out loud. "That smell! I will remember that foul stench for as long as I have breath!"

"As will I."

"The thought of you in that den of horrors . . ."

"There is more. The beast that attacked us was winged."

"Winged? When I led our army to Lamec, we saw no winged beasts. How many did you see?"

"There appeared to be but a handful—the elite among them. However, their numbers are growing. When we were there, we witnessed the birth of one of their kind. It too was winged. Furthermore, the birthing was a celebrated affair, with the full attendance of all the other beasts."

Ciredor pondered what he had just heard. "If there are winged among them—"

"Yes, soon the Gate will be useless in keeping them in." Keris carefully recapped the vial and returned it to its stringed pouch. "So you see, our people face two enemies rather than one. With your help, we can face the beast threat and remove Nephredom from power."

Ciredor shook his head. "It is not that simple. Nephredom has many supporters. You are asking me to help start a civil war."

"I don't believe it will come to that. Once the people see that you are openly opposed to Nephredom's rule, I am certain they will rally behind us."

"And if they do not? The streets will run red with blood because of our false certainties."

"If we do nothing, the blood will still flow, only far worse. Nephredom grows madder each day that passes. If he loses control of the Gate before our forces are mobilized, the beast threat will be far worse."

Ciredor chuckled grimly. "And I suppose I am the only one you could find equally as mad as Nephredom, who would openly oppose him?"

"The people trust you, as do I. This is why Nephredom fears you—why he banished you here, rather than risk the consequences of your martyrdom."

"And that is why you think he has spared my life thus far?"

"If Nephredom wished you dead, you would have been dead long ago. He has a master assassin in his employ—the witch they call Aric."

"Perhaps, but I cannot win a war on my good name only. The people of Soren are not warriors. You know that."

"Is not every citizen required to learn staff fighting and unarmed combat? Are they not expected to practice these skills routinely as part of their daily rituals?"

"Yes, but that hardly qualifies them as war-ready. The purpose of the training is to tune the reflexes and create harmony between the body and the soul—nothing more. Having them take up arms for battle would go against everything this place represents."

"That has not always been so. History speaks often of the epic heroics of Soren warrior priests. The very walls that surround us are covered with the frescos and paintings of their war stories."

"That is history long since past. Now, the only battles fought here are those of the spirit. When your bloodline came to power many years ago, Soren swore itself to peaceful neutrality and to remain as such thereafter. It is the only reason the streets of this city are not overrun with militia and Red Robes. There can be no talk of battles here."

"Then the very bloodline you speak of will end with me, for I am the last of the Bromus line. What irony, that the bloodline that inspired Soren to eschew violence would ultimately suffer a violent end!"

Ciredor sighed. "Even if I were to use my rank and influence to persuade the people of this city to take up your cause, Nephredom's army is sizable—and if what you say is true about the winged beasts, we may be fighting on two fronts."

"Ciredor, you are a famed strategist. I've seen you win battles with worse odds. And in regard to Nephredom's army, I am told that he has weakened his forces by disbanding his true army and hiring West Taren mercenaries in its stead."

"Yes, I've heard of that as well, but his forces are hardly weakened by that fact. The Kuaran Shields they are called—one of the few long-standing mercenary companies still in existence. They are uncommonly well organized for a mercenary band, even after the loss of their captain."

"So their captain is dead?"

"Murdered. She was found horribly slain, along with hundreds of her men, in far outreaches of the Jerelan border. Once the false-king Nephredom heard of her death, he dispatched dozens of agents throughout East Taren to question the people. Many were tortured and thrown in prison, having been accused of harboring information as to the identity of the killers. Many more were killed for speaking out against the atrocities. His mercenary army has been ruthlessly efficient to that end. They've become almost as hated as his Red Robes."

Keris turned away, momentarily distracted by the news. "All of this occurred while I was on my way here? Much can happen in one cycle."

Ciredor's gray robes formed new gathers as his body shifted positions. "These are dangerous times we live in. What you ask of me is too great a risk. Nephredom is expecting such defiance at this time. He will be ready."

Keris gently placed her hand on Ciredor's chin. "Tell me," she asked, "do you fear Nephredom?"

Ciredor stared at Keris. "Now you think me a coward?"

"To fear a man like Nephredom is not cowardice; it is prudence. I fear him too. What I must know is whether that fear keeps you from doing what you know in your heart is right. You say these are dangerous times, yet while we argue they grow more dangerous still. We must act!"

Ciredor remembered what Orin told him: *"It is what you fear most—the consequence of a foolish mistake."*

"You hesitate," Keris said. "Why?"

"Keris, I'm sorry, but I cannot."

Keris heard the cheerless finality in his voice, the sound of her defeat. Standing to her feet, she straightened her posture, stiffening to her usual guarded stance. "Then no more need be said. I will look elsewhere for help."

Ciredor reached out to Keris. "Keris, this is not right—us quarreling like this."

"We will quarrel no more. That I promise." Keris paused before leaving, leaning against the door more than she wished to. "Before I go, there is something you should know. When we first entered East Taren, we came upon a guardsman of mid-age. I had not fully seen his face before I decided to kill him."

"You must not—"

"I will finish!" Keris snapped, fury raging in her voice. "You speak of the potential loss of innocent lives as if you think I know nothing of it. Many have risked their lives, and many more have already died to protect me. If my friends had not intervened on my behalf, I would have gladly killed that sentry and scores like him if necessary." Keris's words suddenly softened; the confession she had spoken lifted a bitter weight. "I have changed, Ciredor," she said. "I am not the innocent, coy Princess you trained with several years ago. I have changed in order to survive, and I can never go back to whom I once was. You are an honorable and noble man, and I will always remember you as such. You have given me your ear and made your decision. I can ask no more of you. Good-bye, Ciredor. I pray my fears are wrong, for all our sakes."

Keris's dry, unflinching eyes spoke a message that words could not convey. It was done; it was over. As Ciredor silently watched Keris leave, he prayed that he had made the right choice, for the sacrifice was great and terrible indeed: He had just lost the only woman he ever loved.

❋ ❋ ❋

Arstinax gathered another flower and added it to the growing bunch in his hand. Sensing he was being watched, he looked up to see Rayna staring in his direction.

"The monks told me I could find you here," Rayna said, adding, "though I never quite pictured you as the flower-picking type."

Arstinax smiled with embarrassment. "When we first passed through this garden on the way to the city, you seemed to enjoy its beauty very much."

Rayna nodded. "I did, but I didn't know you felt the same."

"It is true that I admire and respect the many faces of nature, but that is not why I am here. I allowed myself to become lost in my duties here. Before I left my home in Argat, I had little time for friends or family; my work was my only companion. When my brother was killed before my eyes, I came to understand that my life would mean nothing without those I hold dear. I consider you a good friend, and good friends should never be forgotten."

"Even when there's work to be done?" Rayna quipped.

"Especially when there's work to be done. The fruit of one's labors is of no worth if there is no one to share it with." He handed the flowers to Rayna. "I hoped to make amends with this bouquet."

Rayna took the flowers and held them close. "But how could you?"

"I asked the monks for permission to harvest these blossoms before I began."

"That's not what I meant," Rayna said, holding back laughter. A chill breeze passed, fluttering each petal, sending its sweet fragrance dancing to her nose. She sighed. "I mean," she explained, "I don't deserve these flowers; I don't deserve to be called your friend."

"I don't understand."

Rayna braced herself. "This is it," she whispered, then began. "Arstinax, there's something you should know about what happened that night in the Sharpening Stone—the night before your brother was condemned to death."

"The pain of his death is with me still, though your presence does much to ease it."

"Arstinax, I am the cause of that pain in the first place."

"That is not true! You had nothing to do with his death."

Rayna told Arstinax everything about the night she met his brother, and the details leading up to his Condemning. Arstinax remained quiet, and Rayna feared he would never say another word to her again. Nevertheless, it had to be done. There would be no more secrets, no more pretenses.

When Rayna finished, Arstinax spoke. "Is this the thing that has troubled you? Nothing else?"

Rayna swallowed. "Isn't that enough? You brother is dead because of my stupidity."

"No. My brother is dead because he loved drink more than discretion, and he is dead because the Red Robes made it so."

"But I . . ."

"No. You are no more responsible for Merlott's death than the barkeep who sold him drink, or the Prod Bearers who sent him into the Band." Arstinax smiled, and Rayna forgot what she was going to say next. It didn't matter, whatever it was. What mattered was he didn't hate her. He didn't hate her.

"I am glad Merlott had the chance to meet you," he said. "And I am glad he thought well of you."

Rayna scarcely heard him, still caught up in the revelation of her vindication. Distant-eyed, she mumbled to herself, "I'm on a roll, so I might as well go for the gold."

Earnestly trying to understand what she meant, Arstinax paused thoughtfully before shrugging his large, square shoulders. "That is one riddle I cannot solve. What does it mean to go rolling while searching for gold?"

Rayna burst out laughing, and Arstinax soon followed suit.

"I guess I should put it another way," Rayna said, forcing down another bout of laughter. "According to the customs of your land, when someone finds oneself falling in love, what does that person do?"

Arstinax stepped closer to Rayna. He knew where the conversation was going, but he had never imagined . . . Rayna's eyes showed him that she saw what he was thinking. In the face of the deepening cold, he felt so warm. Was he blushing? "He would declare his love for the woman, and pray she feels the same," he said.

"I don't think there's any question about that. Then what?"

"Then betrothal is announced when the man presents the woman with a necklace."

"In my land, it's a ring."

"But I have neither ring nor necklace."

"But you gave me a bracelet. Good enough. Is there anything else?"

"Finally, the man should offer his beloved a gift—something that reminds him of her."

"Like these flowers?"

"Yes."

"Then I guess that means we're betrothed?"

"Yes, I suppose it does."

Rayna smiled slyly. "Congratulations."

"But . . . is it right for a man to love a Power, let alone design to marry one?"

"But I'm not a Power. I'm just me."

Arstinax held Rayna close, and she felt secure in his embrace. As the icy wind blew harder, they turned to head back. Something caught Rayna's eye, moving down the narrow path toward them.

"Is that Keris?" she asked, squinting her eyes.

"Yes, it is."

"Something must be wrong."

"How so?"

"She normally moves like a cat; we usually don't even see her until she's right upon us."

"It is true that stealth is her way. Perhaps she is distracted."

Keris approached them, her tear-reddened eyes betraying her earlier efforts at wiping them.

"I did not wish to interrupt," she said, lowering the brim of her dark hat, "but I thought you would want to know as soon as my business was concluded here. I take it you are not in each other's arms merely to ward off the cold?"

Rayna proudly raised the arm bearing her bracelet. "We're betrothed!"

Keris smiled sadly. "Heavens be praised. Then our journey here has not been a total waste."

"It went that badly?" Rayna asked.

"There will be no army, no support. I have failed."

"I'm sorry."

"No need. My lot has been cast. I accept it."

"I um, hate to bring this up . . ." Rayna began haltingly, "but we had a deal, remember?"

"Of course, and I intend to keep my word. Let us be off to Dosk, then."

Rayna found herself in the strange position of feeling sorry for the downcast Princess. "Maybe I'm oversimplifying this," Rayna said, "but can't you just command Ciredor to help you? I mean, technically you are his Queen–granted, with serious PR problems–but still . . ."

Keris shook her head softly. "If you were my subject, and I had commanded you to kill that guard on the bridge, would have done it?"

Rayna frowned. "No, and even if I did, I probably would hate you for making the request."

"Which is precisely why some things cannot be forced. Sometimes it is best to judge the wisdom of one's decision through the eyes of others. Ciredor deems my plan unwise. Perhaps he is right." Keris turned her back to them, calling out, "In any case, we waste precious light, which fades every moment we stand here in idle conversation. Do you wish to go to Dosk or not?"

"Can we at least wait until morning?"

"No. We will retrieve our supplies and start out straightaway."

As Keris marched ahead, with Rayna and Arstinax in tow, Rayna whispered to her betrothed, "And to think, I was going to give her a hug."

※ ※ ※

"I take it you turned her away?"

Ciredor sat in the meditation room, brooding. "That is the second time you've asked me that," he said, looking up momentarily to glare at Orin before closing his eyes again.

"Then perhaps you should answer the door, if you wish the knocking to stop."

"I was hoping the knocker would have enough basic wit to stop knocking on his own."

"I take it you turned her away?"

Ciredor sighed. "If I had not, I would have put the lives of five thousand Soren citizens in peril . . . and by doing so, I may yet put the lives of a hundred thousand in peril."

"An interesting dilemma."

Ciredor opened his eyes and stared back at his friend. "Must I drink from Life's cup of perverse irony with every decision I make?"

Orin inhaled deeply, his voice growing distant and faint. "That cup is nearly drained. The drinks to come may be far worse bitter."

"You have an infallible talent for optimism. If you keep pouring on the cheer like this, I fear it will be more than my flesh and blood can stand."

"If you wish to be alone, then I will leave you."

"Don't be so sensitive. You are a Psi-clairvoyant; you know my ways."

Orin rose to his feet, took a bowl of fruit from a nearby table, and brought it back to where Ciredor sat. He handed Ciredor some moodberry fruit and took an apple for himself.

"Do you remember when we were men of war?" Ciredor said.

"Of course."

"Our magic was feared by all. We were lions, then."

"Yes. I remember."

"Now look at us. We have become as lambs. Lambs waiting for slaughter. Our strength—where has it all gone?"

"We are the same as we always were. Nothing has diminished us."

"I wish I could believe as you do. Do you have a poem for a time like this? Something that would assure me I made the right the decision?"

"No."

Ciredor lowered his head wearily. "Then time shall be my judge, and if I am wrong, I pray that history may one day forgive me." He took a bite of the moodberry fruit and found it sour.

CHAPTER
18

Dosk

After several days of travel, the party entered the city of Dosk at the eve of night. Tarnished braziers, scattered throughout the old streets, scented the aged city with the smell of their burning coals. The shops and homes were made of brick, often crumbling, and mortar, often cracked. A few straggling scholars, hugging armfuls of faded and dog-eared papers, hurried their gait to reach the safety of a private study or quiet inn before the "lesser educated" came out to prey.

"Dosk is indeed a unique province," Keris explained as they made their way through the winding walkways. "It is the center of knowledge in Taren—full of libraries, bookshops, and lecture halls. Philosophers and scholars from both Tarens eventually find their way here—some simply to learn and open their minds to better understanding, others to study the twelve Psi-magics."

"You sound like my second Hand," Rayna said. "I thought you said Nephredom outlawed magic."

"That is correct. The new law states that no Taren citizen, other than the court mage or the Red Robes, may practice magic. However, the law does not say that one cannot *study* magic. Many former mages take advantage of this discrepancy and study magic in Dosk. So long as they do not actually cast spells, they are free from Red Robe persecution."

"I suppose it's better than nothing."

Keris scoffed. "It is like trying to master the art of blade fighting by reading about it. There is no substitute for practical skill. The longer our people go without honing our talents, the more inept we will be become."

Rayna turned to get a better look at her disgruntled companion. "I thought you didn't trust mages or magic."

"I do not, but I am Queen of East Taren. Magic is in our blood and should not be denied to those who wish to use it! And simply because my own magic is weak, one should not assume I wish the same for all my people!"

Rayna could tell from Keris's defensive tone that she had stumbled across a touchy subject. Then again, every subject had seemed touchy to Keris since they had left Soren. Rayna felt uncomfortable in the situation and suspected Keris felt the same. She had the unnerving feeling that Keris was secretly hoping Rayna would say, "Hey, forget Ciredor. I'm a great and powerful master mage—we can take Nephredom out all by ourselves!" It would be suicide, but Rayna doubted that Keris would care, in her depressed state. Of course, Rayna had no intention of volunteering to lend her supposed magical powers to a doomed rebellion, though part of her wanted to help. Keris was her friend, after all.

"Where is this guild of the scientists?" Arstinax asked. "The city is large, and night is upon us. An ambush is likely if we do not find refuge soon." The sound of unseen things scurrying in the shadows seemed to affirm his concerns. Once they had come into the light, Rayna saw to her relief that they were only rats. Before she found herself in Taren, seeing rats would have distressed her considerably, but after all she had seen lately, rats were a trivial finding.

Across the way stood an apparently condemned building, rotting planks nailed against its dark windows, hardened drifts of snow and ice piled high against the front door, untouched. Keris pointed to the building. "I believe that is the place," she said, leading them closer.

"You've got to be kidding!" Rayna said, nearly falling over a mound of filthy snow. "It's an abandoned old shack."

Keris made her way to the front door and rapped sharply on the upper portion, not covered by snow. No answer came from within. She repeated this several times before hearing the sound of footsteps; a small voice responded on the other side.

"Who is it?"

"Friends of the Science Guild," Keris replied.

"What is the password?"

"Access denied."

"'Access denied?'" Rayna muttered. "What kind of password is that?"

"I do not know its significance, only that it is the same password they have used since the Guild was founded many years ago."

"They haven't changed it in all that time? Isn't that bad for security?"

Keris gave a surly shrug. "Why bother changing the lock to an empty vault? Most do not care enough about the Science Guild to bother remembering its password, even if it were posted on every streetlamp."

The small, muffled voice responded. "Back door!"

Around back, they were met by a short, wizened man dressed in formal finery. "Inside, quickly!" he ordered, looking outside suspiciously before he herded them through the back door.

Inside, Rayna felt her heart sink. Whatever remaining hope she harbored that this place could show her the way home, died abruptly at what she saw. At the far end of the room, three scruffy-looking figures sat at wooden desks, scribing copiously onto bits of parchment; each had a half dozen or so such bits scattered in front of him. Upon seeing Rayna and the others, they stopped and looked up, their tired, unshaven faces smiling like those of penniless drunks being offered a round of free ale.

Rayna looked past them and made mental notes about the place. The interior was much larger than she expected, and far from tidy. Piles of papers and musty journals cluttered each corner of the room. The surface of nearly every piece of furniture was covered with unfinished equipment, odd bits of metal and wood, and more papers. The floor was littered with a plethora of small candles, as if the scientists deemed their light not quite important enough to take up precious table space; Rayna had to take care not to step on any as she walked. Every window was covered with a dirty blanket, which Rayna assumed was meant to keep prying eyes from seeing inside.

The man who had ushered them inside looked at Arstinax disapprovingly and said, "You are not the one who usually brings the girls." He then looked at Rayna's chest in a way that made her feel uncomfortable. "If you were, you'd know to use the back door. At least this time they sent better looking entertainers!"

"But terribly overdressed!" another man yelled out from across the room.

"Habott, you are a daft one, you are. You can't very well expect them to appear at our doorstep half-clothed in this weather, can you? Even the ugly ones wear coats."

Keris drew her dagger and placed it dangerously close to the short man's fancy tunic. "I have had enough of this foolishness. If I were in a better mood, I could find this somewhat amusing, but not now." Keris stared at the frightened man unnervingly. "Do I look like a dancing whore to you?"

The man began stammering apologetically. "Of course not! I beg your forgiveness! It's just that we have an . . . eh, um . . . *arrangement* with the Thieves Guild to, uh . . . oh, never mind—there's obviously been a terrible misunderstanding." He looked nervously at Keris's blade. "But surely there is no need to resort to violence."

Keris sheathed her weapon, grumbling, "Indeed."

"My name is Authright. Forgive me for asking, but if the Thieves Guild did not send you, then why have you come here?"

"I was kind of hoping you could help locate a place for me," Rayna said halfheartedly.

"Oh," Authright said, reluctant to take his eyes away from Keris and the blade she carried.

"Rayna believes that science is the key to finding her back home," Keris said.

"Lost, is she? There is an excellent mapmaker a few streets over."

"No. You don't understand," Rayna interjected. "I'm not from either of the Tarens. As wild as it may sound, I'm not from this world at all. I was somehow brought here during a lightning storm. The storm may have had something to do with it. I was hoping you could help me find a way to reverse the process."

Authright coughed nervously; otherwise, the room was deathly quiet. "I'm not sure if I can help you with that sort of thing, Rayna," he said slowly, looking at Keris.

"My friend is not mad," Keris said fingering the pommel of her dagger. "You will help her."

Authright shuddered. "Yes, of course. . . . Science goes where the twelve Psi-schools cannot. If the answer exists anywhere, we can find it . . . I hope."

"Good." Keris looked to Rayna, stone-faced. "Then I am done here. My obligation has been fulfilled."

Rayna stared back at her friend. *It would be no good trying to convince her to stay,* she thought.

"What will you do now?" Rayna asked, already knowing the answer.

"I plan to gather my few remaining supporters, and together we will confront Nephredom."

Rayna bit back the comment she was going to make, for it would only have made matters worse. Instead, she said, "All right, fair enough—but you look like you could use some rest. You should at least spend the night in a hotel before you leave town." She added, "A soft bed will do you good."

Keris nodded hesitantly, letting out an unexpected yawn. "Perhaps you are right. I must be well alert for the days to come. This may be the last time I get a chance to sleep all of the night. Very well, there is a small inn near here. I will stay there for the night, and then leave at daybreak. Farewell, noble Rayna Powell of Nightwind. I hope you find all that you seek."

As Keris left, Rayna felt anger rising slowly within her. Keris was nearly as stubborn as she was. All the same, she wanted to believe that, given time, Keris would come to accept her situation and find a new life for herself, one that did not involve futile, desperate raids on enemy strongholds. "Are we just going to let her wander off tomorrow and eventually get herself killed?" she said to Arstinax.

"She is a strong-willed woman," he replied. "She must follow her heart, as you have followed yours."

Rayna sighed. "Do you think she has even a remote chance of winning?"

Arstinax frowned thoughtfully. "It is doubtful, Irel. Nephredom's warriors are many, and she commands only a handful by comparison."

"In other words, it'll be a slaughter."

"Only the aid of a Power could turn the odds in her favor."

Rayna shook her head, laughing at the less-than-subtle hint. "I keep telling you, I'm *not* a Power. I'm not a master mage. I'm not even a *sorcerer's apprentice*." She crossed her arms, pouting. "I'm not going to fall for Keris's 'You-must-help-me-I'm-pathetic' routine. Not this time."

"You believe Keris's plight to be a ruse?"

"No. Her cause really *is* pathetic—I mean . . . that's not what I mean." Rayna looked back at Arstinax mournfully. "I'm being an ass again, aren't I?"

Arstinax shrugged. "That judgment, I leave to you."

"I want you to follow Keris to the inn. Keep an eye on her. Try to convince her to give up the suicide crusade."

"Will you not come as well?"

"No. It's better you go alone. I think she's mad at me—in a subtle, regal kind of way—but angry all the same. If I try to talk any sense into her, it would just fall on deaf ears."

"So you feel her resentment of your refusal has hardened her heart to your reason."

"Exactly. And that's another thing—you are *way* better with words than I am. She'll listen to you. In the meantime, I will be here working with my fellow scientists." Rayna motioned to the men behind her, with a look lacking conviction. "I am where I want to be."

Arstinax looked suspiciously at Authright and the others. "Will it be safe to leave you here? Can these men be trusted?"

"I'll be fine; I have my staff. Anyway, I don't think anyone will try anything after what Keris did."

"Are you certain?"

"Yes. Right now, I'm a lot more concerned for Keris's well-being." She raised her arm to let Arstinax see her bracelet. It was dormant. "If they were really bad news, my talisman would have let me know," she whispered. "I'll be all right; now go."

"Very well. I will be back before the third hour is past."

Arstinax took Rayna's hand and kissed it softly.

Rayna watched him go, smiling to herself. He was a wonderful paradox of a man, she thought, big and strong, yet so sensitive. He professed confidence that she had the power to defeat an army, yet he worried about leaving her alone with a few strangers.

Rayna turned her attention to Authright and the others in the room. "Well, gentlemen," she said, "where do we begin?"

✳ ✳ ✳

Arstinax secretly followed Keris to the Hapless Deer, a small inn with a pub, about a dozen buildings down from the Science Guild. He found when he arrived, that Keris had already taken a seat and was starting on her first drink. His imposing presence caused a few heads to turn. Quietly, he sat down beside the brooding Keris, registering vague surprise that the chairs in this bar had four legs.

Keris gazed at Arstinax casually. "Rayna sent you here to persuade me to accept my failures graciously and give up my plans to claim my mother's throne?"

Arstinax nodded.

Keris took a swig of her drink. "You have come here in vain. I will stay my course."

Arstinax furrowed his brow. His voice was soft as the wind, but just as deliberate. "An act as desperate as the one you are planning is what

Nephredom hopes for. Why do you allow yourself to play into the hands of the enemy?"

"I have no choice. My hand is forced."

"To carry out this mission as it stands will invite certain death."

"And if I fail to challenge the man whose hand is behind the murder of my brother and nearly every blood relative I have known, then I am already dead."

"Then," Arstinax whispered, "challenge him when you are more likely to win."

Keris glared at Arstinax. "I do not take well to your patronizing, Kuaran," she said. "We both know that day will never come. My best hopes had laid with the master mage Rayna Powell, and with Ciredor of Soren, but both have refused to join me."

"We are your friends, but we cannot take part in your self-destruction."

"You are cowards! And I have nothing more to say to you!"

"Then," came a voice from behind Keris, "perhaps you will have something to say to me."

Keris looked up and back to see a young Dosken guard standing behind her, smirking. She took another sip of ale, judging the man with the look one would give a servant who had arrived at an inappropriate time. "Who in hell are you, and why are you in my space? I have broken no laws."

The guard snorted. "Talking disrespectfully of an agent of His Majesty is a law broken, for a start."

"'His Majesty?'" Keris said with contempt. "Let me tell you what I think of your so-called King—"

"No!" Arstinax interjected loudly, turning to the jaded Princess with a presence that that made her put down her cup and listen. "This is *madness*. Now are you to simply throw your life away? Rayna endured much anguish at the loss of my brother. Would you have her endure that again over you?" He whispered, "Let this man do his job, and he will be on his way. We need not make a scene."

"My sister is a little drunk, good sir," Arstinax explained to the guard. "That is, no doubt, why you came over. We appreciate your concern, but all is well now. Please forgive her rudeness. I will take her to her room, where she can offend no one."

"You lie poorly," the city guard sneered. "This woman is not going anywhere."

"Please—" Arstinax began.

"Silence, Kuaran! Go back to pulling plows in the wild. The City of

Learning is the last place I'd expect to see the likes of you." The guard returned his attention to Keris. "But you, Princess, are coming with me."

Surprised at the mention of her title, Keris took notice of the uniformed man fully, for the first time.

"There's no use denying it," the guard said. "Your face matches the posted drawings—the ones that offer that big reward for your head. I will retire a rich man after I turn you in!"

Keris mentally made note of the young man's slack posture, the careless way he moved as he talked, his repeated exposure of his midsection to attack, the awkward position of his feet, and the unadorned bamboo staff he carried—standard issue for new hires. "You are new to your job," she said, resuming her drink. "I'd wager you have not been a guard for more than a week. Your training is far from complete."

For the first time, the fresh-faced guard was ruffled. "How did you—?"

"Leave me be, guardsman, while you still can." Something in her voice dared not be questioned. Arstinax could sense impending bloodshed.

The guard remained indignant. "How dare you speak to me that way?"

Keris slammed her drink on the table and stood fearless before the inexperienced guard. "I dare because I am your Queen!"

"Bah! You are but a brother-killer, and it is I who shall bring you to justice!"

Several patrons of the inn had left in fear; the rest stood near the walls, cautiously waiting to see what would happen next. They did not need to wait long.

Arstinax turned to the door to see another figure approaching, a tall man in military uniform. From his size and manner, he suspected the man was Kuaran, like himself.

Keris could see that this man was different. His battle-ready stance was effortless, and his calm demeanor and steady eyes revealed that he needed to prove nothing. Time-etched creases from combat experience decorated his cragged, bearded face like badges of honor. He was everything, Keris noted, that the young city guard was not. This one was a professional, a professional killer.

The newcomer walked up beside the guard and, with the slightest effort, pushed him aside so roughly that he fell to the floor and slid a few feet. Humiliated, the guard jumped to his feet, his staff ready. "What is the meaning of this?" he yelled, unable to keep the fear from his voice.

The man laughed. "You try to speak like a warrior, but the words fit poorly in your mouth. I have come to Dosk by direct order of the King.

The Princess will come with me."

The young guard limped toward the other man, favoring the leg he had injured while being thrown to the floor. "You have no jurisdiction here, Kuaran! Mercenaries have no rank over the local militia!"

The large Kauran fighter turned to face the injured guard, growling, "For a man living in Dosk, the supposed center of all knowledge, your grasp of current events is lacking. If you took your job seriously, you would have made it your business to know when there were major changes to your chain of command."

"What kind of changes?"

"The King recently hired us into his army on a permanent basis. I have sworn myself to the throne. As commander of the King's army, I outrank guardsmen by far."

"I will not take orders from an illiterate Kuaran!"

"Leave this man alone," Keris said quietly to the guard. "In his eyes, you are already dead. Flee before he makes it so."

"And I will not have you telling me what to do either!" The guard made a move to grab Keris. "I saw her first, Kuaran. If you have a problem with that, then take it up with my captain, over at the—"

The commander's blade slipped into the guard's chest so quickly that he never got a chance to see it. He fell to the floor, dead.

Arstinax gasped, "By the Heavens! The boy posed no serious threat to you. Why did you take his life?"

The Kuaran soldier grinned cruelly. "Because I could." He wiped his bloody blade on the hair of the fallen guard before re-sheathing it. "The locals here think they are high and mighty," he said. "They call Kuarans stupid and savage, yet their storehouses and granaries are full with the fruits of our labors. *Our labors!* Kuara is covered with fertile, green fields. Here, there is only hard icy ground. If it were not for trade, these people would be forced to eat the very parchment they write upon."

The soldier stared hard at Arstinax, noting the brown leather patch on his eye—a weakness. "I have no quarrel with you, brother," he said. "Leave now, and I will forget having seen you here."

"You are no brother of mine!" Arstinax shot back, then hesitated. "And I will not abandon my friend to you, murderer," he finished, more calmly.

"I've heard of you. You are Arstinax of Kuara's Northern Tip. They say you stood before twenty Red Robes with no fear. They say that is how you lost your eye."

"And now I stand before you."

The Kuaran soldier spat on the floor, barely missing Arstinax's foot. "It appears your misplaced loyalty for the Princess has blinded your other eye as well, brother."

"On the contrary. I see more clearly now than I ever have."

"You claim you represent Nephredom's authority," Keris said, partially disrupting the growing hostilities between the rugged soldier and Arstinax. "What is your name?"

"My name is not important," the soldier replied, baring his teeth in a slight scowl. "My title is." I was commander of the Kuaran Shields—and now commander of the East Taren Army. I was sent here by the King to smash the heads of a few who are guilty of breaking the laws forbidding the practice of magic."

"I thought that dirty work was the charge of the Red Robes."

"They have been engaged in another matter, and so we were ordered to come here in their stead. I had no idea I would find you here, Princess. The King will be pleased."

"I am Princess no longer. I am Queen of East Taren."

The commander bowed pretentiously, his dark eyes never leaving Keris's sight. "Majesty," he growled.

"Do you mock me, Commander?"

"I see no queen before me. I see a bounty."

"My mother, the old Queen, is dead. By birthright, I am Queen of East Taren."

The Kuaran military leader chuckled. "Perhaps I've been too busy with my work, but I don't remember being present for your coronation as Queen. If there was one, I would have known. Without a formal coronation, you are queen only of that empty cup of ale in front of you."

"I am your Queen," Keris asserted.

"So you keep saying," the commander replied. He seemed to enjoy the tension between them. "You have no power over me, woman."

"You say you have sworn yourself to throne."

"That is what I said."

"Then you are a servant of the throne, not merely of the King."

"Your word games would have a better chance with a more idle mind. There is no difference. The King and the throne are one."

"There you are wrong. You swore allegiance to the office, not necessarily to the one currently occupying it. It is a small but important distinction that may save your life. When Nephredom is revealed as the fraud he is, you and all your men run the risk of being found guilty of treason, and crimes of treason are punishable by death."

Arstinax realized what Keris was doing and could not help but marvel over her audacious persistence. Through this commander, she was trying to recruit Nephredom's own men against him!

"Go on," the commander responded gruffly, listening.

"You owe Nephredom nothing," Keris said. "He is a play-king who has used lies and deception to steal the throne, and soon the people will grow weary of his mad tirades and demand that the true heir be instated. You are agents to the throne, and I am the only true heir left. If you take up your arms under my banner, I will swear immunity, for you and all your men, against all past war crimes. You will be able to serve East Taren with legitimacy and honor."

The commander slowly brushed a coarse hand down the smooth curve of Keris's jaw. "And how far are you willing to go to gain my support, eh?"

Keris shrugged off his touch. "Not as far as that," she said. "And keep your lust and animal bribery to yourself."

"Then we have nothing further to discuss."

"So you would be content to remain one of Nephredom's dogs?"

"In a single meal, the scraps at a king's table, given to his dogs, are better than what most what people eat in a day. I would rather stand by this King and share in his riches, than follow you and share in your execution—*Your Majesty*." From the corner of his eye, the commander glimpsed three of his men entering the inn, no doubt responding to word that their commander had found the Princess.

Keris also saw them. "It appears your fellow vultures have smelled blood and have joined you," she said.

Bolstered by the presence of reinforcements, the commander stepped back, allowing his subordinates to flank him. "The time for pretty talk is over. You have but one man; I have three. You will either come with me alive and whole, or we can do it . . . the other way."

Keris drew her short blade. The commander smiled and nodded, admiring her decision. "The other way it is, then."

✳ ✳ ✳

"So you say you rode into this world upon a lightning bolt?"

Rayna let out an exasperated sigh. "No, you're not listening. I said I was struck by lightning, and it somehow transported me to the Band."

Authright scratched his head. "Right. And then you were somehow able to walk through the Band unharmed until you reached Lamec."

"No, it was Kuara. Lamec is where I fought the creatures and escaped through Nephredom's Gate."

"Right."

Rayna paused. "You think I'm crazy, don't you?"

Authright shook his head vehemently. "No, no, of course not. We get this sort of thing all the time here at the Science Guild."

A confused voice sounded out. "We do?"

"Shut up, Habott!" Authright laughed nervously. "Of course we do. Now, please continue. I need as much data as you can spare so that we can better understand what happened to you." Authright added sheepishly, "And after we have done all we can to help you, you will tell your friends to leave us in peace?"

"This is a waste of time," Rayna said, throwing up her arms in frustration. "The only reason you are even hearing me out is because you are afraid Keris might come back and attack you."

"And the big Kuaran looks a right menace as well!" Habott cried out.

"That big Kuaran menace is my betrothed!"

"Habott," Authright said, with a veiled edge in his voice, "you appear to be exciting our guest needlessly. Why don't you go the garlic room and finish your work there?"

"But it's smelly in the garlic room," Habott whined in protest, "and it's not my turn to work there!"

"Habott!"

"But the garlic room is in the cellar," Habott sniveled, "and that's where the ghost is. You know how I hate going down there with the ghost. There's only one thing worse than the smell of the garlic room, and that's the sight of that ghost!"

"That's because you keep touching the handprint," Authright said with fake, cheery politeness. "If you don't touch the handprint, the ghost will not appear. It's that simple."

"But you always tell us to touch the handprint whenever we go to the basement, to see if she will say new words, remember?"

"Shut up, Habott! You talk too much. You reveal our guild secrets!"

"Wait a minute," Rayna said, bewildered. "Are you saying that you guys here think there's a ghost in your basement?"

"A woman ghost," Habott said. "A strange ghost she is, dressed in her green overcoat and white shirt."

"Habott!" Authright shouted. "Your gob is larger than your brain! The details of the ghost are a scientific matter, not to be shared with outsiders!"

But Habott was too excited to stop now. "And she wears these strange metal symbols pinned to her garment, like a soldier would, but I've seen no soldiers around here wearing metals like that!"

Rayna shook her head. "And you thought *I* was crazy?"

"I assure you, the apparition is quite real, madam," Authright declared indignantly, tugging the collars of his waistcoat. "I've seen it many times."

Despite the ridiculous claim, Rayna's curiosity was piqued. "All right, then show me," she said.

Authright puffed out his small chest. "Absolutely not. Members only!"

"Fine. How do I join?"

Authright looked surprised. "You mean you wish . . . you wish to join us?"

"Why not? I've done worse since I've been in Taren."

Authright was suspicious. "It's been so long since we had someone ask for membership, that's all. We didn't think you were that impressed."

Rayna grimaced. In truth, she wasn't. She had come to a dead end and was too proud to admit it aloud. Her rational mind told her that Keris was right; the trip to Dosk was a waste of time. She had hoped to find a group of technical specialists who had the means to send her back to her world. Instead, she found a disorganized crew of four misfits who had nothing more to offer than an alleged ghost in their basement.

Yet something beyond her rational mind urged her to stay. These people could help her. But how? They seemed barely able to help themselves. Rayna searched her thoughts deeper. The answers were here, but why was she so sure? Slowly, since her arrival in Taren, something within her was changing, making her . . . aware.

Authright ran to a back room and returned with a heavy, hidebound book. The title was handwritten in faded black: "The Charter and Laws Governing the Guild of Science." He quickly presented it before Rayna, worried she might change her mind any minute. "Now you must swear upon this book and—" Authright stopped mid-sentence. "Surely you know that once you join us, you are prohibited from joining other guilds, including the Alchemy Guild?"

"I didn't know there was any such thing as the Alchemy Guild," Rayna said.

"I'm glad to hear you say that. Damned nuisance, those alchemists! The less you know about them, the better."

"In my land, alchemy was a kind of early day chemistry."

"And what is chemistry?"

"A branch of science."

"I knew it! And that pompous lot had the audacity to call our experiments 'rudimentary.' Wait until I tell them their precious alchemy is but a subset of our science! A minor one, no doubt."

"Authright—"

"I've lost dozens of potential members to that guild and their so-called 'nature magic.' I thought nature involved trees and living things—they spend most of their time studying metallic rocks—*rocks!* What a waste of talent!" Authright scoffed bitterly. "It's not as if the twelve Psi-schools see us any differently, you know. Scientists, herbalists, alchemists—we're all failed mages to them. The Twelve Schools are all the same; if it doesn't involve mind magic, they've got no time for it."

"Authright—"

"If you ask me, the Twelve Schools are jealous, because we actually get to put what we learn to use. Haw! All they can do is read and reread—"

"Authright!"

"Eh, what—? Well there's no need to shout, my hearing isn't failing me, you know."

"You were having me swear membership into the Guild."

"Oh, yes, sorry. I get a little excited when we get new members. It's not very often we do, you see."

Authright placed one end of the book to Rayna's forehead. "Now repeat after me," he began. "I swear my allegiance to the Science Guild."

"I swear my allegiance to the Science Guild."

"I will diligently pursue my scientific duties."

"I will diligently pursue my scientific duties."

"And heed the counsel of my peers."

"And heed the counsel of my peers."

"And promise never to defect to the alchemists."

"You made that part up."

"I resent that! How did you know?"

"Authright!"

Oh, very well. You are henceforth granted membership into the Science Guild, with the current rank of novice. Congratulations!"

"Fine," Rayna said, wiping book dust from her face. "Now let's go see that ghost."

"Not so quickly, novice," Authright stated. "The cellar is restricted to higher ranking members, and that would be me, Habott, Jon, and um . . ."

"Fervis," Habott said.

Fervis, a patchwork-robed fellow, was sound asleep at a nearby table, snoring faintly.

"Yes, of course, Fervis. As a novice, you must stay up here and study the basics before the wonders of the cellar can be revealed to you."

"That's not fair," Habott moaned. "I was hoping she would take my turn in the garlic room!"

"You didn't mention that when you swore me in," Rayna said in an irritated tone.

"Patience, novice. I can tell you have a sharp and curious mind. You should move up to the rank of adept in little to no time at all."

"And how long is that, exactly?"

"Oh, well . . . no longer than say, six cycles. A new record that would be!"

Rayna shook her head in tired frustration. "I don't have time for this," she said. Slowly, she untied her scarf, revealing her ears to the others. "Does this help speed up my rank?" she asked.

❈ ❈ ❈

"You have the heart of a Kuaran, Princess. I'll grant you that," the commander acknowledged. "I promise to say you fought bravely when I bring your lifeless body before Nephredom."

Keris did not reply. She concentrated on her enemy's weapon. It faded in and out of focus as she struggled against the effects of the ale. To her regret, she had ordered the strongest ale the barkeep had in supply, to help her forget her many woes. Now her very life depended on sharpness of wit and skill—the very things the drink had dulled.

"You speak of victories before you have done any work to make it happen," Arstinax chided, trying to divert the commander's attention away from the Princess. "A braggart is the worst kind of idler. You are like the lazy youth who does nothing all day but boasts of his great hunting skills, when he has yet to kill a single large game animal!"

The commander was furious at the insult. Likening a grown Kuaran man to a child was nearly as great an offense as calling him lazy. Having both remarks levied at him at once was a double affront. "You dare compare me to a youngling?" he shouted. "I am older than you, young Arstinax. My blade bears the notches of many fallen men. I am a warrior full born!"

Arstinax ripped a sturdy leg from a nearby table, then readied his newly acquired club for battle. Unbalanced, the great table toppled, spilling its contents of bottles and mugs to the floor with the sound of smashing glass. Arstinax coolly replied, "Then prepare to die like one."

The commander took the bait, feverishly waving his hand to his men behind him. "Take the Princess alive if you can—dead if you must. I will deal with this one-eyed son of a whore myself!"

In spite of herself, Keris breathed a sigh of relief. Arstinax had tricked the commander into fighting him, while sending his lesser skilled underlings to challenge her. Because she was a highly trained knife master, this would have normally given her the advantage—even against three opponents. However, half-impaired with drink, she found herself wondering if the risks Arstinax was taking on her behalf were for nothing.

She parried a blow and countered with one of her own. She missed. A second assailant, hoping to take advantage of her turned back, charged at her, yelling, with his blade aimed for her neck. Keris barely dodged the attack; she struck the man in his chest while he was in the act of bringing down his weapon. He fell to the flood with a thud. Keris's stance wobbled slightly, and she struggled to keep her mind clear.

"Had a bit much to drink, have we?" one of the soldiers jeered, cautiously circling Keris, looking for an opportunity to strike. Her other attacker briefly looked down at his fallen comrade, eyeing Keris contemptuously. "You will pay for what you did to Kanax!" He lunged at her, his drawn blade flashing from the dancing flicker of torchlight. Time had slowed down for Keris; she managed to tear herself away from the entrancing flicker just in time to avoid full impact. Nevertheless, the blade glanced the side of her cheek, leaving a thin, crimson line of blood.

"Stupid!" Keris cursed herself as she spun about to face both opponents at once. She was finding it increasing difficult to concentrate. She knew if she stood any chance of winning this battle, it had best be won quickly. Keris took the offensive, thrusting her curved blade ahead. Her target jumped backed, narrowly avoiding the blade's wicked tip. The other mercenary tried to sneak down low to wound her legs. Instead, his face met the full brunt of her forceful boot. He sprawled backward, landing scarcely conscious on the floor.

The lone remaining mercenary waved his dagger menacingly. Keris knew him to be the most skilled of the three. She also knew, in her current state, that she could not defeat him. Already, the room around her was beginning to turn and shift, like the image in a mirror held by an unsteady hand. Keris could hear the sounds of Arstinax and the commander doing battle elsewhere in the room . . . the sounds seemed so far away . . . so unreal. Three more mercenaries came through the door. One guarded the entrance while the others ran to aid their commander.

Keris's mind began to drift away. She could see a mercenary move toward her with his blade poised for death, but she could do nothing. Her own blade had dropped to the floor, too heavy to be wielded by her loosened grasp. *All is lost*, she thought, and prepared for her end. The sounds of glass breaking jarred her back to her senses. A round, flat face peered at her though the haze of bright noise.

It was the innkeeper. He held the broken remains of an ale bottle in his hand. The mercenary lay at his feet, gripping his bleeding head in pain. The barkeep hastily pressed something into Keris's hand—a key. "The exits are all blocked!" he shouted. "You must go down the stairs to the first room you see. That is my room, and it has the strongest door in the inn. It will keep them out—at least for a while."

As he spoke, Keris saw that the mercenary soldier was coming to his feet, his wildly twitching eyes possessed with thoughts of vengeance.

"We can only pray that a miracle happens in the meantime," the innkeeper said. "Go!"

Keris did as she was told. Summoning all her remaining strength, she ran down the stairs to find the room the innkeeper spoke of. Just before she closed the heavy door to bolt herself in, she heard him cry out. "Not everyone believes you are a traitor, my Queen, and not everyone thinks Nephredom is fit to rule us. Reclaim your throne and—"

Keris heard a terrible scream, then silence. She sat huddled on the floor like a frightened child; the inner strength she so often depended upon was gone. She sobbed heavily and waited for them to come for her.

✳ ✳ ✳

After slavishly apologizing, for what seemed the tenth time, Authright hastily ushered Rayna toward the cellar door. "This way, please, Irel," Authright said, his eyes fixed on Rayna's ears. "And again, welcome to the Guild, Guild Master."

Rayna smiled secretly. Being mistaken for an ancient myth had its advantages after all.

While in Soren, Rayna had learned from her second Hand that Irel was the Science Guild's patron Power—*an interesting choice for a science guild*, she thought, considering that Irel was supposed to be the Power of chaos and change. That would, however, explain the décor.

The stairs behind the door led down to a rather unremarkable room cluttered with stacked books and assorted junk. "Our storage room,

Guild Master," Authright said apologetically. "Please pardon its disordered state. I will get Habott and the others to tidy it when we come back." He pushed hard on a section of wall at the back of the room and it slowly gave way, revealing yet another set of stairs. Authright explained that they had discovered the false wall by accident some time ago.

The long flight of hidden stairs took them much further underground, to a short hallway with a door on each end. To her left was the infamous garlic room Habott spoke of. Even with its door closed, the smell emanating from its direction was sharp and potent. The other door, however, caught Rayna's attention. For the first time since she had seen the Lake Stone in Lamec, she was staring at something obviously more advanced than anything else in Taren.

The door was metallic, with a computerized display console attached at eye level. In lieu of a doorknob was a flat, rectangular glass panel with a flashing red light in its center. The outline of a handprint was etched into the glass. Embedded in the floor, near the base of the door, lay a peal-toned oval platform; it appeared to be inactive.

"Guild Master, please allow me," Authright said, stepping forward and touching his palm to the glass handprint. The console lit up with green, typed characters, scrolling by on its screen faster that Rayna could fully read. She was able to make out a few words as they rolled fleetingly by:

. . . database link initiated . . .
scanning . . .
DNA analysis complete . . .

Before Rayna could ponder the words' meaning further, the oval plate on the floor became alive with illuminated energy. A beam of opaque light streamed upward from the platform, then dimmed gradually, revealing a middle-aged woman in military attire. She turned and looked at Authright with disdain in her soulless eyes. Her dark voice echoed eerily throughout the secret chamber:

"To unspecified Taren Subject.
This area is restricted to authorized personnel.
Access denied."

The image dissipated, and the oval platform grew dormant once again. Rayna felt an unshakable chill take hold of her. The hologram's voice was that of the woman from her accident in the woods, the woman from her nightmares.

"You see," Authright pointed out, "a ghost. She always says the same thing, no matter whose hand we use. Of course, being a ghost, she is of little scientific interest to us. The door she guards, on the other hand, is a different matter." Authright tugged the collars of his waistcoat confidently. "We are convinced that something of great scientific value is behind that door! The problem is, we haven't had much luck getting it open. We've tried everything—tools, brute force—we even tried using a special acid we developed using garlic. Nothing."

Rayna wasn't impressed. She scoffed, "If the best you could come up with is a garlic-based corrosive, it's no wonder the Alchemists don't think much of the Science Guild. Has anyone tried looking for a hidden access panel?"

Authright stared back blankly.

"Never mind. I have a hunch we may not need to find one." Rayna placed her hand on the palm sensor. Authright was right about one thing, her instincts told her: Something important was behind that door. But what, she thought, would she do if her instincts were wrong?

It didn't take long to find out. The console began its previous routine, but then she noted new words running across the screen:

DNA scan positive . . .
   . . . no genetic aberrations found in target area . . .
Bio-identification results negative . . .
Limited access granted . . .

Even as the sequential pop of releasing metallic fasteners sounded and the security door swung open before them, the holographic woman appeared before them again, but this time with a different message:

"Welcome, unidentified visitor to observation post number three of the Testing Area of Restricted Environmental Neo-prison . . . or, as we prefer to call, it—TAREN."

Authright fainted.

* * *

Four men lay half-dead at Arstinax's feet, but the lumbering giant was bleeding and battle weary, and three more men stood before him. He hoped that Keris was able to escape, but he dared not take his attention from his enemies to be sure.

The commander cursed him, shouting, "You will die this night, young Arstinax, and your miserable death will be un-mourned and forgotten!"

Arstinax waved his makeshift club threateningly. "You said as much six men ago," he rumbled. "And yet I still stand, and your men are now but two."

The commander nodded. "I must admit," he said, "you are a skilled warrior, but you are injured and weakened from battle. I promise you, you *will* die before this night is done!"

With those words came the next concerted attack, as the remaining three men sought to wear him down and penetrate his defenses. They spread out, each man slowly approaching from a different direction. Arstinax's club was a force to be reckoned with; the now-semiconscious group that had dared face it in battle—and lost—lay moaning and bleeding on the floor in sobering testament to that. Suddenly, one of the commander's men charged forward with a dagger, forcing Arstinax to engage him. The blade sliced into Arstinax's side; he groaned in agony as he brought his club down hard upon his attacker's back.

A single grunt was all the villain uttered as he fell to the floor and lay still. Now Arstinax faced but two men. He ignored the pain from his fresh wound and stood his ground.

The commander smiled, which puzzled Arstinax at first. Then he noticed how light his weapon suddenly felt. Looking down, he saw that the last attack had broken off the greater part of his club. He held only the remaining stub in his tired grasp.

"As I said," the commander sneered, "you will die this night."

✳ ✳ ✳

When Rayna arrived at the shattered inn, she instantly became aware of an unsettling noise—the sound of an axe hitting something. Quietly, she followed the sound down the inn's stairs to a narrow hallway, where she saw a man chopping at a door with a hand axe. Rayna's bracelet burned her wrist; its fierce glow illuminated the dim area. *Danger!* The light from Rayna's bracelet offended the axe-wielding man, and he stopped his incessant hacking, looking wildly around for the source. Upon seeing Rayna, he turned his weapon to her, madness in his eyes.

Rayna tried to summon the magic, but it would not come. Instinctively, she dodged the man's attack and used her staff the way her first Hand had taught her. Keeping her distance, she disarmed him with series of downward strikes to his wrist. A double-handed thrust to his head with her staff sent the axe wielder slumping against the wall, unconscious. Her bracelet decreased its shine and eventually darkened.

Rather than relief, Rayna suddenly felt a pang of utter sadness at what she had learned while in the restricted-access room at the Guild. She pushed away the feelings of despair and turned her attention to the door. The intruder had nearly chopped his way through; only a few stubborn ribbons of oak kept the door intact. Without fully knowing why, Rayna called out, "Keris? Keris, are you in there?"

"Is that you, Rayna?"

Rayna scarcely recognized the frightened voice as belonging to Keris. "Yes, it's me," she replied.

The splintered door opened, and the two embraced. The gladness Rayna felt was short-lived, however, because she realized there was no one else in the room. "Where's Arstinax?" she asked.

Keris gathered her composure, looking once again like her old self. "Follow me," she said. "I pray we are not too late."

Those haunting words distressed Rayna, and she feared the worst as they raced back to the inn, where Keris saw Arstinax last. To Rayna's relief, she found her fiancé sitting in a chair, grunting from pain. He was alive.

Keris saw the Commander lying still on the floor and quickly confirmed that he was dead. He had been lanced in the neck by a pointed piece of wood, the length and thickness of a small knife, which still jutted from Arstinax's broken club.

Stepping over a mass of defeated adversaries, Keris couldn't help but marvel at the Kuaran warrior's prowess. "You defeated them *all?*" she asked slowly, with slurred speech, still fighting the effects of the ale.

Arstinax nodded, grimacing at the same time. "Yes. All but one. He fled at the sight of his leader falling at my hands."

Rayna quickly searched the bar area until she found a bottle of clear liquor with a potent smell and a clean cloth. She applied the liquor to the cloth and began dabbing it on Arstinax's injuries, much to his discomfort. "You'll have to forgive me," Rayna said, frowning, "if I don't find all this testosterone talk terribly exciting. I think we need to focus on keeping you from joining your friends on the floor."

"Quite right," Keris agreed. She began searching the round sacks tied around her belt. "I'm out of healing herbs," she lamented.

"That's okay, I have something." Rayna reached into her robe pocket and pulled out several cloves of fresh garlic. "Courtesy of the Science

Guild," she quipped. "I had the strangest feeling I would need some, so I took a few cloves with me before I left."

Rayna handed the alcohol to Keris. "Here, finish cleaning and sterilizing his wounds while I prepare the garlic."

Keris was not used to taking orders, but she did as she was told because Rayna's tone was so compelling. "Why garlic?" she asked. She remembered Emawin mentioning an old herbal remedy involving the plant, but her fogged memory failed to recall the details. "Is it not little more than a strong spice to flavor one's meals?"

Rayna shook her head, "It contains certain antiseptic properties to prevent infection and promote healing. It should make a decent salve." Rayna found an empty bottle and began using it as a pestle, hastily crushing the garlic into a lumpy paste.

Keris understood only part of what Rayna said, but she was in no condition to inquire further. She simply replied, "What a strange use for garlic."

Rayna began dressing Arstinax's many cuts and bruises with the fresh paste. "I've heard stranger," she said.

After treating his wounds, she bandaged them tightly. By that time, most of the wounds had stopped bleeding.

"When you didn't return like you promised, I got worried," she told him, inspecting her work. "Well, that and the fact that I just found out something that you both need to know right away."

Keris noticed for the first time that Rayna wasn't wearing a headscarf. Rayna caught her stare.

"Is that wise?" Keris questioned.

Rayna understood her concern. "It doesn't matter anymore," Rayna said. "It's not about me, or my ears—it's Taren. Taren is in major danger."

"Of course, we already know this. Nephredom, the beasts . . ."

"No. I'm talking about something far worse."

Before Rayna could say more, the party was disturbed by the crunch of shoes stepping on broken glass. They had company.

In spite of his injuries, Arstinax stood, ready to face their yet-unseen visitor. Keris had recovered her dagger from where she dropped it, and held it with confidence once more. Rayna felt like screaming a tantrum of protest at having to face yet another crisis, but she held fast to her staff and prepared to fight alongside her friends.

A small figure appeared in the doorway—Quan.

"The man at the Science Guild said I could find you here," he said, blinking in disbelief at the destruction around him. "What happened here?"

"Never you mind about that," Keris replied sharply. "Why are you not in Argat? Did not one of Ciredor's monks accompany you there?"

"He's dead."

"If this is one of your pranks . . ."

"No, I swear, he died while trying to help us."

"'Us?'"

"Everyone. The whole hamlet is under attack."

Keris suddenly felt a numbing chill run down her spine. One of her worst fears had come true. "The Red Robes have come to Argat," she whispered.

"Yes," Quan said, finally breaking down under the weight of the news he bore. Tearfully, he continued with a quavering voice. "Argat is on fire. They set fire to everything, without torch or flint. They did it all with their minds. When people tried to run, they were set on fire too."

Keris noticed that the back of Quan's left hand was badly burned. "They did this?" she asked, running a careful finger across the reddened, blistered spot of flesh.

Quan nodded. "The monk blocked the fire so I could escape and warn you." Quan paused and swallowed hard. "That is how he died."

Keris braced herself as she asked the next question. "What of Emawin and the girls?"

"The Red Robes were heading to the house when I fled. I don't know if they had time to escape."

"Then I will have to go there and find out. You will stay here with Rayna and Arstinax while I investigate."

"I will not!" Quan protested. The boy regained his composure in such a complete, mature manner that it made Rayna wonder if the boy was ever truly a child. "Emawin is the only mother I've ever known," he said. "I fled only to get help, not to cower here while someone else tries to rescue her!"

"Spoken like a true warrior," Arstinax lauded.

"Indeed," Keris said, recognizing the budding signs of manhood in her young adoptive brother. "Very well, you may come with me, but you must follow my every command. If Emawin and the others are still alive, they will no doubt be hiding. We will need to find them with stealth and guile to avoid detection. We must not arouse unnecessary attention, for the Red Robes are very dangerous."

"Which is exactly why I'm going with you," Rayna said, her cracking voice lacking the conviction she intended.

"You do not have to do this," Keris responded, looking her friend in the eyes. Despite their differences, she had come to admire the eccentric master mage from the place called Nightwind. "Emawin is family to us only. You need not get involved."

"You forget that Emawin saved my life. She is a friend, and I owe her this, at the very least. Please, I want to help."

"And where Irel goes, as do I," Arstinax said. "I too consider Emawin a friend."

Keris smiled. "Very well. We will do this together. Quan, how did you get here so quickly? Argat is several days journey from here."

"Tell me about it," Rayna snapped, remembering her sore feet.

Keris pretended not to hear her. "I take it you came by the monk's horse?" she asked.

Quan nodded. "But I don't think the horse can make a return trip so soon. I rode it all the way here without really stopping. It started to limp as we approached here."

"I saw a stable around back, when I first came to the inn," Keris said. Let us hope our valiant innkeeper was well off enough to afford a horse."

They found two horses in the stable. Keris and Quan chose one, and Rayna and Arstinax claimed the other. With docile brown eyes, like shiny saucers, the horses stared at the party complacently. One snorted lazily as it went for some hay strewn near its feet.

"It is time these idle creatures earned their keep," Arstinax said, preparing a saddle for their horse.

"And for the horse I rode here to take a much-deserved rest in their stead," Quan added. His thoughts drifted from the horse to Bard. He had lost contact with the dog when the Red Robes attacked, and hadn't seen him since. He wondered if Bard had had a chance to escape.

Rayna couldn't decide if it was good luck or bad that they found the horses. They were going to a place besieged by Red Robes, after all. Still, there was hope. Her magic did defeat the Red Robes once. Maybe she would be able to pull off a repeat performance—provided she could figure out a way to summon the magic again.

The two pairs mounted their horses. As Arstinax set his and Rayna's horse in motion, Rayna looked up at the dark sky and suddenly became very afraid; the twin stars looked back at her, their meaning now clear to her. She thought back on what she had learned in the secret chamber and shuddered. She wished she had more time to explain to the others what was going to happen, and how nothing—not even this brave rescue attempt—would mean anything in the end. Rayna sighed with frustration. News of Armageddon would have to wait.

CHAPTER 19

Chorus

King Nephredom screamed. "Enough! I've heard enough!" But the chorus had grown relentless. *You have been shamed by your falsehoods,* they said. *The truth is not in you.*

"It had to be done!" Nephredom shouted, his manic eyes darting about his quarters, looking at things no others could see. "The burden could be held by me no longer, and my enemies are too many." He began to whimper like a small child. "I *had* to release the gate."

But the last of the Bromus line has not been destroyed. The Princess yet lives.

Nephredom sank deeper in his chair, as if trying to hide inside it. He worriedly clawed his long nails through unkempt hair. "I could wait no longer! She will die when the beasts come. All here will die when the beasts come."

"You have failed."

Nephredom jerked his body around to see a tall bearded man standing behind him, his dark woolen hair mixed with jagged streaks of silver. He had the presence of hardened steel about him, and his piercing eyes wore an unapproachable stare.

"You have failed me. You can be no son of mine."

Nephredom gasped and tried to lift himself from his chair, but he was too feeble to stand. "Father," he started, "I have not failed you. I have taken the East Taren throne, and soon it shall be destroyed in retribution."

"Coward!" his father cried out. "You were too frightened and weak to rescue me from the beasts, and so you trapped me inside with them."

"No! I could not reach you, Father! There were too many of them!"

"Coward!"

"But I came back! In secret—"

"Coward!"

With trembling hands covering his eyes, Nephredom blotted out the image and sounds of his father; he waited for the reproachful voice to fade away, to become one with the chorus once more. Eventually it did, but then another voice broke away from the chorus to take its place.

"Nephredom, my love."

The panic-stricken King looked up to see his betrothed.

"Cattana?"

"Yes, my love. I have returned to you at last."

Nephredom was taken aback; he thought he would never see her again. "But I was told that you—"

"Had died? Yes. I did. And vengeance is yet to be claimed in my honor."

Nephredom lamented, "I should have never allowed you to leave my side. Who . . . who did this to you?"

"You know who did this. It was the master mage they call Rayna Powell. We both know her true name."

"Irel!"

"Yes, my love. Irel has taken me from you."

Nephredom's wild eyes flared. "She could not kill me, so she killed you instead!"

"Where do you want me to leave it?" another single voice sounded.

"Leave what?"

"Your food, my King."

Nephredom found himself looking at another woman. "Who are you?" he demanded.

The woman looked nervous, but she answered plainly. "I am one of your attendants. I help keep the place in good order, my King."

"Why are you here?"

"You asked me to bring you food, remember?"

"Yes, of course. Where are the other servants?"

"There are only a handful of us left, my King. Many have left."

Nephredom noticed the woman wore a necklace. It was the betrothal necklace he had given Cattana, his beloved.

"Thief!" Nephredom shouted, his voice like burning sand in desert wind. "You dare stand before me with my dead lover's gift about your neck!" His dark eyes squinted with disdain. "You are one of Irel's spies. She sent you here to gloat . . . perhaps even to try taking my life!"

A single gurgling scream was all the servant could utter before Nephredom crushed her throat with a thought. He managed to stand, then walked to where she had fallen. He reached down to retrieve the necklace and found it to be made of plain string, with simple beads. Nephredom stepped back, bewildered. "Impossible," he said.

He noticed a tray of food lying near the body, part of its content scattered across the floor. Nephredom picked up some bread and cheese and sat back down.

The chorus taunted, *The strain of the gate was too much for you. We told you it would be.*

"Silence!" Nephredom's voice was hoarse and raw. It hurt to swallow, and he could taste blood in his throat. He hadn't noticed that before.

They say you are mad and that the strain of the keeping the gate was too great. Can you not hear them whispering? Can you not hear them speaking ill of you behind your back?

"Yes, I hear them. They think I cannot, but I hear them. Their incessant little voices seeping through these stone walls . . . I hear them!"

They say you spend your days screaming in lunacy and your nights wandering the halls speaking to those who are not there.

Nephredom stood unsteadily and gripped the arm of the chair for support. "They say such things of their King?" he said. He lost his balance and stepped forward to regain it, nearly stumbling over the body of the servant. He stared down at her, confused.

"Who is this person?" he asked. "Was she a spy?"

No, she was a servant and washerwoman. She has been dead for some time. You murdered her.

Nephredom laughed hysterically. "Surely you jest. I have never before seen this woman! What was her name?"

Why don't you ask her?

Nephredom squatted down nearer the subject. "Very well, woman. Tell me, what is your name?"

The woman opened her lifeless eyes and spoke to Nephredom in the voice of his dead lover. "I am Death, and soon I will come for you, my love!"

Horrified, Nephredom flamed the speaking corpse until nothing but smoldering ashes remained.

"You were always my best student." An old woman clapped her hands.

Nephredom recognized her as his former mentor, from the days he lived in Dosk as a common student.

"The fire was strong and sure," she said, "just as your magic has always been."

How did she get in here? Nephredom thought. *Why did not the guards see her?*

"I have always been here," the old woman said.

"I don't have time for you now, old hag!" Nephredom growled.

The old woman faded. Nephredom rubbed his temples in pain.

"Then perhaps you would see me." Yet another voice spoke.

Nephredom stared up, his brows raised in surprise. "Aric? Why are you here? I sent you to Argat."

"I bring you good news, my Liege. The Princess has been killed, and the she-mage as well."

Nephredom smiled. "Excellent! You have served me well."

She is a deceiver, the chorus warned. *The last of the Bromus line still lives.*

"Don't listen to them, my Liege," Aric said. "I have proof."

"Where is it?" Nephredom demanded.

Aric pointed to the mass of ashes on the floor. "There. You see, the Princess."

Nephredom looked closer and saw the Princess lying before him."

"She is dead," Aric said boastfully. "I killed her in your name."

Fiery pain flared sharply inside Nephredom's head. He screamed, then shut his eyes in agony. He could do nothing else until the pain lessened to its usual throb.

When he opened his eyes, Aric was gone, and so was his prize: The body of the Princess was missing. Only a pile of ashes lay in her place.

"The Princess was never dead," he said hatefully. "It was only a ruse." He looked upward and cried out, "Why do you toy with me, Irel! Face me, if you dare!"

"Nephredom," A soft voice sounded behind him. He turned, expecting to see Irel herself. Instead, it was Aric.

"You again?"

Aric laughed smugly. "This is not one of your pathetic hallucinations.

If you can see me, it means your mind has deteriorated to a point where you are no longer of use to me."

Nephredom blinked. "What? You dare speak to me that way? I have the power to snuff your life out like a candle's flame!"

Aric was unshaken. "Some time ago, I embedded this . . . interactive vision deep in your mind, to surface only when the time was right." Aric grinned. "If you are seeing this communication, it means one of two things: I have imprisoned you and will soon end your miserable life, or I no longer need you to further my own ends." Aric shrugged. "Or both . . . but technically that would be three things."

"You will regret those words!"

Kill her! the chorus urged. *You must kill her now!*

Nephredom brought forth a great ball of flame and hurled it at Aric, who made no attempt to move. The fire passed through her and hit the wall; its after-blast shoved Nephredom back, throwing him onto his back, with his clothing and hair badly singed.

Aric clapped mirthfully. "What a performance!"

Kill her, kill her now!

Nephredom tried to stand again, but quickly sank to his knees in pain. The voices and the headaches—they were too much to bear. When the pain in his head had diminished, he summoned enough strength to stand, then he stumbled aimlessly about the room like a drunkard. He found himself in front of a mirror. What he saw frightened him. The reflection revealed a haggard wildman with blood on his torn shirt, and with hair that was uncombed, with patches torn out. His beard had grown like an unruly patch of weeds. The worst was his face, which had gone slack on one side. He looked more like a creature than a man. *How long have I been this way?*, he thought.

"Sad, isn't it?" Aric asked. "And to think you were once the most powerful man in both Tarens."

"Who are you?" Nephredom asked, fixated on the mirror.

"Have you forgotten already? I am a hidden message. A note in a bottle, from the one you know as Aric."

"Then give me your message and be gone!"

"My, my, my, aren't we angry today?" the image chuckled.

"My anger is hammered and forged from my hatred of those who oppose me."

"Yes, I know. And who do you think shaped that hatred in your heart all these years? It is true, the hatred was always there, but it was I who kept it strong, who fanned and stoked it into blinding rage. I know about the Gate. I know that the beasts are now free and are heading toward the source of magic that trapped them for so long. They are coming here." Aric paused. "I also know that you are the son of West Taren's King Sunder , and that you were born an *Unnatural*."

Nephredom suddenly turned around, almost losing his balance, and focused his full attention on Aric. "How do you know these things?" he asked.

Aric shook her head. "You never were terribly smart, were you? I am a master Psi-telepath. Your mind is weak. Did you truly think you could keep secrets from me? And you are in no condition to do anything about it, anyway. Ah, the message. Well, here it is."

Nephredom's mind flooded with flashing images and events. He saw himself standing before his father, who told him for the first time what he was—an *Unnatural*. He saw his father sending him away to Dosk, where his burgeoning magic would be tolerated, even encouraged. Nephredom didn't want the moment to end, for it had been so long since he had seen his father, but the scene did end, and then he was standing before the old woman who had been his mentor. The vision showed them training together, and he felt his envy of her great power and his longing to be her equal in all of the magics she possessed. The vision jumped again, and he saw himself sending her away, in a fit of anger. He never knew where she went.

The vision then took him to the Great Lake of Lamec, before the city turned everyone into beasts. Unlike the previous scenes, this vision did not involve Nephredom's personal past—it involved someone else's. Yet, he was allowed to see these events unfold as if he had personally been there when they happened. Nephredom found himself sitting in a small boat with his mentor and an unknown sentry—no doubt the one assigned to guard the sacred Lake Stone. From his childhood, Nephredom remembered that a guard always watched over the Stone. But why was this one taking the old woman, his mentor, so close to the Stone? He saw her touch the Stone, and then a blinding light; the boat came to pieces around them. Nephredom shielded his eyes.

When the light had eased, he could see that he and his mentor were headed toward shore, kicking their legs as they clung to a large floating piece of what remained of the patrol boat. A transformation had overcome his mentor. Her matted, gray hair sprang to life with renewed vigor, and it darkened to a lustrous raven black. The light had washed over her frail body, straightening her curved back and fleshing out sagging skin. Her formerly age-ravaged face was free of wrinkles and full of youthful beauty.

He recognized his mentor by her new face: Aric. Nephredom now understood. Aric had used the Lake Stone to restore her youth.

"Not just my youth," Aric corrected. "The Lake Stone increased my power nearly twofold. No master mage alive can match me."

Lies. She tries to confuse us, the chorus chanted.

"You know I speak the truth," Aric said. "It all makes sense now, doesn't it? Now you know how the Lake Stone was changed and who changed it. Ironic, isn't it, that it was a West Taren guard who allowed me access to the Stone in the first place?"

Nephredom wrapped his arms around his head in a desperate effort to block Aric's image and voice from his mind. He shouted feverishly, "It was East Taren hands that defiled the Stone and the city of Lamec, and it will be East Taren blood that shall pay the price!"

"Oh?" Aric commented wryly. "That's only part of the plan. I agree that East Taren should pay the price—not for any bloody Lake Stone, but for allowing West Taren to exist in the first place. We should have wiped out the West Taren people decades ago. Our rulers chose to compromise and dally, and chat our way from one truce to another. Now, thanks to you and I, that will all change. West Taren finally will fall."

The chorus began to moan. *Her words are poison! Silence her!*

"You speak nonsense," Nephredom said. "It is East Taren that the beasts will come for. You purport to have free dominion of my memories. You should know that."

The image of Aric sneered. "What a hollow little man you are. Your sole reason for living is vengeance. I've always had a fondness for single-purposed men. They are so easy to manipulate and mold, like clay in my hands."

"You have delivered your message, specter! Now leave me be!"

"I think it's a disgrace when a West Taren dog like you can wield stronger magic than an East Taren Princess. Our people have become weak. We very nearly lost the war. That is why the purging must come." The image of Aric looked away from the suffering ruler. "Do you want to know a secret, King? The beasts can be calmed only by Psi-telepathic magic—*very strong* Psi-telepathic magic. All other forms of magic are nigh useless."

"I am too tired for this."

"I decided long ago that Psi-telepathy was a magic superior to all others. I envisioned a new Taren ruled by a Psi-telepathic East Taren queen."

"Never! Now go!"

"It is true that the beasts will first come here, but do you think they will stop here? You think they will be sated from their orgy of spilling East Taren blood, pack up, and go back home to their prison in Lamec? That is precisely why men should leave complex plans to us women. Men simply have no brains for it."Aric laughed cruelly. "There was always a flaw in your plan, and that flaw was the one magic you possess—and you were never very good at it."

"Psi-telepathy," Nephredom answered.

"Of course. Are you beginning to understand now? As I said before, the beasts can be controlled only by the strongest of Psi-telepathic magic."

"I controlled the beasts, and I did not need such worthless magic to do it," Nephredom rebutted wearily.

"Control them? All you did was put them in an elaborate cage—which reminds me—have you seen your father lately?"

"Silence, witch! Is there nothing sacred to you? Are my most private thoughts but mere playthings to you?"

"Is that fear I see in your eyes, Nephredom?"

"Be gone from here, wraith! Leave me in peace! Your insolence remains unchecked only because you lack flesh and blood!

The chorus cried, *Keep her away from us! Keep her away from the secrets we hold! She is not of us, not of us at all!*

"Why, don't you wish to hear the rest of the story?" Aric taunted. "The beasts will kill many East Tareners, as you predicted, but those of us—such as myself—who possess strong enough Psi-telepathic magic will survive. Together, with my help, we will drive them back—"

"Impossible!" Nephredom shouted. "The mind tricks of such few will not seduce the horde! There will be too many of them!"

"Not if we have your famous Red Robes helping us. Or should that be my famous Red Robes? You do know that I control the Red Robes, don't you? I have for some time. They will act as the heart of my Psi-telepathic army. In the face of that kind the power, the beasts will succumb to our will, I assure you." Aric smiled in delight. "That will be when the true fun begins. As a token of our everlasting affection, we will send the creatures to your native West Taren. With no magic to speak of, your people will not fare well in attack. The beasts will slaughter everyone in sight, save perhaps a few hundred, here and there. But don't you worry; I won't allow those brave survivors to go to waste. They will be the slaves to rebuild East Taren and serve our people until we have no further use for them. With Psi-telepathic might, I will retain the beasts as our army against all dissent. With only the strongest of us alive, East Taren will be invincible, and finally worthy of my claiming its throne."

Nephredom shook his head weakly, his listless eyes staring away at nothing. "There are too many of them. The strain of controlling them will be too great, even for one of your power."

Aric tilted her head and leaned forward gloating. "Now doesn't that sound familiar?" she asked. "I recall the same thing being said to you about the Gate. But thankfully, you were too proud and stupid to listen. I, on the other hand, have no intention of saddling the full burden of beast control. That's what the Red Robes are for. Like you, they are of a single mind, a single purpose. Let that purpose be to serve me, and all the things I desire.."

Aric's words blurred, and her image grayed out in Nephredom's mind. He found himself in a dank place of mossy stones, dimly lit by fading torch light—a place that he found familiar, but could not remember exactly. As his vision cleared, Aric stood across from him, disinterested.

"Where am I, and why have you brought me here?" he asked.

Aric scoffed. "You brought yourself here, you fool—with your own two feet! It's a wonder you remember your own name. Don't you recognize your own dungeon? You've certainly sent enough poor devils here to rot."

Nephredom remembered. "But this is not that part of the dungeon," he said, looking around.

"No," Aric agreed. "It is in this part of the dungeon that we keep our dirty little secret."

Nephredom saw the cell door, an enormous slab of coarse, black iron. At the center was a small window with three stout bars. The heavy glass that covered the window was cracked and smeared from the inside with filth, so as to render it opaque. There was no slot or gap under the door to deliver meals. That would be too dangerous. Instead, food was delivered to this cell via a narrow chute from a concealed trap door far above. Sometimes this "food" would include the remains of certain prisoners Nephredom deemed unworthy of a public execution.

The chorus spoke again. *What curious award awaits! The sins of the one must be punished. The unclean one must find union. Then there will be peace!*

Nephredom found himself in Lamec, back at the Gate, in the black of night. He was surrounded by fifty of his best men, well-trained West Taren mercenaries. Six months had passed since the Queen had named him Regent, before retiring to her sickbed. He prayed he would be forgiven for taking so long. They entered the city through an opening he created in the Gate. Nephredom sensed that some of his men had reservations about the mission. They did not know the specifics, of course, but they knew enough to know that many of them would not live to return from this mission. They held fast to their swords, in nervous anticipation of the inevitable.

They had made it to their target destination when they were seen. Glaring red eyes, full of fury, closed in on them. Nephredom remembered his own fear. His men began to panic. He forced them to complete the mission. He nearly failed. Several of his men ran blindly from the attacking creatures and wandered too close to the Lake Stone; they became beasts themselves. Others ran back to the Gate without Nephredom's consent and were speared to death by the glass blades. More died fighting the beasts—especially those who forgot to thrust with their weapon, as they had been told.

Nephredom escaped from the city with only five of his men alive, but that mattered not, for they had fulfilled the mission. He had the five survivors killed later, to ensure that this secret would be known by none other than him.

"But I know," Aric said. "I stole it from your mind. Feeling guilty, are we?"

Aric's voice brought Nephredom's mind back to the present. He ignored her question. From within his badly soiled robes, he produced a plain key that had been painted black. He used it to open the cell door, went inside, and locked the door behind him. The chorus began to stir inside him, sounding loudly. Blinding pain enveloped his head. He blinked. "Father?"

A great scaled beast lay crouched in the corner, watching Nephredom, hissing and baring jagged teeth. On one of its gnarled, clawed fingers rested the royal ring of West Taren Kings.

"I am here, son," replied his father, King Sunder, hand outstretched. Gone was the judging scowl he had borne earlier; he now had the gentle face of the man Nephredom remembered as a boy. Dressed in magnificent robes of white, Sunder smiled.

Nephredom spoke. "Though it cost the lives of forty and five men, I knew I would find you. That was my first promise. It was but one of three vows I swore in your name."

"And your second promise?"

"To end the Bromus bloodline—in that promise I have failed."

"And your third?"

"To cure you of the curse. In that too, I have failed."

"But you have not failed, my son," King Sunder said. "I am here whole, as you can see."

The chorus began to wail, berating Nephredom like spiteful imps, clawing viciously at the mangled tatters of his tortured mind. Louder they chanted, hellish screeching from within.

Sunder beckoned "Come, son, be with me."

Nephredom hesitated, confused. He saw his father calling for him, forgiving him. But something was wrong. An alternating image of a great beast and his father seemed to flash in an unstable fashion before his eyes. In one moment, he saw his father, in the next, he saw the beast in his father's place. The beast growled in a low, guttural fashion, then crept closer to Nephredom.

The confusion passed, and Nephredom saw his father once more, asking that he join him. With the last effort of his faltering mind, he caused the black key to float before him, and then he set it ablaze. It melted away to nothing. Suddenly, Nephredom was a child again back in Lamec, long before he was exiled to East Taren. Long before the war . . . before he was ever called *Unnatural*. He excitedly ran into the arms of his father. He had thought he would never experience that joyous feeling again. He was back home.

Green venom covered his face, and soon numbness came. The beast ripped into the smiling King and began to devour his flesh. Its final note rendered, the chorus grew silent. At last, King Nephredom was at peace.

CHAPTER 20

Firesend

Rayna, Keris, and the rest of the party rode for many hours before arriving in Argat—or, rather, what was left of it. Like bones rising from devoured carcasses, blackened sticks of consumed buildings jutted from the ashes. After dismounting from her horse, Rayna turned and looked all around, seeing nothing but a panorama of ruin. There was no one alive in the street save themselves. A haze of acrid soot permeated the air, burning her nostrils. The party approached Emawin's house cautiously, weapons ready. The reek of death greeted them before they reached the house. Arstinax pushed lightly at the door, which fell forward and crumbled to the ground.

As she stepped over the threshold, Rayna caught her first grisly glimpse of what had happened inside the house. Emawin's home bore no resemblance to the cozy apothecary shop she remembered. Six small, lifeless bodies lay on the floor like discarded driftwood among the wreckage. Their arms and legs took awkward forms, as if they had been strewn about like rag dolls. Soot and ash covered them, providing one small source of solace to Rayna, for the soot obscured the terrified looks on the young faces. The sight of the charred bodies themselves was too much for her. She shut her eyes tightly, warding off the crippling panic she felt growing inside her.

"What manner of evil thing would do this?" Arstinax said, troubled disbelief in his voice.

Tears in his eyes, Quan turned away and ran out the door.

"Please go after Quan," Keris said to Arstinax. "I don't want him out there alone."

Arstinax nodded, but then hesitated for a moment as he looked at Rayna. Then he did as he was asked, and left the house. Rayna didn't notice his departure.

Keris suddenly heard shallow coughing, and she leaped toward the source of the sound. Quickly, she moved fallen sticks and boards away from a previously ignored pile of debris at the end of the main room.

"Emawin!" Keris shouted. Her joy soon lessened, however, upon seeing the dire condition her foster grandmother was in. Her robes were in tatters, and Keris could see areas where dried blood had glued the cloth, which clung fast onto her burned skin, so that it could not be removed without further harming her. A heavy board had fallen across Emawin's chest, and Keris struggled to remove it. Once Emawin was free of the debris, Keris decided to take the risk of moving her broken body to a corner of the room, which was better protected from falling debris. As if it had patiently waited for the old woman to be moved to a safer place, the roof where Emawin had lain collapsed, covering the floor below with more heavy boards and plaster.

Gingerly, Keris laid Emawin down near where Rayna stood. "Can you hear me, Grandmother?" she asked. The fire had burned out, but its smoke and heat had taken its toll on the frail woman and robbed her of her sight. Her eyes, now a milky gray, stared out at nothing; she lay on the floor dying, barely able to keep her breath. Turning her head in the direction of Keris's voice, Emawin called out to her, her wavering voice wheezing from the effort: "Keris, is that you?"

Keris quickly kneeled, close to Emawin's side. "I am here," she said.

"They came during the nighttime," Emawin said. "I tried to fight them off, I did . . . but there were too many of them. I—" Emawin broke off in a fit of coughing.

Keris searched the floorboards around them. "Where is your hidden stash of herbs, Grandmother? It is somewhere here, I'm certain."

"No time, precious. No time for me. . . . Listen to a dying woman, for stubbornness is what kept me alive. I had to see you just once more before the Heavens claim me."

Keris clawed at a loose floorboard and pulled it back. Underneath was a small niche filled with dried plants and medicines. "You are not going to die, Grandmother," Keris reassured Emawin as she gathered the herbs in her hand.

"Listen," Emawin said sternly, her rasping voice fading. "Take care of my children—so that their spirits can rest peacefully. Do you understand?"

Keris nodded. "They will be given decent burial and rites, I promise."

"Good . . . good. The old ways say that the dead . . ." Emawin paused. "The old ways say that the Heavens will claim *all* children, the unwanted and all. Rich or poor. It makes no difference. I taught you this, yes?"

"Yes."

"Then prepare them for me. They are one with the Heavens now, but it is . . . not good for them to be remembered like this. Bury them properly for me."

"I will."

Emawin smiled. "I stayed alive to see you. I may be blind, but I can still see you with my heart. I am proud of you. . . . They must never hurt you. As soon as you have seen to the children, you must run. Never let them find you."

Keris smiled, holding Emawin's hand snuggly inside her own. "You must rest. No more talking. I will prepare these herbs, and you will feel better."

Emawin coughed, and the light in her clouded eyes faded. "You shouldn't lie to your grandmother," she said. Her breath became more ragged and irregular. "We both know . . . well, we both know . . ."

Emawin's grasp became limp, and her tired breathing came to a rest. She was gone. Keris held the old woman's frail body close to her own for some time, wailing tearfully. Then, gently, carefully, Keris once more took Emawin up into her arms, carrying her. She looked over at Rayna. "Will you help me with the burials?" she asked.

Trauma stricken, Rayna was nearly shut off from the world, and Keris's words registered barely above a distant whisper in her mind. She sat on the floor, hugging her knees close to her body. "I'm not touching any dead bodies," she said softly, not looking up.

"I need your help with the burials," Keris insisted.

Rayna shook her head, saying nothing.

Keris stood quietly for a few seconds, at first watching Rayna, and then Emawin, whom she still held. "Very well," she said. "I will bury them on my own." Keris left with Emawin's body.

Rayna battled a distant war of will somewhere in the far reaches of her subconscious mind. She had fled, hiding within herself, where she was safe.

The eerie sound of shoveling startled Rayna from her dreamlike state. With the aid of her staff, she stood up and listened. The sound of shoveling continued. It was coming from outside. Stepping over dead bodies, Rayna followed the sound around to the back of the building, where she saw Keris burying Emawin. They exchanged no words; Rayna quietly found another shovel and began to help. Rayna did not know how much time had passed, but all the bodies were eventually given decent burials. Keris spoke the proper rites, as she had promised Emawin, and it was done. Rayna tried to find hope in the fact that they could find only seven bodies to bury. She remembered Emawin once telling her that there were about fourteen children in her care. Could it be that some of them escaped?

Rayna tensed. The shoveling had aggravated the pain in her lower back, which was already sore from hours of horseback riding. She felt guilty thinking of her own discomfort at a time like this.

Keris stared down at Emawin's grave. "Thank you, Rayna. I know that was difficult for you."

Rayna looked at Emawin's grave, remembering her gentle, sweet spirit, and how she nursed Rayna from the edge of death, never asking for anything in return. Rayna's tears came suddenly, like a rushing river that has broken through a dam. Once she started, Rayna couldn't stop crying. She knew her tears couldn't bring Emawin back, but they flowed all the same.

She felt a familiar hand touch her shoulder and turned to see Arstinax. She drew close to him.

True strength is seen in the fruit of one's works. Emawin's own hands sewed the belt I now wear. It is as strong as leather, but humble, like its creator. Above all, she saved the life of the woman I both awe and love. I will never forget her.

Rayna turned to Arstinax, touched by his words. "And neither will I," she said.

Arstinax looked at her, puzzled. "Neither will you do what? I didn't say anything."

"Of course you did, you just mentioned how Emawin made your belt—" She stopped cold, fearful of what was happening to her.

"I was thinking that," Arstinax said, confirming what she already knew.

"Forgive me," Rayna said, pulling away. "I didn't mean to—"

A dog was barking. "Bard?" Rayna questioned.

"Yes," Arstinax answered. "Quan and I were looking for him near the woods, when he came out from nowhere at the sound of the boy's magic flute. I had thought him dead, like the others, but he is fine."

The barking turned into growling. Rayna looked at her wrist and found it alit with magic, like white fire.

"I think we have company," Rayna said, getting a better grip on her staff. Keris saw the wild glow as well and unsheathed her blade. The party hurried their way back to the front of the house; they found Quan and Bard staring down the street. Bard's fur bristled as he snarled viciously.

Rayna saw it too: approaching from all directions—Red Robes. Hundreds of them. Her group had been caught in an ambush.

A slender woman with cold eyes swaggered into view, proud and sure. The Red Robes had stopped moving, and Aric approached the party alone.

Rayna's bracelet pulsated in union with the quickening rhythm of her own heart; she shuddered in revulsion. The unwholesome, foul nature of the being before her was unmistakable. She felt herself cringing from her own magic—it was telling her more than she wanted to know. She knew without doubt that this was the Aric of whom Keris had spoken, and that she murdered Keris's brother . . . and so many others. The psychic residue of Aric's past crimes washed over Rayna like an obscene shower of death.

"Some might say," Aric said, "burning down an entire hamlet is overdoing it a bit for a single bounty, but I've always had a flair for the dramatic. So at last, we have found our evasive Princess. I don't suppose you are going to surrender without a fight, and allow me to take you back to Jerel alive?"

Keris merely shook her head slowly, her curved dagger poised for a death-strike.

Aric closed her eyes and smiled. "Words cannot adequately express how *pleased* I am with that. And I must say, the people here certainly knew how to put on a show! Especially the ones who lived in that old hovel behind you. Did you know them? What a sight! Barefoot children, and an old woman armed with a rusty sword, trying to fend off my Red Robes. Pathetic! We dispatched them with no trouble at all."

A lone tear trickled down Keris's face, but neither her expression nor her stance changed.

"Have you no gratitude?" Aric jeered. "Are you not going to thank me for allowing you time to bury your dead, before I add you to their number?"

Arstinax took a step toward Aric.

Rayna intervened, shouting, "Arstinax, she's toying with us—she's trying to bait you!"

Aric gazed at the raging Kuaran curiously. "'Arstinax'? That's a surprisingly large number of syllables for a Kuaran name. An odd name. Do me a favor, dear Arstinax," she moaned in a breathy voice, "*grunt* for me."

Rayna looked at Arstinax; her eyes locked with his. "She would have flamed you dead before you got halfway to her," she said.

"Psi-clairvoyant, I presume?" Aric said, her appraising attention now fixed on Rayna. "So this is the famed mage I've heard so much about. You have become very popular—particularly amongst the rabble. Their tales about you become grander with each passing day. Some even say you are the incarnation of the Power Irel. And now finally, I have the opportunity to look upon your flesh with my own eyes—and see but a frightened little creature barely into womanhood. I must say, it is something of a disappointment. However, the round ears are a nice touch."

Rayna remained calm and forced herself not to look away from the malevolent master mage. For an unnerving moment, she and Aric both hesitated—each seemingly uncertain of what the other might do.

"That cheap trinket on your wrist," Aric said, pointing to Rayna's bracelet. "What does its glow mean?"

"It means it doesn't like you," Rayna replied coolly.

"Psi-clairvoyant *and* witty, I see. Well, if you were truly any good, you would know that your one-eyed friend is going to die anyway. In fact, you are all going to die."

"If I am to die today," Keris said, "I will take you with me, I promise."

Aric laughed. "Armed with a dagger, accompanied by a strongman, a single mage, and a boy with a mongrel dog? Is that *all*?"

"And about 3,000 armed men," Rayna said, looking ahead.

Aric turned and saw, in the distance, a legion of warriors ready to engage her Red Robes in battle. Clad in white, they shone brilliantly in the sun.

"They are practically on top of us!" Aric exclaimed. The main army was only a mile or so away, and there were smaller forces even closer. "How did so many get so close without me knowing?"

"I blocked their presence from your mind," Rayna said. "The fact that you like to hear yourself talk helped a lot."

The Red Robes also were caught by surprise. The warriors descended upon them with no fear and no hesitancy. The Red Robes were not accustomed to such bold challenges.

"I underestimated you," Aric said to Rayna.

"And not for the last time."

Aric walked closer to Rayna. "Do you have any idea whom you are speaking to, little girl?"

Rayna nodded. "As a matter of fact, I do. You're Aric Telvanni of Dosk, second born and illegitimate daughter of—"

Aric cut her off with a hiss. "Enough! So you are a Psi-telepath as well. Good. Then let us dispense with tedious words."

Rayna felt a slight shift in her awareness. She shuddered: Aric had linked their minds. Gradually, the sounds of fighting around her dimmed, and she was aware only of Aric. Aric's thoughts sounded in Rayna's mind like the haunting notes of a flute:

Welcome to my domain, Rayna Powell. Now, let us see who is the greater mage.

* * *

Her mouth agape with uncharacteristic amazement, Keris watched as the unknown army drew the Red Robes into battle, coming in waves of about fifty to a hundred at a time. They were no ordinary fighters, for though each carried a staff in one hand, the other flowed with the deadly flicker of Psi-Pyric magic. Some took position at a distance, using fire magic to attack the enemy, while the others fought directly with their staffs. One man led the charge, and he brought forth a volley of fireballs, each the size of a round melon, from raw, blue-white energy that surrounded his arms and hands. The fireballs pelted a small cluster of five Red Robes, taking them down. The Red Robes were on the defensive against the deluge, with their frantic counterattacks wildly reflexive, like the erratic bite of a wounded animal. Fire against fire, spell against spell— it was a spectacular display. Then Keris saw the leader's face, and her heart leapt: It was Ciredor. Barely within earshot, she could hear his voice.

"It's a shame," Ciredor yelled, preparing another volley of fireballs, "that two years of exile and disuse of my magic has made me a bit rusty. Fortunately for me, Nephredom was kind enough to supply me a generous offering of Red Robes to practice on!"

Even though the Red Robes had turned their backs to Keris and her party, to face Ciredor's army, Keris found herself frustratingly unable to take advantage of the situation. All of the Red Robes had joined together and engaged Ciredor's men on their right, while Keris, Rayna, and the others of their group stood at a safe distance from the army's magic. She longed for a bow, though she was but a novice archer at best.

"Stay!" Quan commanded his restless dog, who also seemed eager to join the fray. "They'd kill you just like all the rest!"

Bard whined but remained still, looking up questioningly at his master. Quan had a new, hardened look about him. Keris feared that part of his soul had died with Emawin and with the accursed fires that took his childhood home away forever. Moreover, Keris could tell, from the stony stares he gave her, that he held her responsible—that she had brought this tragedy down upon their heads. Keris suspected in her heart that he was right. Anyone having ties with her—however innocent they may be—risked the persecution of her many enemies. Quan knew that Keris had never told Emawin that she was Princess of East Taren, in hiding—wanted for murder by her own government. Thus, Emawin never fully knew the grave risks she was taking by having Keris in her company.

Her thoughts went back to Quan. She felt a schism growing between them, and that made the sting of the day's events all the worse to bear. She tried with limited success to refocus her mind on how the battle was progressing. She prayed that Ciredor and his army would at least right some of the wrongs done today—for all their sakes.

Arstinax was not as concerned with the battle between the Red Robes and the monk army as he was with the smaller conflict apparently going on between his beloved Irel and the powerful witch they called Aric. The two stood facing each other, motionless. He sensed a great battle of wills being tested between them, but he could not tell who was winning. He did not like the grimace on Irel's face. If she was in pain, how could he stand idly by and simply watch? He knew little of the ways of magic, but instinct warned him that attacking the witch Aric while she and Irel were in such a state could do his betrothed great harm. So he waited, a helpless giant forced to watch the woman he loved do silent battle—quite possibly for her very life.

Meanwhile, the warrior-monks' foray had taken an abruptly bleak turn. Initially, the Red Robes had been ineffective and clumsy in their defense. Many dozens had fallen. The element of surprise had expired, however, and their shock was replaced with seething hatred. Even as Captain Ciredor commanded the second wave of the attack, the Red Robes had already adapted. Like floating wraiths of red, they came together to form a large circle, then began to chant. Something about the manner of their mantra worried Ciredor deeply. He knew the Red Robes to be formidable enemies due to their ability to draw upon each other's power and increase it many-fold, but he had never seen so many of them unite in such a way before. More than a hundred Red Robes remained.

The chanting continued. Ciredor felt a baleful force brewing, and he was compelled to stop it before it was complete. He ordered his two hundred remaining men to assail the living circle from all sides with their deadliest magics, hoping to dismantle it. More Red Robes staggered under the impact of the army's offensive and collapsed. The circle adjusted for its missing members by closing tighter into itself—diminished but still intact. Then it was too late.

A wall of shimmering green light surrounded the crimson circle, then shot up like a great cylinder, blocking all subsequent attacks. The cumulative effect of the Red Robes's combined magics had created a shield larger and stronger than Ciredor had ever seen. But that was not all the Red Robes had done. A large area of ground just outside the circle began to warp and contort, writhing and rising. A small, quivering hill developed—pregnant with something foul.

"Fall back!" Ciredor ordered, praying that he and his men had time to escape the wake of whatever dark force the Red Robes were about to unleash. Myriad bald warrior-monks retreated, few daring to look back at the unholy event that was quickly unfolding behind them.

Ciredor felt a disturbing tremor, and he looked back to see that the hill had split open, spewing forth a great geyser of molten rock and billowing smoke. Soon, the heavy haze cleared, and Ciredor gasped, "Merciful Heavens!"

There, on the tortured patch of earth that bore it, stood a creature that Ciredor recognized only from folktales and from spoken accounts of adventures long past. It was an abomination he prayed had never truly existed, yet his eyes did not deceive him. It was a fire golem.

It stood more than twice as tall as his tallest man, and although it possessed the shape and form of a man, it was an inhuman thing born of flame, reeking of brimstone and lava-smoke. Its flickering red skin glowed with Red Robe magic, and its ominous eyes shone like miniature suns.

Frantically, Ciredor and his division continued to flee, hoping to meet up with their main army, which was more than a mile away. With haste, Ciredor used his magic to send up a fiery flare, his signal to his Second, Orin, to bring reinforcements quickly.

Ciredor suddenly felt a terrible heat upon his back. *Fire?* He looked back again, and saw to his horror that the fire golem was closer than he expected—scarcely forty or so feet away.

The giant golem had been running in pursuit; scalding lava and flaming fragments of glowing-hot rock burst from beneath its thundering feet with every rushing step it took. As it gave chase, it emanated wave after of wave of searing heat that spread out and flowed from its superheated body. The heat produced by this creature was no natural heat—it was like gaseous fire, scorching and blistering flesh. In its wake, the unfortunate monks who were too slow with their retreat were broiled alive, and their dead bodies erupted violently in flame as the golem came upon them in passing. The acrid smell of burning flesh from the small army's dead seemed to join the golem in the chase, for the scent somehow reached the noses of Ciredor and his fleeing men like a plague, like a ghoulish memento of the harrowing events happening around them.

Still awestruck, Ciredor managed to tear his eyes away from the fire-thing pursuing them. Though it was part of myth, the creature that pursued them was as real as the death it was dealing. It made him feel better about his decision to run from the fire golem at first chance. However, the golem was gaining ground, and his forces could not run forever.

No time to gather additional forces, Ciredor concluded resolutely. They would have to take a stand alone. He led his men to the highest ground he could find in the mostly flat hamlet—a hill lay ahead. An abandoned stone watchtower sat atop its peak. *Strategically, the watchtower would be the best location to hold our ground against that monstrosity,* Ciredor thought, *if we can reach it in time.*

✳ ✳ ✳

You will make an excellent Red Robe, Rayna Powell. I will bind your will to mine and you will serve me! But first, I think I will burn you so horribly that no man could stand the sight of you—not even your faithful Kuaran friend.

Rayna barely heard Aric's threats; her focus was elsewhere. Rayna did not how much time had passed since Aric linked their minds together. Seconds? Hours? There was no way she could tell safely, with Aric's slippery, dark presence inside her mind—ready to infest and burrow past her defenses at the first opportunity. Rayna suppressed a sickening shudder. It was like trying to stay calm with a swarm of scorpions crawling over her face.

To an outsider, Rayna and Aric appeared as motionless figures, confronting each other in a timeless face-off. Inside their minds, however, the waters were far from still. Like a young lion trying to defend its territory, Rayna fought back Aric's constant psionic attacks, using more instinct than skill. She was still coming to terms with the powers inside her . . . but she was learning. She was no longer worried about the "awakening" she had been undergoing since she had arrived in Taren. She now embraced her newfound abilities and was curious to discover what more she could do.

Aric's thoughts reached out to her again. *Are you listening, Rayna Powell? Can't you mind-speak? It's dreadfully rude of you to ignore your guest. Now is not the time to be bashful, for this may be the last time you get a chance to think as your own person before I enslave your will. I suggest you use it.*

Rayna responded to Aric's intimidation with a mental reply of her own: *I'm not afraid of you, Aric Telvanni—not anymore.*

Then you are a fool. I am Master Psi-kinetic, among other things. With a mere thought, I could rend—

Rayna interrupted. *I don't think you can do anything right now. Since you joined our minds together, you've tried twice of get free, so that you could attack my physical body, but I won't let you. You are stuck here—with me.*

Perhaps . . . but so are you. Release me at once!

No! As long as I have you like this, you can't lend any help to the Red Robes, and you can't escape.

It should be you worrying about escape. Even without my assistance, my Red Robes are winning. They have unleashed a force that the attacking army has no hope of defeating.

You're referring to the fire entity capable of emitting enormous amounts of thermal energy. I think you call it a "fire golem."

How—how did you know this?

I can sense the same things you can while we are linked. Unlike me, you haven't been doing a very good job shielding your outer thoughts.

Aric's "voice" grew louder in Rayna's mind. *You play a dangerous game, little girl. Eventually I will find a way through the troublesome barriers you have put up to block me out from your inner mind—and when I do, you will beg me to kill you before I am done!*

*** *** ***

Captain Ciredor and his men made it to the watchtower, but at a cost: Nearly a fifth of the small contingent he commanded had died before they were prepared to defend themselves. The bulk of his forces were still some distance away, too far away to help. Ciredor heaved a heavy sigh of exhaustion. He was drenched in sweat, with his skin badly blistered from the tremendous heat the fire creature was radiating. He ordered half of his men to take shelter behind the watchtower, while the rest scrambled to the front and sides of the building. Many yards away, the Red Robes stood in their circle, watching and waiting.

"Shields!" Ciredor yelled to his men in front, and they each summoned forth a man-sized shield of shimmering magic. Side by side, the monks pressed themselves tightly together, so that their individual shields acted as a single barrier, providing protection to the front and side flanks. Their "surround-shield" did not look as impressive as the Red Robes's version, Ciredor thought, but he prayed it would work all the same.

Seconds later, the golem attacked, this time with actual fire instead of heat. From its flaming hands, it sent forth a fearsome sheet of fire toward the defenders, who braced themselves against the impending firestorm. The fire clashing with their shields produced an angry roar—*krsssuuurrr!*

Miraculously, their shields held and protected them from most of the driven heat and flame. The golem's fire attack washed over them and bathed the stones behind them with flames so hot that they began to redden and glow. At Ciredor's command, the side flanks countered with an assault of their own. Synchronizing their attacks and using their Psi-kinetic power, they unleashed a concussive force powerful enough to topple a great oak. The fire creature staggered backward but did not fall. The golem attacked with fire again, with the same results. Ciredor and his men had encircled the watchtower, and they frequency rotated the battle weary and magic-spent among them to the relatively safety at the rear of the stone structure, while the more rested ones—shields ready—moved to the front to face the creature.

Seeing that its fire attacks were being impeded, the fire golem tried moving forward, to strike from a closer range. Its advance was hastily repulsed by another forceful push from the monks' magic. The golem fell back again, but not as far as before. The monks' shields prevented most of the intense heat and flame from getting through, but not all, and some of the monks began to fall unconscious from the heat alone. Streams of perspiration flowed from the crown of Ciredor's head. Keeping his shield up against such an onslaught required both hands, so the sweat freely trickled down into his eyes, burning as it went in. They were losing ground. Ciredor knew he needed a new strategy, and soon.

He spotted a drinking well a short distance away, and a desperate plan came to him. He ordered his men to run for the well, explaining his intentions along the way. A small contingent lagged behind to buy the main group more time by slowing the creature's advance with force magic; they soon ran to join the others, before the deadly creature got too close. Knowing that the creature would follow in pursuit, they had to act quickly. At his command, a group of about thirty men used their magic to pull away the well's brick housing, leaving an ugly, dark hole of jagged earth. Ciredor peered briefly into the exposed pit's depths. It was their best hope for survival.

No sooner had they finished than the fire golem arrived. The captain's men had their shields ready—and so was their trap. The plan was to trick the golem into stepping into the well, so that it would plunge into the underground waters below. In the rear of Ciredor's unit, as far back as they could go and still be in magic range, several of the monks concentrated deeply to cover the opening to the well with a floating cover of dirt and sand, disguising the hole and making it appear as solid ground. Ciredor prayed the golem did not see through this deception.

As the fire golem moved closer to the well hole, another blast of fiery heat bore down on the monks' conjured shields, like the weight of a giant's hand. The air began to ripple so badly with heat waves that the men could scarcely see ahead. The creature was now less than twenty feet away from where Ciredor and his men stood, and only three feet from the hidden well hole. The strain of maintaining their defensive magic under such conditions proved too taxing for a few; the shields of some of the monks failed, and they were instantly killed from the overwhelmingly high temperature.

The golem suddenly stopped moving. It looked at the ground directly ahead of it, as if it had sensed something wrong. Ciredor held his breath. Was the accursed thing aware of the trap? "What's the matter?" Ciredor yelled at the golem. "Are you afraid? We are right here! Why don't you claim your prize?"

The fire golem looked at the captain with eyes that shone like ominous torches; they began to flicker wildly, irritated with his goading.

"Why do you wait?" Ciredor continued. "You have us beaten—you need only finish the job! Or have your creators made you too stupid to know such things?"

The fiery behemoth opened its mouth and let out a bellowing howl that Ciredor could feel in his bones. Apparently angry at Ciredor's words, the golem took another step forward. Ciredor suspected that the creature's limited sentience was somehow linked to the consciousness of the Red Robes, and was therefore as vulnerable to emotional provocation as they were. The golem let out anther hostile cry and looked as though it would take another step. *Only one more step to go*, Ciredor thought. The trap was nearly sprung—*closer!*

The creature paused at the lip of the concealed hole and lifted its head to the air, as if testing it for signs of magic. It looked down again and took a step back.

Ciredor felt his heart sink with disappointment. The golem was aware of the trap—the ploy had failed. Affirming Ciredor's conclusion, the golem began to walk around the hidden hole, careful to avoid getting too close. Somehow, it could "see" the hole despite the monks' attempts to conceal it. Once the fire golem cleared the obstacle, it resumed its pace toward them. With the trap discovered, the assigned monks ceased to suspend the dirt over the hole and prepared themselves for battle.

Bent and leaning like an old man, Ciredor gasped and heaved ragged breaths in the sweltering heat. His white robes were soaked with sweat and marked with black streaks of grime and soot. More of his men began to pass out from the hellish heat of the approaching golem. Ciredor didn't bother giving the command to pull away—they had no hope of getting back to the relative safety of the watchtower in time. In a matter of seconds, the creature would be in close enough range to resume its fire attack.

Ciredor thought briefly that he could endure no longer, but then he shook his fist angrily, refusing to give in. He shouted obstinately at the fire golem, "This is not how my life will end—not like this, being cooked alive by the likes of you! One way or the other, *you are going in there!*"

With all their remaining strength, Ciredor and his men rallied and assailed the golem once more with their force magic, pushing the creature back toward the hole. "Back into the depths of darkness whence you came, fire demon!" Ciredor screamed, squeezing the last ebbing current of magic from his heat-blistered hands, before his exhausted body buckled to the ground.

The fire golem stumbled back to the fringe of the hole. It teetered there on its massive feet, struggling to regain its balance. Like Ciredor, the monks had given all they could; they could only watch and hope it was enough. Ciredor looked up ruefully at the sky and softly muttered a brief prayer: "Heavens grant us victory."

As if in answer to his prayer, the heavens seemingly blew their breath, and the fire golem fell in the hole. As it descended down the pit, the creature let out a deep yowl of discontent. The chilling sound haunted Ciredor's consciousness, and he would not soon forget it. Despite their weakened condition, the monks cheered excitedly. Struggling back to his feet, Ciredor was surprised to see that these normally quiet, pious men were capable of such a loud and joyous noise. Seconds later, they heard a distant splash, and a powerful spout of steam, smoke, and ash jetted from the hole, sending the foul stench of sulfur everywhere. This display went on for several minutes, then finally subsided into silence. It was over. The cheers resumed.

"That well is probably dry now," Ciredor joked as the joyous yells of his comrades died down. His familiar smile had returned. He reached under his damp robes, pulled out a water flask, and said, "But luckily, we already had these filled before we came!" As Ciredor took a long, thirsty gulp from his flask, the other monks did the same, happily drinking to their miraculous survival. According to myth, fire golems were invincible creations of dark magic and could not be defeated. Ciredor, however, never believed in an invincible enemy. He recalled the barbarian tribes he had defeated when he was new to his command. They too were said to be invincible.

He thought of the Red Robes—the red-clad devils in the distance—and poured some water over his head, feeling the cool wetness mercifully trickle down his face and neck. Tired though he was, he knew his forces could not afford to rest too long. He knew that it was only a matter of time before the Red Robes conjured another fire golem, or some other hellish thing, and sent it their way, and the monks had run out of wells to use. Ciredor hoped the exertion of creating the first golem would delay the Red Robes's efforts in creating another—long enough to give him and his men time to join up with the rest of the army and swell their ranks by thousands. That would be more than enough men to push any new golem all the way back to where the Red Robes stood, forcing them to either break their concentrated effort in sustaining the creature or be consumed alive by the unforgiving heat and flame of their own creation—surround shield or not. It was a simple plan, and Ciredor liked it.

As the captain prepared to gather his remaining men, he saw the main army heading his way, led by Orin. He grinned broadly; the reinforcements had arrived. Ciredor led them to his exact location by sending up a flare. Soon, Orin and the army met up with Ciredor and his small contingent.

Orin looked at his captain and then at the well hole, which was sporadically puffing wisps of white smoke. "Judging from the state of things," he said, as he began coughing from the lingering ash in the air, "my suspicion that the Red Robes had unleashed a fire being was true. We could see it, even from our location, but we at first believed it to be but a trick of the sun on our eyes. When we saw your first flare, we came as fast as we could."

"You were late," Ciredor said casually, "so we couldn't resist starting on the first golem without you. No matter—I promise you can have the next one."

"I'm sorry, Captain," Orin replied, failing to see the humor in the comment, "but we arrived as soon as we could. I did warn you that leading our vanguard so far ahead of our main forces presented considerable risk."

"Fewer numbers move faster," Ciredor said, wiping more sweat from his face. "We arrived just in time to draw the Red Robes's attack away from the Queen."

"Then she is alive?"

"Yes, thank the Heavens. I caught sight of her and the rest of her party just before the Red Robes attacked and threw that horror at us."

"Is the master mage with her?"

"Yes, I believe I saw her as well. Why?"

"She is the key. She must not die, if at all possible."

"It would be nice if you expressed as much concern for your Queen," Ciredor said, trying not to let his personal feelings show.

"I meant no disrespect."

"One of your visions, I take it?"

"Yes. Only a few visions revealed to me show the master mage alive at this point in time, but those paths are the most desirable, I think."

"You don't sound terribly certain."

"Can one be certain of how much rain will fall on a given day—or even that it will rain that day at all? What I do know for certain is that the paths I've seen without the presence of Rayna of Nightwind are bleak and full of despair."

"I don't suppose you are willing to be more specific."

"I regret I cannot.."

"It's good to know some things never change," Ciredor said, much too tired to press the matter further. "Some of our men will stay here, to tend to the wounded . . . and to bury our dead. The rest will come with me to do battle with the Red Robes." *The so-called invincible servants of Nephredom,* Ciredor thought as the army began to move. It was time to see if his forces could disprove yet another myth.

✳ ✳ ✳

Leading the army, Ciredor and Orin came upon the Red Robes's circle, expecting to meet great resistance. Instead, they found the Red Robes wandering around, appearing dazed and disoriented. Some of them had removed their hoods, revealing pale, gaunt, but very human faces.

No wonder they didn't create another fire golem after we defeated the first, Ciredor thought, watching the Red Robes with disdain. *They have all taken leave of their senses.*

One of them stumbled up to Ciredor, his head hanging. He did not look up when he addressed the captain. "Sir, forgive me, but where am I? Surely this is not Jerel."

Ciredor resisted the impulse to immediately strike the man down with magic or blade. Instead, he spoke with an angry tremor in his voice "You claim to be ignorant of your purpose here, villain? Look around you!" Ciredor gripped the man's face and chin, then forced his face up. "I said *look!* The ground is littered with the dead, the village scorched beyond recognition—your handiwork! And you and your ilk killed scores of my men with your vile creation!"

The red-robed man dropped to his knees, in a posture of pleading, clutching the lower half of Ciredor's robes. "Spare me your wrath, good sir! My name . . . I think my name is Keron—yes, yes, it is Keron of Jerel! I am but a simple man. I am no murderer!"

Ciredor could scarcely believe what he was seeing and hearing. He turned to his Second. "Orin, is there a Psi-telepath in our ranks?"

"Yes, there is one," Orin replied. He left, then returned a moment later with a tall, thin man.

"You are a Psi-telepath?" Ciredor asked him.

The tall man nodded.

"Then," Ciredor said, "tell me if this man's thoughts match his words." Ciredor returned his attention to the man calling himself Keron. "Tell me, is it true you know nothing of being a Red Robe? And that you know nothing of the foul deeds you have done while in service to the false King, Nephredom?"

Keron lowered his head and shook it slowly from side to side. "No, that is untrue. I did become a Red Robe. I needed to feed my wife and four sons, and I heard that the families of Red Robes do well. I was accepted because of my strong Psi-illusionic talents. I remember some of the training, yes . . . but I can't remember—this is the second year following the War of Kings, yes?"

Ciredor stared at the kneeling man, torn between pity and contempt. "No, Keron of Jerel, it is not. It is the fourth year."

"I . . . I cannot recall any of this. These killings you speak of—surely I had no part in them! You say that Nephredom is now King? I do not remember!"

Ciredor looked at the Psi-telepath. "Does he speak the truth?" he asked, secretly hoping Keron's assertion was yet another Red Robe deception.

"He speaks the truth," the Psi-telepath declared. "He truly does not remember."

Keron began to weep, "I have a . . . two-year hole in my mind? I was told I would be an enforcer of law . . . but this?" Keron looked at the destruction and death around him. "For two grand cycles I have done things like this?" The Red Robe saw that Ciredor wore the ring of a high priest and noted his shaven head. "Reverence? High Priest?" he asked with a trembling voice.

"I was," Ciredor responded simply.

"Can there be any forgiveness of an act such as this?"

Ciredor turned away, stiff-shouldered and aloof. "I am here as a man of battle, not of the cloth. I resigned my position as High Priest to fight as Captain of the Queen's army. There will be no forgiveness here, and we are a long way from Soren!" The words burned in his heart even as they left his lips.

Keron nodded solemnly. Orin started to say something, but instead remained silent.

Ciredor watched the confused Red Robes with ever-rising, unresolved anger within him. He said to his third in command, "Keep the remaining divisions here and watch over this lot. Make sure none of them escape. Their fates will be decided later."

The monk-fighter nodded stiffly in acknowledgment.

"Orin, you and your division will come with me. We still have a very powerful witch to deal with."

✳ ✳ ✳

Rayna was running out of time. Aric's mental probing was wearing her down, and she began to sense the walls of her defenses beginning to fracture. She could feel Aric's insect-like presence scurrying around the barriers of her inner mind, looking for a crack, a chink—any opening to get inside. Rayna suddenly felt her self-control slipping, and she desperately wanted to pull away, to flee. She restrained her panic, knowing that losing her focus would most certainly give Aric the opportunity she wanted.

She concentrated on gaining access to Aric's thoughts. Her surface thoughts had been relatively easy for Rayna to read, but her deeper thoughts were far more elusive. Rayna's instincts told her there was a well-guarded secret deep within the inner sanctum of Aric's mind, and Rayna needed to find out what it was. To her amazement, she found something.

At the same time, Rayna heard Aric's dreaded voice in her mind. *Rayna of Nightwind. I'm afraid your time is up, dear.*

Rayna felt something sinister and sadistic crawling around inside her private thoughts, violating her most intimate memories. Aric had broken through. Hideous, dark eyes opened wide, gazing deeply into her soul, as slithering, hooked tentacles of Aric's will spread out and took hold in Rayna's mind like a fulsome disease.

What a curious life you have lived, Rayna of Nightwind! Aric chirped gleefully. *Amazing! This wondrous world you come from—like Taren in some ways, and yet so different.* Aric began to mock Rayna, speaking of the two of them as one person: *The secret place we found, while in the company of the fool scientists in Dosk—it showed us a way we can return to our world—and see our mother again, yes? You remember Mother, don't you—the one we were going to abandon in our pursuit of independence? We've been a bad girl—left Mommy all alone. Awww, poor Mommy. Haw! What a sheltered life you have led, Rayna of Nightwind, to have allowed such a trivial matter to concern you so. That will all change, now that I'm in charge.*

Aric's excited voice echoed in Rayna's mind. *Why are you hiding, Rayna? It doesn't matter which little corner of your mind you retreat to. I am gradually taking over your consciousness, and soon our minds will think as one—mine being the dominant one, of course. I think I like your world better than my own, Rayna. We must go there soon. Once my mind and yours are fully linked, we will return to Earth and see dear Mother. I will allow her to see you one final time, Rayna—let her get close enough to embrace you . . . and then, when I tell you, you shall slit her throat! What a day that will be!*

Aric's creeping presence suddenly stopped moving. *What's this? Biofeedback loop disrupted? Psionic network downlink completed? Sleep command acknowledged? Why are you thinking in these strange terms? What do they mean?*

Rayna replied, *I've been thinking in these terms since you first entered the core of my mind. If you spent more time stealing my knowledge instead of my personal memories, you would know what they mean. Then again, if you had done so, you would never have allowed me to sever the Red Robe connection.*

What? No!

'Fraid so. It was Rayna's turn to mock. *They are no longer telepathically linked. I also told the Red Seers to enter into a meditative state for an indefinite period of time. They won't be adding their abilities to the Red Robes anymore. Also, while you were distracted with my memories, I accessed the Red Robe network via your mind. You remember your mind, don't you—the one you left unprotected while you tried to breach mine? Anyway, the Red Robes have been unplugged, and I couldn't have done it without your help.*

Damn you! Rayna Powell, you have upset a plan that has taken me years to carry out!

If you mean your scheme to get thousands of innocent people killed, and then ruling over the survivors—then good.

I will personally make you regret what you have done, Rayna of Nightwind—I am in your head! Your thoughts, your ideas—indeed, your very soul is at my mercy! I will place unthinkable nightmares in the deepest recesses of your mind, and they will wake you screaming every night until madness and despair drive you to take your own life!

And you will die too—only much sooner. While we have been in each other's minds, getting to know each other, our physical bodies have been left vulnerable. Ciredor and his men are heading our way right now. You have two choices: You can try to destroy my mind—and I promise you, I won't go down without a fight—or you can run while you can, and save yourself. You don't have time to do both. You know that I'm telling you the truth, because—as you continue to remind me—you are in my mind.

Aric's presence moaned in displeasure.

Rayna continued. *Unlike Keris and Arstinax, Ciredor will not hesitate to strike you down, even if it means harming me in the process. He's coming closer. Can't you feel his anger? He despises you. He will attack any minute now.*

Aric's presence raged with unbridled hate. Suddenly, Rayna felt Aric's mental tendrils dislodge themselves, pull away, and recede from her consciousness. Then the tentacles and feelers withdrew, and finally the many eyes of Aric were gone from her mind. Rayna had never in her life felt such a sense of relief. The sights and senses of the outside world had returned. *Thank God it's over*, she thought.

Rayna saw Aric running away but was too weak to do anything but watch her enemy flee. Her recent experiences left Rayna drained, and she collapsed into the arms of Arstinax when he reached her. An overwhelming sense of love and selfless concern flowed over her, washing away some of the filth and slime she felt inside as the result of merging minds with Aric. Rayna visibly relaxed and took tight hold of Arstinax's hand.

"Don't let the witch escape!" Ciredor yelled to his men as they tried to capture Aric. Keris had joined the chase, eager to see at first hand the capture of her brother's killer. Aric fled in the direction of the Edgewoods, and his men in pursuit. Now, the trees grew larger in their sight, as they came closer to the woods—which loomed less than a hundred yards away. Keris felt a stirring sorrow inside her when they passed the remains of Emawin's house; she stared at the ruined orphanage once more. Heartache nearly overwhelmed her before she managed to tear her eyes away from the death scene. Steely-eyed, Keris reset her sights on Aric, and forced herself to run faster. Aric, for a pampered aide in the service of the false King, ran surprisingly fast, and was proving to be a formidable test of Keris's athletic skill.

Seeing that her chasers were gaining ground to capture her, Aric suddenly turned around and uttered a string of obscenities. She then invoked an immense, thick cloud of black smoke that burst forth from the center of her body with violent force, shaking her small frame as it escaped. It swirled and flowed freely, a force of living malevolence, blotting out all light it touched. At the heart of the cloud was a visually impenetrable zone of blackness, and the grayish edges of the cloud spread upward to create a false dusk in the middle of day.

As with the fire golem, Ciredor had never witnessed such sorcery before. Without hesitation, however, he summoned his Psi-pyric magic and hurled a large fireball through the zone of darkness, aimed at the spot he had last seen Aric standing. He heard a scream of pain, then silence. The dense black smoke did not dissipate, which told Ciredor that his fireball had not killed Aric; she was still maintaining the spell. Ciredor did not favor the idea of sending his men blindly into that mouth of darkness, for he had no idea what effect it would have on them. He decided it was best to have his men attack the cloud's core from a distance, with magic, and kill the witch where she hid. Before Ciredor could give the order to bombard the cloud with fire, he heard a horse whinnying, then the sound of rapid galloping.

The black cloud cleared soon afterward, and the sun emerged to shine brightly upon their faces again. With the smoke gone, Keris could plainly see Aric riding off into the Edgewoods, having taken the horse she and Quan had used to get to Argat.

"Let her go," a weary voice sounded. "She is beaten, and we have no horses to give proper chase. In any event, I am not willing to risk any more lives today." The voice was that of Ciredor.

Keris agreed with him, in spite of herself. She could have pursued Aric by taking the other horse, the one that Rayna and Arstinax had ridden to town, but she decided not to. Too much already had been lost, and so much blood had been spilled. Her hunger for revenge would not be sated this day.

"Are you all right?" Ciredor asked her. To her surprise, she realized that he had been standing close beside her for some time. With a sudden rush of anxiety, Keris turned and looked at him. It was true that Ciredor and his army had come to the aid of her and her small party, and she was grateful for that, but their last encounter, at Soren, had placed a stain of unforgivingness upon her heart. Awkwardly, she walked past him without saying a word, heading to check on Rayna and the others. A pall of silence followed in her wake as Ciredor watched her go. Disillusioned, Ciredor began to walk in the opposite direction, instructing his men to stand guard. Orin followed him.

"You shouldn't take her actions as a personal offense," he heard Orin say. "The Queen probably is tired; the day has been a long and difficult one."

Ciredor didn't respond; he was trapped in a tempest of contemplation. "It's getting dark," he mumbled absently, after a few seconds had passed. "We need to gather all our men in the town and make preparations to spend the night there."

"I will take care of the matter personally. Perhaps you should go after her."

"No. It is plain to see that she wants none of my company."

"She cares more for you than you know."

"I thought you were Psi-clairvoyant, not Psi-telepathic."

"You will have to take my word for it."

Ciredor let out a begrudged chuckle. "Taking your word put me in this mess to begin with. I remember your words clearly: 'the consequence of making a foolish mistake.' Bah! Well, I can think of nothing more foolish than risking life and limb by marching off to fight Red Robes, fire golems, and beasts—only to be thoroughly ignored by the very person for whom I performed these feats!"

"The new Queen was never known to be lavish with her gratitude, and the decision to take this path was your own."

"You knew full well that I could not just–." Ciredor paused. "I know most people think of her as some sort of villain, but I know her much better than that." Ciredor paused again, then confided in hushed voice, "I love her, Orin." He was almost certain Orin knew this already, but it felt right to speak the words. "Her refusal to even speak to me hurts far more than it would if my personal feelings were not an issue."

"Then the culprit lies within your own self. You have my sympathies."

Ciredor threw his head back and guffawed. "For a man with no sense of humor, you always manage to find a way to make me laugh–in spite of my every effort to put on a good sulk!"

"Unhappiness is a baneful guest. It is best to keep your doors closed to it as long as possible."

"A most difficult proposition, my friend, when the battering rams of life are involved."

Orin nodded silently.

Ciredor said, "I suppose, as a captain soon to face the greatest battle of my career, I should be concerned with more important things than a former lover's scorn."

"Perhaps, but lover's scorn or not, you would not have regretted your decision to come to the Queen's aid, even if she had slapped your face, rather than simply passed you by."

Ciredor looked astonished, and before he could inquire further, Orin smiled faintly and said, "I have seen it."

At that moment, a young monk approached them at a full run. Ciredor recognized the youth as one of his scouts. Before he and his army left for Argat, he had sent a band of scouts to Jerel to locate potential traps or unpleasant surprises that awaited his men. Something was wrong; this scout had arrived a full day earlier than expected. Ciredor noticed that his appearance was disheveled, his breathing heavy and strained. "Do you bring news of Jerel?" Ciredor questioned.

The scout's eyes were wide with fear. "I ran most of the way to get here . . . you must know . . ."

"Know what?"

"The beasts!" the young scout cried out hysterically. "They are free–traveling in great numbers–thousands! Thousands! My comrades–all dead! The beasts, they killed–"

Ciredor put a heavy hand on the youth's shoulder and held it there firmly. "Present yourself with control and calm when you speak to me!" he barked. The rebuke appeared to restore the young monk's self-control; he straightened, and his face took on a neutral expression.

With a restrained voice, he said, "Captain, I report earlier than planned because of urgent news. The beasts are free of the Gate and were last seen headed toward the royal city of Jerel at great speed. After departing from Soren, our party had reached the southernmost region of Jerel Province when we saw them. From a distance, we spied their movements, and we thought we were undetected. When they attacked us, we were caught unaware. Their scouts—the flying beasts among them—must have seen us from overhead. I was the only one to escape, sir."

"I thought Nephredom had the beasts caged with his will, in the form of the Gate. How is it that they escaped while under his watch?"

"Nephredom is missing, sir. No one knows his fate. We were told this by several Jerelan residents before we encountered the beasts. The Jerelans said the palace is abandoned now, and no one dares go inside for fear of the unknown horrors they might find."

"Why Jerel? What is there that could possibly be of interest to the beasts? It seems against their nature to desire territory or treasure. Are you sure they were not simply roving in that general direction?"

"No, sir. As far as we could tell, they were heading deliberately in the direction of the city. Their path did not waver."

Ciredor dismissed the scout, pondering what he had learned. He had hoped to do battle with Nephredom's forces first, before dealing with the beasts. At least the enemies within the city of Jerel were *men*. He knew how men thought, and he could plot his strategy based on their expected behavior. Even the fire golem was at least created and controlled by men, and it had acted accordingly. Having fought the beasts in the past, Ciredor knew that they were a different matter altogether. They were feral, unpredictable creatures that savagely hurled themselves at their enemies at one moment, then craftily launched concerted sneak attacks in the next. Orin echoed his concerns.

"If the beasts reach and overtake the capital city before we do, our chances of victory will surely go from bad to worse," Orin said. "They are hard enough to kill out in the open, and with walls and buildings behind which to hide, the task will be even more difficult. The beasts are immune to magic, and our weapons require a clear and direct path of attack. Having the creatures leaping from behind blind corners and jumping down from rooftops will make defending ourselves difficult, to say the least. Our best hope is to get to the city before they do."

Nodding in agreement, Ciredor replied. "A depressing assessment, but accurate."

"Shall we ready our troops for departure?"

"No. The march here was long and difficult, and an exhausted army fights poorly. The men should rest at least half the night before we set out for the royal city. The threat of encountering the beasts, and possibly Nephredom's army, will make for a difficult journey, with little chance of solid rest after tonight."

Ciredor sighed. "With luck, we may yet still reach Jerel before the beasts. The scout said the beasts were traveling through the lower region of Jerel Province. From that point, it should take them at least four days to reach the main city.

Orin raised a brow, "Are you certain of this, Captain?"

"During the War of Kings, I had a chance to see how quickly the beasts moved—they are faster than the average man, but not extremely so.

"What of the winged beasts?" Orin asked.

"The flying beasts are a different matter, I do not know how fast they can travel, but I suspect they will stay with the others for strength and safety. If what I learned from the Princess is true, their numbers are limited and not enough to form their own division yet. Here in Argat, we are closer to the city than the beasts are. If we start before daybreak, we should reach the palace in two days."

"That would not give us much time to defeat Nephredom's army and then secure the city against the horde of beasts."

"Perhaps, but remember that we are dealing with mercenaries. The Kuaran Shields were trained to fight, not to defend. Despite their recent elevation to royal army status, the Throne is nothing more than an employer, the surrounding land nothing but cold dirt, upon which they carry out their assignments. They have no strong love or loyalty for Jerel, and no real desire to protect it, unless explicitly told to do so. They are much more likely to engage us in open warfare than to draw us into a prolonged siege of the city. In addition, we can use our magic on them. Our victory therefore should come within a day or two of reaching Jerel. Our victory—or our deaths."

"Do you think our cause to be ill-fated?"

Ciredor was struck off guard by the question, which seemed out of context, and the faintly fearful tone in which it was asked. He thought it was a strange question to be asked by an experienced soldier such as Orin, and a vaguely frightening one from a man who could see multiple futures. Times like these told Ciredor how little he knew of his friend.

Ciredor's tone turned gravely serious, almost apologetic. "I brought with me no conscripts on this journey. All who have joined me to fight have come freely and willingly, with their eyes wide open. If the Heavens wish us victory, then we shall have it. And if we die, we will die well."

Orin seemed reassured; his shoulders straightened, and furrows disappeared from his brow. "When we stepped down from our positions in the temple to join the Queen, I knew this day would come. I have no regrets."

Ciredor often forgot how young Orin was, because he was so mature for his age. In truth, they were all young. Only the young would be audacious and brazen enough to attempt to change the future, to alter the path of fate. He briefly thought back on Orin's peculiar question, and suddenly it didn't seem so peculiar. *Ill-fated causes.* Surely, every vision that Orin saw had at least one ill-fated version. It seemed more of a curse than a blessing to see visions of the future, as Orin did. Ciredor tried to imagine what it would be like to see many possible versions of the future, to look at friends he might never meet, to view places he might never see, or even to look into the ghostly faces of his own children, who might never be born because time or circumstance would not allow their births.

No wonder Orin is such a melancholy soul, Ciredor thought. *Long before the future shows him its final vision of how things will truly turn out, it first floods his mind with enough possibilities to drive the average man mad.* An odd thought came to Ciredor's mind: *In how many possible futures,* he asked himself, *did Orin see me lying dead in my own blood for this cause? Ill-fated, indeed.* Ciredor turned, and then slowly started walking back to the ruins of what had once been Argat.

CHAPTER 21

Rayna's Revelation

Rayna could hear faint, tinny bleeps coming from nearby machines, but the area was too vast and poorly lit to determine exactly where these machines were. The sterile, white tiling beneath her feet, along with the ghostly pale fluorescent lighting on the ceiling high above, assured Rayna she was indoors. She nevertheless felt displaced and vulnerable in the endlessly wide room with no doors, windows, or visible walls. As she walked slowly through the room, she occasionally felt forced air from overhead ventilation fans blowing across her face, hissing harshly in her ears. The busy sounds of electronic beeping grew louder and more frequent, as if she were entering an important zone.

An uneasy sensation passed over Rayna; she looked over her shoulder and saw something in the corner of her eye. She turned completely around to get a better look and was taken aback. There, standing immediately in front of her, was a middle-aged woman in military attire. Rayna recognized her immediately as the woman she had nearly hit with her car, so many weeks ago, before the lightning storm had brought her to Taren, and as the same woman whose holographic image had stood before the secret room in the Science Guild cellar. The woman's twisted smile revealed a cold curiosity that chilled Rayna to the marrow of her bones. "Now, do you understand why you are here, little ghost?" the woman asked in a monotonic voice.

Rayna shuddered. She tried to move away from the woman, but her legs would not move. "Do you understand why you are here?" the woman repeated. She grabbed Rayna's arm with a grip like death. Rayna refused to answer, intent on breaking free.

"Stubborn one," the woman chided her, as one would scold a disobedient pet. "You cannot stop what has started. You are here to serve us. You *belong* to us."

"No!" Rayna shouted. Her staff was suddenly in her hands, and she held it ready.

The older woman's form suddenly warped and shrank until Rayna found herself staring at the young girl she had met soon after arriving in Taren. She recalled that the girl had poisoned herself to avoid Red Robe retribution. Her large, limpid eyes blinked at Rayna.

"You're not real!" Rayna accused, trembling at the sight of her. Seeing the girl again flushed old, painful feelings up to the surface. Tears began to well in her eyes. "I saw you die!"

The girl smiled and began to speak in odd, varying tones—not quite singing, but close:

> *And they shall build their houses with rotten sticks,*
> *for nothing will last past a season.*
> *Demons shall snuff the light from men's mortal wick,*
> *Rayna of Nightwind knows the reason.*

The child's rhyme seemed to echo hauntingly in the hollow, expansive room. To Rayna, the brief verse was both cruel prophecy and taunting condemnation. Since her return from the Science Guild, she had learned many things about the fate of Taren—*terrible things*. Rayna began to lose her will to resist. She dropped her staff, and it dissolved into the floor, leaving no trace. She looked down at herself and saw that she was wearing the same kind of uniform as the older woman had worn.

Rayna awoke with a start, sitting upright in bed. Her rapid, ragged breathing gradually eased to a normal rate. The words from her dream remained with her, haunting her consciousness with the ominous ending of the rhyme: "Rayna of Nightwind knows the reason."

✷ ✷ ✷

The old watchtower of Argat had four levels. The first floor was a large foyer, prominently displaying a winding stairwell in the center. The second and third floors held the sleeping quarters, mostly communal areas containing several beds. However, a few rooms on this level served as private quarters, and in one of these rooms, Ciredor sat on a simple, narrow bed stuffed with unruly straw that playfully poked its tips through the bed's porous mattress, feeling like the stiff whiskers of an unshaven man.

The leader of the monk army had been deep in thought. He pulled himself away from his ponderings and looked around the room—a welcome distraction. The opaque darkness of the night allowed but a small amount of light in the room, but he could clearly see the silken highlights of brightly dusted cobwebs that draped every corner, and "windows" that were little more than vertical slits in the walls, just wide enough to permit an archer's arrow through. As far as he could tell, no one had used this watchtower in a long time, but Ciredor felt a certain affinity toward the neglected building; it did protect him and many of his men from the fire golem's attacks, after all.

The watchtower was one of but a handful of structures left standing in the village after the Red Robes torched the town—its pitted gray stone exterior endured to the end. Although the exterior of the watchtower bore the ugly, charred scarring of the fire golem attack, the interior was undamaged. It was Orin's idea that Keris and her party, as well as Ciredor and several of his best men, occupy the tower, while the great remainder of their forces camped just outside the fallen hamlet. Ciredor was not the kind of man to take special privileges, but he understood that Orin was merely trying to protect him, as was the duty of any good second in command. It mattered little to Ciredor anyway, for he was in no mood for debates over his safety. He had other things on his mind.

A knock sounded at the door. "Ciredor, are you in?" a familiar voice called out.

"Come in, Keris," said Ciredor. "I was just thinking of you."

"I do not wish to intrude."

"You're not intruding. Please come in."

Keris walked in, closing the door behind her. It creaked in a low, whining fashion as it swung shut. There was no light inside. "Shall I light a candle?" she asked.

"Please forgive me, but I have seen enough fire and flame for one day, and I find the peace of a darkened room soothing."

Keris strained to make out his image in the darkness. "I came to say

'thank you,'" she said. "I also came to apologize for my rudeness earlier."
She waited for Ciredor to say something. When he did not, she
continued. "When I saw you and your men arrive, I was shocked, to say
the least. I thought you were not interested in my plight. You had told
me the risks were too great."

"I had a change of heart," Ciredor said, sadness in his voice. Keris
now remained silent. "Why didn't you tell me?" he said.

"Tell you what?" Keris asked.

"That you made an arrangement with an underworld overlord."

"How did you find out?" Keris heard rustling as Ciredor moved his
body. As her eyes became adjusted to the dim light, she saw him bend
down and pick up his staff. He pressed down on its top, and a long blade
forcibly sprang from the other end.

"You can imagine my surprise when I received a large shipment of
these—cartloads, in fact. Not exactly standard issue."

"Not exactly," Keris agreed with sad resonance.

"Although Nephredom has permitted us to use staffs, I suspect he
would not have approved of this variety." Ciredor put the blade away.

"It is true, I made an arrangement to have the weapons sent to you,
but I was given every assurance that Jharet and his men would contact
you only *after* you had agreed to help me."

"You expect honor from those who know not the meaning of it."

"So they came anyway."

"A rather shifty fellow dressed in funeral gray delivered them to me."

"And it was he who told you that I requested the shipment?"

"No, not at first. It was only after I refused to pay for such items that
your name suddenly spouted from his lips, like wine from an overturned
basin. You should pick your business partners more carefully."

Keris turned away and looked out the thin window, which revealed
no view other than the blackness of night. "I had no choice," she said.
"He was the only dealer I could find who was willing to take the risk."

Ciredor sighed, his normally cheerful voice sounding tired. "I was
worried enough at the thought of Nephredom's loyalists hunting you
down. Then to discover that the Thieves' Guild had gotten involved . . ."
He repeated his earlier question. "Why didn't you tell me?"

A maelstrom of past hurts seemed to surge in Keris's voice, giving it a
bitter edge. "It was hardly worth mentioning at the time," she said. "You
had made up your mind that my cause was lost—or have you forgotten?"

"It was the most difficult decision of my life."

"Then why did you change your mind—why bother?"

"Because I love you."

Keris fell silent once more, and Ciredor wondered if he had just made a fool of himself, and if Keris had seen their past moments of love as nothing more than a temporary diversion.

"When I needed you most, you turned me away," she said.

"Yes, and now I am here."

Keris's voice softened. "Perhaps I asked for too much."

"No," Ciredor replied. "It was not asking too much that I help free our people from the grip of a tyrant—one who I helped introduce to the throne in the first place. That failure lies with me, but the failure that hurt me most was my failure to keep your trust. I am sorry."

Keris walked over to Ciredor and sat down on the bed beside him. She gently caressed his face and found it slightly damp to the touch. "I thought I never wanted to see you again," she said.

"You certainly had me convinced," Ciredor answered.

She allowed him to drape his arms around her, then closed her eyes and appeared to draw comfort from the warmth of his touch. "Promise me you won't turn me away again," she whispered. "Promise you will always be here, with me."

"I promise."

"Once more."

"I promise."

Keris smiled. "I believe you mean it."

"I do."

A quiet moment passed before Ciredor broke the silence. "If it were not for meddling monsters and mad usurpers, I may never have had the opportunity to seek you out and redeem myself. I suppose I am in their debt."

Keris laughed. "Well, as far as meddling monsters and mad usurpers are concerned, I think it is best we keep that debt unpaid—especially as we intend to do war with them."

"Agreed."

Keris stood and removed a stout candle from a nearby wall sconce, then placed her finger near its wick. She closed her eyes in concentration, and a small blue spark arched from her fingertip, lighting the candle. A soft, pale glow filled the room. "As you can see," she declared, replacing the candle on its sconce, "poor as I may be with magic, even I can manage to light a candle." She sat back down beside Ciredor. "I needed the light to see you better," she explained. Ciredor took a moment to silently admire the remarkable beauty of his Queen. The flickering image of the candlelight reflected in the sheen of Keris's dark eyes as they stared back at him. "And incidentally," Keris whispered, "I love you too."

Ciredor leaned closer and kissed her gently, her soft, full lips trembling noticeably while pressed against his. His fingers softly stroked her ebony hair as her body shifted closer to him. He felt her arms around his neck, and feelings of wild excitement overcame him. What had started as a display of polite affection quickly turned into a torrid exchange of ravenous kisses and caresses. Ciredor found himself looming over Keris, shaking with desire. Suddenly, nothing in either East or West Taren mattered half as much as the closeness they shared at that moment. The softly lit room seemed to sway and swirl as savage passions erupted into a frenzy of utter abandon. Garments were hastily shed and discarded, and soon Ciredor could feel Keris's soft flesh pressed hard against him as they surrendered to each other. Keris muttered faint words he did not hear; he was aware only of the rhythmic movements of their bodies as they made love in the dim candlelight.

Keris carefully unwrapped herself from Ciredor's arms as he slept. A couple of hours had passed since they had laid together, and yet she could not sleep. She stood and got dressed in the dark; she feared relighting the candle would wake her lover, and he needed all his rest for the troubling days ahead. Rather than put on her own traveling clothes, she decided to wear Ciredor's robes, open and loosely fitting, so that the coarse rubbing of cloth would not soon erase from her body the memories Ciredor's warm, gentle touch. On curious impulse, she decided she would explore the top of the watchtower. Ciredor's trusted second in command, Orin, had personally searched the tower prior to her arrival to ensure that it was safe, so she left her weapon in her room.

She took the candle from the wall and left the room, closing the door gently behind her. In the darkened hallway, she could hear faint sounds of snoring from neighboring rooms. As everyone else slumbered, she lit the candle, then proceeded up the winding stairs to the fourth and highest level. The topmost level of the tower was a bit of a disappointment to Keris, nothing more than a musty storage room, filled with crates of old farm implements such as wooden spades and small hand axes for chopping thin branches into kindling wood.

She noticed another door in the room and opened it. It led outdoors to a gray stone balcony that encircled the upper tower. Great parapets walled the balcony, partially blocking the splendid view of the full moon and distant, swaying tree line of the Edge Woods. Keris stepped out onto the balcony and was greeted by a refreshing night breeze. "Now this is more like it," she whispered to herself. Moonlight shone down on her and comforted her soul. She found it hard to believe that such a beautiful night stood on the eve of what could very well be the most terrible war Taren had ever known.

As she walked along the balcony, she saw to her surprise that Rayna was also there, on the other side of the tower, quietly and motionlessly staring out through the parapets into the dark skies. Keris tightened her robes. "Greetings and pleasant night to you, Rayna Powell of Nightwind," she called out formally.

Rayna jerked and turned her head, startled. "You've got to stop doing that! How long have you been standing there?"

"Not long," Keris replied.

"I thought I was the only one up this late," Rayna said.

Keris momentarily diverted her gaze toward the bright moon. "Ciredor and I had been . . . going over various battle strategies for the approaching war. Afterward, I decided to go for a stroll and experience the upper tower."

Rayna made a sour face. "Battle plans, huh? Not my idea of a good time—" Rayna belatedly noticed that Keris was wearing Ciredor's robes. She smiled with embarrassment but chose not to comment.

Keris sighed and smiled back, knowing that Rayna had seen through the ruse. "It *was* a good time, actually," she said. "But never mind that— why are you up at this hour? I didn't know you were an avid star gazer."

"I had a bad dream," Rayna said. "I couldn't sleep after that, so I came up here to clear my head."

"Well, don't clear it too thoroughly. We will need the potent magic it commands to better our chances of winning the war."

"You always have so much faith in me," Rayna said, a forlorn tinge to her words.

"Faith well placed, I would say. Our recent victory over the Red Robes has proven it. When you told me what you did to them, I could hardly believe it, but once I saw the state of them with my own eyes—"

"Keris, we've got to talk. It's important," Rayna blurted out.

"Very well. I am listening."

"Remember back at Dosk, when I was trying to tell you something I had learned while with the Science Guild?"

"Yes, I recall that moment." Keris could tell from the distressed look on Rayna's face that something was deeply bothering her. "We never did get around to hearing your report. I think I would like to hear it now."

Rayna took in a deep breath, exhaling slowly. "It's a long a story," she said.

"Stories—even the long ones—usually have a beginning. I suggest you start there."

"While I was with the Science Guild, I gained access to a secret room in their cellar."

"The cellar?"

"Right." Rayna affirmed. "That was after they made me Guild Master."

"They named you Guild Master of the Science Guild?"

"Yeah—different story. Anyway, they thought the entrance to the room was guarded by a 'ghost,' but it turned out to be some kind of holographic guardian. Luckily for me, a successful biometric hand-scan got me past it."

Momentarily nonplussed, Keris arched one of her brows. "I think I'd better sit down for this one," she muttered. She sat on the cool stone floor, crossing her legs.

Rayna went on. "Well, it turned out that the room was actually a huge underground computer lab—I think the hologram called it 'observation post number three.' There was no one inside; whoever occupied it must have abandoned it a long time ago. Anyway, the database gave me read-only access, so I could only view the archive files, skim through a few entry logs, and—"

"Wait!" Keris said, her hand raised in objection. "Half of what you are saying sounds utterly cryptic, and that's a bit excessive—even for you."

Rayna wore a surly frown. "It wasn't *that* bad," she said, her hands resting on her hips.

"Yes it was," Keris countered bluntly. "You should keep in mind that you are *not* talking to a fellow scientist!"

Seeing Keris's comically frustrated face, Rayna cracked a smile that threatened to erupt into full laughter. "OK, maybe I got a little carried away," she confessed, managing a straight face. "I'll try to keep the language simple—I promise." Keris looked much relieved, and Rayna said, "I was just getting to the part that explains the origin of Taren."

"The tale of Taren's beginnings is common knowledge," Keris said. "If that is all the science room taught you, then I am afraid that your trip was a waste."

"All right," Rayna responded, taking Keris's remark as a challenge. "Let's hear this common knowledge. You tell me what you know about early Taren, and I'll tell you what I found out. Then we will see which account makes the most sense."

"Now is an odd time for a history lesson."

"Humor me."

Keris answered, "Very well. It is said that one thousand years ago, Taren was a wild land discovered by twelve Powers, simply known as the Twelve. They named the land 'Taren' and befriended the natives who inhabited the land. The Twelve noticed that these people possessed no magic, and so they decided teach them. Each Power taught these new Tareners a different kind of magic, which many believe to be the Twelve Schools of Psi-magic today. All was well for a time, and peace abounded. Then legend speaks of a thirteenth Power—an extremely powerful one."

"Let me guess—Irel," Rayna scoffed.

"Irel indeed. The stories I've heard describe her as a jealous Power who resented how the people adored the Twelve. She plotted against the other Powers by telling the people of Taren that there were many more types of magic, which the Twelve were keeping from them. This sowed seeds of mistrust among the people toward the Twelve, and many began to follow Irel and use the many types of magic she taught—magic of frightening power. This angered the Twelve, for they felt the people of Taren were not ready for Irel's teachings. They commanded her to stop."

"I'm guessing she didn't," Rayna said.

"No, and a great civil war erupted, splitting Taren in half."

"East versus West."

"Yes. The Twelve ultimately defeated Irel, in spite of her formidable magic, and created a terrible outdoor prison for her that encircled all of Taren like a crimson chain, where night and day did not exist, and unbent lightning fell from the skies forever."

"Nicknamed 'The Band' for short, I presume?" Rayna quipped.

Keris nodded. "Irel was thrown into the Band and made to sit upon a crystal pedestal—the only safe place there. She was told never to leave the Band, lest she die from the lightning."

"What happened to the people?" Rayna questioned.

"Those who had followed Irel were shunned, and the Twelve placed a spell of forgetfulness upon them so they could no longer recall any of the spells Irel had taught them."

"The *Wild Magic Chaotic*," Rayna mumbled, remembering something her second Hand had told her.

Keris's eyes widened a little, surprised that Rayna was familiar with the obscure term. "Precisely," she said. "As further punishment, they were also forbidden from using any of the magic taught by the Twelve and were forced to go back to living without magic. These outcasts, who mostly inhabited the western region of Taren, became known as 'West Tareners,' and their land called 'West Taren.'"

The night was heavy with the distant chirping of crickets, accompanied by an occasional hooting owl. The ambient sounds had a tranquilizing effect on Rayna, and she yawned softly as she listened to Keris. "Sorry," she apologized.

Keris nodded, then continued. "Those who had stayed loyal to the Twelve inhabited the part of Taren known today as East Taren. The subsequent wars and treaties to follow would eventually settle on the Taren River as the border dividing the two lands." Keris's voice took on a slightly smug tone. "It's interesting to note that West Tareners tell a slightly different version of this tale, in which the Twelve are the villains, and Irel their hapless victim."

"Which version do you believe?" Rayna asked.

Sitting on the stone floor had begun to feel uncomfortable, and Keris shifted her weight to a better position before answering. "Neither," she said. "It is legend and folklore, nothing more. Most of the noble and educated classes agree that no one really knows how Taren was founded, and because no written accounts have survived from that time, it will forever be a mystery."

"Not anymore."

"I take it you are about to present yet a third version of how Taren came to be."

"Yes, but I think my version is the truth. At least it makes more sense than myths about Powers and pedestals."

Keris reached under her black straw hat to smooth stray hair back from her face. "This should prove interesting," she murmured.

"You were right about one thing," Rayna said. "Taren did come into existence here on Earth a thousand years ago, but it was not so much founded as it was *built*. 'Taren' stands for 'Testing Area of Restricted Environmental Neo-prison.'" Rayna paused for a moment to let the implication sink in. "We are standing in a massive prison—a sort of research prison, to be exact. According to the records, an old but advanced civilization known as the Geni somehow—"

Keris raised her hand again. "Wait! Though you say we are prisoners, I see not the prison you speak of—only the land around us."

"The land *is* the prison. The entire land of Taren was created by the Geni to contain their enemies."

"How can one possibly create a land—in common tongue, please."

Rayna shrugged and shook her head. "The underlying technology is way over my head, but I think I understand the gist. As a solution to earlier overpopulation problems on Earth, the Geni had found a way to cause underwater volcanoes to erupt, rise to the surface, and create new landmasses and islands. Over time, the new lands would cool, grow plant life, and be fit for habitation. Animals would be introduced, then people. Not only did the Geni perfect this process, but they found a way to get it done really fast." Rayna made a sweeping pass with her hand. "Taren is but one example of their work. The logs didn't go into much technical detail beyond that, but from what I know, it is scientifically possible— not that science carries much weight around here."

Keris momentarily stared into the night, trying to envision her homeland as once a smoldering mass of lava and ash. The thought of it was intriguing, but what Rayna had said earlier still bothered her to the point of deep offense. "Taren may be far from perfect," Keris said, "but I would hardly see myself as its prisoner. A prison has its walls, a jail its bars. Taren and Tareners are not held bondage by fence, nor with unsightly stone. Taren is free. We are free!"

Rayna sniffed impatiently. "*The Band*, remember? Anyone who tries to cross it gets zapped. Taren is essentially a small peninsula, and the Band surrounds it, acting as a lethal buffer zone to cut us off from the mainland. I'm pretty sure the Band is active in all directions, including the surrounding waters. Has anyone ever tried to sail far into the sea?"

Keris nodded her head. "There have been many accounts of sailors who ventured too far beyond the safety of Taren's coastal waters, and wandered into the Band by mistake. They say it is a horrible sight from the sea—even worse than it looks from land. They say that the sky is a dark red that ripples and churns like the waters below, and that unbent lighting falls like rain. No seafarer who has entered the Band by sea has ever returned alive."

"That's because we are trapped inside an enclosed environment—a *prison*. There's a whole world outside Taren that has been purposely kept from you."

"Very well," Keris conceded. "Tell me more of this version of Taren's past . . . and of these Geni."

"The Geni government came to power following a terrible war," Rayna said. "It was called the Psionic War. It started at a time when people suddenly began to demonstrate powerful psychic abilities—what your people call magic. They used their new abilities to wage a kind of war that had never been fought before—one fought using various mental attacks, rather than the conventional weapons of that time. A lot of people died. The logs I read say only that the people gained these new powers due to a 'natural evolution of the human mind,' but I have a feeling there's a little more to it than that, and I think the Geni had something to do with it."

"The criers of history seldom utter the whole truth, Rayna of Nightwind," Keris said. "Go on."

Rayna continued. "After the war, anarchy took hold, and the world plunged into a New Dark Age, from which it did not emerge from for many years. The logs didn't give me much information on the New Dark Age, but I don't imagine it was a very nice time for anyone."

"Perhaps the less said about it, the better. What occurred next?"

"The Geni eventually gained dominance over all the other factions, and united them under Geni rule. In doing so, they brought stability and relative peace back to the world."

"Then the Geni were ultimately a force for good?"

Rayna's forehead wrinkled to show her disagreement. "Not exactly," she answered. "Of course, all the records I read painted the Geni with a very rosy brush. After all, the observation post, and all the information it contained, was once maintained by them, before they abandoned it. All of the historical data inside came directly from their perspective. It wasn't until after I looked at some of the entries more closely did I see the truth—or at least as much truth as is possible to find in a biased source."

"Such as what?" Keris asked. She listened as Rayna explained that the Geni used false benevolence and suppression of truth to retain the power they seized. They forbade the history of the Psionic War from being taught, lest their dubious role in that war be brought into question. They destroyed writings, books, and any accounts that told things they did not wish others to hear. Eventually, even ancient history that occurred long before the rise of the Geni was censored to include positive remarks about the Geni, or banned from being told altogether.

Rayna scratched her head. "It was like they were trying to convince the world that the Geni were always in power, and they were willing to change the facts of history to do it."

"Such things are not unheard of among the powerful," Keris said, unsurprised. "History is often written and told by the mighty, for the quills of the weak and oppressed hold little ink."

Rayna went on to say that those who spoke out against the Geni's practices, or who openly criticized them, were given an opportunity to recant—provided they agreed to undergo a process called "reeducation." The logs Rayna read did not elaborate further on what "reeducation" meant, only that it was used on reformed dissidents before they would be accepted as lawful citizens again. If a protester refused this option, he was considered an enemy of the government and arrested.

The victims of these persecutions came from many backgrounds— warriors, lawmen, philosophers, historians, teachers. Even playwrights and storytellers who wrote unflattering portrayals of the Geni government, or who failed to include historical tribute to the Geni leadership, were arrested and detained. But such prisoners were not publically executed, nor killed in secret, nor were they incarcerated in common jails. To appear positive in the public eye, the Geni government had forbidden killing of any kind, and public prisons were reserved only for the most violent of citizens.

"And so," Keris surmised, "the Geni relocated thousands of their detractors and adversaries to a newly formed land, made especially for them—*Taren*."

"Yes," Rayna said, "and once the majority of their enemies were in Taren, the Geni created the Band to prevent them from escaping. From what I read, they called this exile a 'gentle, peaceful solution for those who refused reeducation.'"

Keris raised her eyebrows in silent exclamation.

"There's more. Before being sent off to Taren, all prisoners were 'genetically branded' to separate them from the regular citizenry— supposedly as an easy way to identify them in the event any of them escaped."

"Branded? Where?"

"The ears," Rayna stated. "That is why *all* Tareners have pointed ears. The Geni found a way to manipulate the gene that controls ear shape and get instant, visible results."

"'Gene?'" Keris questioned.

"Oh, yeah . . . Genes are things inside us that we inherit through birth and determine how our bodies look and behave."

"And you say the Geni somehow changed these genes in Tareners, as a way of marking them, and even their unborn children?"

"Yeah—branded, like cattle—only worse, because it marked future generations as well. Apparently, the Geni loved playing around with genetics, and performing experiments at other people's expense."

"Was there no public outcry?"

"Not much," Rayna said. "The Geni leaders controlled practically all information by that time; the common people knew only what the Geni government wanted them to know. After genetically altering all prisoners of Taren, the Geni argued that they were technically no longer human, and not protected by the same rights and laws that governed the rest of the Geni people. Even those who knew better dared not complain, in fear of ending up in the same situation as the new Tareners."

"I'm beginning to despise these Geni," Keris remarked. Rayna told Keris that the Geni government had also made a dark deal with some Geni scientists, who planned to use Taren and its inhabitants as "guinea pigs" (which she had to explain to Keris) for all manner of experiments that would be illegal or too dangerous in the Geni's main territories.

"How did the prisoners fare once they arrived in Taren?" Keris asked. "Surely they must have sought vengeance for what had been done to them!"

"They were stripped of everything but the clothing on their backs, and they were taken to Taren by heavily armed men," Rayna replied. "There wasn't going to be much vengeance going on at that point. Besides, many of the exiles had brought their families with them—some with small children. When they first arrived, Taren was mostly forests and wilderness. They had to build shelter for themselves, find food, and decide who would lead them—all before they could seriously entertain any thoughts of retaliation." Keris sighed.

"Believe it or not," Rayna went on, "not everyone saw exile as necessarily a bad thing, and even the ones who wanted to get back at the government couldn't agree on the best way to do it."

Keris scoffed. "That's a polite way of saying the exiles squabbled among themselves, even before the ground beneath their feet had fully settled."

"It's not all their fault," Rayna said. "It was what the Geni scientists wanted. They had hoped that the Taren Project, as they called it, would pit the Tareners against each other. They had hidden observation posts throughout the land so they could secretly watch the drama unfold and record the results." As she listened, Keris learned that Taren ultimately split into two tribes—the Settler Tribe and the Resistance Tribe. The Settler Tribe wanted to start new lives for themselves. They eschewed magic and advanced technology, and wanted only to live a simple life. They saw Taren as a place to live as their ancestors did centuries ago, and they embraced the notion.

"The Resistance Tribe disagreed," Rayna said. "They used magic religiously to keep their skills sharp, and they missed the technology and comforts they once had. They wanted to challenge their exile, and cross back over into Geni territory—their real home. The tribe was convinced that if they could appeal their case to the Geni public—let enough people know the truth—the government would be forced to accept them back."

"Understandable," Keris said.

"Maybe, but crossing the Band unprotected was out of the question. It was tuned to detect and destroy anyone with the genetic anomalies all Tareners had been given. They tried thinking up ways around the problem, but ironically, some of their best engineers and scientists had chosen to go with the Settler Tribe."

"You pride yourself as a scientist, Rayna of Nightwind," Keris said. "Tell me, if you were among the scientists during that time, what would you have done?"

Rayna laughed. "Are you kidding? I would have been with the Resistance Tribe, focusing all my efforts on finding a way to get back to Geni territory without ending up as another Band statistic—meaning no offense to your Taren, of course."

"No offense taken. In fact, your words do you honor. So, if the Resistance Tribe found that they could not return to their homeland for revenge, what did they do? Did the logs speak of this?"

"They did. The tribe eventually organized themselves into a well-structured society, but their progress was slow. By that time, hundreds of years had passed, and each succeeding generation knew less about the reason they were in Taren than the one before it. Wars broke out between the two tribal nations, which by now were known as East and West Taren. To make matters worse, most records and documents about their political exile were destroyed in various fires and enemy raids."

Keris leaned back, clasping her hands around her knee. "What were the battles fought over?" she inquired.

"Resources and ideological differences, mostly," Rayna answered, with a tired shrug. "I don't remember the specifics, but it doesn't really matter, because in the end, the truth of who they really were, and all knowledge of the Geni's role in their history, were lost." Rayna paused, studying Keris's face carefully. "You don't believe any of this, do you?"

"Your tale was a most fantastic one," Keris said, in measured tones.

"That doesn't answer my question."

"You have to forgive my skepticism, but I don't see how this story is any more believable than the 'Powers and pedestal' story, as you call it. I want to believe you—but without proof, you are asking me to trade one implausible explanation for another."

"*Implausible?*" Rayna shouted.

"This claim that Taren was literally made by an ancient civilization known as the Geni as a prison for their amusement . . ."

"All right, all right. I see your point," Rayna said, frowning. "To be honest, I guess I wouldn't believe my story either without proof." Rayna pointed at the sky. "But there's my proof," she said. "It's one of the Geni experiments I wanted to warn you about."

Keris followed Rayna's finger with her eyes and saw two stars—one red, the other blue—shining in the night sky. Keris looked puzzled, and replied, "The Twin Stars of Taren? What do they have to do with these Geni?"

Rayna shook her head. "Those are not stars. They are specialized satellites—machines placed in the sky, by the Geni, over a thousand years ago."

Keris let out a heavy laugh. "The Twin Stars of Taren—sky machines? Now I think this tale of yours has gone a bit far."

Keris watched as Rayna fished through her pockets and produced a silvery, cylinder object the length of a long knife, with strange, glowing symbols etched on its surface. Keris's laugh died in her throat as she stared at the object with curious amazement. It resembled a small rune-covered wand. "What kind of talisman is that?" she asked, instinctively reaching at the side her hip for a short blade that wasn't there.

Rayna explained. "Don't worry, it's not dangerous. It's a remote control—a device that's used to send a special command to the Twin Stars."

Keris looked on with reserved caution. "The stars are for no one to command. They simply are." She observed Rayna point the strange object at the sky, toward the Twin Stars, and press down on one of the runes. The red star emitted a single, sudden burst of intense, red light, and then returned to normal brightness. "That's the red one," Rayna announced, then pressed another rune on the silver wand. "Here's the blue one," she said, and the blue star also pulsated brilliantly one time. "And last but not least, we have the hidden one." Rayna pressed down on a glowing, spiral-shaped rune, and the heavens suddenly rolled back their dark coverings to reveal a previously unseen "star." It glowed a ghastly green, and although it was slightly smaller than the Twin Stars, there was something about this celestial object that disturbed Keris. Its emerald shine throbbed brightly two times before fading back against the black nightscape, invisible once more. Keris blinked her eyes in disbelief.

"How is that possible?" she marveled aloud. Keris noticed that Rayna was momentarily enthralled with the strange wand with the power to influence stars, like a child who had discovered a new toy. She hadn't heard Keris's question. Keris asked again, "How is that possible?"

Rayna turned her gaze from the wand to Keris's face. "I found this device in the science room while I was looking around, "Rayna said. "At first, I had no idea what it did, but then I came across a data file describing its function. It's an amazing piece of technology."

"How . . . how did it cause the very stars themselves to flash so?"

"I told you, they're not real stars. The Twin Stars are manmade machines in low orbit around this world. This device tests the Twins, and their hidden counterpart, for problems—basically a diagnostic tool. It was programmed to make the machines flash twice if all systems were normal, and only once if it detected a malfunction. Rayna brought the strange wand device closer so that Keris could get a better look. "You see, the red and blue icons are up here, the green icon is down here; this icon displays the power reserves, and this is the view-screen . . ."

Perplexed, Keris peered warily at the handheld, wand-like device, and began to rub her temples, wondering if she was adequately prepared to hear such revelations—or if she should hear them at all. Perhaps there were some kinds of lore best kept among master mages, she thought. With tentative reservation, she asked her next question. "Though powerful as they obviously are, why would these ancient people wish to create false stars?"

Rayna sat down beside Keris and explained. According to accounts Rayna found in the secret room, the Twin Stars were weather-changing machines—the blue Twin capable of making a land colder, the red Twin, capable of making it warmer. Originally, the machines were built by the Geni, with the intention to make their deserts and tundra green and fruitful. They dared not risk using the devices on their own land before the technology was properly tested.

"True to Geni form, they decided Taren would be the test," Rayna said. "That is why half of Taren is always very hot, while the other half is constantly cold—even though Taren is a relatively small peninsula and shouldn't experience such temperature extremes."

"Darkly clever creatures, these Geni," Keris commented softly. "But surely by now their tests are done. You said the machines have been in the skies for over a thousand years."

Rayna agreed. "Yes, they abandoned the project a long time ago, but the logs didn't say why."

"But are not the machines still active, trained on Taren?"

"Right—the Geni didn't bother to turn them off. And as my demonstration showed, two out of the three machines only flashed once, which means they have started to malfunction."

"I fear to ask how."

Rayna peered gravely once more at the handheld device, looking specifically at a small, square, glowing window, upon which ever-changing writings mysteriously appeared and changed, according to which rune Rayna touched. Rayna had called the magic window a "view-screen." Keris looked away, disturbed by the sight. "According to this," Rayna said, "the machines have been experiencing a slow but steady temperature deviation, increasingly putting out more energy than what their original parameters called for."

"In common tongue, please," Keris said in an uneasy voice.

"Oh, sorry. In a nutshell, each year, the blue Twin is making East Taren colder and the Red twin is making West Taren hotter. It had been only a fraction of a degree in the past, so it probably wasn't very noticeable, but in recent years, it's gotten much worse." Rayna resumed reading from the glowing view-screen on the device. "In fact, this year alone, East Taren experienced a five degree temperature drop and West Taren experienced a temperature increase of roughly the same amount. At this rate, neither East nor West Taren will be habitable in ten years. Everyone would die from exposure."

Keris blanched. She had noticed that East Taren lately had seemed colder than ever before, while West Taren felt the hottest she remembered it being. "Did you learn of a way to turn the machines off? Perhaps the rune wand you found can do it."

Rayna shook her head. "It looks like its only purpose is to test the overall health of the machines. As far as I can tell, the remote can't alter the Twins' orbit, or change any of their settings—I tried."

"The place where you discovered the logs, then?"

"I wasn't given full access to the facility, and even if I were, I don't think it's possible to shut the machines down from an observation post. The logs did mention a building that houses a master control room—deep in Geni territory. From there, it may be possible to deactivate the Twins."

"Does not Geni territory lie beyond Irel's Band?"

"Yep," Rayna sighed. "Which poses a problem."

Keris let out a mirthless chuckle. "Indeed." A moment of silence passed, and another question came to her mind. She said, "What of the third machine—the hidden one in the sky that flashed its vile shade of green at the command of your rune wand. What does it do?"

Rayna looked apologetic. "Sorry," she said, "I thought I told you: That machine is responsible for maintaining the Band."

Keris regretted having left her lover's side. Hearing these revelations was enough to drive a person mad. "You certainly know how to ruin one's night, Rayna Powell of Nightwind," Keris declared, only half joking. She found herself becoming angry with Rayna, in spite of the close bond they had recently shared. She thought to herself, *How could someone find out so much secret knowledge without themselves being a part of the secret?*

"Does that mean you believe me now?" Rayna asked. She hadn't noticed Keris's sudden change in mood.

Keris nodded ruefully.

"Good, because there's more that you need to know."

Keris nearly groaned out loud. "Perhaps it should wait until the morning. Ciredor wants us up before dawn, so—"

"Please, Keris, this is important. It involves the beasts."

Keris involuntarily shuddered. "You have my attention," she stated coldly.

"The beasts are victims of another Geni experiment—the Lake Stone. It wasn't a 'gift from the Heavens,' as the people of Lamec thought. Like the Twin Stars, it's an ancient Geni machine, and it was launched—catapulted to Taren—like a missile, where it landed in the Great Lake. It was supposed to activate immediately upon impact. I don't know why it didn't, but it took centuries before something or someone managed to turn it on—which became a very bad day for the people of Lamec. That's because the Lake Stone was designed by Geni scientists to mutate the people of the city into monsters—the beasts!"

"To what end? Why would they do this?"

"Mainly, they wanted to see if it could be done. They also wanted to see what effect it would have on the greater Taren population."

Keris began to look annoyed and snapped back. "Other than butchery and death, I presume?"

"Look, I don't pretend to understand their twisted logic."

"I don't see why you shouldn't! You are one of them, are you not?"

The accusation left Rayna stunned and shocked. "You think I'm a Geni?" she stammered.

"You said yourself that you come from beyond the Band—Geni territory. And you lack the 'genetic branding,' as you call it, for your ears are quite round. You were able to cross the Band into Taren unharmed, because the Band is trained to kill only Tareners, and that explains why you were able to save Arstinax from the Band without fear of dying."

"Trust me, I had plenty of fear of dying!"

"It explains why you were able to enter a secret post designed to permit only Geni, and your ability to understand their evil tools and use them so comfortably. Most important, it explains why you so conveniently cannot find a way to turn off the foul machines that curse the skies above our heads!"

"I am not a Geni!"

Keris crossed her arms, unconvinced. "If you are not a Geni, then what else could you possibly be?"

"Something else."

"What does that mean?"

"I don't want to talk about it."

"I see."

In those two simple words, Rayna heard the foundation of their friendship crumbling with the shrill resonance of suspicion. She felt like a fool. *Why didn't I see this coming?* she asked herself. "You just have to trust me," Rayna said feebly.

In reply, Keris stood and began to walk away. Keris hesitated, then turned to face Rayna once more. "I trusted you with my life once. I want to trust you again, so I will give you one final chance to speak the truth. *Who are you*, Rayna of Nightwind?"

Rayna felt sick hearing the suddenly cold, almost hostile tone of voice coming from her friend. "If I were a Geni, why on Earth would I tell you Geni secrets?"

"To gloat, perhaps," Keris answered. "Or perhaps to judge the effects of my reaction—something I understand to be a favorite pastime of Geni scientists."

Tears began to well up in Rayna's eyes, but she ignored them. "I'm not a Geni," she said. "I was *made* by the Geni."

Keris took another step back and took on a guarded stance. "'Made'? I will not believe such nonsense. Geni may have created the ground beneath our feet, but never flesh and blood!"

Rayna sighed sorrowfully, trying to regain some of her composure. "I'm a clone, Keris," she whispered.

"What is that?"

"A living copy of a person."

Seeing the predicable baffled look on Keris's face, Rayna patted a spot on the cold, moonlit stone floor next to her. "Have a seat, and I'll tell you the whole story—this clone doesn't bite." She added, "Do you want to know who I am, or not?"

Keris relaxed her stance and sat down, but at a safe distance from Rayna. "I am listening," Keris said.

"I found out I was a clone—or a 'replicant,' as the Geni call us—while in the observation post. I didn't want to tell you, or anyone else. I guess I was still trying to come to terms with it myself. Or maybe I was just in denial. The Geni experiments didn't stop with Taren. I am just as much a victim of Geni experimentation as are Tareners. Many years ago, the Geni discovered backward time travel—a way of physically revisiting Earth's past. After the novelty wore off, the Geni began to fear this technology, and later prohibited its use."

Keris interrupted. "Why would they fear this? Did you not say they wished to control history? What better way than to change and mold the past to their liking?"

Rayna shook her head. "It's not that simple. The majority of Geni leaders were afraid that altering historical events would have unintentional results on the present. They thought too many things could go wrong that could jeopardize the Geni government's current place in power, and they weren't willing to take the risk." Rayna digressed, pondering the notion. "I never thought time travel was even possible. Scientists from my day would give anything to experience it just once."

Keris cut in again, her sharp voice rising with impatience. "What does any of this have to do with whether are not you are Geni?"

"I am but one example of how the Geni solved their time travel dilemma. Rather than going to the past and risking contaminating the timeline, the Geni decided to bring the past to them—well, a piece of it, anyway. The Geni devised a way to locate and molecularly scan a person from the past, at a particular point in time, and then produce an exact copy of that person, complete with all of his or her memories, in the Geni's time period—all within a matter of seconds. It's like making a detailed sketch of a painting, and then going home and producing a replica indistinguishable from the original. I know it sounds crazy, but the Geni found a way to do it."

"What sort of interest would the Geni have in a twin made from a person in the past?"

"Think about it. If the Geni wanted to meet or learn from a famous person from history, they could simply have a copy of that person sent to them. It was their safe solution to the conventional concept of time travel. I saw the records of hundreds of heroes and leaders from my past who were duplicated by the Geni at some point in their lives. Some were copied multiple times. Albert Einstein, a scientific genius, roughly from my time, was a particularly popular choice." Rayna found herself clenching her jaw. "When I came to Taren I thought I had somehow traveled to Earth's past. In reality, I was the one from the past—well, at least my original self was from the past."

"Then," Keris surmised, "you were made as a copy because of your past fame—or rather the past fame of your other self."

"Maybe," Rayna replied with a sardonic tone, "but the logs never mentioned what my other self did to deserve the honor."

Rayna, anticipating Keris's next question, said gruffly, "Don't ask me how they did it—because contrary to popular opinion, I'm not a Geni. All I know is that the scanning process they used was designed to mimic a natural occurrence—such as a lightning storm—so that the original subjects would not be any wiser and would go about their lives completely unaware that they had been used to make their own identical twins."

Keris found herself drawn in once again by Rayna's intriguing words. "According to your own accounts," she said, "the lightning storm that brought you to this land seemed hardly a subtle or natural affair."

Rayna shrugged. "Somehow, I think my experience was unique." She recalled her constant dreams of the mysterious woman, who was standing in the road, and later appeared in the lower chamber of the Science Guild. She thought of her new powers, which had not manifested until she came to Taren. "I think the Geni were trying something new in my case. I just don't know what it is yet."

"'Something new' . . . I suppose that would explain why no others have been known to come here from beyond the Band, as you have. If not the Band, then where were the other replicants brought into existence?"

"From what I learned, replicants were almost always 'materialized' inside of Geni Territory—usually in a government lab, where they could be inspected for possible flaws. Then they would be used for Geni experiments, or sometimes sold to a small segment of the public, or to corporations, for large sums of money. Like Tareners, replicants are not considered Geni citizens, so they are treated more like property than like human beings." Rayna shook her head. "It's not fair. They—we—are just as human as our originals, right down to our birthmarks and fingerprints— I even have the same scar on my elbow from when I—I mean, Rayna—fell and scratched herself with a tree branch trying to climb the old oak in her backyard. She was only nine years old at the time. Rayna's mom came running out of the house when she heard her cry . . . ." Rayna choked back tears from the memories she knew were not her own. She laughed bitterly. "And now I'm reduced to talking about myself in the third person. My mom was never my mom. She died more than a thousand years ago, along with her real daughter." Rayna sobbed. "All this time I wanted to go back home and see my mom again—it was the one thing that helped keep me sane since I came to Taren. Now I know that will never happen."

Keris got up, walked over to Rayna, and quietly placed a comforting arm over her shoulder. "I believe you speak the truth. Please forgive me for doubting you."

Rayna replied with a teary tremble; her thoughts were elsewhere. Keris said, "Taren folklore speaks of creatures called doppelgangers—false twins with evil hearts said to be harbingers of doom to whomever they meet."

"Thanks," Rayna grumbled. "I feel better already."

Keris smiled. "I was not my intention to call you evil, for you are far from such. Rather, it is my way of saying that I have recently seen many wondrous and terrible things—things that could easily pass for folklore and fantasy tales, but are very real. You have opened my mind to things that I would have once dismissed or ignored as having no value."

"Like science?" Rayna asked.

"Yes, like science. It is a far more powerful brand of magic than I could have ever imagined. If you are indeed a doppelganger, then the Geni scientists made a mistake in their twinning, for you are one of the noblest people I have ever met."

Rayna wiped the tears from her eyes. "I appreciate you trying to cheer me up," she said, "but nothing can be said that can change the fact that I am a fake—a copy made at somebody's whim, for God knows what reason. What am I—three, maybe four months old? I never did any of the things I thought I did. I never majored in science, I never graduated from college . . . every memory I have is a lie; everything I thought I was is a lie!"

"I disagree. You are no one's pale reflection. You are a whole person, no doubt every bit as clever, and stubborn, as the one who bore your name before you." Keris chuckled. "Even if you are a lesser form of your other self, as you claim, then I am grateful I never met the original, for you are as much Rayna Powell of Nightwind as any person can reasonably stand."

"I'm glad you can find something funny in all this!" Rayna shot back, anger flashing in her dark brown eyes.

Keris stared back at Rayna, hard and unflinching. "I fear that you have become so entangled in the thorns that you fail to see the roses. You have been given a chance to live again; it is something that most people only dream of, so stop this self-pity nonsense and know that you are truly fortunate." Keris paused and added, "I say this because I consider you a dear friend."

"But I don't even know *why* I was chosen for this, or why I can suddenly do things that I could never do before—"

"You have been restored to experience a second lifetime, Rayna Powell—never mind the reason." As Rayna reflected on what Keris said, Keris continued. "You must remain strong, Rayna Powell. Did you not know that I sometimes draw my strength from you?"

Despite her angst, Rayna managed an incredulous laugh. "Me?" she sniffled.

"Yes. Your inner strength is a quality I have much admired in you."

"Funny, I've thought the same thing about you."

"Then let us draw our strength from each other. The foul manipulators known as the Geni should be found and held accountable for their deeds. You said yourself that the machines they placed in the sky will one day destroy Taren. Somewhere on Geni soil is the source of the machines' power. If we were to find a safe way to pass through Irel's Band, we may be able to destroy that source. I believe you are the only person capable of accomplishing such a thing."

The compliment galvanized Rayna's confidence and helped bring to her memory a bit of obscure information she had run across while in the secret room. She snapped her fingers. "Come to think of it, there just may be a way. I remember seeing a few vague references to something called the 'Catacomb Passage.' I think it may be some kind of underground network that connects Geni territory to Taren. It would explain how the Geni were able to set up multiple observation facilities throughout Taren without detection."

Keris nodded thoughtfully. "I believe I understand your reasoning: If we cannot pass *through* the Band, then perhaps there is a way to pass—"

"*Under* it. Precisely. I would need to return to the observation post to gather more data, and try to pinpoint exactly where in Geni territory the satellites are getting their power. I will also need to find out where the entrance to the Catacomb Passage is. Depending on the size of the passage, we may be able to send a small task force through, to permanently shut down the both Twins and Band."

"It's good to see the fiery light of ambition in your eyes again," Keris said with a smile.

Rayna smiled back briefly, but the smile soon turned to a familiar frown. "We're a bit ahead of ourselves, aren't we? We first have to survive the war."

Keris sighed. "Yes, the war . . ."

No more words needed to be spoken. Rayna was well aware that the impending war did not favor them, even with Ciredor and his formidable army on their side. A stray thought taunted her with a verse from her earlier dream: *And they shall build their houses with rotten sticks, for nothing will last past a season.* Those words alluded to a secret knowledge that Rayna had about the war, but this knowledge came not from the logs she read while in Dosk; it came to her in a bleak vision.

In the vision, the beasts had won. They spread over the land of Taren like a blight—destroying everything in their path. Death was everywhere; all hope was lost. The few humans who remained alive were forced to live as nomads—forever roaming, in fear that if they stayed in one place too long, the beasts would find them. Rayna kept this dark revelation to herself. If it was indeed a premonition, as she feared, she hoped it was merely one possible outcome. She thought about Ciredor's second in charge, Orin. He was supposed to be able to see future visions. She wondered if he, too, had ever seen what she had seen. Something else deeply disturbed her about her vision: It revealed that the beasts had become—

Keris broke Rayna's contemplative silence with a question: "Do you still doubt who you are?"

In response, Rayna looked at the Twin Stars of Taren, wincing with revulsion at the thought that the same beings that built and placed the climate-changing machines in orbit were responsible for her existence. *Why did they bring me to Taren—why here?* she thought, half hoping a Geni representative would appear from nowhere with an answer. Far stranger things had happened of late.

Rayna replied to Keris in a low voice. "I suppose, for all intent and purposes, I'm still Rayna Powell."

"Your words lack conviction."

"I just don't know. . . . How can I claim to be someone who died more than a thousand years ago?"

"If you cannot claim to be Rayna Powell by birthright, then you must claim her by *soulright*." With that said, Keris turned to leave. It was late, and the sleep once denied her, now threatened to overtake her. She also had learned that Rayna preferred solitude in times like these. Walking away, her back turned, Keris could still feel Rayna's stern stare behind her.

"Do I even have a soul?" Rayna questioned out loud to herself.

Before Keris rounded the corner to the tower door, she paused for a moment, turned to look in Rayna's direction, and answered back softly, "By asking that question, you have already shown that you do."

Here ends
Rayna of Nightwind,
Book One of
The Taren Series

ACKNOWLEDGEMENTS

I want to give thanks to my readers, and to all of those who encouraged and supported me in the preparation of this novel. Thanks to my mother, Janie Baker, and my wife, Avis Baker. Many thanks to A. J. Sobczak for seeing this book through the editing process, and for his support. Thanks to Rich DiSilvio for the great cover art and design. Special thanks to Tina Williams for her professional advice and moral support. I am fortunate and blessed to have friends and family who have consistently expressed a sincere interest in the completion of this book. Thanks for everything.

ABOUT THE AUTHOR

R. A. Baker was born in North Carolina in 1971, and was raised in Richmond, Virginia. A writer since high school, he went on to receive an undergraduate degree from Virginia Commonwealth University, having double majored in Psychology and Rehabilitative Counseling. Presently living in Southern Virginia, the Taren series marks his debut as a novelist.